BOOK THREE

THE FRIENDSHIP LETTERS

Letters *of* Wisdom

BOOK THREE

THE FRIENDSHIP LETTERS

Letters of Wisdom

WANDA & BRUNSTETTER

BARBOUR
PUBLISHING

ISBN 978-1-63609-622-3
Adobe Digital Edition (.epub) 978-1-63609-623-0

Scripture taken from the New King James Version®. Copyright © 1982 by Thomas Nelson, Inc. Used by permission. All rights reserved.

All German-Dutch words are taken from the *Revised Pennsylvania German Dictionary* found in Lancaster County, Pennsylvania.

This book is a work of fiction. Names, characters, places, and incidents are either products of the author's imagination or used fictitiously. Any similarity to actual people, organizations, and/or events is purely coincidental.

Home remedies mentioned in this book are not to be taken as medical advice.

For more information about Wanda E. Brunstetter, please access the author's website at the following internet address: www.wandabrunstetter.com

Cover model photography: Richard Brunstetter III;
Cover background photography: Doyle Yoder Photography

Published by Barbour Publishing, Inc., 1810 Barbour Drive, Uhrichsville, OH 44683, www.barbourbooks.com

Our mission is to inspire the world with the life-changing message of the Bible.

ecpa Member of the
Evangelical Christian
Publishers Association

Printed in the United States of America.

Dedication

To all my special Amish friends who have shared their
wisdom with me so many times over the years.

———≈———

"If you forgive men their trespasses,
your heavenly Father will also forgive you."
MATTHEW 6:14 NKJV

Chapter 1

Mount Hope, Ohio

After putting her two-year-old daughter, Myra, down for a nap, Irma Miller grabbed the mail and went outside. There, she found her middle child, Clayton, crouched in one of the flower beds with a bunch of rocks he'd piled into a mound.

Irma shook her head slowly and kept walking until she came to the wooden bench she'd placed under a shady maple tree at the first sign of spring. Eager to read the letter she'd received from her friend Doretta Lengacher, she placed the rest of the mail on the bench beside her, ripped the envelope open, and started reading:

> *Dear Irma,*
>
> *I hope this note finds you well and enjoying some lovely spring weather. It's been beautiful here in Grabill, and I love spending time in the yard. The feeders are full, and there are birds aplenty. Yesterday, I spotted two Eastern bluebirds eating at one of the feeders. Although they're fairly common here in Indiana, I always enjoy seeing the beautiful blue feathers that cover most of their little bodies. The cardinals are out too, and I love the remarkably vibrant red color of the males and the red crests above their heads. Remember*

how you, Eleanor, and I used to play at Riverside Park?
You two used to tease me because I was always pointing
out pretty or unusual birds. I'm still doing that as an adult,
telling anyone who'll listen.

Irma smiled as she thought of Doretta Lengacher and Eleanor Lapp, her two best friends from Grabill, Indiana. They had attended the Cedar Creek Amish school together until Irma was seven and her loving father had died in an accident. Within a year, her mother had married Homer Schmucker, and he'd moved the family to Ignatius, Montana. Things were never the same for Irma. Homer constantly criticized her and treated her as an outsider compared to his four flesh-and-blood children. She frowned, dismissing her bad memories and focusing on her friend's letter again:

Things are going well at the nutrition center, and I
still enjoy working there with Warren. Even so, I won't be
there once the baby comes. Yes, you read that right—Warren
and I are expecting our first child, and he or she is due in
six months. Of course, as you might guess, we're both very
excited about becoming parents.

Enough about me, though. How are things in Ohio with
you and your family? I imagine the children are growing
and keeping you busy.

It was wonderful to see you at our wedding last year,
and we enjoyed getting to meet LaVern and the children.
Maybe you can come here for another visit soon, and we'd
like to visit you in Ohio sometime too.

Well, it's getting late, and I must close for now and get
ready for bed. Take care, friend. I hope to hear from you soon.

Your friend for life,
Doretta

Irma set the letter aside and sighed. Although happy for Doretta, she was glad she herself wasn't expecting a baby. She had her hands full enough with three active children to care for and couldn't imagine having another child added to the family. "*Jah*," she mumbled, "better her than me. If I had another little one to raise, I think I'd go crazy. I can barely keep up with the *kinner* I have now, let alone manage the care of a new baby."

Although Irma loved her children, they sometimes tried her patience. Brown-haired Brian, six going on seven, was the most mischievous and could be a bit sassy at times. Clayton, with his jet brown hair, was full of energy at the age of four and often brought the rocks he collected into the house. This got on Irma's nerves because she had told him many times that rocks belonged outdoors, not in the house. Clayton was also a tease and liked to frustrate his little sister by hiding her toys. Myra, with her pretty blond hair, was a daddy's girl and often whined when he was gone from home too often or for any length of time. Irma couldn't blame her little girl for that—she also missed LaVern when he was away from home due to some event where his services as an auctioneer were required. Sometimes when her husband had to travel, it meant him being away for a night or two, which left Irma alone with all the responsibilities, inside and outside the house, as well as dealing with their children. She tried not to feel sorry for herself, but there were times when she felt lonely and a bit resentful of her husband's job, even though it did pay the bills and provide them with the necessities of life.

"I'm home, Mama. . . . I'm home!" Brian shouted as he raced into the yard, pulling Irma's thoughts aside. He held up his lunch pail. "I ate all my lunch today, even the stinky tuna fish sandwich."

Irma walked over to her son and took the lunch pail from him. "I'm glad you ate the sandwich, even though you don't care for tuna. Tomorrow, I'll fix you cheese and bologna. How's that sound?"

A big grin spread across his oval face. "Real good! *Danki*, Mama."

"Hurry now and change out of your school clothes. I'll fix you a snack, and then there are a few chores that need to be done."

Brian frowned and scuffed the toe of his shoe against a clump of grass. "I wanna play with my *katz*."

"You can play with the cat after you've finished doing your chores."

The boy shrugged and took his time climbing the porch stairs and getting into the house.

Irma rolled her eyes. *That boy is going to make me old before my time. Jah, I'll probably have gray hair by the time I'm thirty.* She grimaced. *Which is only two years away, so I'd better enjoy having dark brown hair while I can.*

———≈———

When Irma went into the house, she found Myra on the kitchen floor, playing with several pots and pans she'd taken from the bottom drawer of their gas stove. The little stinker hadn't slept very long, and Irma wondered how long ago her daughter had left her little bed and made her way to the kitchen to play.

"You little *schtinker*." Irma shook her finger, but she couldn't help smiling at her daughter's cuteness as she looked up at her with all the innocence of a child. It looked especially funny when Myra set one of the smaller pans on top of her head.

Irma let the child play while she cut up an apple and some cheese to have ready for all three children after Brian changed his clothes.

Once the apple and cheese were arranged on a platter, Irma set it on the kitchen table. Brian hadn't come downstairs yet, so she stood at the bottom of the stairs and shouted up to him: "Your snack is ready, Brian!" Then she opened the front door and called for Clayton to come inside.

Irma's brows furrowed when she noticed Clayton's rock pile in the flower bed had grown larger, but the boy was no longer there. *I wonder where he went now.*

"Clayton," she called. "*Kumme*—come in now and have some apple and cheese with your brother and sister."

No response.

Irma glanced around the yard, thinking he'd probably found another place to pick up some more rocks, but she saw no sign of her mischievous son.

Irma stepped off the porch and headed for the barn. *I'll bet Clayton lost interest in the rocks and went out there to play with the* katze. *He's probably sitting on a bale of straw with one or two cats in his lap right now.*

Irma dodged a few toys in the yard and headed for the barn. Upon entering the rustic building, the aroma of horse flesh and manure assaulted her senses, and she wrinkled her nose. "Ick." Apparently, LaVern hadn't taken the time to clean their horses' stalls before he'd left this morning.

Irma poked her tongue against the inside of her cheek and inhaled a long breath. *The least my husband could have done was come back to the house and let me know those chores still needed to be done,* she fumed. *He couldn't have been in that big of a hurry to leave.*

Forgetting about Clayton for the moment, Irma made her way to the stalls. Her mare, Misty, as well as LaVern's gelding, Buck, were inside their stalls, munching on the food he'd given them. *Well, at least he did that much before his driver picked him up.*

Irma opened the gate and led Misty out of the stall, calling Clayton's name as she walked back through the barn. Her facial muscles tightened when she got no response. *Where is that boy, anyway, and why doesn't he answer my call?*

She paused at the door a few seconds, holding tight to her horse's bridle, and then she walked the mare on out. After letting Misty into the pasture, Irma went back for Buck. Once more, she called for Clayton, but there was still no response. *Strange. Unless he's left the yard, which is doubtful, surely he should have heard me by now.*

LaVern's horse must have been eager to be out of his stall, because he flipped his head several times and nearly got away from Irma. She was quick, though, and grabbed his bridle firmly. With a determined set of her jaw, she led him into the pasture.

Irma was about to close the fence gate when she spotted something way out in the field, under a tree. She squinted and shielded her eyes from the glare of the sun, but she couldn't quite make out what appeared to be lying beneath that tree. She stepped inside and moved slowly along the

11

fence line, being careful not to spook the horses by any quick movements, which had happened on occasion when they were first let out to run. Once Irma knew that Buck and Misty were a good distance from her, she headed across the pasture to take a look at what she'd seen. As Irma drew closer, she realized it was a child lying, facedown, under the tree. She recognized his clothing and jet brown hair before ever seeing the boy's face. Her heart raced at the thought of what may have happened to him.

"Clayton!" Irma screamed as her legs moved faster, despite the fact that they had begun to tremble. When she reached the spot where the boy lay, Irma dropped like a stone beside him. He wasn't moving and didn't respond when she repeatedly called his name. Irma's body broke out in a cold sweat. *Oh, dear Lord, please let my son be all right.*

Chapter 2

By the time Irma made it back to the house, carrying her son in her arms, Clayton had opened his eyes and begun to wail.

"It's all right, Son. You're gonna be okay." Irma breathed a sigh of relief as she laid him on the couch and examined the wound. It wasn't as bad as she'd first thought, and thankfully the bleeding had stopped. Apparently, it was only a surface wound and didn't appear to need any stitches. It would, however, have to be cleaned and bandaged—and she would definitely keep a close eye on Clayton to make sure he had no signs of a concussion. Irma knew about concussions firsthand, because she'd suffered one herself when she was thirteen and had run into a tree.

She shook her head. *I won't think about that now. Clayton needs my attention, and it's my job to make sure he's okay.*

"Where's my *felse*, Mama?" Clayton whimpered. "I tried to get it, but then I fell."

"Don't worry about the rock you were after right now. I need to take care of the cut on your forehead."

Irma heard Myra in the kitchen messing with the cooking pans again.

"What happened to my *bruder*?" With huge eyes, Brian stared down at Clayton, lying on the couch.

"I found him out in the pasture. He hit his head on a rock."

"Is he gonna be okay?"

"Your brother will be fine, but I need to clean up his wound and put a bandage on it," she replied. "Will you please go into the kitchen and keep an eye on your little sister?"

At first, Brian hesitated, but then he nodded and hurried down the hall.

Irma was about to head for the bathroom to get what she needed when she remembered she kept a first aid kit in one of the kitchen cupboards. Since that was closer, she told Clayton to lie very still and rushed off to the kitchen.

Upon entering the room, Irma saw that her daughter still played with the pots and pans and that Brian stood near the table, watching. "My sister is silly," he said. "Why does she wanna fool around with your pots and pans all the time?"

"She probably thinks it's fun to pretend she's cooking." Irma moved across the room and called to Brian over her shoulder. "Would you please give Myra a piece of cheese and make sure she stays here in the kitchen?"

"Okay, Mama. Can I have some *kaes* too and maybe an *appel?*"

"Of course. But save some cheese and apple for Clayton, because he may be hungry."

Irma went to the cabinet where she kept the first aid kit and rushed back to the living room.

Clayton lay still, staring at the ceiling, his eyes filled with tears. But at least he had calmed down and no longer sobbed, which had torn at Irma's heart. *No child should ever be left to cry alone—for any reason,* she thought.

She opened the kit and picked out the items she needed to dress his wound. Clayton turned his head to face her, watching Irma's every move. "Don't hurt me, Mama," he whimpered.

"I'll be gentle and try not to press too hard while I clean the cut with this antiseptic." Irma wiped the area as lightly as she could.

"Will I have a big bandage on my head?"

"No, it will be one of these." Irma held up a sterile-packaged bandage. "Here, why don't you hang on to it for me until I'm ready to put it on your forehead?"

Clayton took it and gave her a brief smile.

As Irma administered first aid to her son's wound, his eyes closed and he murmured, "I'm real tired, Mama."

She shook his arm firmly. "Don't go to sleep, Clayton. You must stay awake."

He opened his eyes and blinked several times. "How come?"

"Because you hit your head, and I need to make sure you're all right." She helped him sit up and put a small pillow behind his back. "Let me have the bandage you're holding." Irma took it, unwrapped the sterile strip on the bandage, and applied it over Clayton's wound. "Now stay like this while I go to the kitchen to get you a snack."

"I'm not *hungerich*, Mama. I'm *schlaeferich*."

She shook her head vigorously. "No, Son, you must stay awake, even if you do feel sleepy. If you're not hungry, I'll bring you a glass of water."

"Okay."

Irma gathered up the things she'd used from the first aid kit and returned to the kitchen. Brian now sat at the table, eating an apple, while Myra remained on the floor, one hand holding a piece of cheese and the other hand hanging on to the handle of a small kettle. If Irma wasn't so concerned about Clayton, she might have joined the children with a snack of her own.

Brian looked at Irma with his head tipped to one side. "Where's Clayton? How come he ain't comin' in for some kaes and an appel?"

"He is not hungerich, but I'm taking him some *wasser*." Irma filled a glass with cold water from the faucet and went back to the living room. She was pleased to see that Clayton had remained upright with his eyes open. He seemed to be fixated on something across the room and paid no attention when she offered him the glass of water.

"Clayton, what are you staring at?"

"A *maus*." He pointed. "Oh, it just ran off."

She groaned. *Not another mouse in the house! Haven't we dealt with enough of those already?* "Don't worry about it, Son. I'm sure your *daed* will set a trap for the critter when he gets home from work this evening." Irma bit the inside of her lip. She had no fear of mice, but they were dirty rodents that gnawed holes in things and got into food supplies whenever they could. One way or another that nasty little mouse would have to go. The big problem was, LaVern had not taken the time to figure out how the mice were getting into the house or plugged up any suspecting holes.

My husband can't expect me to do everything, Irma thought as she handed Clayton his water. *I have enough on my hands taking care of the children and doing household chores. He should understand that and make more effort to get the necessary things done around here. I'm going to speak to LaVern about this as soon as the kinner go to bed this evening.*

St. Ignatius, Montana

"Have you heard from Irma lately, Mama?"

At the sound of her fifteen-year-old daughter's voice, Dorcas Schmucker turned and set her sewing project aside. "No, I haven't, and it's doubtful that I'll hear anything soon."

"How come?"

Dorcas' lips pressed together in a tight grimace. "Your sister rarely writes unless I've written to her first, and then it's usually just a brief note about the children. Irma never talks about coming here for a visit, and not once has she invited all of us to come to their house in Ohio."

Caroline's coffee-colored eyes seemed to darken further. "I'd sure like to go there sometime. I've never been anyplace but here, and it'd be nice to see what it's like in Ohio."

Dorcas wasn't sure how to respond. Even if she or any of her children wanted to leave St. Ignatius to go on a trip, it seemed doubtful that Homer would give his approval. He'd been in a sour mood lately and seemed to say no to every request. Of course, things had been busy at the lumber mill, and he needed the boys' help there, but that was no reason Dorcas and the girls couldn't make a trip. *If I brought the topic up, Homer would probably say it would be too expensive to hire a driver to take us to Ohio.*

Caroline tugged on Dorcas' apron, pushing her thoughts aside. "Did you hear what I said, Mama? Do you think we could make a trip to Ohio sometime?"

Dorcas shrugged her shoulders. "I don't know. We'd need an invitation from Irma first, and then it would be up to your daed if we could go there or not."

Caroline's chin lowered as her hands went limp at her sides. "That'll never happen. Papa gets mad if we even mention Irma's name. He wouldn't wanna go there, and it's not likely he'd let any of us go either."

Dorcas gave a slow nod and quickly changed the subject. "You'd better go upstairs and get changed out of your school clothes, because we have chores to do."

The girl frowned, and her chin jutted out. "Seems like there's always chores around here. Wish I could just go off someplace when I get home from school and have fun."

"There will be time for that when school's out for the summer. Besides, this is your last year of school, and then you'll be home with me learning everything you should know to run a household when you meet the right fellow and get married someday. In the meanwhile, though, please do as you're told." Dorcas gestured toward the hallway leading to the stairs. "Get going now, Caroline, and I don't want to hear any mumbling either."

With slumped shoulders and arms crossed, her youngest daughter shuffled out of the room.

Dorcas watched her daughter's form disappear up the steps. She sensed the raw emotions that remained in this house from Homer's cruel treatment of Irma while she'd lived here, but none of the other children had ever talked about it. Was it wrong of Caroline to desire to have things normal in her family's life? She wanted to visit her big sister, and the truth was so did Dorcas, but she knew there was nothing normal about how this family functioned. It was unfortunate, but Homer had never been interested in acting in a loving and kind manner toward his non-biological daughter, and worse yet, Dorcas had stood by and let it happen. That was in the past, though, and there was nothing she could do about it now.

She heaved a sigh and resumed sewing the new dress she was making for herself. *Caroline is too much like Irma to suit me. Always asking questions and wanting something she shouldn't have. If we're not careful, Caroline's likely to run off with the first boy who takes an interest in her, the way Irma did when she was eighteen.*

———————— ≈ ————————

Mount Hope

After the children were tucked in bed that evening, Irma served her husband a bowl of chocolate ice cream, and the couple sat around the kitchen table. While he ate dessert and she drank a cup of relaxing herbal tea, Irma told LaVern about Clayton's accident, the mouse she and Clayton had seen, and what a rough day she'd had.

"I'm sorry to hear that, but I'm glad Clayton's injury wasn't serious," he said in a sincere voice. "I also wish I could be home more, but I can't quit my job. The money I earn pays the bills."

Irma nodded. "I understand, but I can't do everything here on my own. Taking care of the children and doing all the cooking, cleaning, and other things it takes to run a household is a full-time job. Sometimes I have chores in the barn to do too because you don't have time to do them."

"I realize that, and I'm sorry, Irma. I promise to set some more mouse traps before we go to bed. Also, on my next day off, I'll spend some time looking for places where the mice might be getting in." LaVern got up from his chair.

"Where are you going?"

"To set some traps in the attic and down in the cellar. And I'll probably put one way in the back under the kitchen sink. For the safety of our kinner, I won't put the traps out in visible places where they might be tempted to fool with them."

Irma nodded. "And it would be upsetting for the children, especially Myra, to see a dead maus in one of the traps."

"Good point." LaVern put his empty bowl in the sink and drank the water left in his glass. "I'll get the traps and start setting them out now."

"Before you do that, there's something else I'd like to talk to you about."

"If it's concerning Clayton's bonk on the forehead, he seems to have no signs of a concussion, so there's no need to worry about him, Irma."

She shook her head. "It's not about Clayton. It concerns a letter I received from my friend Doretta today."

LaVern went back to the sink and put more water in his glass. "What did she have to say?"

"Why don't you sit back down, and I'll tell you about it?"

"Okay, but if you want those traps set, I can't sit very long."

"It'll only take a few minutes."

After LaVern took the seat across from Irma, she shared with him the things Doretta had said in her letter.

"I bet they're excited about having their first baby," he commented.

"Jah, and I was thinking how nice it would be if we could go to Grabill for a visit."

"That would be nice, but as you know, I have several big auctions coming up, and I can't be away from the area right now. Besides, Brian is still in school, so we won't be able to make any trips for a while."

"Maybe sometime this summer, after he's out of school for a break, we could take the kids to Grabill."

"I can't make any promises, Irma. We'll have to wait and see how it goes."

"Okay, but the last time we were there, it was only for Doretta and Warren's wedding. Since we couldn't stay in the area very long, there was no time to visit any of the stores in town or even drive by the house where I used to live with my *mamm* and daed, until he was killed in that horrible hunting accident."

"Wouldn't seeing the place make you feel sad?"

"Maybe, but I have good memories of living there when Daddy was alive. After my mamm married Homer and we moved to Montana, I was miserable—at least until I met you." Tears welled in Irma's eyes. "Danki for taking me away from that place and bringing us to your home state."

LaVern got up and went around to the other side of the table where he bent down and kissed Irma's cheek. "I like it here too, but there were some things about living in Montana that I enjoyed as well. After hearing that the hunting and fishing was good there, I was curious and wanted to try it out, so that's why I left home and ventured out to Montana. I wanted to try some things on my own." LaVern pulled Irma to her feet and held her gently in his arms. "Of course, meeting you was the best thing that happened to me while I was living in St. Ignatius, and I'm glad you were willing to move here with me when I got a job offer and decided to come home."

Tears rolled down Irma's cheeks and dripped onto his pale blue shirt. LaVern had no idea just how glad she'd been to leave her mother and stepfather's house. She would have followed her husband to the ends of the earth in order to get away from St. Ignatius.

Chapter 3

Irma glanced out the kitchen window and sighed. The first day of April had brought rain to Mount Hope, which was good for everything growing in the yard, but it meant the two youngest children couldn't play outside today. It was also doubtful that either of the two teachers at the school-house Brian attended would let the children play outdoors when it was raining so hard.

Selma Troyer taught the younger grades—one through four—and when asked, Brian had nothing but good to say about his teacher. Grades five through eight were taught by Mae Schrock, and from what Irma had heard, the young woman seemed to be equally liked by her students.

Sure wish I could have been a schoolteacher when I was old enough, Irma thought as she moved away from the window. *But no, Homer said I was too dumb for teaching, so he wouldn't let me apply to our local Amish school board after I graduated the eighth grade. Even though I got fair grades when I attended school, he insisted that I was stupid and wouldn't make a good teacher.*

Irma's posture stiffened, and she let out a forceful breath. *He said all I was good for was cleaning the house, slopping his smelly hogs, and doing all sorts of other dirty outdoor chores.* Irma thought Homer was the one who was dumb. His criticism only created a wider divide between Irma and her stepfather. It had been easy to see that he had never been on Irma's side, and in her heart, she felt that he had no business voicing his narrow-minded opinion. Irma's feelings had taken quite a hit that day when he'd called her stupid. If only her mother could have defended Irma instead of remaining silent as she often did in those types of situations.

Get a hold of yourself and stop thinking about the past, Irma told herself as she opened the refrigerator to see what she might fix for supper. *I have a new life here in Ohio, and Homer is more than two thousand miles away, so I don't have to answer to him ever again.*

Irma's thoughts scattered when Myra toddled into the room, carrying her favorite stuffed toy. During her last visit, LaVern's mother had said, "Little Myra is the spitting image of her mommy." Even though their hair color wasn't the same, their facial features and blue eyes were similar. Truthfully, Irma had always thought her daughter resembled LaVern, at least with the color of her blond hair.

Myra looked up at Irma and pointed to the drawer where the pots and pans were kept. It was hard not to give in to her youngest child's wishes, but knowing Myra was always happy when she played with the pots and pans wouldn't change Irma's desire to have the house quiet for a while.

Irma shook her head. "Not today, little girl. Mama has things to do here in the kitchen. And I can't have you underfoot or making a bunch of racket that will end up giving me a headache." Irma spoke in Pennsylvania Dutch, since Myra knew very few English words yet. She had, however, learned to say a few things in English by being around Brian, since he'd been learning English at school.

Irma picked up her daughter and placed her in the wooden high chair that LaVern's father had made when Brian was born. Paul was such a good grandpa to the children. If it weren't for the fact that he and his wife, Mildred, lived in Baltic, where his woodworking shop was located, LaVern's parents would probably come to visit a lot more. However, Mount Hope was almost eighteen miles from Baltic, which meant hiring a driver to bring them there. That, coupled with the fact that Paul's business kept him quite busy, meant their visits were often several weeks apart. That was fine with Irma. Whenever company came, the children got too excited and often did or said things that embarrassed her.

Myra let out an ear-piercing scream and pounded on the high-chair tray.

"Okay, okay. . . I hear you, loud and clear." Irma filled Myra's sippy cup with some of the goat's milk she'd purchased from a neighbor and placed it on the tray. Myra was sensitive to cow's milk, and Irma was glad the child was able to drink goat's milk without any problems. Since Myra was sensitive to cow's milk, even the cheese Irma gave her daughter was made from goat's milk. She would have given it to the boys too, but neither of them liked goat's milk—not even the cheese.

I wish my kids weren't so picky, Irma thought as she took out the meat and other ingredients to make a meatloaf. *Maybe I should insist that they eat whatever I give them, the way I was raised.* Her brows furrowed. *At least, that's how it was after Mama married Homer. I never understood what she saw in him, other than as a provider since she had no job to take care of us after my daddy died.*

That's enough thinking about the past, Irma told herself when Myra looked up at her with a milk mustache and a dimpled grin.

She kissed the little girl's cheek, blotted her lips, and resumed her project of making LaVern's favorite meatloaf.

A few minutes later, Clayton and Brian entered the kitchen, each holding their favorite cat. She hadn't even realized Brian had arrived home from school.

Irritation welled in Irma's chest, and she had to take a few deep breaths before speaking to her sons so she wouldn't shout. "How many times have I told you boys that those katze don't belong in the house?"

"But Mama, Stripey is real good at catching *meis*." Brian lifted his cat a bit higher.

"Mittens is good at catching mice too," Clayton put in, looking down at the black cat with white paws he held in a protective manner.

Irma shook her head. "I'm sure both of your cats help to keep the mice down in the barn, but we have no need for them here in the house.

Your daed took care of our mouse problem when he plugged up the holes where they'd been getting in." She ushered her boys to the back door and opened it. "Now go put the katze back in the barn and come inside. I don't want you playing outside when it's raining like this, and I don't want you bringing those katze in here again."

"Okay, Mama," they said in unison on their way out the door.

"I hope they mean it," Irma muttered as she returned to the kitchen. *Sure wish their dad could be here more often so all the discipline didn't fall upon me.*

Grabill, Indiana

Doretta Lengacher sat at the kitchen table, going through the mail she had picked up when their driver dropped her and Warren off after work. While she'd done that, Warren had gone to the barn to feed the horses and do a few chores.

After thumbing through the bills and advertisements, Doretta found two letters. One was from her friend Eleanor and the other had been written by Irma. It was hard to know which letter to open first since she was eager to hear what both of her friends had to say, but she decided to read Eleanor's first as she hadn't heard from her in a while. Doretta tore open the letter and began to read:

> *Dear Doretta,*
>
> *Greetings on this beautiful spring day. I just brought the laundry in from outside, and everything smells so nice and fresh. I love the aroma of clean clothes that have dried on the line outdoors. I took Rosetta outside with me to play while I removed the clothes from the line, and she ended up picking a few of the early spring flowers blooming in the flower bed near our house. When we came inside, I put them in a vase. Rosetta was happy about that, and she pointed to the flowers and said she wanted to smell the blumme. I had*

to chuckle, because I was the same way when I was a child—always wanting to smell the pretty flowers.

The baby is growing by leaps and bounds. It's hard to believe our precious little Stephen is already fifteen months old. I wish children didn't grow up so fast.

Enough about me and my kinner, though. Congratulations on your good news! I was so happy when I received your last letter announcing that you and Warren are expecting your first child. I bet your folks and his parents are really excited. Be prepared for all the spoiling that will go on from the grandparents after the baby is born. Although Vic's parents get to see our kinner more than my folks do, they all do a pretty good job of treating their grandchildren special.

Well, guess I'd best end this letter and go check on Stephen. I hear him fussing, which means he's probably hungry or needs his diaper changed.

Take care, and I'll look forward to your next letter, or maybe a phone call.

> *Love & Blessings,*
> *Eleanor*

Doretta smiled at the little red heart that had been stamped beneath her friend's name. It was nice to know that, even with two children to look after, Eleanor still had time to do a little something with her rubber stamping.

Doretta glanced at the clock across the room and decided that she still had time to read her other friend's letter before starting supper. She opened it and began to read:

Dear Doretta,

I received the letter announcing your pregnancy. Congratulations, and I hope you are feeling well, with no morning sickness. For me, that was the worst part of being pregnant.

Things are about the same with me as the last time I wrote. Nothing much new to write about. The first few weeks of spring have been chilly, and I am looking forward to being outside more once the weather stays warm and brings us into the summer months. I've never been much of a winter person and always look forward to the warmer seasons.

Clayton hit his head on a rock a few weeks ago, but it wasn't serious and the wound has healed well.

Brian still likes his first year of school, so he'll probably be disappointed when the end of May rolls around and he won't be back at his school desk until the end of August. But I'm sure he'll find things to occupy his time here.

Myra is fine and growing quickly, but then, so are the boys. Her favorite thing to do is play with my pots and pans. When she's older, I'm sure she will enjoy learning how to cook.

LaVern is fine too, but he's gone a lot due to his auctioneering duties, which means I have more responsibilities around here than I would like. He said if things work out, maybe we can come to Grabill for a visit sometime this summer. That would certainly be something for me to look forward to.

Take care of yourself, and I'll hope to hear from you again soon.

All the best,

Irma

Doretta yawned and stretched both arms over her head. It was nice to receive letters from both of her childhood friends on the same day. She closed her eyes and said a prayer for each of them, then pushed away from the table. It was time to start supper, no matter how tired she felt. If Warren didn't mind, maybe she would fix something simple for their evening meal, like soup and sandwiches.

Doretta thought about getting up from the table to peek into the pantry to see what soups she had on hand and could heat up for the two of them. She wished there was some leftover homemade soup to offer Warren, but tonight they would have to settle for store-bought instead.

Doretta had just put her letters back inside their envelopes and set them next to the rest of the mail when Warren came into the kitchen.

"You look *mied*," he said, approaching the table.

"I am tired," Doretta admitted, "and I probably shouldn't have sat down at the table to look at the mail instead of getting supper started."

Warren stepped behind Doretta's chair and began rubbing her shoulders and the back of her neck. "Maybe working at the store all day is too much for you now that you're pregnant. Maybe I should start looking for someone to take over for you there."

Doretta shook her head. "I'm fine. I enjoy working with you at the nutrition center."

"I like having you there too, but your health, as well as the baby's, takes priority right now."

"If you could find someone willing to work part-time, I could cut back on my hours." Doretta turned in her chair to look up at him. "Would that keep you from worrying about me and our unborn child?"

Warren smiled and leaned over to kiss her forehead. "Maybe a little. But as your devoted husband who loves you very much, it's my job to worry about you and the baby."

"So if I cut down my time at the store, would that at least cause you to worry less?"

He nodded. "For now, at least. But as your September due date approaches, I'll want you to give up working at the store and stay close to home." Warren moved over to the refrigerator and opened the door. "But for now, dear *fraa*, I'd like you to go lie on the couch and rest while I fix supper."

Doretta opened her mouth to protest, but Warren spoke again before she could get a word out.

"No arguing now—I insist."

"Danki." Doretta smiled and pushed away from the table. How grateful she felt to have married such a thoughtful man. She thanked God every day for bringing Warren into her life.

Heading to the living room, Doretta placed one hand against her still-flat stomach. *Heavenly Father, I pray that this child within me will one day grow up and find a Christian mate who will love them as much as my husband loves me.*

Chapter 4

Irma couldn't believe that today was the first day of June, but the perpetual desk-top calendar said so. Today was her mother-in-law's birthday, and they'd been invited to celebrate the occasion with a surprise birthday supper at the home of LaVern's sister. Sylvia would make fried chicken, and LaVern's other sisters—Priscilla, Barbara, and Irene—would each bring an accompanying dish to go with the meal. That left dessert, which Irma had agreed to contribute. It was two o'clock already, and she still hadn't started baking the cake. She'd hoped to have it done already, but with all the interruptions she'd had so far today, Irma was behind on everything she'd planned to get done. With Myra down for a nap, and the boys both playing outside, Irma was finally ready to begin making the cake. It was apparent this one cake wouldn't be enough to feed a big crowd, however. Irma brushed her hands against the apron she wore and started thinking. *I wonder if someone else plans to bring a dessert besides me.* It wasn't unusual for Irma to stress over something like this, and if she wasn't careful, she could end up with an intense headache. *Maybe I should make two cakes to bring to tonight's celebration for Mildred.*

She moved away from the desk and got out the ingredients for her walnut coffee cake, which was also one of her mother-in-law's favorites.

Irma smiled as she thought about Mildred. Like everyone else, her mother-in-law wasn't without her faults, but she and LaVern's father had welcomed Irma into the family when she and LaVern left Montana and moved to Baltic to live with his parents for a time. The kindly way they'd treated Irma had been a healing balm to her hurting soul. Although Mildred and Paul had been disappointed when LaVern and Irma moved to Mount Hope, they'd accepted it and hadn't tried to interfere with LaVern's plans to become an auctioneer, which would include many events at the Mount Hope Events Center.

Irma's jaw clenched as she began mixing the cake batter into a bowl. *If LaVern and I had stayed in St. Ignatius, he wouldn't have a job he likes, and he'd probably be working for Homer still. I'm surprised LaVern stayed there as long as he did, but I guess it was so he could be close to me.*

Irma pushed aside her troubling thoughts to finish mixing the cake batter and get both cakes into the oven. A little batter remained in the bowl. She couldn't help putting a finger into what was left and tasting its sweet, rich flavor. Irma's taste buds understood Mildred's reason for liking this kind of cake so much because it was sure tasty. Irma brought the spoon and empty bowl over to the sink to rinse them off. Meanwhile, she looked forward to the delicious aroma of the baking cakes that would soon permeate her kitchen.

After setting the timer, Irma went to check on the boys. She found them both on the front porch steps, each with a cat in their lap.

"Hi, Mama." Clayton offered her a grin. "Wanna hold Mittens for a while?"

She shook her head. "I have two cakes in the oven, and I need to keep an eye on them. I only came out to see what you and your brother were up to."

"We ain't done nothin' bad," Brian was quick to say. "Just sittin' here, pettin' our katze."

"That's fine," Irma said. "Make sure you don't leave the yard, though. Okay?"

Both boys nodded and continued stroking their furry friends.

She paused a moment, taking in the children's activity and the decent weather they'd been blessed with today. Irma watched as Brian scratched under the cat's chin, and she smiled when the animal closed its eyes, as if in approval.

"Stripey sure likes it when I do this to him, and I enjoy listenin' to the kitty's purr."

Clayton eyed his older brother and tried to do the same with Mittens. Irma held back a giggle because he had rubbed the cat's chin instead of scratching it. She leaned over to show her son exactly how to move his fingers. Soon, with Irma's demonstration, Clayton's cat was purring loudly. Irma gave Mittens a few scratches behind the ears. "This is another place cats like to be scratched," she told the boys.

They nodded simultaneously and continued stroking their cats.

Irma brushed away the cat hairs that clung to her hands. "I'm going back inside now, boys. I need to check on the cakes."

"Can we have a piece when they're done?"

"No, Brian. The cakes are for Grandma Miller's birthday. We'll all have some after we've had supper at your Aunt Sylvia's house this evening."

"*Daadi* is goin' too, right?"

"Yes, Clayton. We'll leave here after he gets home from work and has had a chance to clean up and change his clothes."

"Do we hafta change too?" Brian asked.

Irma nodded. "We all need to look nice for Grandma's birthday."

"How come we never go to our other *grossmammi*'s house?" Brian stopped petting Stripey and looked at Irma with a sober expression.

"Because she lives far away in Montana."

"Can't we go there?"

Irma shook her head. "It's doubtful." Truthfully, Irma didn't care if she ever saw her mother again, and she had no desire to be anywhere near Homer. He was a horrible person, and she wouldn't want her children around him either.

Irma grasped the doorknob. "I'm going back inside now, but I'll call you when it's time to clean up and get changed."

"Okay," the boys said in unison.

When Irma entered the kitchen, she was relieved to see that the timer hadn't gone off yet. The last thing she needed were two overdone cakes to take to her sister and brother-in-law's house this evening.

Baltic, Ohio

All the noise inside Sylvia and Ray's house gave Irma a headache. In addition to her, LaVern, and their three children, LaVern's other three sisters, along with their husbands and children, had all come to celebrate Mildred's fifty-fifth birthday. Mildred's parents, Andy and Patricia Yoder, lived in the *daadihaus* that had been added onto Paul and Mildred's place about five years ago and had naturally been included in their daughter's birthday gathering as well. Mildred's three brothers—Daniel, Richard, and Ivan—and their wives had also been invited. None of LaVern's cousins had shown up, which was a good thing, because the house, although quite large, was bursting at the seams with a total of thirty-five people, who all seemed to be talking at the same time. Irma hadn't realized so many of LaVern's relatives would be here, and she didn't think the two cakes she'd made were large enough for everyone to have a piece. She was glad when Sylvia brought three-dozen chocolate cupcakes. Then Sylvia's husband took three tubs of vanilla ice cream from the freezer, so there was plenty to go around. Now, as everyone sat around eating their dessert, the chatter that had been going on all evening increased and grew louder.

When Irma thought her head would burst open from pain, Sylvia must have noticed her discomfort, for she came up to Irma and whispered, "You appear not to be feeling well. Why don't you go lie down in one of our guest rooms for a while?"

"I've developed a *koppweh*." Irma touched her forehead. "It's the kind that makes me feel nauseous."

"Maybe you should call it a night and go home where it's quiet so you can rest. Although I love having all of the family here at the same time, the noise level can get pretty high, which is enough to give anyone a headache." She patted Irma's shoulder. "Should I tell LaVern you have a koppweh and need to go home?"

Irma shook her head. "He and the kinner are having a good time, and I don't want to be the reason our evening is cut short. Besides, our driver will be here in less than an hour."

"Would you like to go lie down until he arrives?"

"No, that's okay. I'll just step outside for a while. Maybe the quiet plus the cool evening air will make me feel better."

"All right then. Would you like me to get your shawl?"

"I'm sure I'll be fine without it." Before Sylvia could respond, Irma slipped out the back door and closed it behind her.

Irma stood on the porch a few seconds then wandered out into the yard. The sun had already set, and now the full moon above cast a soft white glow over the yard. It provided just enough light to reveal the shape of the outbuildings. The shed where Ray kept their two buggies was to the left of Irma, and so was the barn.

Irma smiled, despite her headache that had lessened a bit since she'd come outside. LaVern had shared some cute stories with Irma about growing up with his siblings here in Baltic. His brother-in-law's house, the barn, and buggy shed had a welcoming feel compared to the buildings on Homer Schmucker's land in St. Ignatius. Irma was aware that LaVern's upbringing was a good one and that this buggy shed wasn't a threat to her. Even so, she found herself staring at the darkened structure while a cold feeling crept in around her.

Irma's smile faded, and she shuddered as she thought about the buggy shed where her stepfather had often doled out whatever punishment he thought was appropriate for Irma's misdeeds. He'd only used the buggy whip on her once, when she'd tried to escape his wrath. Irma could still feel the sting of that whip as it made contact with her back. She'd screamed, hoping her mother would hear and come to her rescue, but that hadn't happened. Mama had never interfered with Homer's disciplinary measures, which rarely involved his flesh-and-blood children. There was no doubt about it—they were the lucky ones or, more to the point, the favored ones.

It was no wonder Irma and her mother's relationship was strained. *Where was the love and support a mother should give?* Irma wondered. *What kind of a mother would allow her husband to treat one of her children so harshly?* Irma grimaced. *And Mama wonders why I won't come there for a visit or invite her to our home.* This seemed like a situation that may never be resolved. Would her mother ever apologize for the wrong deeds she had allowed to happen? And if, by some chance, Mama ever did say she was sorry, Irma wasn't sure she could forgive her. One thing Irma felt sure of was that Homer would never utter one word of remorse in his lifetime.

Although the evening air was cool, Irma was surprised that she'd broken out in a sweat. *I wish my real daed hadn't died. He never abused me physically, and Mama was a lot nicer back then too. If my husband was abusing any of our kinner, I would never stand for it. Mama must have loved her other children more than she did me.* Tears sprang to Irma's eyes. *If she loved me at all—which is highly doubtful.*

"Irma, are you okay? Sylvia said you came out here a while ago, and I was worried about you."

LaVern's deep voice startled Irma, and she whirled around to face him. "I—I have a koppweh and thought some fresh air might help." She didn't bother to mention that she'd been bothered by all the noise inside the house. LaVern probably wouldn't understand, since he seemed to enjoy being with lots of people. That was evident by the occupation he'd chosen. Many auctions drew in huge crowds.

He slipped an arm around her waist and pulled her close. "You should have told me you had a headache. I would've called our driver and asked him to pick us up sooner. He's here now, though. I saw his vehicle pull into the front yard a few minutes ago. When I told my mamm we'd be leaving, she said she'd get the kinner ready to go. So let's go back inside now and say our goodbyes, and then we can be on our way home."

Irma had no desire to go back into that noisy house. But it would be impolite to leave without saying goodbye, so she clasped LaVern's hand and went with him back to the house.

"When we get to home, why don't you fill the bathtub with warm water and have a nice soak?" LaVern suggested as they stepped onto the back porch.

She shook her head. "I can't do that. I'll need to get the kinner ready for bed."

"I'll take care of doing that tonight." He leaned down and gave her a kiss on the cheek.

"Danki, I appreciate it." Irma didn't know what she had done to deserve such a kind husband, but she was ever so glad she'd agreed to marry LaVern—and even happier that they'd left St. Ignatius and settled in Ohio.

Mount Hope

LaVern had gotten the children put to bed, and Irma was still soaking in the tub. He figured now was a good time for him to relax a bit, before his own bedtime.

He got a glass of milk from the kitchen and sat down in his favorite chair in the living room. *Ah, that feels better.*

LaVern thought about his wife and how quiet she'd been all evening. She didn't do well in crowds—he knew that much—but this had been a family gathering. If they'd been at an event with a bunch of strangers, it might have made sense, but these were all people Irma knew.

Maybe the koppweh was what kept Irma from socializing, he thought. *No one wants to carry on a conversation when their head is throbbing.*

LaVern finished his milk and took the empty glass out to the kitchen. Then he headed for the bathroom to check on Irma. She'd been in the tub quite a while, and he worried that she may have fallen asleep.

Stepping into the hall, he nearly bumped into his robe-clad wife. "Oh, good, you're out of the tub. How's your headache? Are you feeling any better?"

"A little." Her mouth drooped at the corners. "But I'm exhausted and more than ready for bed."

"Same here. I'll make sure all the battery-operated lights are turned off and join you in our room shortly."

"Okay." Irma yawned. "I may be asleep by the time you get there though."

He stepped forward and kissed her lips. "I'll say *gut nacht* now then."

"Good night, LaVern." She turned to the right and stepped into their room, closing the door behind her.

LaVern smiled. *I bet she'll feel better in the morning, when things are quiet and calm around here.*

Chapter 5

The weeks had seemed to fly by, with never-ending chores, and Irma struggled to get everything done. Tomorrow was Brian's birthday, and there would be another family gathering—this time at their home. Thanks to the warm summer weather, most of the festivities could take place outside rather than crowding into the house. There also wouldn't be as many people as there had been for Mildred's birthday gathering, since only LaVern's parents, grandparents, and his siblings with their young children had been invited. LaVern had promised to grill hot dogs, and Irma would serve baked beans, macaroni salad, and potato chips. For dessert, she planned to have vanilla cupcakes and chocolate ice cream, which Brian had requested. It was hard to believe that he'd be turning seven or that Irma and LaVern's eighth wedding anniversary would take place next month. Time sure went by quickly, even when a person was not having fun.

In the last few days, Irma had been cleaning the house, making sure things looked tidy for Brian's birthday party. Even though most of the festivities would be outdoors, some people would be coming inside to use the facilities or help in the kitchen. Irma had spent time dusting the furniture and cleaning the floors throughout the house. It wasn't the easiest thing to accomplish, what with taking care of the children, plus an added chore that her husband had asked her to do. Before LaVern's driver had showed up this morning, he'd said to Irma, "I have a few minutes to feed the horses before heading to work, but I don't have time to fill the stock tanks in their stalls with water."

It wasn't unusual for her husband to drop a task like this on Irma. LaVern's job was important, and being called away from Mount Hope to the outlying areas happened too often in Irma's mind. *I wish my husband could work every day in town and not have to travel away from his family.* It was hard not to be envious of other Amish women whose husbands had jobs that were closer to home. Some even had their business on the same property as their home.

Irma paused from washing the breakfast dishes and stared out the kitchen window as she reflected on the day LaVern had asked her to marry him. It was a day she would never forget. . . .

―――――≈―――――

St. Ignatius

"You seem kind of quiet this evening, Irma. Is something wrong?"

LaVern's question caused Irma to turn on the buggy seat to face him. "I was just thinking, is all."

He reached for her hand. "About me?"

"Jah. If you should decide to return to Ohio at the end of summer, I would miss seeing you every day."

"I was thinking maybe I should stay here and keep working for your daed. Then we can join the church and get married."

Irma's pulse raced at the thought of becoming LaVern's wife, but the idea of remaining in St. Ignatius held no appeal. "Homer is my stepfather, and I don't want to stay here." Irma almost choked on the words. She'd already told LaVern that Homer was a harsh man, but she'd never mentioned that he'd physically abused her, while not laying a finger against his biological children. Irma figured that if she told LaVern the truth, he probably wouldn't believe her. Homer knew quite well how to put on an act in front of people he wanted to impress. He was very good at pulling the wool over people's eyes.

"Irma, did you hear what I said?"

She blinked against the tears obscuring her vision. "I heard, and I do want to marry you, LaVern, but I can't live here, where everything I do and say will always be scrutinized."

"Then we'll move to Ohio. We can join the church there and get married. I'm sure my daed would let me work in his shop till I can find something I like better."

Irma blinked in rapid succession. "Really, LaVern? You'd be willing to move back to Ohio even though you like it here and had thought you might stay?"

"Jah. I love you, Irma, and I'd do anything to make you happy."

Irma sagged against the back of the buggy seat and gave a sigh of relief. Even though she had never been to Ohio or met any of LaVern's family, anything she might encounter there would be better than remaining here, under the watchful eye and criticism of her stepfather and spineless mother.

Mount Hope

The shrill cry of her daughter brought Irma's thoughts back to the present, and she turned away from the window. "For goodness' sake, Myra, what are you fussing about this time?"

Irma hurried from the kitchen and found her daughter on the living room floor with one of the boys' cats in her lap. The streak of red down Myra's arm suggested the cat had scratched her. Irma bent down, grabbed the cat, and hauled it outside. Then she picked up her daughter and took her to the kitchen to clean her arm and put some antiseptic ointment on the scratch. Once that was taken care of, Irma put Myra in the high chair and gave her a few crackers and her sippy cup filled with water and a small amount of apple juice.

While Myra ate her snack, Irma went to the back door and looked out into the yard to see what the boys were up to. They each had their favorite cats and were pulling them around in the little red wagon. She was relieved to see that they weren't up to any kind of mischief at the moment but figured the cats probably wouldn't stay in the wagon very long—and then her sons would no doubt find something else to do.

Irma returned to the kitchen to finish doing the dishes and get started making the cupcakes for Brian's birthday celebration. She figured it would be best to make an extra dozen, knowing that her children (especially Brian and Clayton) would not want to wait till tomorrow to have one. That would be better and easier on her nerves than listening to them whine.

<hr>

The following morning after breakfast, Irma put Myra in her stroller and headed down the driveway to the mailbox while the boys took turns on the swing in their front yard. She was glad they were sharing and smiled when she saw Brian pushing his younger brother.

"Not too high," Irma called as she continued her trek to the mailbox. She glanced back and saw Brian bob his head a few times. *Good boy. At least you understood and are paying attention to what I said.*

Myra squealed and clapped her hands when a colorful butterfly fluttered past them.

"*Fleddermaus*—butterfly," Irma said, teaching Myra some English words. "So *schee*—pretty."

The little girl cried when the butterfly flew off in the opposite direction. Irma knew she had to do something to divert Myra's attention, so she stopped walking, bent down, and plucked a purple wildflower growing along the end of the driveway, which she then handed to her daughter. Myra settled down right away, revealing the dimples in her cheeks as she grinned up at her mother.

Lifting her gaze to the cloudless sky, Irma released a breath of relief. Now she wouldn't have to listen to anymore crying—at least not for a while. Like many other two-year-olds, Myra was likely to find something else to fuss about before the day was out. Irma hoped all three of her children would behave themselves today so she could get everything done in readiness for Brian's birthday gathering this evening.

At the mailbox, Irma found a couple of advertising catalogs, along with three envelopes. One was from her friend Doretta, one from Eleanor, and a third envelope postmarked St. Ignatius had been addressed to Brian. *I wonder if Mama remembered that today is his birthday and sent a card.*

Irma slipped the mail inside the tote bag she carried over her shoulder and pushed Myra's stroller back up the driveway. The swing was empty now, and the boys were on the porch, each holding a cat. Irma was glad they hadn't taken the felines inside. After having thoroughly cleaned the house in preparation for the party, she certainly didn't need any cat hair floating about the place.

She lifted Myra from the stroller and took her inside. Irma would let her daughter play on the kitchen floor with a few pots and pans while she looked at the mail. After seating herself at the table, Irma opened Eleanor's letter first. It was filled with news about her two little ones, and Eleanor had also asked how things were going for Irma these days.

"They'd be going a lot better if I didn't have so much work to do," Irma mumbled as she put the letter back in its envelope. She opened Doretta's letter next and read with interest about some of the things her friend had written about her pregnancy. Doretta had also mentioned that a new business had opened up in Grabill. Irma thought about the conversation she'd had with LaVern a few months ago regarding a possible trip for the family to Grabill. Unfortunately, LaVern had become even more in demand as an auctioneer this summer, and it didn't appear that they would be making a family trip anywhere outside Ohio this year.

Irma set Doretta's letter aside and picked up the one addressed to Brian. She pursed her lips and stared at the envelope. *Should I call him to open the card now or wait until this evening to give it him? Maybe I should let Brian open the card now so I don't have to think about it for the rest of the day.*

Irma got up and went to open the front door. Brian and Clayton were still on the porch, but their cats were not. Apparently the critters had gotten tired of being held captive by the boys and made their escape to the barn or found some other good hiding place.

"Brian, please come inside," Irma said. "Something came for you in the mail today."

The boy leaped to his feet and whizzed past Irma so quickly her skirt fluttered. Not to be outdone, Clayton also made a beeline through the open door.

When the three of them entered the kitchen, where Myra still sat pounding a wooden spoon against one of the pans, Irma suggested that Brian open his card in the living room where it was quieter. He took the envelope from her and raced out of the kitchen with Clayton on his heels. Irma followed and stood near the couch where Brian was tearing open the envelope. He grinned up at her when a ten-dollar bill slipped out of the card. *"Geld!"* he shouted. "Can we go to town now so I can buy something?"

"Not today," Irma said with a shake of her head. "There's too much yet that needs to be done in order to be ready for your birthday party. Maybe tomorrow we can go shopping." She reached for the card. "Don't you want to see who it's from?"

"Oh, jah." He gave a firm nod.

Irma read the birthday greeting and told Brian that it was from his grandma who lived in Montana.

"Can we go there so I can thank her for it?" he asked.

She shook her head. "That's not possible, Son. Tomorrow, you can write her a thank-you note, though."

His brows furrowed. "I don't know how."

"I'll help you with the words."

"Okay." Brian set the card on the coffee table, and holding onto his money, he dashed for the stairs.

"Where you goin'?" Clayton called.

"To my room to put the geld someplace safe!"

Clayton started to follow Brian, but Irma stopped him. "Why don't you come to the kitchen with me? You can help me figure out what to fix for lunch."

The boy heaved a sigh but did as she said. Irma waited until he'd left the room, then she picked up the card and read it again. A knot formed in her stomach. She wished things weren't so strained between her and Mama. With Homer in the picture, Irma didn't think she and her mother would ever be close like they had been when Irma's father was alive. In fact, she was certain of it, because some of the bitterness Irma felt was toward her mother.

———————≈———————

At four o'clock that afternoon, Irma had just finished making her macaroni salad and placed it in the refrigerator when she heard a commotion outside. She opened the back door and looked out, but seeing nothing, she hurried out of the kitchen and opened the front door. Irma's eyes widened at the sight before her. She had to cover her ears to drown out the shrill barking of a shaggy brown dog as it ran circles around Brian, who was whooping, hollering, and clapping his hands. LaVern stood off to one side, arms folded and a big grin on his bearded face. Clayton stood next to him, also smiling ear to ear. What in the world did these three have to be so happy about, and why was this mangy-looking dog in their yard?

Irma stepped off the porch, nearly tripping on a pile of small rocks near the door, and walked straight up to her husband. "What's going on here, LaVern? Where did that *hund* come from?" She pointed at the frisky dog.

"I got him for Brian. Thought it'd be a nice birthday present and a good way to teach him the responsibility of taking care of a pet."

Irma frowned. "And who do you think will actually end up caring for that mutt?" She pointed to herself. "Me, that's who! And you should know that I don't have time to do one more daily chore."

Seemingly oblivious to their parents' conversation, Brian and Clayton chased the yapping dog around the yard.

Struggling not to give in to the anger she felt, Irma whirled around and went back into the house. It frustrated her to think that LaVern would get their son a dog without talking to her about it first. Didn't her opinion matter at all?

———— ≈ ————

That evening, when their guests all arrived, Irma forced herself to put on a smiling face. It wouldn't be good if LaVern's parents, or anyone else for that matter, knew how irritated Irma was with her husband this evening. What happened to the pleasant relationship they'd once had, when LaVern tried to please Irma more than anyone else? Now he seemed more interested in his job as an auctioneer and fooling around with the kids whenever he was at home. Of course, LaVern had certain chores to do too, but there didn't seem to be a place in his schedule for him to spend the quality time with Irma that she felt she deserved.

Maybe he doesn't love me anymore, she thought as she took Myra out of her high chair. *He might wish he'd never married me at all. Does he think my opinion on important matters, such as getting a dog, doesn't have any value? Have I not been a loving, helpful wife to LaVern since we got married?*

Tears sprang to Irma's eyes, and she quickly whisked them away. *I must not allow my frustrations to ruin Brian's birthday. No matter how unimportant or neglected I feel, I need to make every effort to be cheerful and a pleasant hostess this evening.*

Chapter 6

Irma spent the next few weeks either reminding Brian to feed, water, and clean up after his dog or taking care of the mutt herself. From the moment Buster had come to live with them, she'd known it would turn out like this. Why couldn't LaVern have seen it too? Irma couldn't help feeling frustrated with her husband. This was yet one more thing she'd have to contend with—another chore that would need her time. Irma would have appreciated having less on her list of things to do around their place, but that list seemed to be growing all the time. Why was LaVern so unaware of her stressed-out situation? *I need to speak to my husband about this,* she told herself. *But I'm sure he'll only play it down. LaVern will probably say that I am overreacting.* She released a heavy sigh. *If I am, then what is my problem?*

Irma bent to pick up a pair of Clayton's socks that he'd left on his bedroom floor. How many times had she reminded him about putting them away? What if Brian's dog had gotten into the room and chewed up the socks, the way the hund had done a few days ago when he'd snuck into Brian's bedroom and torn one of his shirts that hadn't been hung in the closet. *I'd have to say that Buster is an added* unflaat. *I doubt that I could ever warm up to the idea of having any animal in the house, much less a nuisance like him.*

Irma went to the utility room and grabbed a dustpan and broom to sweep up the piles of dog hair she'd discovered in the hallway leading to the bedroom stairs. Cleaning up the dog's hair, not to mention the messes Buster made, seemed to be a never-ending job. *I can't help but think that I've gained another child. If my husband thinks having this dog is such a great idea, maybe he should be the one to go behind Brian's hund and clean up after him.*

"That animal's place is outside," she grumbled. "If LaVern would keep his promise and build a dog run, I wouldn't have to put up with Buster's messes in the house."

Of course, the messes weren't limited to the house. Whenever Brian's dog was outside running free, he dug up plants and flower bulbs in Irma's flower beds and had even snatched some of the vegetables from her garden. Unless LaVern found the time to build a dog run, it seemed like a no-win situation for Irma and continual reminders for Brian to keep an eye on his dog.

Maybe I could hire someone else to build the dog's outside enclosure, she thought. *I bet one of the teenage boys from our church district could do it, and he would probably be glad for the chance to earn some extra money.* She gave a crisp nod. *I'll go out to the phone shed sometime today and make a few calls to some of the mothers I know and see if any of their boys would like to tackle the job and earn some extra cash. LaVern will probably be pleased that there will be one less job I'm asking him to do.*

Irma started sweeping again. *And I'll be a lot happier when Buster is confined and I have less to do.*

Grabill

After getting the bed made and starting a load of laundry, Doretta thought she'd take a break. At six-months pregnant, she didn't have as much stamina as she used to. Doretta glanced out the window. *Should I stay indoors and take a seat on the sofa or go outside to soak up some sunshine?* She opted for the latter, which would be more fun and relaxing.

Doretta went out the front door and smiled as she took a seat on the front porch bench to watch the hummingbirds flitting from the feeders she'd set out earlier in the summer. Doretta felt blessed to be sitting in the warm sun, enjoying nature, and eagerly awaiting the birth of her and Warren's baby. Just three more months, and their son or daughter would be here. Doretta could hardly wait to be a mother, and she knew that Warren was equally happy about taking on the role of fatherhood.

She patted her ever-growing stomach. *He will be a good daadi, because he's loving, patient, and kind.* She closed her eyes. *Thank You, Lord, for bringing Warren and me together and blessing us with a cozy home and a business that's doing so well. I also thank You for all our family members. Please bless them and fill their lives with the joy and peace that comes from knowing You.*

Doretta thought about her friends Eleanor and Irma and said a prayer for them. She hoped they were both well and enjoying their summer as much as she was. Too soon, the warm weather would be gone, and fall would set in.

Mount Hope

Irma had just stepped out of the phone shed, where she'd left a message for Glen Herschberger's mother about the possibility of him building a dog run, when she caught sight of her three children through the open doorway. Myra and Clayton were seated inside the children's little red wagon, and Brian had hooked the dog on its leash to the handle.

"Come on, Buster!" He clapped his hands and tugged on the dog's collar. "Get going!" he hollered.

Buster didn't budge, but when Brian smacked Buster's rear, the dog took off across the grass like he'd been stung by a hornet. Apparently, the younger ones in the wagon thought it was funny, because they laughed and waved their hands in the air.

Irma raced up the driveway, shouting at Brian, "Stop that dog right now!"

"I can't, Mama—Buster's going real fast, and he's getting away from me."

The wagon zigzagged back and forth through the grass. It was going so fast, and the children made such a racket, causing several blue birds to swoop out of the maple tree and scatter in every direction.

Before Irma could reach the dog, he broke free, but the wagon kept rolling. She gasped when it hit a bump and toppled onto its side, dumping out both screaming children. Brian chased after Buster, while Irma hurried to see if Myra and Clayton had been hurt.

Kneeling on the ground, Irma checked Myra and Clayton for scrapes, bruises, or possible broken bones. Fortunately, all she found was a small bump on Myra's head and plenty of grass stains on both children's clothes. She shuddered at the thought of how much worse it could have been and gently patted Myra's back to calm her down and stop the sobs. Clayton, on the other hand, didn't seem to be as shaken, and he jumped up and joined his brother in the chase to capture the dog.

Irma took Myra inside, cleaned her up, and gave her some water to drink. In no time, the little girl stopped crying and went to play happily with her toys. Irma remained in the kitchen until she heard the back door open and close, letting her know the boys had come in. She moved toward the door and told Clayton to go wash up. When he disappeared down the hallway, Irma grabbed Brian by the shoulders and gave him a good shake. "What were you thinking? What possessed you to hook your hund to the handle of that wagon? Didn't you know how dangerous that could be for your sister and brother?"

His chin quivered a bit, but he did not give in to tears. "I thought it would be fun to see if Buster could pull the wagon. Besides, Clayton and Myra said they wanted to go for a ride."

Irma gave him another firm shake. "That was a foolish thing to do. Your brother or sister could have been seriously hurt when the wagon toppled over."

"S—sorry, Mama. I didn't do it on purpose. I just thought—"

With the flat of her hand, Irma gave his backside a swat and said, "Now go to your room, and don't come out until I say you can!"

Without looking back, Brian ran down the hall and scampered up the stairs. Irma collapsed into a chair at the kitchen table. She hated disciplining the children, but what Brian had done was wrong, and he needed to learn a lesson. *At least I wasn't too harsh with him*, she told herself. *If I'd done something like that when I was a girl, I can only imagine how severely Homer would have punished me. I probably wouldn't have been able to sit down for a week. Brian got off easy with just one swat.*

≈

Kidron, Ohio

Carrying a package in one hand and wearing a satisfied smile, LaVern left Lehman's Hardware and headed for his driver's van. He had bought Irma something special—an item she'd been wanting for a long time, but he would wait to give it to her until their anniversary next week. In the meantime, he would need to locate a good hiding place so neither Irma nor the snoopy boys would discover it. LaVern remembered how last Christmas he'd hidden a few toys for the children in the toolshed, thinking no one would be going in there except him. That had been a mistake. He hadn't anticipated Clayton would pick the shed as a place to hide from Brian during a game of hide-and-seek. LaVern was beyond surprised when the little stinker came into the house with two paper sacks containing gifts the children were not supposed to see until Christmas morning.

I learned my lesson that day and won't make the same mistake again, LaVern thought as he climbed into his driver's van and closed the door. *Where I put Irma's gift, it'll have to be in a better place and up high enough so none of the kinner will be able to reach it.*

"Did you get everything you needed?" LaVern's driver Carl asked.

"Yep, sure did." LaVern set the sack on the floor by his feet.

"Don't forget to put your seatbelt on," Carl said after turning the key in the ignition.

LaVern rolled his eyes. "Have I ever?"

"Not in my rig, but there's always a first time." Carl pulled out of the parking lot and into traffic. "You probably heard about the accident that occurred last week outside of Walnut Creek. Two Amish passengers were hurt real bad because they weren't wearing seatbelts."

LaVern nodded. "I did hear about it. They were from Pennsylvania, passing through on their way up north to attend the funeral of a friend."

"Yep, and they were lucky, 'cause if they'd been killed, it could have ended up being their own funeral others would have had to attend."

LaVern looked out the side window at the passing scenery. *Carl is throwing cold water on my happy mood. I can't wait to get home for the day and relax.* At times, it wasn't easy to listen to certain topics of conversation. A lot of crazy things were going on in the world, and sometimes it could be overwhelming. But when LaVern hired any driver, he was kind of at their mercy. They were liable to talk about any topic at any time. Today, he really didn't want to hear about funerals.

Since LaVern thought it was time for a topic change, he mentioned the warm weather they'd been having.

"Yes, indeed," Carl agreed, "but I'm always glad when summer comes. The only thing I don't like is when too much humidity takes over. Makes it hard to do outside chores when sweat begins pouring off you like someone's squeezed out a wet sponge."

"I know what you mean. And when the humidity gets really bad, it doesn't matter whether you're outside or in."

"You're right about that. But even so, I still prefer the warmer months—humidity and all—rather than the cold, snowy days of winter when the roads get nasty, making it hard to drive."

For fleeting moments, LaVern sometimes found himself wishing he could have a car to drive for long distances, but he really did prefer the horse-and-buggy mode of transportation. In fact, he liked the Amish way of life and had no regrets about his decision to get baptized and join the Amish church. LaVern felt thankful that televisions and the internet were not permitted in Amish homes. He also appreciated the fact that the Plain people's way of life fostered a strong family unit and a special sense of community, with a willingness to help others in need. Although LaVern would be the first to admit that being Amish did not make one perfect, he felt blessed every day to have grown up in an Amish home with godly parents. He hoped that his and Irma's children would feel the same way when they came to the age of accountability and eventually entered adulthood.

Mount Hope

When Carl pulled his vehicle up LaVern's driveway, LaVern paid him, grabbed the sack beneath his feet, and said goodbye. After he stepped down from the van, LaVern started for the barn but turned to the left at the sound of steady hammering. *I wonder what's going on over by my buggy shed.* He headed in the direction of the noise and stopped short when he saw Glen Herschberger hammering two pieces of lumber together.

LaVern went straight up to the teenager and asked, "What are you doing?" He couldn't help his dismay when he discovered what looked like a dog run was half made. *Irma shouldn't be so impatient with me. I would've taken care of this chore one evening this week.*

Glen looked up and grinned at LaVern. "I'm buildin' a dog run for Buster. Your fraa called my mamm and asked if I'd be willing to do it."

"Oh, she did, huh?"

"Jah, and she said she'd pay me for doin' the job too."

Irritation welled in LaVern's soul, and he clenched his jaw. This bit of information from a teenage boy in their community had thrown cold water on the excitement LaVern had felt moments ago about the anniversary gift he'd bought for Irma today. Now, he needed to hide the gift someplace safe and go up to the house to confront his wife about this dog-run situation. Of course, he would need to be careful how and when he told her the way he felt about her going behind his back to get a dog run built. The last thing the children needed was to hear their parents quarreling. And with LaVern's irritation mounting, he could very well say something that might lead to a heated argument.

Chapter 7

After hiding Irma's gift way back in the hayloft, LaVern entered the house through the back door. When he stepped into the kitchen, he was relieved to see that Irma was alone in the room, tearing lettuce leaves into a serving bowl. No aromas emanated from the oven or stovetop, indicating that supper wasn't in the process of being cooked. But that didn't really matter right now. LaVern had something to say, and if the children were not within earshot, he planned to say it. "Where are the kinner?" he asked without saying hello or giving his wife the kiss he normally produced quite happily when he arrived home from work.

"Clayton and Myra are in the living room, playing with toys." She turned to face him. "I sent Brian to his room a few hours ago and told him to stay there until I said it was okay to come out."

"I assume he did something he was told not to do?"

"Not exactly." Irma pushed a wayward strand of hair back under her head covering. "He did something he shouldn't have done, without asking, and because of his foolish act, Brian's siblings could have been seriously hurt."

Blinking rapidly, LaVern pulled his fingers through the ends of his beard. He guessed what he had to say could wait until he heard the details of her complaint. He joined her at the table and said, "Tell me what happened."

"Okay." Irma's shoulders hunched a bit, and she gave a heavy sigh.

LaVern recognized his wife's frustration. *She's obviously upset over the children, so I'll try to be supportive and hear what's on Irma's mind.*

LaVern listened attentively as she explained that Brian had hooked Buster to the wagon handle with the intent of having the dog pull the wagon around the yard. Irma's lips trembled as she told LaVern that after a bit of a wild ride for Myra and Clayton, who were riding inside the wagon, the dog had broken free, and the wagon had tipped over, dumping Myra and Clayton out onto the ground. Irma paused. "I'm just glad our daughter only had a small bump on her head, and it was nothing serious. Clayton was fine other than some grass stains on his trousers." Her forehead wrinkled. "I was really upset with Brian for doing something so foolish. Either one of his siblings could have been seriously hurt, and he should have known better than to try to make his hund pull the wagon."

LaVern held back from saying anything at first. *I'm not trying to excuse our eldest son's actions, because he was at fault, but Brian's only a few years older than Clayton. It sounds like my fraa needs to watch the boys more carefully.* "You are right, Irma," he said. "It wasn't a smart thing for our boy to do. However, Brian is an impulsive boy, and he obviously didn't think it through."

She quirked an eyebrow. "What are you saying? Do you think I was wrong for sending him to his room?" Before LaVern could respond, Irma quickly added, "Brian is lucky I didn't give him a sound *bletching*." A pink flush spread across her face.

LaVern frowned. "I don't think what Brian did was deserving of a spanking. I am sure he didn't do it on purpose in the hope of hurting his little sister and brother. Since our horse pulls the carriage that we all ride in, maybe Brian was trying to mimic that, by seeing if Buster could pull Clayton and Myra in the wagon. I bet he thought it would be fun, and his brother and sister obviously did too or they wouldn't have gotten into the wagon."

Irma lowered her gaze and then cleared her throat. "If we're done with this conversation, I'd better finish the salad I have barely started."

"Could you please wait on that a few more minutes? There's something else I'd like to discuss with you."

"About the kinner?"

He shook his head. "It concerns the teenage boy building a dog run out by the buggy shed."

"What about it?"

"When I spoke with Glen, he said you had asked him to do it."

"That's right, I did."

LaVern pushed his shoulders back. "I told you I would build Buster a dog run, so why did you go behind my back and ask Glen?"

"I did ask you, LaVern, and you agreed to do it. But that was several weeks ago, and you haven't even started the project." Her nostrils flared. "After what happened today, can you blame me for wanting to get that hund in a safe place that will keep him out of trouble?"

"I thought you had put the blame on Brian since he's the one who hooked him to the handle and made Buster pull the wagon." LaVern spoke through his teeth with forced restraint. "Isn't that why you sent Brian to his room?"

"Yes, it is, but that troublesome dog is always doing something naughty when he's free to roam around the yard, such as digging holes where they're not wanted, destroying some of my plants, and snitching things from the garden." Irma clasped her hands so tightly that her knuckles turned white. "And in the house, it's just as bad. Buster not only sheds his hair all over the place but he chews everything in sight. I am sick of it! He belongs outside but shouldn't be free to roam all over the place, because Brian does not keep a close eye on him."

"Guess I could give the dog a good brushing weekly—outside, of course. I could also show Brian how to do it. That would help minimize the loose hairs being found around the inside of the house."

Irma unfolded her hands. "Am I not making myself clear, LaVern? If you took the time to show Brian how to brush Buster, how long do you think it would take till he forgot about doing it regularly?" She gave a huff, and her arms dropped to her sides. "With your busy schedule and Brian's forgetfulness, I'd be the one who ended up brushing the hund. Besides, the dog hair is not the whole problem. As I said previously—"

LaVern held up one hand. "Okay, I get it. But you can't keep a dog caged up all the time. He needs the freedom to run and play, just like our kids."

"I understand, but when Buster's not supervised, he needs to be in an outside dog run."

"All right, but the kids won't like it. I can tell you that. Buster was Brian's birthday present, and it won't be any fun for Brian if his dog is cooped up in a pen most of the time."

Irma planted her hands against her hips as she stood from the chair. "So I guess our son and his hund's needs are more important than mine?"

"I did not say that."

"Sure sounded like it to me."

LaVern could see from the determined set of his wife's jaw that he was not going to win this argument. And as much as he hated to admit it, she had made some valid points about the trouble Buster caused, which put more work on her, having to clean up after him all the time. He pushed his chair aside and stood. "I'll go out and help Glen finish building the enclosure. Between the two of us, we can get the job done a lot quicker than with him working on it by himself."

Irma's lips parted in a brief smile. "Danki, LaVern. I appreciate that very much. I'll plan on serving supper a little later than usual so you have more time. Oh, and feel free to invite Glen to join us for the meal."

"Sounds good." He went around the table and gave her a hug. "I love you, and I'm sorry I didn't make the time to build the dog run sooner. I should have been more considerate of your feelings."

She leaned her head against his shoulder and sighed. "Danki, dear husband. I love you too."

When Irma called the children for breakfast the following morning, Clayton came into the kitchen, along with Myra, but there was no sign of Brian. "Where's your bruder?" Irma asked, directing her question to Clayton.

"Said he wasn't hungerich and went outside to see his hund," the boy responded. "I heard him cryin' last night. Guess he was sad 'cause Buster couldn't sleep in his room."

"I'm sorry he's sad, but Buster's place is not on Brian's bed."

Clayton tipped his head back and looked up at Irma with a slack expression. "How come?"

"Because, like most dogs, he probably has fleas. And besides, that mutt sheds hair all over the place, and I get stuck cleaning it up." Irma picked Myra up and placed her in the high chair. She looked back at Clayton. "Would you please go outside and tell Brian to come in for breakfast?"

Clayton looked at the empty table. "There ain't no food ready for us to eat."

"We are just having cereal this morning, and it will be on the table by the time you and Brian come in."

"Okay, Mama. I'll go get my bruder." Clayton shuffled out the door.

Irma got out four bowls and spoons and placed them on the table. LaVern wouldn't be joining them, since he'd left early for an auction near Apple Creek and said he would grab a few doughnuts and some coffee at one of the stands after he got to the event. Irma was pleased that LaVern and Glen had finished the dog run for Buster last evening. Now, she wouldn't have to worry about her garden or flowerbeds being torn up by the mutt, and Buster wouldn't be sneaking into the house all the time.

Irma got out the cereal and the goat's milk. Myra was getting fussy, so she poured some cereal and milk into a bowl and placed it on her daughter's wooden tray, along with a spoon. Once Myra started eating, Irma poured orange juice into her and the boys' glasses. Since Clayton hadn't returned with Brian yet, Irma decided to sit at the table, pray, and begin eating her own breakfast. She was certain they would be along any minute and would probably gobble down their cereal before she had the chance to finish her meal.

After fifteen minutes went by and there was still no sign of the boys, Irma took Myra out of her high chair, because the child had finished eating, and so had she. Then, Irma opened the back door and hollered, "Clayton! Brian! Your breakfast is ready!"

No response. Irma looked around. She saw no sign of either one of the boys. Irma pursed her lips. *They're probably out there by the dog run, and now I suppose I'm going to have to go get them.* She picked her daughter up and carried the child on her hip. Although Myra could have walked on her own, it would be much quicker to carry the little girl across the yard than holding her hand while they trudged through the thick grass that needed to be mowed. *One more job for me to get done,* Irma thought. *With LaVern gone so much, it seems like my chores are never-ending.*

As she approached the newly built dog run, Irma saw Brian and Clayton kneeling inside the enclosure, petting Buster. Apparently, LaVern had put the latch on the door low enough that Brian could reach it and have access to letting the dog in and out on his own.

"Boys, your breakfast is on the table," Irma said, lowering Myra to the ground and moving closer to the dog run. "Please go inside now and eat."

Brian turned to look at her with tears in his eyes. "I can't leave Buster. He's really sad being out here all by himself. He was whimpering when I came outside."

"You can let him out to play for a while after you've finished your cereal, but you must watch him closely so he doesn't do any digging. And you'll need to put him right back in the pen before you come into the house again. Is that clear?"

"Jah, Mama, and I promise not to let him do nothing bad." Brian gave Buster a few pats on the head and stood. Clayton did the same.

Irma opened the gate, and once the boys were out, she closed it again. Buster let out a few loud barks and pawed at the wire fencing.

"It's all right, Buster," Brian called over his shoulder. "We'll be back to see you soon, and I'll bring a ball so we can play fetch in the yard."

Irma was thankful that the boys had cooperated and hadn't put up a fuss. She did not want to be in a position where she'd feel the need to dole out more punishment and feel guilty about it afterward. Hopefully, the rest of this day would go well, with all three children doing what they were told. She had several things on her list to do today, and she was determined to get them all done without interruption or any problems with her children.

As Irma made her way back to the house, this time holding Myra's hand, she thought about her friend Doretta and the excitement about her pregnancy she'd shared in her last letter. Once more, Irma felt relieved that it was not she who was expecting a baby. Although she'd never mentioned it to LaVern or anyone else, Irma always felt relieved each time her monthly came on schedule, indicating that she was not pregnant. Thankfully, this month had been no exception.

Chapter 8

Irma stared at the calendar and shook her head. This was her and LaVern's eighth anniversary, and it was hard to believe they'd been married that long. Where had the time gone?

The first half of her day would be busy, making sure everything was done from the list she had made. Irma was excited about getting away for their anniversary, even if it was for only one night.

Since the animals would be alone while he and Irma were gone, LaVern said he would make sure to fill the water dishes for the dog and cats and set out plenty of food for them. He would also put the horses out to pasture to eat in the field and make sure their water tank was filled.

Irma smiled as she looked out the window. *I have grown to love this area and the community we're a part of, although I still miss the life I used to know when my daed was alive and I could spend time with my friends Doretta and Eleanor.*

Irma thought once again about how thankful she was that LaVern had chosen to live in Ohio and hadn't stayed in Montana where she would have been forced to see her mother and stepfather on a regular basis. The thought of it caused Irma to shudder.

"Are you cold, Mama? Is that why you're shivering like that?" Brian asked, stepping up to her.

"No. In fact, I'm quite warm. And it wasn't a shiver. It was a shudder."

His brows lowered as he repeated what she'd said as a question.

Irma nodded. "Jah, it was a shudder from thinking about something I'd rather forget."

"Is it about Buster and the holes he used to dig before Daadi and Glen built the dog run?"

"No, it wasn't about that. It was something about my past." In order to end the conversation, Irma asked Brian a question. "Why don't you go on upstairs to your room and start packing for your stay at Grandpa and Grandma Miller's tonight? Maybe you can help Clayton put some things in his small suitcase, and I'll take care of packing for Myra."

"What about Buster? Can he go to Grandma and Grandpa's too?"

"No, he will be fine in his dog run until we get back tomorrow evening."

Brian frowned. "But that's a long time, and my hund can't be cooped up in that cage till we get home."

"It's only twenty-four hours, and Buster will be okay. We'll give him plenty of food and water. Also, since part of his dog run is in the shade, he won't get too hot. Besides, he can earn his keep by watching the house for us while we're away."

"He will miss me, and I'll miss him. I don't wanna spend the night at Grandma and Grandpa's while you and Daadi stay at some fancy hotel."

"The Carlisle Inn in Sugarcreek is very nice, but it's not what I would call fancy."

"Can't I stay here by myself so Buster won't be sad and lonely?"

"You are too young to be left alone overnight." Irma clasped Brian's shoulders and turned him toward the kitchen door that led to the hallway. "Now please go upstairs so you can pack whatever you need, and ask Clayton to do the same. As soon as your daed and his driver get here, we'll need to leave."

Brian opened his mouth but then closed it and darted out of the room.

Irma stepped into the utility room and opened the closet door. She'd hidden LaVern's gift in there and wanted to put it in her suitcase before he came home. She would wait until they were at the hotel to give it to him, either before they ate dinner at the hotel restaurant or afterward when they returned to their room. She looked forward to this evening and being able to spend some quality time alone with her husband. They didn't get away by themselves very often, and she appreciated the willingness of LaVern's parents to keep the children overnight.

I'd better get Myra's suitcase packed, and mine as well, Irma thought. *Then, I'll check on the boys and make sure they've both packed their pajamas and toothbrushes.*

Sugarcreek, Ohio

By the time they had dropped the children off at their grandparents' place in Baltic, it was five o'clock, and by six, their driver had taken them to the lovely inn in Sugarcreek. They'd checked in, quickly put their bags in the room, and walked over to the Dutch Valley Restaurant, where they now sat, looking over the menu. Irma thought it was nice that the restaurant was on the same property as the inn. It appeared to be a popular place to eat, as evidenced by the number of people sitting at the various tables in the dining area. Also, the parking lot had many vehicles in it, but the nice thing was that their driver didn't have to hunt for a spot to park. He had simply pulled right up to the inn's entrance to unload their things.

"I'm having trouble deciding what to order," Irma said, looking at LaVern from across the table. "There are several delicious choices."

He smiled. "I agree, but if we do the buffet instead of ordering off the menu, we won't have to wait for our food."

"You must be hungerich. I should have given you a snack when you first got home."

"I'm not that hungry. Just anxious to get back to our room at the inn so I can enjoy your company and give you the *geschenk* I bought at Lehman's a few weeks ago."

"I have a gift for you too." Irma was eager to see what LaVern had gotten for her. From the twinkle in his eyes and the grin on his face, she figured whatever he'd bought must be something he knew she would like. Irma hoped LaVern would appreciate the gift she had for him too.

"Guess if you want to do the buffet, I'll do it as well. That way we can pick and choose what we want," Irma said.

"Sounds good to me."

They walked across the room and joined a line of other people waiting to dish up from the delicious-smelling items on the buffet.

———————— ≈ ————————

When Irma and LaVern entered their hotel room an hour and a half later, Irma stood inside the doorway, taking it all in because she hadn't when they'd hurriedly set their luggage inside the room.

"Oh, my. . . This is such a lovely corner room," she exclaimed. "I had no idea it was so beautiful."

"It's called the Deluxe Executive Room." LaVern put his arm around Irma's waist. "It offers more than the standard rooms, and I wanted to do something special for you."

Holding hands, they wandered around the room, looking at every detail. In addition to the king-size bed, they had a sitting area with a gas fireplace and a small dining table with two chairs. In the middle of the table sat a fresh flower arrangement, along with a bottle of sparkling grape juice, two fancy goblets, and a gift basket filled with cheese, trail bologna, assorted chocolates, crackers, and a pretty tea towel.

"I certainly never expected all of this," Irma murmured.

LaVern kissed Irma's cheek, and then trailed butterfly kisses down her neck. "I ordered these items to make our stay here tonight even more special."

"It certainly does." She twirled around. "And this room is so nice."

"Jah, and look over there near the bed." LaVern pointed to the Jacuzzi tub. "I believe that's big enough for the both of us."

Irma's face warmed. Even after eight years of marriage, he could still make her blush. "Oh, look. . . There's even a balcony over there." She moved in that direction and wasn't surprised when LaVern joined her.

"Would you like your gift now?" LaVern asked after nuzzling her ear with his nose.

She bobbed her head. "As I said earlier, I have something for you too."

"Okay, but I want to go first."

"All right." Irma took a seat on the end of the bed and waited until LaVern took an oblong box from his suitcase. He wore a big grin as he handed it to her. She fumbled with the flaps but finally got it open. Her eyes widened when she reached inside and withdrew a lovely wind chime. The tag attached told the name of the chime: "Just a Breeze." She held the chime with one hand and gave one of the copper-colored tubes a gentle push with the other hand. A rich, melodious sound filled the room and she gasped. "Oh, LaVern, it's beautiful! I've always wanted something like this to hang in the yard. Thank you ever so much."

"You're welcome. One of the best things about the chime is that it's made to last with poly wood, six powder-coated aluminum chimes, and it's weather-resistant. It was also hand-crafted right here in the USA."

"I'll treasure it for years to come." Irma placed her gift on the bed and went to her suitcase to retrieve the present she had for LaVern. She'd wrapped it in blue tissue paper and tied a red bow around the item to keep it closed. "This used to be my father's, and it was the only thing given to me when he died. I've kept it hidden away all these years, but I felt it was time to give it to you." She handed the package to LaVern and waited breathlessly as he opened it.

He tore the tissue paper aside in short order and held up the pair of binoculars inside. "Wow, these are great, Irma! I'll use them when I go hunting in the fall." LaVern set the binoculars on the table and pulled Irma into his arms. "That was a thoughtful gift, and I'll treasure them, knowing they belonged to your daed. Danki."

"You're welcome. I'm glad you like them."

"Happy anniversary, my sweet wife," he said in a hushed voice. "I love you more than words can say."

"I love you too." Irma closed her eyes, and her lips parted slightly as his mouth touched hers in a sweet, tender kiss. When the kiss ended, she looked up at him and said, "Thank you for such a nice evening."

"It's not over yet," he responded. "And tomorrow morning we can sleep in for a while if we want to. We don't have to check out of the inn until 11:00 a.m., and our driver won't be here to pick us up until noon. So let's take advantage of our time alone and enjoy every minute of being together." He leaned down and kissed her soundly one more time.

⸎

The following morning, Irma and LaVern slept until eight. After showering and getting dressed, they walked over to the restaurant for breakfast. They could have eaten the continental breakfast the hotel offered its guests, but LaVern had insisted on treating Irma to a nice breakfast of bacon and eggs, which she couldn't say no to because she was famished. She couldn't remember the last time she'd slept so well or woken up with such a hearty appetite—except on their last anniversary when they had stayed farther away for a couple of nights at the Little Slice of Heaven Cabin. His parents had pitched in some money to help LaVern out, and they'd even watched the children for those few days away. That location was great, because it was off the beaten path, and Irma thought it would be nice to spend time there with LaVern again sometime in the future.

LaVern held Irma's hand for a little bit and spoke in Pennsylvania Dutch. "I wish we could've gone up to the cabin again this year."

Irma smiled and, also speaking in Dutch, replied, "I know. That was a great place, but this has worked out nicely for us. And I've heard it said that variety is the spice of life."

"That's what I've heard too." He grinned. "I'm always happy to be anywhere when I'm with you, though."

Irma looked up at him as they walked side-by-side, soaking up this alone time with her husband because their anniversary celebration was almost over.

"How nice it has been to celebrate our anniversary with just the two of us and no responsibilities," Irma commented as they took seats at a booth inside the restaurant.

LaVern nodded. "I agree. This time together, although shorter than I would have liked, has been good for both of us, and I'm glad we could make it happen."

"Not we—you." She smiled. "You did all the planning and made the arrangements for the driver, the hotel, and meals, as well as asking your folks to keep the kinner overnight."

LaVern shrugged his shoulders. "What can I say? I've always been a planner. Even when I was a boy, I liked to plan things out."

"Really? Like what?"

"Fishing trips for one thing. Whenever my grandpa invited me to go fishing with him, I immediately started planning everything I would need to take along. Days in advance, I would get it all together and be ready for the day when Grandpa Miller came to pick me up." LaVern paused and drank some of his water from the glass their waitress had filled when they'd first sat down. "When I became a teenager and graduated from school, I started planning for my move to Montana."

Irma felt a twinge of guilt. "You really liked living in St. Ignatius, didn't you?"

"I did, but you weren't happy there, and I had no problem with moving back to Ohio."

"I'm glad." Irma looked up when their waitress returned to the table and asked if they were ready to order. "Yes, I'd like scrambled eggs, bacon, and a side of hashed-brown potatoes," she responded to the young woman's question.

"And I'll have two eggs over easy, sausage, and toast with strawberry jam," LaVern said after the waitress turned to him.

"Would either of you like something to drink besides water?" she questioned.

"Two coffees, no cream or sugar," LaVern spoke up.

When the waitress left the table, Irma smiled at LaVern and said, "You know me so well, you probably could have ordered my breakfast too."

"Yep," he said with a nod. "Knowing my wife's habits, likes, and dislikes are important to me."

She toyed with her napkin. "I chose well."

LaVern shook his head. "No, it was me who did the smart choosing, and I couldn't have planned it better."

Irma blinked. "You planned to marry me?"

"Sure did. From the first day I met you, I knew you'd someday be my fraa." He reached over and clasped her hand. "And I've never once regretted it. We may not always see eye-to-eye on things, but I've never doubted my love for you—and nothing and no one can ever tear us apart."

Chapter 9

St. Ignatius

Carrying an empty wicker basket, Dorcas headed for the clothesline to check on the towels she'd hung out earlier in the morning. Given the sun's steamy heat beating down on her body, she felt sure the towels must be dry. If so, she would bring them into the house, fold, and put them away, and then Dorcas planned to take a much-needed break on the shaded front porch with a glass of iced tea. In addition to doing a few loads of laundry, Dorcas and her daughter Caroline had baked this morning while Hannah pulled weeds in the garden. She figured the teenage girls were probably ready for a break by now too.

Dorcas set the basket on the ground and glanced at the dark purple spot on her right arm. She hated how easily she bruised. It embarrassed her when people would point out a bruise and ask how it had happened. She sometimes said she was clumsy by nature. Then these well-meaning people would offer their opinion on the best way to shorten the duration of a bruise. Dorcas didn't like being the center of attention—especially when it came to her physical appearance. She wished folks would just mind their own business and quit asking questions or telling her what to do.

Dorcas reached up with both hands and felt two of the large bath towels. *Good, they're dry. That means the rest of them most likely are too.* She removed the clothespins from each towel and washcloth on the line and dropped them into the basket. Hearing the call of a dove to its mate, she stood and listened. It comforted her to hear the noise the various birds in their yard made as they congregated in the trees or flew from one branch to another. Their twitters and the other pleasant sounds they made always helped Dorcas feel calmer and more relaxed.

She leaned down to pick up the basket and was about to head for the house when her eighteen-year-old son, Aaron, raced into the yard, waving both arms over his head. As he approached, Dorcas noticed that his face was red and tendons stuck out from the sides of his neck. She knew right away that something was wrong. "What's going on, Son? What are you doing here in the middle of the day? Why aren't you at work with your bruder and daed?"

"Papa keeled over, and we couldn't rouse him. Irvin called for help right away, and the paramedics are probably at the lumber mill with Papa right now." Aaron paused and drew in a few breaths of air. "You'd better come right away, Mama. It doesn't look good for Papa. When Irvin found his pulse, it was real faint, and even with us both hollering, 'Papa, open your eyes,' there was no response at all."

Dorcas' fingers slipped from the basket handles, and as it dropped to the ground, the clean towels tumbled out. Paying them no heed, Dorcas dashed out of the yard behind her son without taking time to tell the girls what had happened or where she was going. The lumber mill was a quarter of a mile away. Dorcas hoped the paramedics would make it there quickly, and if Homer was not meant to survive, she prayed for a chance to at least say a proper goodbye.

***

Baltic

Mildred sat in the rocking chair, holding Myra on her lap and listening to the creak of the chair as it moved back and forth against the wooden floor beneath her feet. She hoped her son and his wife were having a nice time celebrating their anniversary. It was obvious that the youngest of their three children wasn't pleased with her parents' absence, though. The child had been fussy last night and probably hadn't slept well, which was no doubt the reason Mildred had found Myra asleep on the floor fifteen minutes ago. Until it was time for bed, the boys had been content playing with some wooden toys their grandpa had made for LaVern when he was a boy. They'd both been full of energy when they woke up this morning and were currently out in the barn with Grandpa, checking on a mama cat that would soon be delivering a batch of kittens.

Mildred smiled as she rocked back and forth while rubbing the small of her granddaughter's back. She always enjoyed having any of her grand-kids here to spend the night or even when they came with their parents for a meal or a short visit. She missed those days when her own children were little, as she'd always felt that her purpose in life was to be a loving mother. Now Mildred had been given the opportunity to be a grandpar-ent and, hopefully, set a good example for each of the children in her life. Mildred wasn't a perfect person by any means, but every day during her prayer time, she asked God to help her be the kind of grandmother that all her grandchildren needed.

Mildred's thoughts changed direction when she heard a vehicle pull into the yard. She figured it was probably LaVern and Irma's driver, which meant that soon she would have to say goodbye to Brian, Clayton, and Myra. The thought saddened her, because she didn't get to see these grandchildren often enough. Like many other times since LaVern and Irma had moved to Mount Hope, Mildred wished her son and his family lived closer.

"How did the kinner do while we were gone? Did they all behave themselves and go to sleep when you put them to bed?" Irma asked when she and LaVern entered the living room where Mildred sat with Myra in her lap.

"The boys had fun playing all day, and they went to sleep soon after I tucked them into bed," Mildred responded. "Myra was a little fussy last night, but that's to be expected for a two-year-old. I think she missed her mamm and daed, but she finally settled down." She nodded with her head at the sleeping child in her lap. "As you can probably guess, I've enjoyed sitting here for a while with my granddaughter in my lap."

"That's good to hear, Mom," LaVern said. "If anyone can make a child relax and put them to sleep, it's you."

"Actually, Myra fell asleep on the floor before I came into the room, but then she started to fuss, so I picked her up and got busy rocking and rubbing her back."

"Where are the boys?" Irma asked.

"Out in the barn with their *grossdaadi*, waiting for a batch of new *busslin* to be born."

"I'm not surprised. Guess I'll wander out there and see if there are any kittens yet."

LaVern was almost to the door when Irma turned to him and said, "Don't stay too long, please. I have a few things to do at home yet today, so we should get going soon."

"No problem," he replied. "We'll all be back here in the house soon, because I don't want to keep our driver out there waiting for us much longer. He's probably eager to get home too." LaVern headed out the front door.

"Did you and LaVern enjoy your time in Sugarcreek?" Mildred asked when Irma took a seat on the couch.

"Jah, very much. Our room at the inn was lovely, and we had a tasty supper at the restaurant last night and an equally good breakfast there this morning."

"I'm glad. It's always nice to do something special for an anniversary."

Irma nodded. "The time we had together went by so quickly, though. LaVern is always kept so busy with his auctioneering responsibilities, and the kinner and I don't get to see him as often as we'd like."

"He does have a demanding job," Mildred said. "It's too bad LaVern wasn't satisfied to work in his daed's woodworking shop. If he had been, you'd probably still be living here in Baltic, and I could be a big help to you with taking care of the kinner."

Irma fidgeted on the couch as her gaze flicked upward. "I appreciate the thought, but I'm managing fine with the children, and LaVern is satisfied with the job he has."

"Oh, I didn't mean to imply—"

LaVern and the boys, along with Mildred's husband, rushed into the house and joined them in the living room.

"Mama!" Brian and Clayton hollered at the same time as they ran across the room to Irma.

She opened her arms and gave them both a big hug. "Did you miss me and your daed while we were gone?"

They bobbed their heads. "But we had a fun time here with Grandpa and Grandma," Brian said.

"And we had a fun time with them," LaVern's father interjected.

"We certainly did," his wife agreed.

"Our driver is waiting for us, so we need to go." LaVern looked at the boys. "You'd better get your things now, and then it's time to say goodbye to your grandpa and grandma."

"Okay," they said in unison before skipping out of the room.

Irma stood and went over to stand beside the rocking chair. "If you'll tell me where Myra's things are, I'll go get them."

"Her suitcase is in the downstairs bedroom next to ours," Mildred replied. "I can get it if you'd like to hold your daughter right now."

Irma leaned down and scooped Myra into her arms. The child woke up and started to cry, but when she saw who held her, she settled right down and clung to Irma's neck. "You missed me, little one, didn't you? Well, Mama missed you too."

It wasn't long before the boys were back with their suitcases, and they were all in the van and waving to the grandparents as the van rolled out of the yard. As much as she'd enjoyed her time alone with LaVern, Irma was glad to be with Brian, Clayton, and Myra again. Although they tried her patience sometimes, she wouldn't give her children up for anything.

Mount Hope

After their driver pulled up to the house and the van doors had been opened, Brian jumped down and headed straight for the dog run to let Buster out. LaVern paid the driver and then helped Irma take each piece of luggage inside. "While you're getting lunch made, I'll go back out to check the mail and listen to any phone messages in the shed," he told Irma.

"Okay. I'm sure the kids are hungry, so if you have no objections, I'll just make us all sandwiches for lunch," she responded.

"Fine by me." LaVern kissed Irma's cheek and went out the door with Clayton right on his heels.

"Don't you want to unpack your suitcase?" LaVern asked the boy.

Clayton shook his head. "No way! I wanna say hi to Buster, and then I'm gonna look for my katz."

"Okay." LaVern tweaked his son's nose and headed for the mailbox. He found one letter addressed to Irma and a few magazines they had subscribed to. On his way back up the driveway, he stopped by the phone shed where he took a seat and listened to the messages on their answering machine. There was only one, and it was from Irma's mother. He listened to it twice to be sure he'd heard it right the first time, then stepped out of the shed and ran up to the house.

LaVern found Irma in the kitchen making sandwiches, and Myra was in her high chair eating a cracker. "I have some bad news," he said, pulling Irma aside.

"Oh? What's going on?" She looked up at him.

"I found a message on our answering machine from your mamm." He paused and placed both hands on his wife's shoulders. "Your stepfather had a heart attack this morning at his lumber mill, and the paramedics couldn't revive him."

Irma's eyes widened. "He—he's dead?"

"I'm afraid so."

Irma's face paled, and she sank into a chair without saying another word.

Concerned, LaVern took a seat beside her. "Are you all right?"

"I'm fine." She stared straight ahead with one arm pressed against her stomach.

"Your mamm said Homer's *leischt* will be next Wednesday. They're holding it off a few days so we will have time to get there."

She sat at the table with her arms folded.

"I'll call my folks and see if they can keep the kids while we're gone."

Irma gave a quick shake of her head. "That won't be necessary, because I am not going to his funeral."

"You're not serious, are you?"

"Jah. I have no intention of going."

"But Irma, he was your stepdad, and—"

"I don't care."

"What about your mother, as well as your brothers and sisters? Don't you want to be there to offer them comfort and support?"

"They'll be fine without me."

"I don't see how. The tone of your mother's voice in her message said otherwise. She sounded very distraught, Irma. I think it's important that we go."

"Then you can go without me; I'm staying here."

LaVern studied his wife's stoic expression. There wasn't a single sign of tears or anything else to indicate that Irma felt even a smidgen of grief over the loss of her stepfather. LaVern had known that Irma's relationship with Homer had been strained, but he'd never expected she would refuse to go to the man's funeral where support for her family was surely needed. He would drop the subject for now and bring it up again in the morning before they left for church. Maybe after a good night's sleep and some time to think about it, Irma would change her mind.

Unexpectedly, Irma pushed her chair aside and dashed out of the room, leaving LaVern in the kitchen with Myra.

He put both hands on his cheeks and gave a slow shake of his head. *I'm sure Irma doesn't mean it. She's just upset about the news of his sudden death. I bet she'll change her mind once everything sinks in and she realizes that her family is going to need her at their side on Wednesday.*

Chapter 10

It was all Irma could do to get up Sunday morning and face the day. She'd only slept a few hours last night, and when she had succumbed to sleep, a frightening dream about Homer had awakened her. She'd had trouble getting back to sleep. Oh, how she wished the memories of him would vanish like vapor and never return.

While getting dressed for the day, Irma thought about how she'd been able to move on with her life as long as she didn't have to think about the past. But with her stepfather's passing, her immediate reaction was to somehow resist being pulled into thoughts of the past. Irma felt overwhelmed and numbed by this news, and the thought of going back to Montana made her head ache. It would be hard to travel back to St. Ignatius—and in truth, it was the last place Irma wanted to go. Even so, she tried to put herself in her mother's place. From now on, Mama would be the sole guardian over Irma's half-siblings, although the four of them were old enough to take care of their own needs and help out. Even so, Mama would have to worry about their finances now.

Irma picked off a piece of lint from the white prayer *kapp* she held. *LaVern was right about my mother needing support during this crisis, not to mention the rest of the family I grew up with. Maybe going to Homer's funeral might be what I need to deal with the anger I feel for him,* Irma thought as she stood in front of the bathroom mirror, putting her head covering in place. *Perhaps looking at his dead body and knowing that he's never coming back will give me the sense of peace I've been yearning for all these years. When Homer's casket is lowered into the ground, all the mean things he ever said and did to me will finally be put to rest, and hopefully the nightmares I sometimes have about him will stop.*

With hope welling in her chest, and a determined set of her jaw, Irma left the bathroom and made her way down the hall to the kitchen. She found LaVern sitting at the table with a steaming cup of coffee and his open Bible lying out before him. She hesitated to say anything, not wishing to interrupt his reading of the scriptures, but apparently he'd heard her come in, because he turned his head to look at her. "*Guder mariye*," he said.

"Good morning." She pulled out a padded wooden chair and sat next to him. "I've decided that I will go to St. Ignatius for Homer's funeral after all, and I can call upon one of our drivers and make the trip by myself if you can't get the time off." Irma looked at him directly. "You were right about me needing to go, and I'm glad you urged me in a kindly manner."

LaVern reached for Irma's hand and gave her fingers a tender squeeze. "I'm pleased that you've made this decision, but you won't be going there alone. I am sure my folks will be glad to keep the kinner while we're gone, and I'll make all the arrangements for the trip. The only thing you'll need to worry about is packing your suitcase."

"What about your auctioneering responsibilities?"

"There are other auctioneers in the area who can take over for me."

Irma relaxed a bit. "Thank you."

"No problem. You have a lot going on, and I want to help you get through all of this in any way I can." LaVern let go of Irma's hand. "The less you have to worry about things, the better it will be."

I just need to find some way to get through the whole ordeal once we arrive in St. Ignatius. Irma pushed her chair back and stood. "I'd better get some breakfast on the table so we can get the children up and make sure everyone is ready to head for church on time."

"All right then. While you're getting our food ready, I'll head upstairs and wake the boys. I haven't heard anything out of Myra yet either so I'll get her up too."

"Danki," Irma replied. She felt grateful for her husband's willingness to help and wondered if he knew how tired she was this morning. Irma yawned. *What a long, hard night I had.* It wasn't as though she'd been terribly busy yesterday with the kids or doing very many tasks around the house. Irma's exhaustion was mostly from her emotional turmoil. It had been really rough last night, lying in bed and trying to turn off her thoughts about going back home to Montana. She had lain there wide awake for several hours, trying to fall asleep. Between it all, she'd tried to pray about different things, but negative, frightening thoughts had gotten in the way. Finally, after feeling depleted of energy, Irma had rolled over and fallen asleep.

After LaVern left the room, Irma got out three boxes of cereal and put them on the table. Since today was a church Sunday, she never would have taken the time to cook a big breakfast that might include bacon, eggs, or pancakes. Besides, the kids were always happy with cold cereal for their morning meal. They especially liked eating it with sliced bananas on top and plenty of milk. She glanced at the fruit bowl on one end of the counter and frowned. Only one banana was left, and it was overly ripe. She couldn't make banana bread with just one banana, so she marched over and plucked it out of the bowl, then quickly tossed it into the garbage can. The kids would have to eat their cereal without toppings this morning. If there were any complaints, they could do without breakfast the way Irma had been made to do when she was a girl and complained about not wanting to eat something she didn't like. Homer had a rule about that, even for his own flesh-and-blood children. "Eat what is served, or don't eat at all," he'd said sternly. So without hesitation, they all did as he'd said.

Irma's jaw clenched. *That man had a lot of rules I didn't like, and I always paid the price for breaking any of them. I'm glad he's gone, and after his body is buried, I won't have to think about him anymore. Of course,* she reasoned,

I'll still have Mama to think about. And no matter how hard I try, I can't help remembering all the times she stood by and watched her mean husband punish me so harshly. She shook her head vigorously. *I don't understand it at all. Mama was never like that when my real daed was alive. Of course, he was a kind man and never treated me badly. What changed in my mother after Papa died and she married Homer? Could she truly have loved the man, or did she only marry him so that our family would have enough money to survive?*

———— ≈ ————

LaVern kept a firm grip on his horse's reins to keep the energetic gelding from trotting too fast as they headed down the road toward the home where church would be held. He glanced over at Irma, sitting stiffly on the seat beside him while holding Myra on her lap. She'd been quiet during breakfast, giving only brief answers to any questions being asked of her. And except for reprimanding the boys a few times for fooling around in the back seat of the carriage, Irma had continued her silence since they'd gotten into their family-size buggy. LaVern wondered if she was having second thoughts about leaving for St. Ignatius early tomorrow morning. He'd talked to his mother Saturday evening, and she'd said she and Dad were more than willing to keep the children for however long he and Irma would be gone. Unless Irma wanted to stay longer, they would probably head back to Ohio Thursday morning. LaVern didn't relish the idea of taking too much time away from work, but he would do whatever was necessary without complaint.

His horse's ears perked up as they approached the place where church would be held, and LaVern turned down the lane. A few other horse-pulled carriages were ahead of them, and several other buggies had been parked out in the field. The horses already there were tied to a line in a shaded area, which was where LaVern would take his horse as soon as he'd parked the buggy and his family had climbed out.

He reached across the seat and touched Irma's arm. "Are you okay?"

She gave a quick nod, set Myra on the seat between them, and stepped out of the buggy. Then she waited until the boys had gotten out from the back before reaching inside and lifting Myra into her arms. After she'd headed for the house with the children, LaVern parked the buggy and undid the horse. As he led the gelding over to the line where other horses waited, LaVern spotted his friend Jason near the other end of the line and gave him a wave. Jason lifted his hand in response. After LaVern got his horse secured, he walked with his friend up to the yard, where the ministers and several men had gathered in a semi-circle near the large workshop where the service would be held. After greeting one another with a handshake or a holy kiss, they all filed into the building and took their seats. The ministers were seated on folding chairs and all the other men sat on backless wooden benches.

When the women and children came in, Clayton and Brian came and sat beside LaVern. With Myra in her arms, Irma seated herself on a bench on the women's side of the room and placed the child in her lap. LaVern hoped for Irma's sake that their daughter would be good for the full three hours of the service, but it was doubtful. Most young mothers among the thirty-some families in this church district ended up taking their babies or young children out at least once before church ended. From the way his wife had snapped at the boys on the way here, LaVern figured she was uptight and had very little patience today. It was a good thing they wouldn't be taking the kids on the trip with them tomorrow. He felt sure that Irma would get through her stepfather's funeral easier without any interruptions the children might bring.

Irma had to force herself to open the *Ausbund* during the time of acapella singing. She didn't feel like participating and wished she didn't have to be here at all. Of course, sitting in this building with people she knew and liked was a lot easier than what she'd be faced with when they arrived at her mother's home. In addition to dreading the funeral and graveside service, Irma did not look forward to the thirty-hour drive crossing several states to get to their destination. The plan was for them to get up early Monday morning and travel fifteen hours before spending a night at a hotel. Tuesday, they would drive another fifteen hours and arrive in St. Ignatius sometime that night. She could only hope and pray that she would have the strength to get through the whole ordeal of Homer's funeral. Irma felt thankful that LaVern would be at her side. It would be a lot harder if she had to make the trip without him and only had their driver for company while on the road. It would also be a comfort for Irma to have her husband by her side the day of the funeral. The plan was for them to leave St. Ignatius Thursday morning, which would get them back to Mount Hope by Saturday evening. Of course, they'd stop at Baltic first to pick up the children.

Irma glanced down at Myra, who had fallen asleep in her lap. She heard her daughter's rhythmic breathing and felt the warmth of the child's body pushed up against her stomach. Knowing that Myra would miss her, Irma had thought about taking her youngest child along on the trip. But the long hours of travel would be exhausting, and Myra would probably be fussy most of the way there and back. Besides, the little girl didn't do well around strangers, and she did not know Irma's mother or siblings. Irma released a small sigh as she stroked Myra's soft, warm cheek. *The best thing we can do for all three of our children is to leave them with Grandpa and Grandma Miller, where they will get good care.*

St. Ignatius

Dorcas reclined on the couch with a cold, folded washrag covering her forehead. Last night, she hadn't slept well and had awakened this morning with a pounding headache. She felt thankful that today was their church's off-Sunday and she wouldn't have to face those in their district. With the nauseating headache she had, she would have stayed home anyway. It had seemed strange to sleep in the bed last night without Homer beside her.

She still hadn't wrapped her mind fully around the fact that he was dead. Irma's sons had said very little last night when they'd all come home from the hospital where their dad had been taken and pronounced dead. They would no doubt miss their papa and may even be wondering if either of them would be capable or expected to take over the lumber mill now that Homer was gone.

Maybe I could sell the business to someone else, with the stipulation that Irvin and Aaron continue working there, Dorcas thought. *We will certainly need the money in order to survive. I'll need to talk to the boys about this, but not until after Homer's burial on Wednesday. Sometime on Thursday, I will gather the whole family together, and we'll make some serious decisions.*

Dorcas thought about Irma and wished she still lived in the area. She could really use her eldest daughter's support right now. She tapped her chin a couple of times and blew out her breath. *I wonder if Irma got my message about Homer's death, and if so, will she and her family come here for the funeral on Wednesday?* Dorcas hoped so, because she hadn't seen Irma for a few years and missed her terribly. Right now, she needed her eldest daughter's comfort and assurance that she loved her, more than anything.

Chapter 11

Sunday evening, LaVern's parents showed up in their driver's vehicle to get the children. Since LaVern and Irma would be leaving early Monday morning, they had decided that it would be best to get the kids to their grandparents' home on Sunday.

As soon as Mildred and Paul came in the door, Mildred hugged Irma. "I'm so sorry for your loss. It's never easy to lose a family member. Don't hesitate to let Paul and me know how we can help you through this."

"Homer was not a relative. He was my stepfather—no blood relation at all." A whoosh of breath followed Irma's response, and she couldn't seem to keep the sharp tone from her voice. Referring to Homer as a relative didn't sit well with her. She may not have resented him as much if he hadn't treated her so harshly. Even after all these years, and with Homer now dead, Irma couldn't let go of the anger she harbored toward him.

Apparently unruffled by Irma's terse tone, Mildred patted her arm gently and said, "I'm sure having you and LaVern at the funeral will be a comfort for your mother and siblings."

All Irma could manage was a brief nod. Then she gestured to the children's suitcases lined up in the hall near the front door. "I believe the kinner have everything they'll need for the time we'll be away."

Mildred smiled. "If you forgot anything, I'm sure we can make do."

"That's correct," LaVern's father agreed. "And if they need something we don't have in the house, we'll go to the store and get it. It's always fun to take the grandkids shopping." He looked over at LaVern and winked. "Gives us a chance to spoil 'em a bit when they see something they like."

"My husband is right," Mildred agreed. "We never mind spending money on our *kinskinner*."

"Don't spoil them too much," LaVern said. "We'll have to live with the kinner when we get back home."

"Don't worry, Son." Paul thumped LaVern's back. "Your mamm and I know when to say jah and when to say *nee*."

"Where are the children now?" Mildred asked. "I figured they'd be right here, eager to see their grandma and grandpa."

"The boys are out at the dog run, saying goodbye to Buster," Irma said. "And Myra fell asleep on the couch after we ate supper. I need to wake her up or she won't settle down and go to sleep for you when it's time to put her to bed." Irma turned and hurried into the living room.

Mildred followed Irma and smiled at Myra as she was awakened from her nap. While Irma was overcome with sadness to leave her children behind, she knew it was best to let Myra and the boys with LaVern's parents.

Mildred leaned over to kiss Myra's forehead. Then she reached over and hugged Irma around the shoulders. Irma wondered if Mildred sensed the need she felt to hold her daughter close, not wanting to let go. For a brief moment, it made Irma feel loved and appreciated by her mother-in-law.

When Irma bent down and lifted the child into her arms, a lump lodged in her throat. Once more, she wished she could take her little girl along, but such a lengthy trip would be too difficult for Myra. If the child cried a lot, and no doubt she would, everyone, including their driver, would be miserable and on edge. But Irma had never been away from her little ones for more than a few nights. Oh, how she would miss them. Even though Brian, Clayton, and Myra got on her nerves at times, she wouldn't know what to do without them.

———— ≈ ————

"It was hard saying goodbye to our kinner, wasn't it?" LaVern asked as he and Irma got ready for bed that night.

Irma nodded. "Jah, and it didn't help hearing Myra's pathetic cries when your mamm settled her into the booster seat and then put the seatbelt around her."

"I'm sure she settled down once they got on the road. The boys probably kept her entertained." LaVern plumped up his pillow and climbed into bed. "Brian was close to tears when they got ready to leave too. Even though our closest neighbors will be coming over every day while we're gone to feed and water the livestock, as well as his hund, Brian did not want to leave Buster behind."

"He didn't want to leave Buster when we spent the night in Sugarcreek for our anniversary either." Irma got in on her side of the bed. "The dog will be fine in his pen, and I'm sure the Troyers will take good care of him. Besides, the children will have your daed's black lab, Lady, to play with, not to mention the excitement of running out to the barn to make over the newly born kittens."

"Good point, but Brian will still miss Buster and worry about him." LaVern sat up, took a drink from his bottle of water on the nightstand and got comfortable again. "Gut nacht."

"Good night, Husband." Irma lay there, waiting to see if LaVern would say anything more, but he remained quiet. A few minutes passed, and then she heard the familiar sound of gentle snoring coming from his side of the bed.

How easily that husband of mine can doze off, she thought. *Wish I could shut out all of the disconcerting thoughts that are swirling through my head.* Although Irma had already prayed on her knees before getting into bed, she closed her eyes and prayed again: *Lord, morning will come quickly, so please help me fall asleep right away. Also, I ask that You protect us as we begin our travels tomorrow and keep our children safe at their grandparents' home while we're gone.* She paused, debating about how to end her prayer. *And please give me the strength to get through the ordeal of Homer's funeral without saying something I would regret later on.*

───────── ≈ ─────────

Grabill

Squinting against the morning sun, Doretta opened the flap on her mailbox and reached inside. She was happy to find a letter from Eleanor but had been hoping she might hear something from Irma today as well. It had been several weeks since she'd received any mail from her Ohio friend.

It seemed odd that Irma hadn't responded to the last letter Doretta had sent her. She hoped her friend's lack of correspondence was only because she'd been too busy to write and wasn't due to any problems she might be facing right now. In the last letter she'd received from her friend several weeks ago, Irma had shared her frustrations over LaVern's job as an auctioneer and stated how difficult it was to have him gone so much. Another thing Irma had mentioned was her irritation over Brian's dog and the messes he'd made in the house and sometimes outside in the yard. She'd also brought up the fact that she had asked LaVern to build a dog run for Buster but he hadn't found the time to do it. Doretta figured with the weeks that had gone by since Irma's last letter, the dog run had probably been built by now. She also assumed that with summer almost half over and no word from Irma about the possibility of them coming to Grabill for a visit, it most likely was not going to happen this year.

It's probably just as well, Doretta thought as she made her way back to the house with one hand clutching the mail and the other pressing against her protruding belly. *I barely have enough energy to keep up with my daily chores, let alone entertain company. Maybe after the baby comes and I get my strength back, I'll be ready to entertain and welcome visitors into our home.* She gave her stomach a few gentle pats. *I can hardly wait to become a* mudder, *and it's a wonderful feeling to know that Warren is eager to be a daed.* She smiled and stepped onto the porch to sit and read the mail. *He will be a good father too. I'm certain of it.*

St. Cloud, Minnesota

Irma didn't know it was possible to feel this tired. After a long sixteen-hour drive, they were finally at the halfway point of their trip, and she could hardly wait to take a shower and crawl into bed. Their driver, Carl, had picked them up at four o'clock this morning and made stops only for gas, bathroom breaks, and takeout food for lunch and supper—which they had eaten in the van as they traveled. They'd checked into their hotel near the interstate shortly after ten and planned to start driving again by four o'clock the next morning.

Irma's body felt stiff from sitting so many hours, and she did not look forward to another day of traveling fifteen hours or more. She felt thankful, however, that so far their travels had been uneventful, with no mishaps or close calls. If an accident occurred, riding in a van or some other motorized vehicle was safer than traveling in a horse-drawn carriage. But even when riding in a car, there were no guarantees that a passenger would not get hurt during an accident. Although she disliked wearing a constricting seatbelt, Irma always made sure to buckle her belt, as did LaVern. She knew a few people who hadn't been wearing seatbelts when they'd been involved in accidents, and they'd been hurt pretty bad.

"At least we ought to sleep good tonight," Irma mumbled as she opened her suitcase to get out her nightgown. "I wouldn't be surprised if I'm asleep before my head hits the pillow."

"For sure." LaVern yawned and stretched his arms over his head. "I don't know how Carl could sit behind the steering wheel all day and keep his focus on the road. I'm sure he's as tired as we are and has probably already bedded down in his hotel room."

"I'm glad you stayed awake all day and kept talking to him. No doubt the conversation helped keep Carl alert."

"Jah, that was my plan all along. Sure can't have our driver falling asleep at the wheel." LaVern chuckled. "Of course, he may have gotten tired of me talking his ear off most of the day." He pointed at the bathroom door. "Do you want to take your shower first, while I lay out my clothes for tomorrow?"

"Thanks, I'll do that right now." Irma appreciated her husband's thoughtfulness. No doubt he could see how tired she was. Once more, Irma found herself thinking how glad she was that he'd insisted on making this trip with her. She not only needed him during the trip, but she would appreciate his presence even more once they reached their final destination and she had to face her family and get through the whole funeral.

When Irma entered the bathroom and turned on the shower, her thoughts shifted to the children. She wondered how things went when LaVern's mother put them to bed this evening. Irma hoped the boys had cooperated and gone right to sleep without any fooling around, like they sometimes did at home. Knowing how fussy Myra could be, Irma worried that getting her settled and into bed might have been a bit of a challenge for Grandma Mildred. Irma was thankful for the bond her children had with LaVern's parents—although it would be much stronger if they lived closer. Even so, Irma knew the children would be well cared for while she and LaVern were gone.

Irma hung her nightgown on the hook inside the bathroom. She looked forward to washing away the long day's journey. Irma had already removed her head covering and placed it on the dresser in the other room. It would be nice to finally unpin her long hair from the tightly wound bun at the back of her head.

When the warm water from the shower hit Irma's tense body a few minutes later, she felt herself relax for the first time all day. *If only this feeling could last.*

Chapter 12

Baltic

Mildred fixed the children some lunch, and when they started eating, she made herself a sandwich and covered it with a napkin. She would wait to eat until after she came back into the house from taking lunch to Paul. Mildred told the kids that she would be back soon and asked them to be good while they ate their sandwiches. Then she grabbed the paper sack with Paul's lunch inside and went out to her husband's shop, where she found him at his desk going over paperwork.

"Is it lunchtime already?" he asked when she handed him the sack.

"Jah. I figured you might be too busy to come up to the house to eat, so I brought your favorite sandwich, a few chips, and a beverage." She opened the sack and took everything out.

"Danki. You're a *gedankevoll* fraa."

"I was happy to do it. And don't forget—you've done many thoughtful things for me too."

"What are the kinner up to?" Paul asked.

"The boys are sitting at the kitchen table eating peanut butter and jelly sandwiches, and Myra's seated in a little chair at that small round table you built for our kinner to sit at when they were too young to reach the table from a chair." Mildred leaned against her husband's desk. "I think she likes having her own table to eat at."

"It probably makes her feel like a big girl."

"I believe you're right. I was pleased at how well our grandchildren did last night. The boys got right into bed when I told them to, and I only had to rock Myra a short while before she nodded off. Thankfully, she didn't wake up when I put her into bed. And the sweet little thing slept the whole night with no fussing at all." Mildred stepped away from the desk and casually anchored one hand against her hip. "I'm relieved that all three of the children seem to be happy and content. Hopefully, they'll remain so during the next several days while their parents are away."

"Speaking of LaVern and Irma…When I went to the phone shed to check for messages a while ago, there was one from LaVern. He'd used his driver's phone to make the call and said they had spent last night at a hotel in St. Cloud, Minnesota, and planned to be on the road early again today."

"Oh, that's good to hear. I've been praying for their safety, and it's a relief to know they reached the halfway point last night."

He bobbed his head. "LaVern said the plan is for them to get to St. Ignatius today, and they'll spend the night at a place called Allard's Stage Stop Lodge."

Mildred tilted her head to one side. "I'm confused. If they will arrive in St. Ignatius tonight, wouldn't they go straight to Irma's mother's house and stay there overnight? I would think they'd want to spend some time with her family before the funeral service tomorrow morning."

Paul shrugged. "They probably won't get in till late and wouldn't want to disturb Irma's family at that hour."

"Maybe so, but I would think Irma's mother and siblings wouldn't mind waiting up for her and LaVern, no matter how late they may get in."

"No one in Irma's family will be waiting up, because they don't know for sure that Irma and LaVern are going to her stepfather's funeral."

"What?" Mildred's brows lifted and her eyes opened wide. "Didn't Irma bother to call and leave a message for them?"

"No. And according to LaVern, Irma didn't want to go to St. Ignatius at all, but she changed her mind. When she did, LaVern offered to make the call for her, but Irma said no, they would just show up at the funeral."

"That's inconsiderate, wouldn't you say? I'm really surprised to hear this."

"I was too, but Irma must have her reasons for having made that decision, and the reason behind it is really none of our business."

Mildred stood with pursed lips for several seconds. Deciding it would be best not to say anything more on the subject, she gave Paul's shoulder a tender squeeze and said, "I'm going back to the house now to eat my own sandwich and delight in the grandchildren's company. Enjoy your lunch, Paul."

"Danki, I surely will."

"Oh, I thought tonight, if you would feel up to it, that we could take the children out for burgers and fries."

"That would be something fun to do. I think it's doable too, since I should be caught up here in an hour or two." He gave a little wink. "Besides, you deserve a night off from having to cook."

She smiled and opened the door. *I made a good choice when I married Paul.*

Mildred left the shop, and as she made her way back to the house, she thought about how strangely her daughter-in-law had been acting since they'd heard about the passing of her stepfather. Was it because she felt overwhelmed with grief, or could it be something else? As far as Mildred could tell, Irma had shown no grief or regret over his death.

St. Ignatius

Dorcas glanced at the clock on the fireplace mantle. It was half past nine, and there was no sign of Irma and her family. Not a single message had been left on their answering machine. Aaron had gone to the phone shed several times today, and although there had been messages from several in the community, not one word had been left by Irma or LaVern.

Dorcas got up from her chair and began to pace. *Surely, if they were coming, one of them would have called to let me know what time they might arrive.*

"Mama, why are you walking back and forth like that?" Hannah asked when she entered the living room. "You seem *brutzich*."

"I am fretful." Dorcas stopped pacing and turned to face her seventeen-year-old daughter. "I'm worried because I have not heard anything from Irma since I called and left a message for her about your daed's death." She stretched her hands out wide then forced herself to relax them at her side. "I had hoped that Irma would have the courtesy to return my call." Dorcas looked up at the clock again. "I'd also hoped your sister would come here for the funeral. But if she was coming, she would have been here by now or, at the very least, left a message saying what time we might expect her to arrive."

Hannah moved closer and gave her mother a hug. "I'm sorry, Mama. I know how much you want Irma to be here. You've been sad ever since she and LaVern moved to Ohio. And in all that time, you've only seen her once—when you rode the train all by yourself to see Irma after her first baby was born."

Dorcas sank into a chair and closed her eyes as the memory of that time flooded over her like a tidal wave. She'd been so excited when she'd received LaVern's message stating that Irma had given birth to a baby boy, whom they'd named Brian. He'd invited Dorcas to come for a visit so she could meet her first grandchild. Dorcas had purchased a train ticket right away. The day she'd left, she had asked Homer to call and leave a message for LaVern and Irma, letting them know she was coming and what time her train was scheduled to arrive.

What a foolish mistake that was, Dorcas told herself. *Homer either got busy and forgot to call or he deliberately did not let my daughter and her husband know that I was on the way to Ohio.* She massaged her pulsating forehead. *But why would he have done such a thing? It was probably because he didn't want me to go there. He did say that it wasn't necessary for me to see Irma's baby. Well, at least it worked out in the end, although I don't think Irma was all that happy to see me.*

Dorcas' eyes opened when she felt a hand on her shoulder.

"You're tired, Mama. Don't you think it's time you went to *bett*?"

"I can't go to bed until I know whether your sister is coming or not. Sure wouldn't want to miss a knock on our door sometime during the night."

Hannah's hazel-colored eyes darkened. "If she was coming, Mama, I'm sure she would have called. These last few days since Papa's death have been hard, and you're exhausted. Tomorrow, the day will begin early, and it will be a difficult time as we sit through the funeral and graveside services. Even the meal that will be served here afterward will be tiring, so please go to bed now and get some sleep. If Irma and her family should show up, I'm sure we'll be awakened by their knock on the door."

Hannah was right, and Dorcas had to admit that she was exhausted. "Okay, I'll go to bed, but you must do so also. Caroline and your brothers went upstairs an hour ago and are probably asleep already."

"I'll go to my room when you go to yours," Hannah responded.

Dorcas glanced at the clock one more time. "All right, Daughter. Let's head for *bett*."

After filling his tank with gas at the fuel pump outside of Allard's Stage Stop Convenience Store at ten thirty, LaVern's driver pulled into the parking lot at Allard's Stage Stop Lodge where they would spend tonight and tomorrow. LaVern remembered this place on US Highway 93 with fondness, as he'd visited Allard's Candy and Gift Store on several occasions during the time he'd been living in St. Ignatius. In addition to the gas station, lodge, and candy shop, another rustic building nearby was home to the Huckleberry Jam Factory, where they specialized in huckleberry jams, jellies, and pies. The place was also well known for their delicious milkshakes, ice cream, cinnamon rolls, and empanadas. The owners of the establishment made their own fudge, and it was equally tasty.

Allard's Stage Stop was a unique property, nestled between the base of the Mission Mountains and the National Bison Range. LaVern knew a bit of history about this place, situated on the Flathead Indian Reservation in St. Ignatius. Charles Allard Sr., born in 1852, was the son of Joseph Allard, a Canadian Frenchman. Charles' mother was an Indian woman. Mr. Allard was well known throughout the state as an owner of the large herd of buffaloes on the reservation. He and a man named Michael Pablo played key roles in maintaining buffalo on the North American continent. The men had purchased a few head of bison, and the animals multiplied into a sizable herd as they fed on the lush native grass in the area. The herd was eventually sold to the Canadian government. The stage served as a horse-change stop and resting place for travelers, as they served food and offered shelter to those traveling to and through the Flathead Nation. Joseph Allard had helped his father, Charles Sr., operate a mail and passenger stage service starting in 1887. The Allard family played a role in the return of the bison to the Flathead Indian Reservation and saw it as a great tribute to their family.

LaVern had seen some of the bison housed on the Allards' property while he lived here and had enjoyed watching the herd as they grazed. Perhaps they would have a bit of time in the morning, before they headed for Irma's mother's home, to see some of the buffalo. If so, he would be able to return to Ohio knowing he'd seen something exciting on this unexpected trip that reminded him of what he'd given up when he'd left St. Ignatius and moved to Ohio with Irma. Although there were many things about living in the beautiful state of Montana that he missed, LaVern had never regretted his decision to return to Ohio to marry Irma and raise a family. She was happier there, and he felt confident that he'd made the right decision.

"Looks like a comfortable place to stay," LaVern said after he'd placed their suitcases inside the rustic but cozy cabin.

Irma surveyed the room. A queen-size bed sat against one wall. The bedspread was red and black with a wagon-wheel design scattered throughout. The knotty-pine wall behind the bed gave it an old feel, reminiscent of the 1800s when this property had been a stage stop. A small table, covered with a checkered cloth, had been placed on the other side of the room. Two mismatched wooden chairs sat on either side of the table. Through the open door leading to the bathroom, Irma saw a claw-foot bathtub. *How nice it would feel to soak in that for a while before going to bed,* she thought.

"I see you've been eyeing that tub, Irma." LaVern pointed to the object in question. "Why don't you go ahead and bathe while I hang up our clean clothes for tomorrow?"

"Danki." Irma unzipped her suitcase and removed some things. One of them was a small package of bath salts she'd retrieved from the last place they'd stayed. *The shower was convenient last night, but tonight I can't wait to soak in the tub. This will be even better for relaxation.* She headed back to the bathroom, leaned over, and turned on the water. Not long after, the water was just the right temperature and began filling up the porcelain fixture. Irma set her nightgown aside and grabbed the bath salts to pour into the running water as the tub filled. She breathed in the soft lavender fragrance, and it helped to soothe her.

After Irma lowered her aching body into the tub, she scrubbed herself clean and tried to relax. She was filled with apprehension about tomorrow and hoped that once the funeral was over, she could put to rest the bitterness she felt toward her mother and stepfather. Irma desperately needed to, because that was the only reason she'd agreed to come to St. Ignatius.

Chapter 13

"This is the place," LaVern announced from the front seat of their driver's van as they approached a rambling white farmhouse on Watson Road.

Irma's chest tightened and her insides quivered. Like it or not, they were here—and there was no going back. A tall, young Amish man with dark brown hair came out of the barn and headed their way. Irma leaned closer to the window for a better look. *Could that be Irvin, or is it Aaron, now all grown-up? Does he know I'm sitting here in the backseat? Can he see me through the van's tinted windows?* Irma clutched her purse straps and waited until he approached the van, and then she opened the door and stepped out. LaVern said a few words to their driver and joined her outside of the van.

The young man shook LaVern's hand and gave Irma a hug. "Boy, you two haven't changed much at all, but I bet you don't recognize me—I'm Aaron."

Irma could hardly believe this tall, strapping fellow was the same nine-year-old boy she'd said goodbye to nine years ago. Aaron had to be eighteen by now. "It's been a long time since we last saw you," she said.

"Jah, you're right." He pulled his fingers through the sides of his thick hair. "Mama's sure gonna be surprised. She didn't think you were coming. I'll help with your luggage and we can go inside."

"We won't be spending the night here," Irma was quick to say. "We spent last night at the Stage Stop Lodge, and our luggage is still in the cabin we rented because we'll be staying there again tonight and heading for home tomorrow morning."

Aaron's eyes widened. "You're leaving so soon? Can't you stay around for a few days and spend some time with our mamm and the rest of the family? We could really use your support and input on things right now, because Mama isn't sure what to do with Papa's business."

Irma looked at LaVern, hoping he would speak up and say that they needed to get back to Ohio because of his job. Instead, he looked at Aaron and said, "Irma and I will talk about it."

Irma's skin tingled as perspiration formed on her face and arms. She didn't want to talk about it. She just wanted to get through this day, go back to the lodge for the night, and begin their journey toward home early in the morning. She had hoped that coming here for Homer's funeral would be good enough to satisfy the family.

"Let's go in the house now so we can visit awhile before other people begin showing up for the funeral service." Aaron led the way, and Irma followed, walking close to LaVern on shaky legs that felt like they could give way any minute.

───────────≈───────────

"Mama, come see who's here!"

Curious about the excited tone of her son's voice, Dorcas secured her head covering and hurried from the bedroom. When she entered the living room, her breath caught in her throat at the sight of Irma and LaVern standing beside Aaron. "I—I left you a message about Homer's passing, but when you didn't respond, I figured you weren't coming to his funeral."

"It was kind of a last-minute decision," LaVern said.

Dorcas stepped forward and gave them both a hug. She felt relief when Irma accepted the gesture and didn't pull away. LaVern was cordial too and said he was sorry for her and the family's loss.

"I'm real glad you're here. Homer's death was a shock to all of us." Dorcas glanced past them, toward the front door. "You didn't bring the kinner?"

LaVern shook his head. "We left them with my daed and mamm. The long trip would have been too much for the children. They're not used to riding in a vehicle that long."

"I understand, but it would have been so nice to see Brian now that he's no longer a baby and also have the chance to meet Clayton and Myra for the first time." *Do they even know anything about me or their mother's siblings?* Dorcas wondered. But she didn't voice the question because this was not the time for that.

"Maybe sometime, after things settle down here, you can come to our place for another visit," LaVern said.

"That would be nice. We'll have to see how it goes." Dorcas looked at Irma and couldn't miss the look of uncertainty on her face as she stood close to LaVern, rubbing her forehead.

She doesn't want me to visit her home again. I'm certain of it. Probably doesn't want to be here either. The whole idea to make the trip was most likely LaVern's. I bet he had to coax Irma to do it. Dorcas kept her focus on Irma and offered what she hoped was a reassuring smile. "Do you have a kopweh? If so, I can get you an aspirin for it."

"I don't have a headache. I'm just tired from two full days of traveling to get here."

"That's understandable." Dorcas looked at Aaron, who had been quiet and stood with his arms folded near the front door. "Would you please go get your sisters and brother? Tell them Irma and LaVern are here and that I'd like us all to gather at the kitchen table to talk for a bit before our ministers and others from the church district arrive."

"Sure, Mama." Aaron hurried past her and raced up the stairs leading to their bedrooms.

Dorcas gestured toward the kitchen. "Come take seats at the table. I'll put the kettle on for some tea and set out a plate of *kichlin*."

Aside from a little more gray mixed in with her medium-brown hair, Irma's mother didn't look much different than the last time Irma had seen her. But she seemed stressed out and quite tired. The deep wrinkles on her forehead and dark circles under the eyes were proof of that. It would make perfect sense for Irma's mother to be under a great deal of stress. Preparations for the funeral plus having to worry about Homer's business and how she would provide for the children who still lived at home would be enough to put a heavy strain on anyone at a time like this.

Being here with her mother again had stirred Irma's emotions. On the one hand, she felt a connection between them, but then an incident that had happened in the past came to mind, and the resurgence of Irma's wounded spirit took over. Irma had to squelch the feelings or she might end up saying something spiteful, which would only add more stress to both her and her mother.

Mama led the way to the kitchen, and Irma followed behind LaVern. When they entered the room, Irma noticed her mother's small collection of teapots displayed on top of the wooden cabinets. She'd almost forgotten about them, since the unpleasant events of the past had taken up most of her memories. Irma looked up again and noticed there were a couple of teapots she didn't recognize. *I wouldn't be surprised if Mama found them at a yard sale. Homer was too cheap to let her spend money on collectibles.*

Irma slid out a chair and took a seat at the table, and LaVern sat beside her. The nearness of her husband offered comfort and gave Irma more confidence. Sitting in her mother's kitchen was not easy for Irma, but it was better than being in whatever room Homer's coffin had been placed. Irma was certainly in no hurry to view the man's body.

While Mama prepared the tea, Irma looked around the sparsely decorated kitchen and thought about all the times she'd eaten here with Mama, Homer, and her siblings. She remembered one day in particular when she was sixteen years old and had come to the breakfast table with her hair down and no head covering in place. Pointing a finger at Irma, Homer had said some harsh words and sent her back upstairs to her room with no breakfast. He'd also stated emphatically that she would have extra chores to do for the next week, starting with cleaning out the horses' stalls. Irma remembered the startled look on her mother's face, but she never said a word in Irma's defense or accused Homer of being too strict. Of course, that was nothing new. Mama never stuck up for Irma. At times, she stood with a stony face when Homer punished Irma, as if she didn't care what happened to her daughter.

Irma thought about one time in particular, when she was ten years old and had arrived home from school later than usual with a tear in her dress. Homer had returned to the house from the lumber mill earlier than normal that day and stood at the front door waiting for her. Irma's explanation about why she was late and how the dress had gotten torn fell on deaf ears. Homer called her a liar, and when she'd refuted his statement, he'd slapped her face so hard it had left a mark that lasted several days. He'd then grabbed one of her braids and pulled her over to the sink, where he'd picked up a bar of soap and shoved it into Irma's mouth. Mama had just stood there the whole time without saying one word in Irma's defense. Even now, as she envisioned the scene, Irma could taste the sickening soap that Homer made her hold in her mouth for what had seemed like hours instead of minutes. *Why, oh why, didn't Mama stand up for me that day—or any other time when Homer was so cruel?*

Irma's insides quivered. She didn't like dredging up memories from the childhood she had spent in this house, but it was hard not to when she sat in this kitchen where she had eaten so many meals under the scrutiny of her harsh stepfather. She'd grown to hate him over the years. And even now, knowing he was dead, her soul filled with animosity thinking about all the terrible things he'd done to her.

Irma's thoughts gratefully returned to the present when her other three siblings entered the room with Aaron. Irma was surprised to see how much they'd all grown since she'd last seen them, and she barely recognized either of the girls.

"Remember me?" The shorter teenage girl with light brown hair gave Irma a hug.

"Let me guess—you're Caroline, right?"

The girl nodded. "I was only five when you left home, so I don't remember much about you other than what Mama's told me."

The teenage girl with blond hair, who Irma knew had to be Hannah, also gave her a hug. "I was seven when you left, and now I'm seventeen." She teared up. "How come you waited so long to come see us? Didn't you miss us at all?"

While Irma struggled to find the right words, the taller brother came to her rescue when he said, "In case you haven't figured it out, I'm Irvin, and I was eleven when you moved to Ohio with LaVern. I'm twenty now." He also gave Irma a hug.

Hoping to dodge Hannah's question, Irma commented on how much they had all grown since she'd left Montana. If Irma had met them on the street someplace, she wouldn't have recognized any of them. However, Irma was almost nineteen when she'd left and hadn't changed as much as they all had. Seeing the four of her siblings looking at her now with such pained expressions caused Irma to feel guilty for not keeping in touch with them via cards or letters. Even though she'd turned her back on Homer—and pretty much on Mama too—Irma should not have cut her half-siblings out of her life. It had obviously hurt them. But she couldn't change the past. She had to move forward and would try to do better keeping in touch with her brothers and sisters.

When Mama announced that the tea was ready, Irma's siblings took a seat at the table. Irma felt LaVern's knee touch her leg, and once again, she felt thankful that he was with her. She didn't know how she would have handled any of this if her husband had stayed home and she'd forced herself to come here alone.

Mama had set out the hot cups of water and a box of mixed teas. "Everyone pick out what you'd like."

LaVern pulled out one of the packets, adding it to his steaming mug of water. Irma did the same. *LaVern and I prefer coffee more than tea,* she thought, *but there's no sense being particular about it today.*

Her mother placed a platter in the center of the table with a couple dozen chocolate-chip cookies on it. "This should go well with our tea." She took a seat at the table, pulled out a napkin from the holder, and gestured to the platter.

Irvin, Aaron, Hannah, and Caroline were each quick to take a cookie, and LaVern took two and gave one to Irma. She had to admit that she could use a little pick-me-up right now.

Once everyone had a cup of tea, LaVern started a conversation, asking each of Irma's siblings if they had a job.

"I've been working at the lumber mill with my daed since I was sixteen," Irvin said. "Aaron works there too, but now that Papa's gone, we aren't sure who's gonna run the business."

"Or if it'll get sold," Aaron interjected.

"That has not been decided yet," their mother spoke up. "We'll be talking about it during our family meeting tomorrow, remember?"

The brothers nodded.

"Do either of you work outside of the home?" LaVern asked the girls as Irma took a sip of tea.

"I clean the house for one of our English neighbors," Hannah responded.

"I graduated from the eighth grade this spring, so I've been staying home helping my mamm this summer," Caroline said.

"That's good." LaVern smiled and nodded. "I'm sure she appreciates your help."

The conversation turned to other things as the gas lamp hanging from the ceiling purred overhead, quickly heating up the room. Irma's brothers asked about LaVern's job as an auctioneer. Then Dorcas wanted to know how her grandchildren were doing and whether Brian had received the card and money she'd sent for his birthday. Irma acknowledged that he had gotten it and that she'd meant to help him write a thank-you note, but in her busyness, she kept forgetting. Irma also mentioned a few things about the children's likes and dislikes, and LaVern talked about Brian's love for his dog.

Their conversation was cut short when the bishop and several others arrived at the house, and Mama quickly excused herself to speak with them. Irma fingered her kapp ties as her shoulders curled forward. Within the next fifteen minutes or so, Homer's funeral service would begin—and no matter how much Irma dreaded it, she would be forced to view his body, which she felt certain would bring on a flood of more unpleasant memories.

Chapter 14

Baltic

Mildred pulled a handful of weeds from her garden and glanced at the children playing happily in the yard. It felt good to have the grandchildren with her. Listening to their cheerful young voices brought satisfaction to her soul. Since it was a rarity to have LaVern's little ones for this long, Mildred was determined to soak up all she could from this visit.

Brian was the leader in a game of tag, but Clayton stayed up with his brother fairly well. Myra sat on an old quilt Mildred had spread on the porch for her, playing "little mama" with two baby dolls. It was cute to watch her pretend to feed the dolls with a toy baby bottle. Although the bottle was empty, Myra seemed satisfied that her babies were getting the milk they needed.

I wonder if Irma and LaVern will have another child, Mildred thought. *Even though Myra isn't quite three yet, I'm sure she would enjoy being the baby's big sister. And I wouldn't mind being grandma to another little one either.* Mildred had decided some time ago that grandparenthood was the best part of growing older.

Looking away from the children, she rested a knee in the dark soil and looked back at the row she'd just finished weeding. She was happy with how things looked and pleased that her vegetables were growing bigger by the day. Mildred had noticed while working in the garden that the tomato plants needed more staking. Since each plant was already growing against a tall pole, all she'd have to do was grab a ball of twine and a pair of scissors to fasten them higher onto their own stakes. She would put that chore on her to-do list because it might not get done today.

Mildred yanked a few more weeds and was about to toss them in the bucket she'd set close to her when Brian shouted, "Come quick, Grossmammi! A baby bird fell out of the nest, and that big gray barn katz is gonna get it!"

Mildred dropped the weeds, clambered to her feet, and dashed across the yard to where the boys stood. Brian was correct—a baby crow had indeed fallen from its nest in the maple tree. But at least it had landed in the soft grass and didn't appear to be injured from the fall. The boy was also right about the gray cat now heading in their direction. The furry critter came quick and within close proximity of its prey. Its long gray tail twitched at the sight of the tiny baby crow.

Mildred bent down and scooped up the baby bird just before the cat could pounce on it. She looked up in the tree and saw the nest but no sign of the crow's parents. A few seconds passed, and then suddenly, one of the parent birds swooped down at her.

Brian screamed and started waving his hands, and Clayton joined in. Mildred hollered for Clayton to go get his grandpa and tell him to bring a ladder. Meanwhile, she kept running around the yard while Brian tried to wave off the parent crow that was still trying to dive-bomb Mildred's head. At one point, Mildred was literally running in place, not sure which way to go. Should she run to the left or go to the right? The large, shiny black crow made a terrible racket as it continued its pursuit, and by the time Paul showed up with a ladder, Mildred was completely out of breath.

"Stop running and hand over the baby bird," her husband said after he'd set the ladder by the trunk of the tree. With no hesitation, she did as he'd asked. As Paul ascended the ladder, the full-grown crow stopped swooping and began circling the top of the tree.

Mildred held her breath as she watched her husband climb to the top of their twelve-foot ladder and put the baby crow into the nest. She released her breath as he came back down the ladder. Mildred watched as he removed the ladder, set it aside and looked up toward the nest. Then she stood with him and the boys, waiting to see what would happen.

When the parent crow kept circling overhead, Paul said, "Let's step way back from the tree so the crow doesn't feel that her baby is threatened."

Mildred motioned for Clayton and Brian to follow, and the four of them moved back across the lawn, closer to the house. A few minutes later, the parent crow flew down and landed on the nest. Mildred released a big sigh. "All's well that ends well," she said with relief.

"Just what we needed—a little excitement, jah?" Paul looked over at her and winked.

She lowered herself to the porch step and let out a boisterous laugh.

"What's so funny, Grandma?" Brian asked.

"I was trying to picture how silly I must have looked, running this way and that, wanting to keep the baby crow safe while I attempted to stay clear of the parent bird who was trying so hard to protect her baby that I was so determined to save."

"You did look kinda odd—'specially when you were running and not going anywhere." Brian snickered and clamped his hand over his mouth. Clayton did the same. Myra, still occupied with her dolls, didn't seem to be aware of anything that had gone on in the yard.

These children are so precious, Mildred mused. Then her thoughts changed direction. *I hope things are going well with their parents at Homer's funeral right now.*

St. Ignatius

Irma sat rigidly between her mother and Hannah on a backless wooden bench inside Homer's barn where the funeral service was being held. The building had been thoroughly cleaned, and since it was much larger and could accommodate more people than anywhere in the house, it was the best place to hold the service.

This is Mama's barn now, Irma told herself. *Homer is gone, and he owns nothing any longer. No one does when they leave this earth, because when you die, you can't take any possessions with you.* She tried not to look at the plain wooden coffin that had been moved to the barn from a spare room in the house, where it had been during visitation two days before his funeral. Irma was glad she and LaVern hadn't been here for that. Today would be difficult enough to get through. If they had arrived here two days ago, Mama would have expected them to stay at the house with her and the family, which would have been too stressful for Irma—not to mention knowing that Homer's corpse was in one of the downstairs bedrooms. It was bad enough that she had to view his body today, dressed in white garments that had been newly made for this occasion. She also didn't care for the idea of being expected to talk to other people who had come here to pay their respects to the deceased and comfort his family. What would she even say to someone offering their condolences?

Irma tried to concentrate on the message being preached by one of the ministers, but so many thoughts ran through her head, it was hard to focus on anything being said. She clasped her sweaty hands together, refusing to focus on the casket that had been placed in the center of the room just a few feet from where the minister stood preaching. Irma's face contorted into what she feared was a hateful expression, and she quickly looked down. *I never felt like I belonged with this family. Not like I did when my real daed was alive and it was just me, Mama, and him. Oh, how I wish Daadi hadn't died and that Mama had never remarried—especially to a man like Homer.*

Several women got up at the same time to take their fussy young children outside for a while. Some would probably go up to the house for a diaper change or to feed the babies, while others would walk around outside to stretch their legs and allow their children the freedom to breathe some fresh mountain air while walking or running for a bit. At the moment, Irma wished her children were here. When one or more of them became restless, she would have had an excuse to leave the barn and take them outside or up to the house. Having the children with her would also have given Irma something else to focus on other than the funeral service, which was heading into its second hour.

Irma's face relaxed some, and she stifled a yawn, wishing she'd been able to sleep longer this morning in the comfortable bed inside the rustic cabin they had rented. Irma hadn't told LaVern yet, but she wanted to leave her mother's house soon after the funeral dinner, which would follow the graveside burial service. She figured that if they returned to the cabin early, they could get a good night's sleep before heading out in the morning for home. Irma also wanted to stop at Allard's Candy and Gift Store before it closed for the day so she could buy a little something to take home for the children. She had visited the unique shop a few times when she lived here and remembered seeing a variety of gifts, apparel, and many Montana-made products, including chocolates. Other kinds of candy were available, such as taffy and several flavors of licorice. Black licorice had always been one of Irma's favorite candies, so she might buy the children some of that. If they still had huckleberry syrups and jams available, Irma would get a jar of one or both for her in-laws as a thank-you gift for taking care of the children while she and LaVern were away. Their driver would probably appreciate a special treat too. Irma almost smiled but caught herself in time. *While we are visiting the store, I think I'll buy some goodies for LaVern and me as well.*

Irma glanced over at her mother, dressed all in black, like all the other mourners here today, including Irma and LaVern. Mama's face appeared to be etched in sorrow. Irma didn't understand why. Her mother might not realize it yet, but she was better off without Homer in her life. *Truth was, she should have never married that man in the first place.*

LaVern stood beside Irma at the cemetery, wondering how she was holding up. She'd barely said a word to him as they'd ridden there in Aaron's buggy.

Dorcas, Hannah, and Caroline had gone with Irvin in the buggy ahead of them since there wasn't room for all the family members to ride in the same carriage. Now, along with several people from their church district, Dorcas and her family stood solemnly watching as Homer's body was laid to rest. LaVern wondered what was going through each of their minds. Both Hannah and Caroline had puffy faces and eyes that appeared red from crying. No doubt they missed their father and most likely wondered what things would be like now that he was gone.

He studied Aaron and Irvin's expressions to gauge their feelings as well. Aaron's shoulders curled forward, and his clean-shaven chin trembled slightly as Homer's coffin was lowered into the hole that had been dug previously by the pallbearers. Irvin, on the other hand, showed no outward emotion as he stood straight and tall, staring ahead. Did the young man's thoughts involve the future of the lumber mill or perhaps the responsibility that had now been put on his shoulders to provide for his mother and siblings? It was a difficult position, all right, and Irvin no doubt had some concerns about his new situation.

LaVern looked at Dorcas, standing between her youngest daughters. Her posture was slightly stooped, and his mother-in-law's watery gaze let him know that her grief and concern for her family was very real. As far as LaVern knew, no other relatives of Homer's were here today. During the time he'd lived in St. Ignatius, LaVern had heard Homer say something about having a brother, but LaVern had never met the man. If the brother was present today, surely he would be standing near Homer's widow and her children. One time, while LaVern had been working for Irma's stepfather at the mill, Homer had mentioned that both of his parents were deceased and so were Dorcas' folks. So apparently, other than Homer's wife and children, there were no other relatives to mourn his passing.

If Irma and I had stayed here instead of moving to Ohio, I'd be in a position to look after this family—at least until I was sure Dorcas' sons could handle things on their own, LaVern thought. *But our home is in Ohio now, and I like my job, so I don't feel like I can uproot my little family to move back here. However, I will speak to Dorcas before we leave and offer my financial assistance if it's needed.*

———— ≈ ————

Dorcas was on the verge of collapse, but several people were still here eating and visiting, so she couldn't be rude and excuse herself to go lie down, much as she may long to do so. Dorcas hadn't slept well last night, so she'd been going on sheer willpower all morning and this afternoon.

Dorcas spotted Irma sitting with LaVern on one side of the wraparound front porch, and she decided this would be a good time to talk to them about her situation with the lumber mill.

She took a seat in the chair beside Irma. "Tomorrow, we're going to have a family meeting, and I'm hoping you'll be here for that, because I would appreciate both your and LaVern's opinion on a few things."

Irma shook her head. "No, Mama. We'll be heading for home early tomorrow morning, and we'll be going back to Allard's Lodge soon to spend the night."

Dorcas' lips pressed together in a tight grimace. "Seriously? I'd hoped that you would spend the night here so we could talk during breakfast tomorrow morning."

"I had talked with LaVern before we ate our meal after the graveside service, and I told him that I wanted to get a few gifts to take home to our kinner. Allard's Gift Store will be closing soon, so we'll be going over there when our driver shows up. LaVern went out to your phone shed and called him a while ago."

Dorcas swallowed against the tears clogging her throat. "So you won't be coming back here at all before you head back to Ohio?"

Irma slowly shook her head.

Dorcas pressed both hands firmly against her temples. "I'm very disappointed. I, as well as your siblings, have hardly had any time to talk to you, and I'd really like your and LaVern's input about the future of this family."

"How about this. . ." LaVern spoke up. "We'll go over to the gift store as soon as our driver shows up to get a few things for the kids. And since I can tell that my fraa is really tired, we'll spend the night at the cabin we rented. Then tomorrow morning, we'll come back here and join you for breakfast and talk. After our discussion, we can head for home. Does that sound agreeable to you, Dorcas?"

"Jah, that'll be fine." What else could she say? Seeing the flat look on her daughter's face and her narrowed eyes, Dorcas figured she'd be pushing her luck to ask for anything more than LaVern had offered. She'd known from the moment Irma and LaVern had arrived this morning that her eldest daughter did not want to be here and had only come out of obligation. Well, beggars couldn't be choosy, so Dorcas would settle for whatever time Irma and LaVern would give her in the morning.

Chapter 15

"Girls, would you please set the table?" Dorcas asked when Caroline and Hannah entered the kitchen the following morning.

"Sure, Mama," Hannah replied.

Caroline released a noisy yawn. "How come we had to get up so early? We got to bed late, and I'm really mied."

"We're all tired, Caroline," Dorcas replied. "It must have slipped my mind yesterday with all that was going on here for the funeral and I forgot to mention that I'd talked with your sister and LaVern outside on the porch privately." Dorcas paused a few seconds to collect her thoughts. "I was able to make plans with them, but it had to be early because they'll be heading back to Ohio today." A yawn escaped Dorcas' lips after she'd taken a carton of eggs from the refrigerator. "Since LaVern and Irma will be joining us this morning and they need to get an early start after we've had breakfast, while we eat, we'll have our family discussion about what to do with the lumber mill."

"You don't have to do anything with it," Irvin announced when he entered the room. "Aaron and I talked it over before we went to bed last night, and we decided that we're capable of running the business together."

Aaron, who'd also come into the kitchen, bobbed his head. "That's right. So there's no need to sell the mill."

Dorcas set the eggs on the counter and turned to face her sons. "Are you sure? I know you've both been working there with your daed for a while, but it would be a big responsibility to be in charge of the operation. Are you both up to the task of running things on your own?"

"We believe so, and it's necessary, because we're gonna need money to support our family," Irvin said. "The lumber mill will provide that for us, just like it did when Papa was in charge of things."

"Are you sure about that?"

The brothers nodded simultaneously.

"All right then, it's settled. We'll just have to see about hiring someone to help out, because you boys can't take care of the business end of things and do all the work too."

"I'll see if my friend Thomas would like a job, and we'll put the word out, because we'll probably need to hire more than one fellow to help out." Irvin pushed his shoulders back, displaying a strong posture. "Aaron and I have got this, Mama. You don't need to worry about a thing."

Dorcas smiled, despite her concern and reservations. At this point, she didn't feel that she had any other choice but to let her sons try.

───────── ≈ ─────────

When their driver pulled his van into Dorcas' yard, LaVern invited him inside to join them for breakfast. He felt sure that his mother-in-law wouldn't mind.

"I appreciate the offer," Carl said, "but I'll be fine waiting here in the van with my doughnuts and coffee. Since I'm not part of the family, I would be uncomfortable sitting in on your group meeting. Your family might not appreciate it, either."

LaVern didn't argue. Carl had a point, and LaVern hadn't really thought it through. Whatever was said around Dorcas' kitchen table this morning wasn't anyone's business except her family's.

"We shouldn't be more than an hour or so," LaVern told Carl before exiting the van.

"That's fine, but take your time. I've driven other families to funerals, and I can assure you that sometimes family business can't be rushed."

LaVern opened the back door for Irma, and when she stepped out, he saw from her pained expression that she seemed reluctant to go inside. They were here, though, and had agreed to join Irma's family for breakfast, so they needed to follow through with their promise. Besides, how else was LaVern supposed to bring up the topic of Dorcas' financial situation and present the offer that he and Irma had discussed yesterday evening concerning the amount of funds they would be able to give her? He couldn't understand Irma's reluctance to be with her family, because LaVern had a great relationship with his parents and siblings, as well as with his grandparents. His wife was obviously stressed out by all of this, and LaVern's goal was to ease the tension, so he would continue to give Irma and her family as much support as they needed.

With one hand held gently against Irma's back, LaVern guided her up the walkway and onto the front porch. "Are you okay?" he asked before reaching out to knock on the door.

"Not really, but I'll get through it." She spoke in a tension-filled voice.

He smiled while looking into her eyes. "Just remember, I'm here for you."

LaVern hoped things would go well during breakfast and that his wife wouldn't say or do anything she might later regret. He'd known before they arrived here yesterday that Irma wished she hadn't felt obligated to attend Homer's funeral. He understood that Irma hadn't cared for her stepfather; although she'd never said exactly why, other than that Homer was a harsh man. What LaVern didn't understand was the reason Irma seemed so cold toward Dorcas and hadn't kept in good contact with her mother or any of her siblings since she'd left St. Ignatius with him. LaVern had asked her about it several times since their marriage, but she'd never opened up and stated her reasons. Instead, Irma had said emphatically that she didn't want to talk about it and had always quickly changed the subject. LaVern figured the problem had more to do with Irma's stepfather than her mother or half-siblings. Now that Homer was gone, he hoped Irma's relationship with her family would improve.

———————≈———————

When Irma entered her mother's kitchen, the familiar and delicious smell of buttermilk pancakes and maple syrup assaulted her senses. For the first time since leaving Ohio, she felt hungry and looked forward to eating breakfast. One thing she'd always appreciated about Mama was her good cooking.

"Everything is on and ready to eat, so let's all take a seat and thank God for the food." Mama gestured to the table.

Irvin sat at one end of the table in the chair where Homer used to sit, and Aaron sat at the other end. Mama, Hannah, and Caroline sat on one side of the table, and Irma took her seat next to LaVern on the opposite side.

When Irvin lowered his head for prayer, everyone else did the same. The first thing that came to mind when Irma prayed was to ask God for a safe trip back to Ohio. Next, she asked Him to be with her children and help them to be good for their grandparents. Before opening her eyes, Irma prayed for her brothers and sisters and, also, Mama. Although she felt sure that she would never have a close relationship with any of them, she hoped God would watch over them and provide for their needs.

Soon, Irvin cleared his throat and all eyes returned to looking at the enticing breakfast that awaited their appetites. It was clear to Irma that the oldest of her siblings wanted to take over for Homer. Irvin's strong posture was evident, and he was seated in her stepfather's spot at the table. *It will be good if he's planning to step up and take care of this family. That way, I'll be able to go home today with a clear conscience, knowing that things here will work out as they should.*

As everyone began eating their meal, there was some discussion about what to do with Homer's horse. Dorcas said she thought they ought to sell it, and Irvin quickly chimed in. "I think we should hold onto Papa's *gaul.* You never know when one of ours might get sick or come up lame, so having an extra horse on hand could be a good thing."

Irma tried to tune out their discussion and focus on eating her tasty meal, but it was a challenge—especially when, at one point, two or three of them talked at once. "Was Homer's gaul what you had wanted to talk to me and LaVern about?" Irma directed the question to her mother.

Mama shook her head. "It had to do with the lumber mill and if we should sell or keep it." She paused and appeared to be on the verge of saying something more when LaVern spoke up.

"If you're worried about your finances, Irma and I are willing to help out. Although I can't be here to help run the mill, I'd be happy to send you some money if—"

"There's no need for that." Irvin's cheeks turned crimson. "Sorry, I didn't mean to interrupt, but we're going to get by just fine, because Aaron and I will be running the lumber mill from now on."

"That's right," Aaron agreed. "As soon as we get back to working there, we'll have a steady flow of money coming in."

With a feeling of relief, Irma sagged against the back of her chair. *It seems Homer raised the boys to be responsible. Guess that's something he did right.* She was pleased to know that her mother and siblings would be able to make it on their own, and even more relieved that she and LaVern wouldn't have to part with any money he earned to help this family out. After all, he had his own family to support, and as far as Irma was concerned, she and their children came first.

Dorcas looked around the table at each of her family members. It was so nice having them all here, sharing a meal together. It would be even nicer if LaVern and Irma lived closer and she could see them more often. Dorcas would be willing to start over and try to fix all the mistakes she'd made with Irma, but she wasn't sure how, because the past could not be undone. Oh, how she longed to get to know Irma and LaVern's children.

She wanted to be a part of their lives. But the distance between St. Ignatius and their home in Mount Hope made it difficult and time consuming to travel from Montana to Ohio. If Dorcas could fly on a commercial airplane, it wouldn't be so bad. She'd be able to get there within a few hours, rather than hiring a driver with the long trip taking two full days. But the Amish church didn't allow members to travel by airplane except in some communities, under extreme circumstances considered to be an emergency. A train trip to Ohio would be the next best choice, and for Dorcas, it would seem the most enjoyable.

Allowing her thoughts to change direction, she felt good about the decision her sons had made to take over their father's business. Dorcas was confident that Irvin and Aaron could make a go of it. They were both smart and hard workers. In addition to the income they would make from the lumber mill, Hannah's job as a housekeeper for one of their English neighbors brought in some income too. She'd always been good about giving part of her wages to Dorcas to help with expenses. If needed, Caroline could also find employment outside their home. But for now, at least, Dorcas appreciated having her youngest daughter at home, helping out.

Dorcas watched her eldest daughter from across the table, wishing she could read Irma's thoughts as she sat quietly moving her fork around her half-eaten pancake. *Could she be upset because LaVern offered to help us financially? Does she realize how much I love her? Is she sorry she came here for Homer's funeral? If Irma didn't want to be here, why'd she come at all?* Dorcas clenched the napkin lying in her lap, pushing it between her fingers until it formed a ball. *Maybe it's me she didn't want to see. One thing's for sure: my daughter, whom I love so much, does not feel the same way about me. I really need to talk to her about it and would like to resolve things before she leaves. I just hope she's willing to do that.*

———— ≈ ————

When Irma finished eating and had bowed her head for silent prayer, she carried her and LaVern's plates to the sink and added them to the other dishes soaking in sudsy water. Then she turned to her mother and said, "I'll wash LaVern's and my *gscharr*, but I won't have time to wash anything else, because our driver is waiting and we need to be on our way." She glanced toward the doorway that her husband had just gone through. "LaVern's already gone out to tell Carl that we'll be ready to go momentarily."

"I understand that you're eager to be on your way," Mama said. "And I don't expect you to do any of the dishes—not even your own. I would, however, like a few minutes to talk to you about something."

"If it's about the lumber mill. . ."

"No, we already discussed that during breakfast. This is of a more personal nature." Mama looked at her other daughters, still seated at the table, talking to each other in low voices. "Caroline and Hannah, would you please wash and dry the dishes while Irma and I go to the living room to talk for a few minutes before she and LaVern head out?"

"Sure, Mama," they said in unison. They rose from the table and came over to give Irma a hug.

"I'm sorry you can't stay longer," Hannah said.

"Jah," Caroline agreed. "We didn't have nearly enough time to visit."

"I'm sorry about that too, but I'll try to stay in better touch through letters and phone calls." Irma had to choke back tears when she saw Hannah's chin tremble. She felt guilty for not maintaining contact with her sisters. Neither of them had done anything to hurt her, like Mama and Homer had. Caroline and Hannah didn't deserve to be shut out of Irma's life.

Irma looked at her mother and said, "Okay, I'm ready to go to the living room now so you can tell me what's on your mind."

"Thank you." Mama led the way, and Irma followed. As soon as they stepped into the living room, Irma said, "What did you want to talk to me about?"

Mama placed one hand on Irma's shoulder. "I'd like to know the reason you're so distant with me, and why you haven't kept in touch or come here to see us until now."

Irma took a step back and squared her shoulders. "You know why, Mama. From the time you first married Homer, you never stood up for me when he treated me so harshly."

"I—I know, and I'm sorry about that, but I'd like to explain."

"Don't bother. It's too late for apologies. Besides, there is no way you can change the past." Irma moved toward the front door. "I need to go, so if you want to say goodbye to LaVern, you can follow me out to the van. I think Irvin and Aaron are probably out there too, because they followed LaVern when he went outside."

Mama stood quietly before giving a nod. "All right then, but before you go, I just want to say that I love you very much, and I always have."

Irma stiffened when Mama gave her a hug. It was all she could do to mutter, "Take care of yourself, Mama. I'll let you know when we get home."

Chapter 16

Baltic

"Grossmammi, I sure am bored today. It's raining outside, and there ain't nothin' for me to do." Brian's lower lip protruded. "Wish I was at home with Buster right now."

"Why don't you go to the dining room table and color some pictures with Clayton and Myra?" Mildred suggested, choosing to ignore the boy's use of the word *ain't*.

He shook his head. "I don't like coloring that much. That's boring too."

She picked up her basket of mending and patted the place on the couch where it had been sitting while she'd worked on hemming one of her new dresses. "Take a seat here beside me, and we'll think of something fun you can do."

Brian gave a little shrug and dropped onto the couch with a groan. "Sure wish my mamm and daed would get here so I could go home and see my hund. I keep wondering how he's doin' without me."

"I'm sure the dog is fine. Your neighbors promised to look out for him while you're gone, right?"

He gave a slow nod. "Jah, but I still miss him, and I bet he misses me too."

"I'm sure he does, but your parents will be home soon, and then you'll be back at your own home and can play with Buster again."

"Will they be back today?"

"No, it'll probably be sometime tomorrow evening; although it will likely be quite late, because they left Montana later than they'd planned to this morning. So you and your sister and brother will most likely be in bed by the time they arrive."

"Oh." Brian lowered his head. "I hope they'll wake us up."

"I'm sure they will, or they might decide to spend the night here, and you'll see them the following morning. Then we can all have breakfast together. Wouldn't that be nice?"

"Jah." He lifted his head. "Can we have *schpuck* and *oier*?"

"I think bacon and eggs would be a good idea."

Brian grinned.

She reached over and patted his knee. "Say, how would you like to help me make some homemade bubble solution so we can go outside when the rain stops and blow some really big *wassweblos*? I bet your sister and brother would enjoy blowing bubbles too."

Brian looked at her, his eyes a bit brighter than before. "Guess we could do that. And if it don't quit raining, we can blow bubbles here in the house."

Mildred blinked rapidly and felt a flush cascade across her cheeks. *I'd better pray hard that it quits raining soon or I'll have to disappoint the kids by saying, "No bubbles in the house." Of course,* she told herself, *if it keeps raining, we could always do the bubbles out on the front porch, since there would at least be a cover over our heads.*

St. Cloud

LaVern felt a sense of relief when they stopped for the night and he and Irma entered their hotel room. She had been awfully quiet most of the thirteen hours they'd traveled today, and the questions he had wanted to ask her couldn't be said in front of their driver. If he had chosen to ask her any personal questions while they were on the road, Irma surely would not have responded to LaVern since it was a sensitive topic he wished to discuss.

He couldn't help worrying about his wife. There was no doubt about this trip having been hard on Irma. It wasn't only the dark circles beneath her eyes from lack of sleep he was concerned about. It was the impersonal way Irma had acted around her mother—as if she didn't care about her. There was also the fact that she hadn't wanted to go to her stepfather's funeral at all.

How could that be? LaVern wondered after he'd placed Irma's suitcase on a luggage rack at the foot of the bed and moved across the room to put his suitcase on the small couch. *I know Irma didn't care much for Homer, but surely she must feel something for her mother.* LaVern couldn't imagine having anything but a good relationship with his parents and siblings. He always looked forward to family gatherings, and it seemed odd that Irma had no desire to keep in touch with her mother. It was a puzzle he couldn't figure out. *I truly wish my wife would confide in me, because this matter may not get any better unless we do talk about it. In fact, I can't help feeling that Irma doesn't have any plans to make things right with her mother. It seems that she has managed to push Dorcas away—and her siblings too for that matter. If Irma isn't willing to talk to me about it, then I'm going to feel as if I'm being pushed away too.*

LaVern glanced over his shoulder and noticed that his wife had opened her suitcase and removed her nightgown, but she hadn't uttered a word since entering the room. Having left St. Ignatius later than originally planned this morning, at Irma's request, their driver had agreed to make fewer stops and spend more hours on the road today in the hope of getting to the same hotel in Minnesota that they'd stopped at on the trip going out. LaVern had been surprised that they'd managed to arrive at the hotel before midnight. This would put them back on track so they could be home sometime tomorrow night—although it might be quite late and their kids would probably be asleep by the time they got there.

Irma heaved a big sigh, took a seat on the edge of the bed, and removed her shoes and black stockings. "I'm so tired I may not have the strength to take a shower. I just want to crawl in bed and sleep."

"I know what you mean. It has been a long day, but I think we would both sleep better after warm showers. Besides, we'll need to get up pretty early in the morning so we can make good time and arrive at my parents' place before it's really late."

"True." She yawned and reached up to take off her head covering. When she pulled the pins from her bun, her long, dark hair cascaded down her back.

"Before we take our showers, though, I'd like to talk to you about something," he said.

Irma turned her head in LaVern's direction. "What did you want to say?"

He came over and took a seat beside her. "I've been wondering why you seem so distant toward your mother. Weren't you happy to be with her again after not seeing her for such a long time?"

"My mamm and I have never been close—at least not since my biological father died. After she married Homer, she cared more about him than she did me." Irma rose from the bed. "I really don't want to talk about this, LaVern." She took a few steps forward then paused. "Besides, Mama is perfectly fine without me in her life. She has Irvin, Aaron, Hannah, and Caroline, and they're going to be okay financially." Irma stepped into the bathroom and closed the door before LaVern could say anything more.

He remained on the bed, slowly shaking his head. *Why can't my wife open up to me? What is holding her back?* Irma's attitude toward her mother was hard to comprehend. She'd no doubt been upset when her father died, and probably resented it when her mother chose to marry again. Even so, wasn't it time for Irma to let all that go and work at developing a better relationship with Dorcas and the rest of her family? LaVern couldn't force Irma to do it, of course, but he would try to encourage her to stay in better contact with her family in Montana through letters and phone calls. LaVern would definitely be praying about this matter. He hoped that, in time, the Lord would help work things out between Irma and her family. He hoped that maybe Irma's mother, or some of her siblings, could come to Ohio to see them sometime too. Surely that would help bridge the gap between them. LaVern wouldn't bring that idea up yet, but maybe after they'd been home a few months, he'd find a good opportunity to raise the subject.

<hr />

St. Ignatius

Dorcas pulled back the lightweight blanket and sheet she had slept under and sat up in bed. After tossing and turning for the last two hours, she figured she may as well get up and fix herself a cup of calming chamomile tea. Hopefully, it would help her relax enough that she could finally get some good sleep. Morning would come early, and without proper rest, she wouldn't have the energy to do much of anything tomorrow. They had plenty to do, and that long list of items to deal with would continue in the days ahead.

Dorcas slipped on her robe and, with the aid of a flashlight, padded in her bare feet down the hall and out to the kitchen. Upon entering the dark room, she lit the gas lamp hanging above the table. Next, Dorcas put the teakettle on the front burner and waited for the water to heat.

Her mind replayed the events of the last couple of days. Her heart clenched as she thought about Irma's coolness toward her during the time she and LaVern were here. Tears sprang to Dorcas' eyes and dripped down her hot cheeks. *I know why Irma has hard feelings toward me, and it's with good reason,* she admitted. *I wish she would have let me explain a few things to her before she left. I wanted my daughter to know how much I love her. I should have apologized for not standing up for her when Homer's mean streak took over and he became abusive, but she seemed unwilling to hear anything I had to say.*

Dorcas reached for a napkin and dried her tears. *I suppose I could write Irma a letter and share everything that's on my mind.* She sniffed deeply. *Although, she might not believe me, which could make things worse.*

Dorcas lowered her head and prayed. *Dear Lord, please show me what I should do to make things right with Irma. If I decide to write or call my daughter, please give me the words that will speak to her heart and heal our relationship.*

The teakettle whistled, and Dorcas rose from her chair. Maybe by tomorrow morning she would have a clearer head and a better sense of direction. The one thing Dorcas knew was that she had to somehow make amends for all the pain she had caused her eldest daughter by marrying Homer.

———————— ≈ ————————

St. Cloud

"You're a disobedient child and need to be continually punished until you learn how to obey!"

Irma struggled not to cry, but it was an impossible task. As the leather strap in Homer's hand connected with her back, buttocks, and legs, tears sprang to her eyes, and soon she cried out, begging him to stop. With each subsequent blow, the anger and hatred she felt for this horrible man increased. According to Homer, everything Irma did was wrong and nothing was ever right. And what about Mama, who stood by without saying a single word, watching as Homer practically dragged me out of the house and into the barn to get my "just reward"? Irma thought as she lay helpless across a bale of straw. And all for what—because she'd come home late from school again and wasn't allowed to explain. Homer clearly hated her, and the feeling was mutual. Someday, when she was old enough and had somewhere else to go, Irma planned to leave this place and never look back.

Another blow of the strap came then, followed by several

more. The pain was so intense that Irma couldn't hold
back her screams. "Stop! Stop! Please, stop it!" she shouted
over and over.

"Irma, wake up!"

Irma's eyes snapped open, and her heartbeat raced so fast she couldn't catch her breath. "LaVern?"

"Jah, Irma, it's me. You were shouting in your sleep, saying 'Stop! Stop it!' You must have been having a bad dream. Do you remember what it was about?" He stroked her face gently with his thumb.

She shook her head and sat up. No way was she going to tell her husband about the nightmare that had plagued her since she was a girl living in Montana. Irma chose not to tell LaVern about her dream in order to hide the awful truth concerning her abusive stepfather, rather than open up to the one person in her life who truly cared for and loved her. Her only excuse was that the pain Homer had often inflicted was not something she could talk about freely, because it was too agonizing. It was better to bury the pain and anger she felt than to discuss it with LaVern or anyone else. They might not believe the horrible way Homer had treated Irma, or they could take Homer's side and think she was a horrible stepdaughter who had done bad things and deserved to be punished. Homer had told her that so often, she almost believed it herself. Since her stepfather never treated his own children like that, Irma figured she must have done something to deserve his wrath.

"What time is it?" she asked.

"It's 2:00 a.m." LaVern gestured to the alarm clock on the nightstand by their bed. "We won't be leaving for another two hours, so you should lie back down, close your eyes, and try to get a little more sleep."

She climbed out of bed. "I'm wide awake now, and I'd never get back to sleep. I'm going to get up and fix myself a cup of hot tea. I'd rather have coffee," she added, "but the herbal tea I bought at the gift store in St. Ignatius might help me relax. By the time I get calmed down and dressed, it'll be almost time for us to leave."

125

"All right then," LaVern said, "but I'm going to lie back down and try to get a few more winks before the alarm goes off."

"That's fine." Irma moved across the room and filled one of the cups on the counter with water. Then she placed it inside the microwave to heat the water. While Irma waited, she removed a tea bag from a plastic bag in her suitcase that she'd brought from home. She hoped the chamomile tea would help soothe her frazzled nerves. The thing she wanted most right now was to be back home with LaVern and their children. Irma felt certain that keeping occupied with her own little family, far from St. Ignatius, would help her forget and put to rest once and for all, all thoughts of Homer and Dorcas Schmucker.

Chapter 17

Baltic

It was a little after midnight when Carl pulled his vehicle into the yard of LaVern's parents. LaVern got out and opened the back passenger door for Irma. The full moon above lit the yard fairly well, but LaVern turned on his flashlight to guide their steps to the front door. Irma saw light coming from the living-room window and figured one or both of LaVern's parents must be awake and waiting for them. The children were probably in bed asleep, and she hated to wake them, but maybe if LaVern carried the kids out to the van while they were still asleep, they would find themselves in their own beds at home when they woke in the morning.

Irma and LaVern had no more than stepped onto the porch when the door opened and Paul stepped out. Mildred was right behind him. "The kinner are in bed, but we stayed up to wait for you." She stepped forward and gave them both a hug. Paul did the same.

"We're glad you're back. Any problems along the way?" Paul asked as he ushered them into the house.

LaVern shook his head. "It was just a very long trip, and we're both exhausted."

"That's right," Irma agreed. "So we should get the kinner now and head for home. I'm sure our driver is eager to get some sleep too."

"You should spend the night here," Mildred said. "It would be a shame to wake the children at this hour. You and LaVern can take the downstairs guest room and sleep as late as you like."

Irma swiped a hand across her warm cheeks, and then shook her head. "It's nice of you to offer, but if we stayed the night, we'd have to call our driver again in the morning to come get us."

"You've made a good point," LaVern interjected. "It's probably best if we head home now."

"Not to worry," his dad was quick to say. "In the morning, I will call one of our own drivers to take you home. I'll see if he can come here after we've all had breakfast. How's that sound?"

Before Irma or LaVern could respond, Mildred chimed in. "That's a good idea, Paul. And since I promised Brian bacon and eggs for breakfast in the morning, he will be happy about that. I'm also positive that all three of the kids would be real excited to wake up and discover that their parents are here."

LaVern looked at Irma and tipped his head. "Well, what do you think?"

"Okay," she agreed, devoid of emotion. Spending the night here was not what she wanted, but under the circumstances, and with the late hour, it was probably the best thing for everyone involved.

LaVern nodded. "Good, then I'll go out to the van to get our luggage and tell Carl to go on home and that we'll get a ride home with one of my daed's drivers tomorrow."

"I'll go with you," Paul said.

Before the men went out the front door, Irma said, "LaVern, would you also remember to bring in that large canvas satchel and my bottle of water in the cup holder?"

"No problem, in fact I've got my water out in the vehicle, too, and I also need to grab my sunglasses, the small cooler, and our snack bag." He followed his father out the door.

Irma yawned and fiddled with her purse strap. She remained silent while waiting for LaVern and his father to return with their things. *It would be nice to be able to sleep in late and not have to worry about getting breakfast ready in the morning, especially after traveling the whole day.*

Mildred reached out and pushed a wisp of unruly hair lying on Irma's cheek back under her head covering. "You poor thing...I can only imagine what a stressful, tiring trip it must have been for you."

"It was." Irma dropped her gaze to the floor. *You have no idea how stressful it was.*

———— ≈ ————

The following morning, Irma was roused from a deep sleep by the sound of laughter. When she opened her eyes, she saw all three children clambering onto the bed. She held out her arms and welcomed each of them with a warm hug. Then, glancing to the left side of the bed where LaVern had slept, she saw that he no longer occupied the space. She figured he must have already gotten up and told the children to wake their mother.

"Did you miss me?" Irma placed a kiss on each of her children's foreheads.

"Jah," they all responded, one after the other.

Myra crawled up closer to her mama and rubbed her little nose against Irma's.

"I missed all of you so much," Irma said with a catch in her voice. "And I brought everyone a geschenk."

Clayton clapped his hands. "Oh, boy! What present did you get for me?"

She tweaked the end of his nose. "After breakfast, I will hand out the gifts. Now why don't you go find your daadi and head to the kitchen? I bet your grossmammi has already started cooking."

"We're having schpuck and oier," Brian said excitedly. "Grandma promised she would make 'em if we were still here this morning."

"And so you are." Irma smiled. "Your daed and I got in really late last night, and since you three were sleeping, we decided it would be best to spend the night here too."

"I'm glad you did." Clayton bobbed his head.

"When can we go home?" Brian questioned. "I can't wait to see my hund."

"We'll go soon after the gifts have been passed out, but not until we've finished eating breakfast."

Seemingly satisfied with her response, the children hopped off the bed; and with giggles and arms swinging by their sides, they bounded out the door.

Irma was about to get out of bed when LaVern stepped into the room. "From the happy expressions I saw on our kinners' faces, I figured you must be awake." He leaned over and kissed Irma's cheek. "Mom's got breakfast almost ready. Can you get dressed and join us in the kitchen within the next ten minutes?"

"I think so." She pushed back the covers and slid out of bed. "I slept well last night. Better than any night we were on the road or at the lodge in St. Ignatius."

He smiled. "I'm glad to hear that. Even though we aren't at our own home yet, it sure is good to be back in Ohio."

Irma nodded. "I couldn't agree more."

———— ≈ ————

"You sure outdid yourself with this tasty meal, Mom." LaVern gave his mother a thumbs-up. "I don't know which tasted better: the biscuits and gravy or the scrambled eggs and bacon."

She smiled at him from across the table and pointed to his empty plate. "I'm glad you enjoyed your breakfast."

LaVern's father patted his belly a few times. "It was really good, Mildred, and I can honestly say that I ate myself full."

"When are we gonna open our geschenk?" Brian asked.

"Right now, Son." Irma got up from the table and picked up the large satchel she'd brought to the kitchen when she came in for breakfast. "And I have something for everyone." She reached into the canvas bag and pulled out a pink, plastic plate with a matching cup and spoon, which she gave to Myra. The little girl grinned and began hitting the plate with the spoon. Everyone laughed. LaVern wondered if their daughter might give up banging on pots and pans and play with the child-size plate and spoon instead. Irma would probably appreciate that because it would be less noisy.

"The next gift is for Clayton," Irma announced. She gave him a coloring book, along with a small box of crayons. "This is a Montana coloring book, and it's full of pictures to color—all things you might see if you visited the state of Montana."

Clayton thumbed through the pages and grinned. "I like that big animal." He pointed to a picture of a buffalo.

"There was a herd of buffalo like this one near the lodge where we stayed in St. Ignatius," LaVern commented.

"Buffalo are also called *bison*," LaVern's father put in.

Clayton opened the box of crayons. "What color should I make him?"

"Brown would be good," Clayton's grandfather said. "I've never been up close to a live buffalo, but I've seen pictures of them in books and magazines."

"Montana is full of wildlife," LaVern stated. "It's a beautiful state, with lots to see and do for those who enjoy being outdoors."

"I like being outdoors. Can we go there and see for ourselves?" Brian asked.

"We'll see. Maybe someday." LaVern glanced at Irma, but he couldn't see her expression because her back was to him as she reached into the satchel again.

Clayton picked out a brown crayon and began coloring.

"What'd you get for me?" Brian asked when Irma pulled her hands out of the bag.

"It's something I think you might like." She brought a bright blue ball with the word MONTANA written on it over to Brian. "I thought you and Buster would enjoy playing fetch with this."

Brian nodded as he held the ball close to his chest. "Danki, Mama."

"You're welcome. Oh, and I also have some licorice for each of you." Irma handed a piece to each child and then reached into the satchel again. When she came back to the table, she handed LaVern's mother a jar of huckleberry jam and a recipe book that had been compiled by some of the Amish women who lived in St. Ignatius.

"Thank you very much, but you didn't have to bring me anything," Mildred said.

"I wanted to. It's just a small way of saying thank you for keeping the kinner while we were gone."

"We were glad to do it, and we certainly enjoyed our time with them." LaVern's mother looked over at his father. "Isn't that right, Paul?"

"Most definitely. And remember, we're more than willing to watch our grandkids anytime."

Irma brought over one more item from the bag and handed it to LaVern's dad. "I know how much you like *schocklaad,* so I thought you might enjoy this. Since it was warm in the van at times, even with air conditioning, I kept the box in our small cooler so none of the chocolates would melt."

A wide grin spread across Dad's face. "Danki, Irma." He opened the box, removed one of the chocolates, ate it, then handed the box to Mildred. "Care to try one?"

"Not right now, but maybe later."

"Who else would like a piece?" LaVern's father held the box out toward Irma.

She shook her head. "Those are all for you and Mildred, if you wish to share. LaVern and I bought some taffy, which we ate on the trip home."

"That's right," LaVern agreed. "And I hate to admit it, but I ate more than my share."

A horn honked, and LaVern's father got up from the table to look out the window. "My driver's here. I'll go out and tell him that you're not quite ready to leave."

"We can be ready as soon as the dishes are done," Irma said, rising from the table.

LaVern's mother shook her head. "Don't you worry about the dishes, Irma. I'll take care of them. I'm sure you are eager to get home and settle back in, and there's no reason to keep Paul's driver waiting."

LaVern couldn't miss the look of relief on his wife's face. Irma truly did want to go home—maybe even more than the kids, who were already talking about what they wanted to do when they got there.

———— ≈ ————

Mount Hope

When the driver's vehicle pulled into their yard, Irma heaved a sigh of relief. Although the ride from Baltic to home hadn't taken long, it had seemed like forever to her. The kids had all chattered like magpies the whole way, which got on Irma's nerves and left her with a headache. Even so, she was happy to be home and figured she would feel better once they all got into the house.

After everyone exited the van and the suitcases had been unloaded and taken into the house, Brian and Clayton ran outside and took off across the yard to let Buster out of his dog run. LaVern headed for the barn to check on the horses, and since Irma wanted to get the mail, she got out Myra's stroller and put her in it.

The little girl squealed as they headed down the driveway, and she swatted at a bug that flew past her face. Irma chuckled. *A lot of children Myra's age would have cried if a bug had come that close to them. But not my daughter,* she thought. *She's not the least bit frightened of flying insects.*

When Irma reached the mailbox, she took her key out and unlocked it. Inside were several bills as well as some magazines and a few advertising flyers. There was also a letter from Doretta, which would be the first thing Irma would open.

Back at the house, Irma put Myra in her high chair and gave her a snack. Then she took a seat at the table and opened her friend's letter.

Dear Irma,

It's been some time since you've written. I hope you and your family are doing all right. I've been thinking about you a lot lately and looking for a letter. I guess maybe you've been real busy, which would make sense since Brian is out of school for the summer, and no doubt you have a garden to tend and many other chores to do.

Warren and I are both doing well and eagerly awaiting the birth of our baby in September. I've said this before, but I'm truly looking forward to becoming a mother. I'm not working at the health food store anymore—just staying home, preparing for the baby's arrival and getting several other things done. I get tired easily, so I try to pace myself, but I guess that's to be expected as my time draws closer to the big day.

I hope you will write back soon, as I'm eager to know how you're doing. Take care, and God bless.

Love,
Doretta

Irma placed the letter back in the envelope and set it aside. She had been neglectful about writing. She'd planned to do it, but then after getting the news of Homer's death, her well-meaning plans went awry.

Tomorrow morning after the breakfast dishes are done, I'll sit down and write to Doretta, Irma told herself. *I will tell her all about our trip to St. Ignatius.*

Chapter 18

Grabill

On the first day of August, after Doretta had finished cleaning up the kitchen from breakfast, she went out the front door with the intent of getting the mail. She had no more than stepped off the porch when she caught sight of a squirrel running along the fence that separated their yard from the pasture. She paused to watch the chattering little critter as it scurried along, then jumped down and quickly raced up the nearest tree.

Doretta chuckled. She remembered how her father had always said squirrels were a nuisance. *They could be,* Doretta supposed, *especially when they steal food from the bird feeders.* Even so, Doretta enjoyed watching their antics and had ever since she was a child. It was entertaining to watch the squirrels collect nuts and bury them. They were playful critters too, leaping from tree to tree while chasing other squirrels.

Doretta's attention went to three yellow finches getting a drink from the birdbath she had placed in one of the flowerbeds close to the house. It didn't take long until the birds decided to take a bath, and soon some of the water had splashed over the edge and onto the ground. It was one more thing to smile about, but Doretta needed to move on or she would never get the mail.

As Doretta approached the mailbox, she heard a rhythmic *clip-clop, clip-clop* from a horse pulling a buggy down the road. She turned to see if it was anyone she knew. As the open buggy drew closer, Doretta realized their bishop was the driver and that his wife was on the seat beside him. Doretta waved, and they lifted their hands in a friendly greeting as the horse and buggy went on by.

I wonder if those two are heading to town, or maybe they'll be making a call on someone from our church district. Doretta pursed her lips. *The ministers in our church, along with our deacon, have a heavy responsibility. I need to remember to pray for them more often.*

Doretta turned to the mailbox and opened the flap. Only two pieces of mail waited, and one of the envelopes had Irma's return address on it. Doretta smiled. *I'm glad she finally wrote back, and I can't wait to find out what she had to say.*

Doretta was tempted to take the letter inside the house to read it, but today's weather was so hot and humid that her dress stuck to her back. She made a quick decision that it would be cooler to sit outside at the picnic table, under the shade of the huge maple tree in their backyard.

Doretta went into the house, placed the second piece of mail, which appeared to be a bill, on the kitchen table, and headed out the back door with Irma's letter.

After taking a seat at the picnic table, she tore the envelope open and began to read:

> *Dear Doretta,*
>
> *A lot has happened since I last wrote to you, and when a major event occurred, there was no time to write. My stepfather, Homer, died from a heart attack a few weeks ago while he was at work at his lumber mill in St. Ignatius, Montana. So LaVern and I hired a driver to take us there for the funeral. The kinner stayed with LaVern's parents while we were gone.*
>
> *The funeral went okay, but it was hard to be there. I've*

never told you this before, but my stepfather was a cruel man—at least he was to me. When I was a child, and even into my teen years, I could never do anything right. I got severely punished for things I had done that did not meet with his approval as well as for things I didn't do but was accused of by him. You probably won't understand this, and you may think I'm a horrible person, but I'm glad Homer is dead. I've been angry at him for a long time, but now that he's gone, I'm going to put all thoughts of him behind me for good.

Enough about me. I received your last letter, and I'm glad you are doing well. I know how difficult pregnancy can be. But take heart, dear friend, once the baby is born, you'll forget all about the discomfort you feel right now and will no doubt feel during your delivery.

I'll try to keep in better touch. Please let me know when the baby comes.

As always, your friend,
Irma

Irma's letter slipped out of Doretta's hand and dropped to the picnic table as she closed her eyes. *Heavenly Father, my friend Irma has been through a lot recently, and I can tell by what she said in her letter that she's really hurting. Even though she says she's going to put it all behind her, living with an abusive parent is not something to be taken lightly or forgotten about because the person is gone. Please give me the wisdom to know what to say in response to Irma's letter. I want her to feel that she can confide in me, and I hope what I say in return will offer Irma the encouragement that she needs.*

Doretta opened her eyes and rose to her feet. She would go to the phone shed right now and call Eleanor, asking her to pray for Irma too. Then Doretta would return to the house and go through the supply of all-occasion cards she kept on hand. If there was a "Sympathy" or "Thinking of You" card in the batch, she would enclose a note with it and send it off to Irma tomorrow morning.

***

St. Ignatius

Dorcas entered the house with the mail and placed everything on the kitchen table. She still hadn't received a letter or even a postcard from Irma, even though she and LaVern had been home for a few weeks. At least, LaVern had called and left a message the day they'd gotten home, and Dorcas was thankful for that.

Hannah and Caroline were busy doing the breakfast dishes, so Dorcas decided that this was a good time to remove Homer's clothes from the closet and box them up. The boys had already taken a few items they could wear, like their dad's suspenders and hats. Irvin and Aaron were both taller than Homer, so none of his shirts, trousers, or shoes fit either of them.

Dorcas brought two large cardboard boxes up from the basement and placed them on the floor near the bed. She'd been busy with so many other things since Homer's death and hadn't gotten around to removing his clothes from their room.

"I should have done this sooner." Dorcas spoke out loud, but it came out as a whisper. *Maybe getting rid of his things will make me feel better emotionally and give me some kind of closure. I just want to forget all the pain Homer caused.*

Dorcas would never admit this to anyone—especially her children—but she did not miss Homer and was actually relieved that he was no longer part of her life. She'd made a drastic mistake by marrying him and had paid dearly for her error in judgment.

She rubbed her arm where a nasty looking bruise had been a few weeks ago. She'd received it the day before Homer's death, when she had commented how much she missed seeing her eldest daughter. Her husband's eyes had narrowed, and he'd grabbed her arm and twisted it, then held it behind Dorcas's back until she promised not to mention Irma's name again.

Dorcas never understood Homer's hostility toward Irma. He'd pretended to like Irma when he and Dorcas became a couple, but when Dorcas got pregnant with Irvin, Homer began to criticize everything Irma said or did. By the time Irvin was born, Homer had become abusive toward Irma. Whenever Dorcas tried to talk to him about it, he got angry and said Irma was a belligerent child who needed strong discipline in order to break her will. With the birth of each of their three other children, Homer's harshness toward Irma had increased. There were times when Dorcas tried to intervene on her daughter's behalf, but she always paid the price for it. Homer often reminded Dorcas that he was the head of the house and that it was her duty to respect his wishes and be an obedient wife. He even threatened on many occasions to be harder on Irma if Dorcas didn't listen to him. It did not take long for Dorcas to realize that Homer meant every word he said and that if she took Irma's side on any matter, both she and her daughter paid the price. Of course, Dorcas never told anyone about her husband's abuse, knowing that if she had, it would go even worse for her as well as for Irma.

Dorcas' chin dropped toward her chest as heavy sobs from the depth of her soul poured forth. She felt a sense of self-loathing and wished she could go back and change the past. She should have never married Homer. She could have figured out some way to support herself and her daughter. Dorcas felt certain that if she had done that, she and Irma would both be better off and would have the right kind of mother-daughter relationship today. But all Dorcas could do was hope and pray for an opportunity to make things right with Irma and see if even a thread of their relationship could be mended.

Dorcas took a seat on the bed and reached for a tissue to wipe the tears from her cheeks. *I've made up my mind. I'm definitely going to write Irma a letter of apology, and then I'll wait and see what happens from there.*

---≈---

Mount Hope

As Irma stood at the kitchen table mixing a batch of cookie dough, a wave of nausea overtook her, and she raced to the kitchen sink, thinking she might not be able to hold the breakfast she'd eaten a few hours ago. The same thing had happened to her yesterday while she hung freshly laundered clothes on the line. At first, she'd thought it might have been caused by something she'd eaten that didn't agree with her, but now she wasn't so sure.

Irma placed both hands against her stomach and grimaced. *I hope I'm not pregnant.*

When the nausea abated a bit, she glanced out the kitchen window and saw her sons playing with the garden hose. *Now what do those two think they are doing?*

She moved away from the sink and took a quick check in the living room to see what Myra was up to. When Irma found the child asleep on the floor with a favorite doll in one hand, she quietly left the room and went out the front door.

"Look Mama, *sis en raerricher!*" Clayton hollered as he pointed to the spray of water spewing from the nozzle on the hose that Brian held straight up.

"It is not a rainy day. And Brian, you shouldn't be fooling around with that hose," she scolded. "Please turn it off and put it away."

Brian looked at Clayton and turned the hose toward him. "It is a rainy day, right?"

"*Absatz*—stop that!" Irma rushed forward to grab the hose, but not quickly enough. The next thing she knew, a spray of water hit her face, and she let out a yelp. "Brian Daniel Miller, turn off that water!"

He dropped the hose and ran for the spigot, but before he could get there, Clayton picked the hose up and water shot into the air above Irma's head. "Drop that hose!" She jumped to the left, but the spray followed her when Clayton let the hose fall to the ground. With the force from the water still ongoing, the hose flipped this way and that across the grass. The whole time, Irma kept shouting at the boys. By the time Brian had the water shut off, she was drenched from head to toe and hopping mad.

Irma ran toward Brian, grabbed ahold of his shoulders, and gave him a firm shake. "You little *dummkopp! Schick dich net so dumb aa*—Why are you so stupid?"

Tears welled in the boy's eyes. "I—I didn't mean to be stupid, Mama. I was only having a little fun with the water 'cause it's so hot out today. And I can't help it that Clayton couldn't hold the hose still while I was trying to turn it off."

"You were both in the wrong," she said, swiping a hand across her wet face. "And now just look at me. . . . I'm all wet!" She marched over and grabbed Clayton's arm, pulling him along. "You two get inside and go to your rooms. There will be no more playtime for either of you today, because as soon as I get changed into some dry clothes, I shall find some work for you both to do." Irma's legs trembled and her hands shook like a leaf caught in the wind. This was not turning out to be a good day, and on top of that, she'd lost her temper with Brian and Clayton. She would be glad when Brian went back to school in a few weeks. At least she'd only have two children to look after for most of the day, and she wouldn't have to worry about Brian coming up with things to do that would get both him and his little brother in trouble.

With shuffling feet, the boys headed back to the house with their heads down. Irma heaved a sigh. *Isn't it bad enough that my stomach is upset? Do I have to deal with two naughty boys today? Can't things be simple and peaceful here at this house? That's all I want—just a bit of serenity and some well-behaved children.*

Another wave of nausea hit Irma, and she hurried inside. *Dear Lord, please don't let this sickness I feel be because I am with child. My nerves are on edge and have been since we got home from Montana. I don't think I could deal with having another baby right now.*

Irma had hoped—even prayed—that since Homer was gone, she could bury all her pent-up feelings of resentment toward him and carry on without feeling so upright all the time. But little things that could be seen by some people as humorous—like getting blasted by water from the hose on a hot day—made her lash out at her sons. Thinking about it rationally, Irma had to admit that Brian and Clayton were just being impetuous boys, trying to stay cool on a sultry summer day and having a little fun at the same time. But knowing it and dealing with it were two different things. Truth was, Irma feared that if she didn't get control of the emotions that came over her when she was angry, she might end up doing something worse than pulling Clayton by the arm or calling Brian names and shaking him real hard.

Chapter 19

Irma sat on the couch, going over the mail she'd brought into the house a short time ago. It had arrived later than usual today and had been brought up to the house by their rural mail carrier because there was a package that wouldn't fit in the mailbox. She looked at the parcel, noticing it was addressed to her. *It's from my good friend Doretta. This is unexpected. I wonder what's inside?* Most of the other mail turned out to be bills, so she set them on the coffee table and opened the package. In addition to a sympathy card and letter she found inside, there was a devotional book on the topic of dealing with difficult times.

Doretta must realize from the letter I sent her a few weeks ago that I'm going through a rough time right now. Irma placed both hands against her stomach to quell the queasiness she felt. She'd taken a pregnancy test yesterday, and it had been positive; although she hadn't told LaVern or anyone else yet. Due to the nausea, she hadn't been surprised by the confirmation that she was with child. But the news wasn't welcome. Irma hadn't mentioned to LaVern that she'd been dealing with morning sickness, so he probably didn't suspect that she was expecting their fourth child. Somehow, Irma had managed to keep it hidden. She needed to tell him but would wait until after Brian, Clayton, and Myra had gone to bed tonight. At this point in her pregnancy, there was no need for the children to know.

Irma thought about her previous pregnancies and how, with each one, she'd dealt with morning sickness. The queasiness hadn't been the easiest thing to deal with during the first trimester, but she had managed to find a few ways to help ease the nausea. Irma had kept soda crackers nearby to nibble on or popped a peppermint candy into her mouth and let it slowly dissolve. Peppermint tea had helped some too, but even the smell of coffee made Irma's nausea worse. She'd given up drinking her favorite beverage, which had probably been good, since caffeine made her jittery. The crackers, mints, and herbal tea had helped to calm her stomach sometimes, but other times, she simply had to deal with the nausea until it passed.

Irma sat quietly for a while, wondering how LaVern would react when she told him she was in a family way. *He will probably be pleased,* she thought. *I'm sure that LaVern would be disappointed if he knew I'm not thrilled about having another child.*

After several minutes went by, Irma picked up the devotional book her friend had sent and thumbed through a few pages before setting it on the coffee table. *It was nice of Doretta to think of me, but now that I know I'm pregnant, I'll have a lot more things to keep me busy, and there won't be much time for reading.*

The last thing Irma wanted was the responsibility of raising another child. She had her hands full with Myra, Clayton, and especially Brian. These days, her oldest boy had become quite rowdy, instigating problems with Clayton and sometimes Myra, who couldn't stand up for herself. Irma had become tired of it and given Brian more chores to do, but he still pestered the other children whenever he had the chance. She would be glad when he returned to school next Monday. Maybe then, things would be a little calmer at home.

This morning had been one of those times when Brian had gotten in trouble. He'd hidden some of Clayton's cherished rocks and wouldn't tell his brother where he had put them. Exasperated, Irma had given her son a few good swats on his backside and sent him out to the barn to clean the stalls while the horses grazed in the pasture.

Was I as obstinate as Brian when I was a child? Irma wondered. *Could that be why Homer was so hard on me and doled out such harsh punishment? Like mother, like son. Is that how it's going to be? Will I need to use a firmer hand with Brian when he disobeys?*

Irma shuddered at the remembrance of Homer's disciplinary actions. It was never with a firm hand either. He always used a strap or wooden paddle on her—sometimes with brute force. Irma shook her head. *I would never treat any of my children in such a cruel way. That would be child abuse.*

Deciding it was not good to dwell on the matter, Irma read the letter her friend had included with the sympathy card:

> *Dear Irma,*
>
> *I was glad to receive your letter but sorry to hear about your stepfather's passing. It's good that you and LaVern were able to go to the funeral to be with your mother and siblings.*
>
> *I want you to know that I'm praying for you, and I hope you will find the devotional book I've enclosed to be encouraging and helpful in your journey of emotional healing.*
>
> *Take care, and please keep in touch. I'll let you know when my baby is born.*
>
> *Blessings,*
> *Doretta*

Irma put the letter back in the envelope. *I am certain that Doretta cares about me, but she doesn't really understand what I am going through or what a rough childhood I had. Only someone who has been abused can truly sympathize or relate to what it's like to be abused physically or emotionally.* She clamped her teeth together. *I suffered both at the hands of my cruel and unfeeling stepfather.*

Irma thought back to when she had lived in her mother and stepfather's home. *I wonder why my mamm would marry a man who wasn't spiritually grounded, when Mama liked to read her Bible and enjoyed attending the bi-weekly Amish church services. Surely, she must have known that Homer wasn't spiritually grounded before agreeing to marry him. Could Mama have seen something in Homer that made her want to become his wife? If so, I can't imagine what it was, for I've never liked anything about that man. Even when I was a young girl, he seemed harsh and demanding.* She clenched her fingers in the palm of her hands until her nails bit into her flesh. *Oh, Mama, what were you thinking? You certainly made a mistake choosing a fellow like Homer. I hope you realize that now. Of course, even if you do, it won't change anything about the past.*

———————— ≋ ————————

When Irma heard the familiar sound of LaVern's boots clomping into the house that evening, she wasn't surprised when he entered the kitchen a few minutes later. The chicken-and-broccoli casserole was almost finished baking in the oven. She'd gotten out a bag of fresh veggies a while ago and had begun cutting carrots into slender pieces.

Irma shivered when her husband stepped up behind her and kissed the back of her neck. "It's sure good to be home, and something smells *wunderbaar* in here. What's for supper?"

"Chicken-and-broccoli casserole."

"Sounds good to me. How did your day go?"

She turned to face him and frowned. "Not as well as I would have liked."

"What went wrong?"

"Brian kept pestering Clayton and Myra, and when they got upset and made a fuss, I'd had enough. So I gave Brian a few swats and sent him out to the barn to clean the horses' stalls. He's upstairs in his room now, getting changed into some clean clothes before he comes down for supper."

"Sorry you had to deal with that. How did things go in the barn? Did he do a good job with the stalls?"

146

When Irma nodded and said she had checked to be sure, LaVern mentioned the dark circles beneath her eyes. "You look mied. Didn't you get enough sleep last night?"

"I never get enough, but I can't take a daytime nap, because I wouldn't know what the kinner were doing while I slept."

"That makes sense. Maybe you should make them all lie down for a nap."

Irma shook her head. "Brian's too old for naps, and since Clayton tries to copy his big brother, he'd most likely say that he's also too old. The only one who might actually sleep is Myra, but even she can stay awake most of the day. When she does take a nap, it's usually while I'm busy doing something that needs to be done. It's not likely that she would cooperate and lie down with me. Whenever I've tried lying down with her on my bed, she usually squirms around and demands my attention."

LaVern pulled Irma close and gave her a hug. "Maybe I should take a week off from work and stay home to watch the kids so you can get some rest."

"It's nice of you to offer, but since we took almost a whole week to go to Montana and back, you can't afford to take any time off right now."

"You're right, but if you really needed me to—"

She shook her head a second time. "Maybe I can go to bed a little earlier than usual tonight. It'll give me a few more hours of sleep than I normally get. Besides, there's something I need to talk to you about, and I don't want to do it until we're alone." Irma gestured toward Clayton, sitting at the table, coloring a picture from his Montana coloring book while Myra sat in her high chair with her little plastic dishes.

"Going to bed early is a good idea. Things were really busy at the auction today, and I could use a few extra winks tonight too."

Irma forced a smile and turned back to getting supper ready.

After Irma got the children tucked into bed, she headed to her and LaVern's bedroom. It felt right to put some effort into getting an early start on a good night's sleep. Irma wondered once again how her husband would react to the news about the pregnancy.

When she entered their room, Irma removed her sandals and looked at her husband sitting on the edge of their bed, hoping this was the right time to announce the news.

LaVern yawned and stretched his arms over his head. "Guess I'm more tired than I thought. It'll sure feel good to get into bed."

"Jah, it will. But before we do, remember, there's something I wanted to tell you."

"Oh, that's right." He turned to look at her. "What did you want to talk to me about?"

"I'm pregnant." Irma figured she may as well get right to the point—no beating around the bush or hoping LaVern would guess what was on her mind. Saying it right out was the best way. At least, that's how she saw it.

His head jerked back, and he slapped both of his cheeks. "Wow! That's good news. How long have you known?"

"I've suspected it for several days, because I've had a severe case of morning sickness that sometimes stays with me into the early afternoon. I took a pregnancy test yesterday morning, and it was positive. According to my calculations, the baby should be born next year—sometime near the end of March."

LaVern leaped to his feet, grabbed Irma, and pulled her into his arms for a hug. "I'm real excited about becoming a daed again, and I'm eager to tell my parents that they're gonna be grandparents again."

"Let's wait awhile on that, okay? At least until I'm further along. Same thing with the kinner. I don't want to tell them yet either."

"I agree that it's too soon to tell the children, but I think it might be good to let my mom and dad know about the pregnancy so they can be praying for you. Also, if you're not feeling well, my mamm will probably want to come over here and help out a few days a week."

Irma took off her head covering and placed it on top of their dresser. "I don't need any help, LaVern. In fact, I'm perfectly capable of taking care of the kids and the house myself."

"But you said you've been feeling sick to your stomach, so I thought—"

She shook her head. "It's not that bad, really. I'm sure I'll be fine." Irma didn't need her mother-in-law coming here and taking over, the way she'd done before and after Myra was born. Mildred was a good person, but she was a doer, and doers liked to take over and manage things their own way. Irma didn't appreciate that at all. She had her own way of doing things and didn't want anyone coming into the house and changing things up.

LaVern lifted his shoulders in a brief shrug as he pulled back the bed-covers. "Okay, have it your way. But if your morning sickness gets worse, please let me know, and I'll make a call to my mamm for help or ask one of the ladies from our church district to come over to assist you a few days a week." He held Irma at arm's length and looked directly into her eyes. "I can't help feeling a little disappointed, though, because you don't want to share our good news with anyone right now. For that matter, you don't seem too excited about having another baby. If you are, you haven't said so." He bit down on his bottom lip. "Your lack of enthusiasm makes me wonder if you dislike the idea of another child joining our family. If that is the case, then I don't understand it at all."

She dropped her gaze toward the floor. "It will be an added expense and a lot more work for me. Not only that, but Myra has been the baby of this family for almost three years, and she might feel jealous when the baby comes."

"We'll make sure that all of our kinner know that we love them very much," LaVern said. "For me, though, when our baby is born, it will be a joyful occasion—something to celebrate. From the way I see it, and from what I've read in the Bible, children are a blessing from God."

"Jah, of course. I just wish. . ." Irma's voice trailed off as she slipped her nightgown over her head. "It doesn't matter how I feel or what I think anyway. What's done is done, and we'll work through any problems we might encounter when the baby comes." She crawled into her side of the bed and pulled the covers up to her chin. "Goodnight, LaVern. Sleep well, and I'll see you in the morning."

He rolled onto his side and kissed her cheek. Irma hoped he didn't notice the tears that had moistened her cheeks. She did not wish to hurt her husband and would never have admitted to him that she wished she hadn't gotten pregnant.

Chapter 20

St. Ignatius

Dorcas thumbed through the mail she'd brought in and placed it on the kitchen table. To her disappointment, there was nothing from Irma. It had been a month since Dorcas had written a letter to Irma and then given it to Hannah to mail when she went to town. Surely, she should have heard something from her daughter by now. It couldn't take a letter more than a week to travel between Montana and Ohio.

What could be taking her so long to respond? Dorcas wondered. *Were my words not clear enough to read? Maybe she didn't believe what I said. Or worse yet, Irma might not be willing to accept my apology. Should I write another letter or call and leave a message for Irma? I really need to know how she feels about what I said.*

Dorcas got up and went out the front door. She was almost to the phone shed when she saw Hannah walking toward her with a hand lifted in a wave. Dorcas waved in response.

"You're home early today," Dorcas commented when Hannah came alongside of her. "I didn't expect you'd be home from your housekeeping job till closer to suppertime."

"Mrs. Williams didn't have as much for me to do today as she normally does," Hannah responded.

"That's good. Can you help me and Caroline with supper?"

"Of course." Hannah smiled. "Where are you headed, Mama?"

"To the phone shed. I'm going to call Irma and ask why she hasn't responded to that letter I sent her a month ago."

Hannah blinked rapidly and became unnaturally quiet.

"What's wrong, Daughter?" Dorcas felt concern as she reached out and touched Hannah's arm. "Did you forget to mail the letter?"

Hannah lowered her gaze. "Not exactly."

"What does that mean?"

"I—I lost the letter and was too embarrassed to tell you."

Dorcas was glad she hadn't made that phone call to Irma, but Hannah concealing the fact that she'd lost the letter did not sit well with Dorcas.

She tried to process this information. Then she lifted her daughter's chin, so she looked directly at her. "I'm *umgerennt* that you lost the letter, but even more upset because you didn't tell me about it. What I said to Irma in that letter was important, and I've been waiting all this time for a response from her. If you hadn't owned up to it just now, I could have been waiting forever." Dorcas took short, fast breaths due to the tightness she felt in her chest from trying to suppress the anger she felt.

"I'm so sorry, Mama." Tears seeped out of Hannah's eyes and dripped down her reddened cheeks. "I should have told you right away, but I was afraid you'd think I was irresponsible."

Dorcas recalled how Homer hadn't appreciated deceit from her whenever he felt that she'd held something back from him. Homer's discipline tactics with her and Irma hadn't made a bad situation better. It had only made things worse.

Dorcas struggled not to lash out because of her daughter's carelessness. What good would that do? It wouldn't bring back the missing letter. "Do you have any idea where you were when you lost the letter?" she asked instead.

Hannah shook her head. "I had it with me one minute, and the next second, it was gone. I've looked everywhere, and I can't imagine what happened to it, Mama. I really can't."

Dorcas' heart went out to her daughter. She could see clearly how upset Hannah was, and she had apologized. She gave her daughter a hug. "It's okay, don't fret. I'll go to the phone shed right now and leave Irma a message. If she's willing to call me at noon tomorrow, I will tell her what I'd written in the letter."

"Okay." Hannah gestured toward the house. "Guess I'll go inside now and rest awhile before it's time to start supper."

"Good idea. When I leave the phone shed, I might lie down and take a little catnap too."

After Hannah headed for the house, Dorcas stood for a moment longer, soaking up the fragrance of the honeysuckle bush nearby. *I made the right choice by not allowing my anger to control how I treated Hannah.*

When Dorcas entered the phone shed, before placing the phone call, she checked the answering machine for any messages that may have come in recently. There was only one, and it was from her friend Mary, asking how Dorcas was doing and extending an invitation for the two of them to go out for lunch one day next week. Dorcas made a note on the writing tablet she kept near the phone to call Mary back and see what day might work best for her. It would be nice to get out of the house and do something just for fun. She hadn't gone out to eat or done anything out of the ordinary since Homer died. Her friend's kindness made a difference in Dorcas' mood, and she smiled. *I'll need to give Mary a call as soon as possible. Maybe after I've left a message for Irma.*

Dorcas thought about how well the business had been doing, in spite of her husband's absence. Irvin and Aaron were doing a good job running the lumber mill and keeping up with the orders that had come in. The other fellow Irvin had thought he could count on had found some other job, so he'd hired a young Amish man named Harley to work at the mill. He seemed dependable and had proved himself to be a hard worker. If their business kept growing and doing well, Irvin had told Dorcas that they would need to hire another employee in order to keep up with orders. How thankful Dorcas felt that they didn't have to struggle financially or rely on others outside their family for help. Some widows in their church district didn't have a family-owned business that could provide income to pay the bills. They either had to find a job or move in with a family member who would provide for their financial and physical needs.

Dorcas picked up the phone. It was time to leave a message for Irma and hope she would respond to it. If not, Dorcas didn't know what she would do.

Mount Hope

Since Brian was still at school and Clayton and Myra had dozed off while playing in the living room, Irma decided this was a good time to check for phone messages. These days, with Clayton getting older, it was rare that he slept during the day unless he was sick. He'd obviously been playing harder than usual today. Irma missed those days when she and the children took naps after having their lunch. She glanced over her shoulder to give the children one last look, and certain that they were both still sleeping, Irma went quietly out the front door.

An orange kitten, almost fully grown, rubbed against Irma's leg when she stepped onto the porch. The kids had named this cat Peaches. Normally, Irma would have seen it as a nuisance, but for some reason, she found the kitten's affection to be comforting. Irma bent down and stroked the cat's head, enjoying the silky feeling of its soft fur against her fingers. She was rewarded with a sweet *meow*, followed by gentle purring. Irma smiled. "Pretty kitty, I bet you need some comforting."

More purring ensued until Irma moved on, leaving the young feline to chase after a butterfly. There was usually bird activity in their yard, with the feeders keeping the birds happily fed, and today was no exception. Irma enjoyed watching them eat and seeing how the different birds interacted with one another. As she walked along to the phone shed, the familiar sound of a red-winged blackbird's song filled the air. She paused to listen for a bit and moved on.

Once Irma entered the small wooden structure, she checked for messages. The first one was for LaVern from an Amish couple wanting him to act as the auctioneer during a sale day for their home. Irma wrote the man's number down and listened to the next message. This was just an advertising call, which she quickly deleted. When the third message came up, Irma froze. She recognized Mama's voice right away.

"Hello, Irma, this is your mudder. I wrote you a letter several weeks ago, but the letter got lost and never made it to the post office. So rather than writing another letter, I thought it would be a good idea to call. I have something important to tell you, so if you get this message today and are free to talk tomorrow, I'll be in my phone shed at noon—your time—and will call you then." There was a short pause and what sounded like a clearing of her mother's throat followed. "I hope you'll be free then, and if so, I look forward to talking to you."

Irma was tempted to delete that message too, but she decided that she should probably go to the phone shed at the appointed time tomorrow and wait for the call. It could be something important. Maybe one of her siblings had been injured or was seriously ill. She certainly wanted to know about it if that were the case.

Irma bit the inside of her cheek. *I wish Mama would have simply stated what she wanted in her message instead of making me wait till tomorrow to find out what she wants to talk about. Since LaVern has tomorrow off, he will be home all day, so at least I won't have to worry about leaving the kids alone while I talk to my mamm.*

She picked up the phone and dialed her mother's number. When the answering machine came on, Irma said, "I got your message, Mama, and I will be in the phone shed tomorrow at noon."

The following day, a few minutes before the noon hour, Irma told LaVern that she was going out to the phone shed to wait for her mother's call. Last night, she had told him about Mama's message, and he'd agreed to oversee the children while she waited for her mother's call. LaVern also said he felt it might be important and that Irma should follow through.

"Okay," he responded from where he sat at the desk inside the small room he'd turned into his home office. "The kids are all playing in Brian's room, but if I hear too much racket coming from there or any fussing going on, I'll check on them and take care of the situation."

"Thank you." With a feeling of dread, Irma went outside and headed for the phone shed. Once inside, she took a seat and clicked on the answering machine to listen, just in case her mother had called and left another message for her. No messages waited from Mama, but Doretta's husband, Warren, had left a message, and Irma listened closely to it.

"Hello, this is Doretta's husband, Warren. I'm calling to let you know that Doretta gave birth to an eight-pound, two-ounce baby boy early this morning. Mother and son are both doing well, and we are thanking the Lord for a safe delivery and a healthy boy. We named him William after my twin brother. I'm sure if William was still alive, he'd be happy to know that his nephew has inherited his name."

The phone rang, and Irma saved Warren's message. After seeing the caller's number, she reached for the phone. "H–hello, Mama."

"Hello, Irma. It's good to hear your voice, and I'm glad you had the time to talk to me today. How are you and your family getting along?"

"We're all fine. What did you want to talk to me about?" Irma wanted to get right to the point. If someone had been injured or taken ill, she needed to know.

"It's about your stepfather, and—"

"I don't want to talk about Homer, so if he's the reason you called, we may as well end this conversation right now." Irma's face heated, and it wasn't from the warmth inside the small shed. Just the mention of Homer's name made her skin feel hot and caused her stomach to churn. Talking about him would make her feel even worse. "I've been trying not to think about that horrible man, and I don't want to talk about him, Mama."

"I understand, but what I have to say is *wichdich*. It's something I should have said a long time ago."

Irma pulled a tissue from the band of her apron and swiped it across her sweaty forehead. "All right. If you think it's that important, then go ahead and say it."

She heard a quick inhale of breath on the other end, followed by a slow release of air. Was her mother feeling as stressed as she was right now?

"Well, the thing is. . .Homer was an abuser."

"Of course he was, Mama. That's why he said hurtful things and often punished me so severely—sometimes for things I didn't even do." Irma clenched her fingers tightly around the phone with the heat of anger burning in her brain. "And you just stood by and let him do it!"

"I know, and I'm sorry, but please let me explain."

"I don't need your explanation. You are just as guilty as he was, and if you really cared about me, you would have left Homer and taken me and my siblings with you." Irma trembled as her animosity increased. She wanted to forgive her mother but, under the circumstances, didn't see how she could.

"I—I had no place to go, Irma, and—"

"You could have gone back to Grabill. We had friends there, and I'm sure one of them would have taken us in. Homer didn't deserve a family; he belonged in jail!"

"That may be, but—"

"I can't talk any longer, Mama. I need to get back to the house."

"Irma, please don't hang up yet. I have more to say. . . ."

Irma's hand shook as she clicked off the phone. Her mother's apology was too little, too late. The past was behind them. She needed to move on.

Chapter 21

St. Ignatius

Dorcas remained in the phone shed with tears running down her hot cheeks. *Irma did not say that she accepted my apology, and she wouldn't give me the chance to explain the reason I didn't try to stop Homer from abusing her.* She swallowed around the thickness in her throat and sniffed. *I let fear get in the way of good judgment. Irma was right—I should have taken my children and returned to Indiana or gone someplace else where Homer couldn't find us. I am a cowardly person and a terrible mother. And because of it, I've ruined the relationship I once had with my eldest daughter.*

Dorcas bowed her head and prayed. *Dear Lord, Please forgive me for allowing Homer to abuse my child. Fear of making things worse for Irma and me is my only excuse, and remaining silent only made things worse for her. I should have done something to stop the abuse. Perhaps if I'd gone to our church leaders and told them what was happening, they would have stepped in and gotten Homer the help he needed.* Her lips pressed together and she sniffed. *If he'd been willing to accept it, that is. He was a stubborn man, who always thought he was right; and maybe if I'd gone to the church leaders he would have told them that my accusations weren't true. Homer had a way of fooling those he wanted to impress. He could be hateful and violent one minute and sweet as peach pie the next. It was almost as if I was married to two different men.*

Dorcas opened her eyes and sat up straight. *Could Homer have had multiple personalities?* She'd heard of that disorder but had never really thought about the possibility that her husband had it until now. *I guess I'll never know for sure, since he's gone and can't be evaluated.*

Another thought popped into Dorcas' head. *I hope none of my children have inherited their father's mean streak that could be passed from one generation to the next. That would be horrible.* She shivered, despite the heat and humidity inside the little building where she sat. Dorcas rubbed her temples as she allowed the idea to sink deeper. *No, no, I don't believe that will happen. Irma is not related to Homer by blood, and none of our other children have shown any signs of aggression or bad temper. I should just put that concern out of my head.*

Mount Hope

Irma's legs trembled so badly she could hardly walk as she made her way back to the house. *I can't believe my mamm would expect me to forgive her for allowing Homer to treat me so badly.*

When Irma made it to the porch, she took a seat on the wooden bench to catch her breath and try to calm down before going inside. If the children noticed her shaky hands or saw tears in her eyes, it would upset them, and she'd have some explaining to do.

Irma leaned forward and pulled one corner of her apron up to wipe her eyes. *I sure can't tell them that their Grandma Schmucker called and then relate the things we talked about. They would not understand, and if they knew the way Homer used to treat me, it would frighten them and could lead to a lot of questions I don't wish to answer.*

A hummingbird flew past Irma's head, heading for one of the feeders, but she barely took notice. Nor did she find any pleasure in the tinkling sound of the wind chime LaVern had given her for their anniversary. Irma placed both hands against her belly and massaged it. *I suppose I should have told my mamm that I'm in a family way, but it probably wouldn't have mattered to her. If she cared anything about me, she would have done something about Homer's abuse when she had the chance and not waited till now to apologize, after the damage has been done.*

The screen door creaked open, and Irma turned in the direction of the familiar sound. LaVern stepped out onto the porch and took a seat beside her. "How'd it go with your mudder?"

"Not good. She called to say she was sorry."

He tipped his head. "For what?"

Irma swallowed hard and moistened her lips with her the tip of her tongue. *Should I tell him about the beatings Homer used to give me, and how Mama knew about them but said nothing?* For all the years she had known LaVern, Irma had never said anything about the abuse she'd suffered at the hands of her stepfather. He was aware that she didn't care for the man, and several times while they still lived in St. Ignatius she'd almost told him, but something had always held her back. Truth was, Irma had been afraid to tell LaVern, certain that if he knew what Homer had done, he would have confronted him about it. Homer would have denied it, of course, but Irma didn't think LaVern would have believed him—especially if she'd shown him some of the welts left on her legs after Homer had used the strap on her. Irma also felt sure that if she had told LaVern and he'd spoken to Homer about it, Homer would have punished her even more severely. But that wasn't the sole reason she'd kept quiet about the abuse she'd suffered. Irma's main concern was for LaVern and the probability of him losing his job at the lumber mill. If he had confronted Homer, he'd have most likely gotten fired. And if LaVern had lost his job, he probably would have returned to Ohio, which would have left Irma all alone to deal with Homer's wrath. Now, however, with Homer gone, she saw no reason not to tell her husband the truth.

"Are you all right?" LaVern put a hand on Irma's shoulder. "Your chin is quivering, and you appear to be quite umgerennt."

"I am upset," she acknowledged with a nod. "And even though it's upsetting to talk about it, I will tell you what my mamm said, because you have the right to know."

"Know what?" he asked. "What did she have to apologize for?"

Irma pulled in a quick breath to steady her nerves and told LaVern the whole story of how her stepfather had abused her physically and emotionally. "He hated me," she said, chocking back a sob. "As far as Homer was concerned, nothing I ever said or did was right, and I believe he actually took pleasure in punishing me. To make things worse, Mama never even cared. She just stood by and let it all happen. Never once did she come to my defense."

LaVern sat very still, with his hands pressed against both sides of his head as though he was trying to process what she had told him. "Why didn't you tell me all of this when you and I were dating and lived in St. Ignatius? I would have talked to Homer about it, and—"

"And what? Would you have hit him or tried to make him pay for all the times he beat me and called me names?"

LaVern shook his head. "Of course not. I would never intentionally strike another man—not even one like Homer, who I know now was abusing the woman I love." He lowered his hands and reached over to clasp Irma's trembling hand. "If I had known back then, after I'd gone to Homer and given him a piece of my mind, I would have left Montana right away and taken you with me. You should have said something sooner, Irma. Not waited till now."

"I was afraid you would lose your job if you told Homer that you knew about the horrible way he had treated me."

"I wouldn't have cared. Your stepfather needed to be put in his place. He needed to stop what he was doing."

"It's too late to think about that now."

"But I just learned about this, and I can't help being enraged by how you were treated by that man. Also, you've concealed this from me for more than eight years." His eyes filled with tears. "I'm not going to hide the fact that it hurts deeply, knowing you took this long to finally confide in me. I can't help feeling that you didn't trust me enough to come forward and tell me what you were going through back then. I wasn't even given the chance to try to help you." LaVern slowly shook his head. "I'm sorry, Irma, that I've made this about me when the situation is undoubtedly about you. I know it's too late to be thinking of how I could've dealt with Homer about his abuse." A muscle on the side of LaVern's neck quivered as he looked directly at Irma. "So your mother knew all that time that he was abusing you, yet she never tried to stop it?"

"That's right. But now, all of a sudden, she's feeling guilty about it and wanted to apologize."

"Did you accept her apology?"

"No, I did not. I told her that I needed to get back to the house. Then I hung up the phone and came here to the porch."

"After you pray and think more about it, I feel certain that you will change your mind. The Bible says in Matthew 6:14, 'If you forgive men their trespasses, your heavenly Father will also forgive you.' What that means is—"

"I know what it means, LaVern, but I am not able to forgive." Tears stung the backs of Irma's eyes, but she wouldn't allow them to escape. "There's no point in praying about it either, because I've made up my mind. There is no way I'm going to excuse my mother for her actions—and I may never talk to her again. She had her chance to be a good mother and do the right thing, but she didn't have the courage to face up to that evil man, and now it's too late to make amends." Irma rose from the bench. "I'm going inside to fix lunch now. Are you coming?"

"I'll be there shortly. There are a few things I need to do in the barn."

"Okay. I'll have lunch on the table in thirty minutes."

"I'll be there. Just ring the dinner bell."

Watching LaVern head off, Irma began thinking back to her childhood. *I wonder if anyone from our church district in St. Ignatius ever noticed anything about Homer that would indicate his bad temper. If they had, maybe one of them could have offered to take me in so that I would be safe.*

Irma stood and hurried into the house. She was glad she had told LaVern the truth, but in another way, she wished she hadn't said anything about Homer's abuse. All it did was reopen Irma's wounds, but at least she had been truthful with LaVern. Hopefully, he wouldn't bring up the topic again of Irma needing to accept her mother's apology, because that was never going to happen!

———— ≈ ————

LaVern entered the barn through the double doors and collapsed onto a bale of straw. He needed to be alone for a while and hoped to digest all that Irma had told him about her phone call from Dorcas and the abuse she had suffered from the man he had worked for and thought he knew.

If I had known about Irma having been abused when I lived and worked in St. Ignatius, I could have helped her deal with it. I would have spoken to Homer about it, even if it meant losing my job.

LaVern leaned against the wooden post behind his back, thankful for the needed support. He felt weak and sickened trying to imagine what it must have been like for Irma to have been severely beaten by her stepfather on many occasions. *When Homer married Dorcas, it was his job to look after his new wife as well as her daughter. Irma was just a child and didn't deserve to be spoken to so harshly or physically abused. She deserved a father's love and protection, as all children do.* He remembered something one of their ministers had preached awhile back. He'd said that a father knows best when he knows Jesus. LaVern didn't see how Homer could have known Jesus very well if he'd treated his stepdaughter so harshly and said hurtful things to her.

He shifted on the prickly bale he sat upon and stared at the nose-tickling straw scattered across the floor where other bales had been previously opened. When he'd first met Irma after moving to Montana and being hired by her stepfather at the mill, he'd thought she was just a shy young woman with some insecurities. LaVern had never suspected that Irma had been the victim of abuse.

His nostrils flared as he reflected on what Irma had told him about her mother—how she'd known about her husband's abuse but never stepped in to protect her daughter. LaVern did not understand why Dorcas didn't take her children and leave Homer or try to get him some help. Surely, their church leaders would have offered some suggestions if Dorcas had told them what her husband had done to Irma.

Although it was wrong not to accept her mother's apology, LaVern understood why it was difficult for Irma, because he was also angry about the situation and hurt because his wife had hid all this from him. Regardless of that, if Irma did not forgive Dorcas, the resentment she felt would fester and spill out into every area of her life.

LaVern bowed his head and prayed out loud: "Dear Lord, I am asking You to give me the right words to help my wife see that she needs to forgive her mother. And please heal Irma's heart from all the heartache and pain she had to deal with for so long with no one to protect her from an angry man. Help her to see that she not only needs to forgive her mother but her stepfather too, for that is what Your Word says we are supposed to do."

LaVern heard the dinner bell ring, and he opened his eyes. He felt a bit better about things now that he'd talked to God. From this point on, he would continue to pray for his wife and try to be more supportive of her.

Chapter 22

Grabill

Doretta tenderly cradled her precious son in her arms as she gently rocked him while sitting in her favorite chair. The rocker had been a gift from Warren's parents as a celebration of the birth of their first grandchild. Both sets of grandparents doted over baby William, and the fact that they'd chosen to name him after Warren's twin brother had deeply touched his parents' hearts.

Doretta leaned forward and kissed her son's forehead. It was hard to believe that he was already two weeks old. She knew from watching her siblings grow up that babies didn't stay babies very long. Therefore, Doretta planned to savor every moment of little William's babyhood. His daddy had said the same thing last night as he'd held his son while Doretta sat beside him, looking at some of the cards and gifts they had received for the baby from friends and family members. Doretta had admired the blue knitted sweater, cap, and booties—a gift from her dear Pennsylvania friend, Eleanor. The note Eleanor had written inside the congratulations card stated that she had knitted the little outfit for William.

I can't imagine how Eleanor would have the time to knit, Doretta thought. *With two little ones to look after, plus a household to run, I wouldn't think she would have any free time for things like knitting.*

Irma had sent a card, too, with a check for fifty dollars inside. A small, hand-written note had been included, saying that Doretta and Warren should use the money for whatever their little boy needed. Irma hadn't said anything about how she was doing these days, and Doretta was a bit disappointed. She'd hoped for an update so she would know better how to pray. In Irma's last letter, letting Doretta know how she felt about her stepfather, Doretta had detected her friend's anger and frustration. She hoped that, by now, Irma had come to terms with her feelings and found a place in her heart where she felt a sense of peace.

As Doretta continued to enjoy the gentle rhythm of the rocking chair and the warmth of her baby, she reflected on the hopeless, sad feeling she'd had after the accident that had left her with a serious injury and taken her future groom's life. *I was full of bitterness and self-pity back then,* she told herself. *I am thankful for the letters of comfort Eleanor sent to me. She never gave up but kept encouraging me and offering her support. My mamm was always there for me too, but sometimes I was too proud to accept her help. Dear, sweet Warren was also a big help to me, and I thank the Lord that I allowed Warren to be part of my life. All the special people in my life, along with the Bible verses I read, helped me get through a difficult time in my life. God's Word is what my friend Irma needs too.*

Although Doretta's days were busy with the care of her baby, she would still make time to write letters of encouragement to Irma—or anyone else God placed on her heart to encourage.

--------------≈--------------

Mount Hope

Irma got out everything she needed to make chocolate chip cookies and placed all the ingredients on the kitchen table. With Clayton and Myra enjoying each other's company in the living room, she figured this was a good time to get some baking done.

Soon, the aroma of sweet chocolate chip cookie dough permeated the kitchen, and Irma was ready to put the first batch on the cookie sheet to bake in the preheated oven.

Feeling a wave of nausea coming on, Irma paused to drink a cup of peppermint tea she'd brewed earlier. She didn't care that it was now cold. Whatever the temperature, peppermint tea usually stopped—or at least lessened—the nausea, for which she felt grateful. When the cup was empty and her stomach had settled, Irma returned to the job at hand. She'd no more than put the sheet of cookies into the oven when she heard Myra crying. Her son and daughter had been getting along and playing nicely together, so Irma wondered what was up. *I suspect my son may have caused the problem in the other room*, she thought.

Irma quickly set the timer and hurried into the living room to see what was wrong. She found Clayton holding his sister's favorite doll over his head while Myra jumped up and down, screaming, "*Geb's mir*! Geb's mir!"

Clayton grinned at Myra with a taunting expression as he continued to wave the doll over his head.

It didn't take Irma long to size up the situation. *What is causing Clayton to act out like this? I've told him before not to tease his sister, yet here we go again.*

"Your sister asked you to give it to her," Irma said. "So please let go of the doll right now."

"I was only having a little fun. Myra's a big *brille boppli*."

"Your sister is not a bawl baby. That's her favorite doll, and you should not have taken it. I want you to give it back to her right now." Irma's tone deepened as she squinted at Clayton and crossed her arms.

"Okay then. . .here you go, baby sister!" Clayton let the doll fall to the floor, which made Myra cry even louder. Irma felt like screaming herself. Why couldn't her son learn to play nicely and resist the temptation to pick on his little sister? Irma would have enjoyed a few hours of peace, but now she had to deal with this.

She marched over and grabbed hold of her son's arm. "That was not nice. I want you to apologize to Myra right now!"

He dropped his gaze to the floor.

"Clayton, did you hear what I said? Tell your sister that you are sorry."

"Oh, all right." He moved close to Myra and said, "I'm sorry you're a bawl baby!"

I can't believe he's acting like this. He is only getting himself into deeper trouble with me. Irma's pulse picked up speed, and her body tensed as she whirled the boy around and placed several hard swats on his backside. Clayton let out a yelp, and Myra cried even harder. Irma was sure that she was going to scream. She gulped in a few breaths in an attempt to calm down. Then she pushed Clayton toward the stairs and shouted, "Since you've been rude and can't get along with your sister, then you can spend the rest of the day in your room!"

The timer went off, letting Irma know that the cookies were done. She watched Clayton scramble up the stairs, then swept Myra into her arms and hurried back to the kitchen. *I am beginning to think that I should never have gotten married, because I don't have the patience needed to raise my children.*

Irma put Myra in a chair, grabbed a potholder, and opened the oven door. Just in time, too, for the cookies were starting to turn a little browner than she liked around the edges. Irma had planned to ask both children if they'd like a cookie, but now only Myra would be offered one. Irma had never imagined things would go sour like they had today. She needed a nap more than anything.

When Irma placed the tray on the cooling rack, Myra stood up and reached for one. "Not yet, Myra. The kichlin are too hot to eat right now."

Myra's lower lip protruded, and Irma figured she was about to cry. "You can have a cookie when they have cooled enough." Irma moved the tray out of her daughter's reach and began filling another tray with spoonfuls of dough for the next batch of cookies to be placed in the oven. Myra pointed at the first one Irma had dropped on the tray and reached out her hand to grab it. Irma caught hold of her daughter's hand and firmly said no.

Myra tipped her head back and howled. Exasperated, and still a bit shaken from the situation with Clayton, Irma ground her teeth. She was tempted to give her daughter a swat too and send her out of the kitchen. Pulling from deep within, Irma gave Myra a cracker, and that seemed to satisfy her.

Irma's hand trembled as she finished forming the cookies on the tray. *I definitely do not have any patience today.*

St. Ignatius

Dorcas sat on the front porch with her head down and eyes closed, rubbing her temples. She'd had an emotional dream about Irma last night and couldn't stop thinking about it. At the beginning of the dream, Irma had been a little girl, playing happily with her baby doll. Then Homer appeared in the dream. He held a switch in one hand. Tightness surrounded his flinty eyes, and his mouth contorted as he stomped across the room like an angry child. The fear Dorcas saw on her daughter's face made her want to reach out and pull the little girl to safety, but she did nothing except stand there and watch. Irma let out an ear-piercing scream, clambered to her feet, and started to run, but she was not quick enough to escape the angry switch as it hit the back of her legs. Dorcas shouted for Homer to stop, but he pushed her aside roughly and shouted, "Just sit down and shut up or you'll be next!"

Dorcas' eyes snapped open, and she began to weep—deep, uncontrollable sobs. Thankfully, it had only been a dream, but it was a reminder that she had not been a good mother. If she had been, she would have protected her daughter at all costs. *Why didn't I leave that man? What kind of power did he have over me?*

Caroline came out of the house and sat beside Dorcas. "Mama, why are you crying? Is it because you're sad that Papa is gone?"

Dorcas' conscience battled to keep anyone else from knowing about the ugly past she had suffered. But another part of her longed for liberation from the struggle of pain and guilt she had been living with for so long. *I'm tired of covering up the past, and it's made me nothing but miserable all these years. I don't want to continue living this way. It's time to unburden my heart.*

Dorcas dried her eyes as she struggled with the best way to respond to Caroline's question. When she had herself under control, she said, "It is sad that your daed died so unexpectedly, but I was thinking about Irma just now."

"What about her?"

"I set up a time to call her a few weeks ago, but our conversation didn't go well."

"Was it about Papa and how terribly he treated her?"

Dorcas' head jerked back, and her eyes opened wide. Until now, none of her children had ever mentioned the way their father had mistreated Irma. They'd obviously known about it—at least the boys, since they were a little closer to Irma's age and would have seen or heard what had been going on. Dorcas hadn't expected that the girls—especially the young-est—would have been as aware of their half-sister's abuse. *Or mine either*, Dorcas thought.

Caroline touched her mother's arm. "Was it Papa you were talking to Irma about?"

Dorcas nodded. "She's very angry and blames me for some of it too."

"But Mama, I never saw you hit Irma—not even when she was sassy."

"You're right, I never did."

"But Papa hit her a lot, didn't he?"

Dorcas nodded.

"He never gave me or Hannah a whipping—at least, not a hard one like he gave Irma." Caroline's face contorted. "I remember once when I was about six years old, I saw Papa grab hold of Irma's arm and practically drag her across the yard. When I saw what he was doing, I asked where he was taking her, and he said, *'Es kind bletsche war notwendich.'*"

Dorcas released a deep moan. "Your father may have said it was necessary to spank the child, but your sister did not deserve the kind of severe whipping he gave her on numerous occasions."

"Why didn't you stop him, Mama?"

Caroline's question cut into Dorcas like a sharp knife piercing her soul. "I tried to—many times, in fact—but whenever I did, your daed became angry and—"

"He hit you too, didn't he? That's how come you had so many bruises, isn't it?"

Dorcas swallowed hard and slowly nodded.

Caroline leaned her head against Irma's shoulder and took hold of her hand. "I'm not the only one who knows this, Mama. I think Irvin, Aaron, and Hannah knew what Papa had been doing, but we were all too scared to say anything."

"Were you worried that he would become abusive toward you?"

"Jah, but mostly I was worried about you. I thought if I spoke up about it, Papa might do even more mean things to you. I'm sorry if we did wrong by keeping quiet. Maybe if we'd all said something, Papa would have stopped."

Tears welled in Dorcas' eyes and spilled over onto her cheeks as she gave her daughter a hug. "None of you are to blame. If anyone is guilty, it's me. I should have packed up my children when the abuse first began and left St. Ignatius until your father got the help he needed. By not speaking up and seeking help, I only made things worse for all of us."

"No, Mama, you can't go blaming yourself. You were scared too, and you didn't know what to do."

Dorcas had to admit that she had been very frightened, for herself as well as her children. But that was no excuse, and she didn't think she would be able to forgive herself.

"Did you tell Irma everything you've shared with me?" Caroline asked.

"I'm afraid not. She wouldn't give me a chance and hung up the phone before I could say anything more than that I was sorry."

"Maybe you should write her another letter or try talking to her on the phone again," Caroline suggested.

"I've thought about it, but Irma is very angry with me, and she probably wouldn't listen to anything I had to say."

"I'm really sorry, Mama." Caroline patted Dorcas' hand. "I think you should pray about this situation, and I'll pray too."

"I have been praying, and I appreciate knowing that you'll be praying as well."

Chapter 23

Mount Hope, Ohio

By the time Brian got home from school, Irma's nerves were frazzled. She'd spent most of the day struggling to get her work done. After two hours of confinement because he'd picked on his sister, Irma had allowed Clayton to leave his room—only to punish him again when he'd brought several rocks inside and her bare foot had tripped on them, nearly causing her to fall. Fortunately, she'd regained her balance in time. After giving Clayton a good tongue-lashing, she'd ordered him to take the rocks outside and sent the boy back to his room.

How many times does that son of mine have to be told about not bringing his rock collection into the house? Irma wondered as she brought a batch of dry laundry into the house. She placed the wicker basket on the dining room table and sighed. *By spring of next year, with a new baby in the house, I'll have even more laundry to do—not to mention, another child to look after. If we lived closer to LaVern's parents, I'm sure his mother would help out.*

Whenever Irma felt overwhelmed or full of self-pity, she found herself wishing, yet again, that her husband's job was closer to home so he wouldn't have to be gone so much. The responsibility of being an auctioneer, always in demand, sometimes took him out of town for a day or two, and those were the worst times for Irma. She needed her husband's support and help even more these days, but she'd chosen not to tell him how frustrated she felt. He also didn't realize how she felt about having another child. Once Irma had seen how happy LaVern was when he'd learned she was pregnant, Irma figured there was no point in voicing her thoughts. Besides, it was too late to be thinking about that. Come spring, she would be having this baby whether she wanted to or not.

Irma turned her attention back to the laundry in her basket and began folding the towels and washcloths, which she placed in stacks on the table. When the basket was empty, she noticed that a blue-and-white-striped bath towel was missing. She clearly remembered washing and hanging it on the line and wondered if she may have left it on the line or if it had fallen out of the basket. With her preoccupation over the events of the day, she guessed it could have easily been either possibility.

Irma went down the hall and peeked into Myra's room to see if the child had awakened from her nap. Seeing that her daughter was still asleep, Irma walked softly back down the hall and went out the front door. She headed around the side of the house where the clothesline was located and nearly got knocked off her feet when Brian's dog plowed into her.

"For goodness' sake." Irma marched over to where Brian stood, holding the ball she'd brought him from their trip to Montana. "Would you kindly go somewhere else to play with your *hund*?"

"I'm teachin' Buster a new trick with the ball." Brian slapped his thigh with his free hand and called, "Come here, Buster! Let's show Mama what you can do."

Before Irma could offer a protest, Brian tossed the ball in Buster's direction. *Woof! Woof!* The dog leaped into the air, smacked the ball with his nose, and it sailed across the distance between him and Irma. She jumped out of the way just in time to avoid being hit. "Put that dog away in his run, and do it *schnell!*"

"But Mama," Brian argued, "I don't wanna go quickly, because we haven't been playing very long. Besides, Buster needs more practice with that trick."

Irma's finger shook as she pointed toward the dog run. "Do as I say, Brian, or you'll be sent to your room until supper. And if you don't do what I say, you won't get any supper at all!"

Brian's shoulders slumped, and he called Buster to follow him. Irma grabbed the towel she had left hanging on the line and watched until the rambunctious dog had been put away. Even though Irma hadn't been hurt by the ball or the dog, she could have been. The incident had irritated her to the point that she struggled to keep from doing something more than just hollering at her son. "I need to go lie down for a while," Irma mumbled as she headed back to the house. "Maybe I'll feel a little calmer if I get a short nap."

When Irma entered the house, she knew right away that a nap was out of the question. Myra was up and bawling like a wounded heifer from where she stood in the living room with a runny nose. Releasing a weary sigh, Irma scooped the child into her arms. *I just can't win today, can I? Is there no rest for the weary?*

———————≈———————

That evening, after the children had been put to bed and Irma discovered LaVern sprawled out on the couch with a book, she went to the kitchen, got some notepaper, and sat down at the table to write a letter to Doretta. She had received a note from her friend that morning, thanking her for the check she'd sent so that Doretta could buy something her baby needed. Although Irma did not need to respond to a thank-you note, she felt compelled to write her friend and let her know that she was expecting a baby. Doretta was a prayer warrior and a young woman with a gift for offering good advice. Irma figured Doretta must have a closer relationship with God than she did, because Irma's prayers never seemed to get answered. Maybe if Doretta prayed for her, it would make a difference in helping Irma cope with her pregnancy—as well as dealing with the three children she already had.

Irma set pen to paper, and soon she had a letter written and ready to mail in the morning. She rose from the chair and yawned. *Now I need to see if LaVern is ready for bed, because I'm exhausted.*

When Irma entered the living room, she discovered that her husband had fallen asleep with the book he'd been reading lying across his chest. *Poor guy. He must be as tired as I am tonight.* Irma hated to wake him. She felt tempted to cover LaVern with a blanket and let him sleep. However, the couch wasn't nearly as comfortable as their bed, and if he spent the whole night there, he'd probably wake up feeling stiff in the morning and might be miffed at her for not waking him up when she was ready for bed.

Irma bent down and gave his shoulder a gentle shake. "LaVern, *die zeit fer ins bett is nau.*"

He opened his eyes and looked up at her with raised brows. "Did you just say that the time to go to bed is now?"

"Jah. It's getting late, and I'm tired. Apparently, so are you, because you dozed off and probably didn't get much reading done."

He sat up and stretched his arms over his head. "It was a long day, and this heat we're having near the end of September must have put me to sleep." LaVern covered a yawn with his hand. "I tried not to let on, but I could barely stay awake to eat my supper this evening."

"I wondered why you were so quiet."

He nodded. "That was partly the reason. But mostly I didn't talk much because I couldn't get in a word with the way Brian talked nonstop about the new tricks he's been teaching Buster." LaVern chuckled. "That boy sure does like his hund."

"Uh-huh. He used to talk about his favorite cat all the time, but since you bought him the hund, that's all Brian talks about anymore." Irma didn't mention how she had hollered at Brian to put Buster away when he'd been working with him on a trick with the ball.

LaVern clasped her hand. "How was your day? You were pretty quiet during supper too."

"It went okay, I guess. I did the laundry, baked a few batches of cookies, and got some cleaning done." Irma debated on whether she should say anything about how she'd lost her temper with Clayton and Myra when they'd misbehaved and then again with Brian when she'd nearly gotten hit by the ball. She decided not to mention any of it. LaVern was more easy-going than Irma, and he may have thought, or even said, that she should have gone a little easier on the kids.

"Should we get ready for bed now?" Irma asked.

"Jah, tomorrow's another day, and we both need our rest." He stood and placed one hand gently against her stomach. "How's this little guy doing? Is he being good to his mamm?"

Irma rolled her eyes. "Our baby could be a girl, you know."

"You're right, so I'll reword my question. Has *she* been good to her mamm?"

"I didn't have quite as much nausea today. Does that answer your question?"

"It does. It means our little one is a good baby."

This baby may be good while it's in my belly, Irma thought as they made their way down the hall toward their bedroom, *but what will our child be like after it's born?*

St. Ignatius

Caroline rapped softly on her sister's bedroom door, hoping she was still awake and not wanting to disturb her brothers in their rooms across the hall. A few seconds went by before Hannah opened the door. With her hair hanging down nearly to her waist and dressed in her night clothes, she looked at Caroline through squinted eyes.

"Did I wake you?" Caroline asked.

Hannah shook her head. "I was about to get into bed, though. Did you need something?"

"Jah." Caroline kept her voice low. "I want to talk to you about something important."

"Come in." Hannah opened the door wider, and Caroline went inside. After Hannah closed the door, she told Caroline to take a seat on the bed, and she did the same. "What's this about, Sister? You look sort of *anscht* right now."

"If I look serious it's because I'm concerned about Mama."

"Is she still grieving hard for Papa?"

Caroline swallowed hard before slowly shaking her head. "I don't think she misses him at all."

Hannah's fingers touched her parted lips. "Oh, dear. I thought the reason Mama has been so sulky lately is because she misses our daed."

"Mama might miss him in some ways, but she doesn't miss his sharp tongue or the times when he hurt her."

An unnatural stillness settled into the room as Hannah looked down at her hands, clasped tightly in her lap as though not wanting to respond.

Caroline bumped elbows with her sister. "This is a topic we should have discussed a long time ago. I'm only willing to talk about it now because Mama opened up to me today and said some things that made me realize the abusive way Papa treated her and Irma should have been brought out into the open and talked about a long time ago."

"What good would it have done to talk about it?" Hannah asked. "I am sure that if we'd said anything to Papa, he would have punished us harshly too."

Caroline nodded and sighed. "You're right. I was afraid of him, and now I know you must have been too."

"Jah."

"I wonder if Irvin and Aaron have ever discussed the issue of Papa's abuse, and if so, were they also fearful that he might lash out at them if they said anything about the way he treated Irma and Mama?"

"Do you think we should ask them? Would they even want to discuss it?"

"I—I'm not sure. I think it might be good for all of us if we opened up and talked about it—especially Mama, because she's the one hurting the most right now."

"But Papa's gone, so he won't be causing her anymore pain. Can't she just put this behind her and move on?"

Caroline shook her head. "Mama blames herself for the way Papa treated Irma, and the worst part is that Irma blames her too."

"Seriously?"

"That's right. Mama said she talked to Irma on the phone recently, and Irma wouldn't accept Mama's apology or hear the rest of what she had to say." Caroline covered her face with her hands briefly, before pulling them away. "Irma said she needed to go and hung up the phone."

"I'm sorry to hear that. Things can never get resolved when one person refuses to listen to what the other person has to say."

Caroline paused, deciding what to say next. "I've been thinking I should write Irma a letter, telling her about the way Papa abused Mama."

Hannah reached up and scratched at a small pimple on her cheek. "Surely Irma must know about that. Mama sometimes had ugly bruises on her arms, and maybe other places too that we couldn't see."

"Which, if you remember, she always made excuses for."

"True."

"If Irma knew the truth, maybe she would have more understanding and be willing to forgive our mamm." Caroline got up from the bed and began pacing. "What do you think I should do?"

Hannah tipped her head from one side to the other as though weighing the situation. "I don't know. Have you prayed about it?"

"Just once—after I spoke to Mama and she told me everything. Guess I should pray some more before I make a decision."

Hannah rose from the bed and gave Caroline a hug. "I'll be praying too—that you'll make the right decision. And if you do decide to write the letter, I'll pray that Irma will be open to what you have to say." She paused near the door. "Maybe it would be best for you to ask our mamm about going forward with this plan. If she's okay with your idea of sending Irma such a letter, then you'll know it's okay. Oh, and maybe Mama might like to read the letter before it's mailed, just to make sure you've written an accurate account of the past."

Caroline frowned. "Of course it would be accurate. Why would you think otherwise?"

Hannah held up one hand. "Please don't get defensive about this. I only thought you might want to let Mama know before you send off a letter to Irma."

Caroline tapped a finger against her chin. *If I decide to write the letter and tell our mamm about it, she's likely to get upset. No, if I'm gonna do it, then Mama does not need to know. If Irma gets in touch with Mama and things get better between them, then I will know I did the right thing.*

Chapter 24

The following morning, Caroline got up early and went to Hannah's room. Before she lifted a hand to knock on her sister's door, Hannah opened it. She was glad to discover that her sister was awake and dressed.

"I was going to come to your room to see if you were up yet, but you beat me to it," Hannah said. "I prayed about things last night after you left my room, and I think the two of us should have a talk with Irvin and Aaron about what we discussed concerning our mamm."

"I'm glad we're in agreement, because I believe we should talk to them too. When do you want to do it?"

Hannah glanced at the clock on her nightstand. "Since our brothers are usually in the barn feeding the horses at this time, it might be good if we go out there now, before we all have breakfast. Mama's probably still asleep in her room, so if we hurry, she won't even know we're not in the house."

"Good idea. And I'm ready to go now." Caroline pointed to her bare feet. "All I have to do is slip into my shoes, which are by the back door."

"That's where mine are too." Hannah motioned to her sister. "Follow me, and let's be real quiet so we don't wake our mamm."

Caroline followed her sister down the stairs, being careful not to put her full weight on the creaky treads. When they reached the bottom, she peered down the hall and saw that their mother's bedroom door was closed. They made their way quietly to the kitchen, slipped on their shoes, and went out the back door.

———≈———

"What are you two doing' in here?" Aaron asked when the girls entered the barn and found him cutting the ties on a bale of straw.

"We came to talk to you and Irvin," Caroline replied.

"Can't it wait till we're at the breakfast table?"

She shook her head. "It's about Mama, and we don't want her to hear what's being said."

Aaron opened his mouth, but Hannah spoke first. "Where is Irvin? He needs to hear this too."

"He's cleaning his horse's *schtall*, and I was getting ready to do the same in my horse's stall."

"Could you please ask him to come out here for a few minutes so we can talk?"

"I guess so, but we could all go back there, and then you can tell us what's on your mind."

Hannah shook her head and took a seat on one of the other bales of straw. "It smells better out here, and it'll be easier for the four of us to talk."

"Okay." Aaron headed for the back of the barn and returned a few minutes later with their brother.

"What's this all about?" Irvin stood in front of where the girls had both been seated and crossed his arms.

Hannah looked over at Caroline. "Maybe you should explain, since you were the one who talked to Mama."

"What'd you talk to our mamm about?" Aaron tipped his head. "Is she having some sort of a health problem?"

"No, it's nothing like that." Caroline took a deep breath in an effort to calm herself. This was not an easy thing to discuss, especially with her brothers. She released her breath slowly and plunged ahead. "We've never spoken of this among ourselves before, although I'm sure we all knew about it."

"About what?" Irvin asked.

"When Irma still lived here, weren't the two of you aware of the abuse she suffered at our daed's hands?"

Irvin and Aaron looked at each other, then back at Caroline. "Well, jah, we did notice," Irvin responded. "How could we not? Sometimes when he hauled her out here to the barn, we could hear her screams all the way in the house."

Aaron bobbed his head. "We discussed it a few times with each other, but never said anything to you or Hannah."

"How about Mama?" Hannah questioned. "Did you ever talk about it with her?"

"Tried to once." Irvin swiped at the sheen of sweat on his forehead with the back of his hand and grimaced. "Mama said there was nothing I could do about it, and not to say anything to Papa or he might give me a hard licking too."

"Jah," Aaron put in. "She told me the same thing."

Hannah stood and planted both hands against her slender hips. "So we all knew, but we remained quiet because we were scared." She winced, as though she'd been slapped. "And Brothers—were you aware that Papa was also abusive to our mamm?"

"Jah, but I didn't realize it till I was about twelve years old." Irvin's voice cracked, and he dropped his gaze to the floor. "I heard her hollering, and when I went to see what was wrong, I saw Papa slapping her around."

"What did you do?" Caroline asked.

"I turned and ran." Irvin pressed his elbows against his sides as he slowly shook his head. "I was scared that, if I said anything, he would hit me too."

"So, basically, we're all just a bunch of cowards." Aaron scrubbed a hand over his face. "We let our sister and our mother be subjected to our daed's abuse because we were scared he might do the same thing to us."

"What else could we have done?" This question came from Irvin.

"We should have talked to Mama about it, and tried to get her to go for help." Caroline gestured to her sister. "Hannah and I talked about this last night, and we think something should be done now."

Irvin's brows furrowed. "What can we do at this point? Irma moved away, and Papa's dead, so there is no more abuse in our home."

"True," Caroline said. "But Mama blames herself for allowing it to happen, and she tried to apologize to Irma on the phone, but Irma did not say she accepted the apology. Then when Mama was on the verge of explaining that she had also been abused, Irma hung up the phone. So of course, our mamm is deeply hurt."

"That's a shame, but I don't think there's a thing any of us can do about it," Aaron interjected. "The best thing we can do is put all of this behind us."

Caroline shook her head. "I think you're wrong. I believe we should all sit down with Mama and talk about it—allow her to share her feelings and regrets, and we should do the same. It's not good for our mamm to spend the rest of her life blaming herself for our daed's hurtful actions. And even though Papa is gone, it might help if Mama spoke to one of the ministers in our church or even went to see a Christian counselor. She needs to find a way to forgive herself and to go forth, living a happier life."

Irvin nodded, and the others did as well.

"I also think it would be good for Irma if she knew that our mamm had been abused. Irma needs to understand why Mama didn't succeed in stopping Papa from disciplining her so often with such harsh measures."

"Maybe we should have discussed this while Irma and LaVern were here for Papa's funeral," Hannah said. "We could have talked it all out and asked for Irma's forgiveness."

"Could be, but I'm not sure Irma would have agreed to it. Mama said Irma sounded quite bitter during their brief phone conversation." Caroline looked at each of her siblings. "I think one of us needs to talk to our mamm and see if she's willing to sit down with us this evening and talk things through."

"I'm the oldest, so I guess it's my responsibility to do that," Irvin stated.

"And if she's not willing?" Aaron asked.

"Well, I just mentioned before that Mama has already opened up to me about her and Irma's abuse from Papa. I truly think she's ready to start unburdening herself about the past." Caroline shrugged. "But if I'm wrong in my judgment about our mamm, then I guess we'll have to pray about it and hope she changes her mind. In the meantime, though, I'm going to write a letter."

Aaron's brow wrinkled. "What letter are you going to write, and who's it for?"

"It will be sent to Irma, and I'm going to tell her about the abuse our mamm received from our daed. Irma needs to know what happened in the past and that she wasn't the only one who suffered mistreatment."

"Does Mama know about your plan to write Irma?" Irvin questioned.

Caroline shook her head and looked away.

He shifted his weight. "I think it would be a good idea to run the idea by her first, and that way she can add some thoughts to your letter if she chooses to."

"But if I tell our mamm what I plan to do, she'll likely say not to write the letter, and then Irma will never know the truth."

Mount Hope

Irma woke up with a pounding headache and her nightgown damp with sweat. She'd had another dream about Homer, and her mother had been in it too. She remembered thinking that forcing herself to attend Homer's funeral would bring closure and she would stop having nightmares about him, but apparently she'd been wrong. If only there was some way to forget about her mother and stepfather and put a stop to the dreadful nightmares. In the dream that had awakened her, Irma had seen herself as a teenager, standing in the yard with her hair down and no head covering. She closed her eyes and relived that dream in her mind.

Red-faced and wearing an angry-looking scowl, Homer stormed into the yard and grabbed hold of Irma's hair. She winced and tried to pull his fingers away, but it was no use—he was too strong for her, and tears sprang to her eyes as he held on tight. "You're an ungrateful, disobedient child, and you deserve to be punished," he shouted before giving her hair another good yank. "We're going to the barn now, so tell your mudder goodbye." Irma glanced up at the house and saw Mama on the porch, leaning against the railing. Instead of coming to Irma's defense, Mama just stood there, waving at her.

She doesn't care about me, and never has, Irma thought when she opened her eyes. *Just like in the dream, she never did anything to stop Homer from hurting me.*

With sheer willpower, Irma pushed the dream out of her mind and pulled the bed covers aside. It was all she could do to get out of bed, and the thought of fixing breakfast for the children caused her stomach to roll. LaVern's side of the bed was empty, and she remembered him telling her last night that he'd be leaving early this morning to preside over the auction of an Amish home in Millersburg. That meant Irma did not have the option of staying in bed any longer this morning. *I need to make breakfast, and I know at some point the children will get up and want food.* She tipped her head toward the door. *Oh, great. . .I think I hear someone coming down the hall.*

Drawing from what inner strength she could muster, Irma got dressed, went to the bathroom to freshen up, and headed for the kitchen. When she entered the room, she was surprised to find Brian sitting at the table, eating a bowl of cold cereal.

"What are you doing up so early?" she asked, without commenting on the fact that he'd fixed his own breakfast.

"I'm eating, Mama, 'cause I've gotta go to school."

Irma glanced at the clock on the far wall. It was seven thirty, and she realized for the first time that she'd overslept. Apparently, she'd forgotten to set the alarm clock in the bedroom last night. She wished LaVern would have awakened her. Now, she had to hurry and get Brian's lunch made before it was time for him to head out the door. School began at eight thirty sharp, and she did not want her son to be late.

Irma got out a loaf of bread, along with jars of peanut butter and grape jelly, and quickly made a sandwich, which she placed in a small, ziplock bag. Next, she grabbed three chocolate chip cookies and put them in another bag. The last item to go in the lunch pail was a thermos filled with cold water. Normally, she would have given Brian milk, but he had used too much in his cereal bowl, so water would have to do. She would make hot oatmeal for Clayton and Myra when they woke up, and the little bit of goat's milk Brian had left in the bottle would be just enough to pour over the oatmeal, cinnamon, and brown sugar in their bowls. They wouldn't like it, of course, because both Clayton and Myra preferred cold cereal or scrambled eggs for breakfast. Unfortunately, they were out of eggs right now, so Irma couldn't offer those to the children either.

Irma massaged her forehead, hoping the throbbing pain would subside. This was not starting out to be a good day, and despite her headache, she would need to make a trip to the store. She would have to take the kids with her, which would make shopping an even bigger chore. If only she could call upon one of their drivers to take her and the children into town. It would be so much easier to get into a vehicle and let someone else drive than it would be to pull out the buggy, put on Misty's gear, and hitch the mare. Irma didn't look forward to this chore, especially while dealing with her splitting headache, but she wasn't sure if she'd have enough money to pay a driver today. Even though it was tempting to make the call for a ride to town, she decided to go through with taking the horse and buggy.

I'm glad Brian managed to get his own breakfast this morning. I should've praised him for his effort. If he'd sat there waiting for me to get his cereal, he wouldn't have had enough time to eat before he left for school.

Irma glanced at the clock again. Mark, one of their neighbor boys who always walked to school with Brian, would be here soon. "Clear your dishes now, Son," Irma said. "And then go brush your teeth."

"But Mama, I still have some cereal left in my bowl."

"Leave it. I'll feed it to the katze. Hurry, now—schnell!"

Brian hesitated and took one more bite before handing her his bowl. She felt relieved when he headed down the hall toward the bathroom. The last thing she needed was having to deal with a defiant boy. Irma tilted her head toward the ceiling and let out a heavy sigh. *Lord, I know I don't pray very often anymore, but please give me the patience I will need for the rest of this day.*

Chapter 25

St. Ignatius

Caroline stood in the hallway outside the bathroom door, waiting for Irvin to come out. She needed to talk to him before he left for work.

Several minutes went by, and then Irvin came out. He grinned at Caroline and said, "Your turn."

She shook her head. "I don't need the bathroom. I need to talk to you about Mama."

"What about her?"

"Have you talked to our mamm about having a family meeting?"

"No, not yet."

She frowned. "It's been a whole week since you said you would do it."

"I know, but things have been really busy at the mill, and I haven't had time to talk to Mama about much of anything."

It appears that my brother doesn't think having a family meeting is important. Caroline scrunched up her face. "It's important, Irvin, so I think you should make the time to speak to our mamm."

Spots of color erupted on his cheeks. "Why don't you try running the lumber mill and see how much time you have on your hands? You're not that busy, so why don't you talk to Mama about having a meeting? As I recall, it was your idea, after all."

I think my brother is making excuses. She recoiled and said sharply, "I am plenty busy, helping Mama with chores in and outside of the house."

"All the more reason why you should be the one to talk to her. You're with Mama all the time."

"True, but I'm not the oldest child living here, and she might be more willing to listen to you. Since you and Aaron are the ones earning a living to support our family, she's bound to listen to what you have to say, more than she would if I brought up the topic."

He shrugged. "Maybe so. . .maybe not."

Caroline tugged on his arm. "Are you gonna talk to her or not?"

"Okay, I'll see if she's in the kitchen and do it right now, even if it means getting to the mill a bit late. Will that make you happy?"

Caroline gave a satisfied nod, and changing her mind about needing the bathroom, she entered the room.

———— ≈ ————

Dorcas took a bottle of milk from the refrigerator and was about to place it on the table when Irvin walked into the kitchen. "I don't have time for breakfast, Mama," he said. "But I do need to ask you a question before I leave for work."

She turned to face him. "What is it, Son?"

He blinked rapidly, and Dorcas noticed a tightness around his eyes. "Well, I. . .umm. . .that is, my brother and sisters and I would like for us to have another family meeting this evening. Would that be okay with you?"

"What is it about?" she asked.

"Oh, we just want to talk to you about some things and ask a few questions. Can we do that right after supper?"

She touched the back of her neck and massaged it before responding. "I suppose it will be okay. As soon as we finish supper, we'll all gather in the living room, and then you can tell me what's on your mind."

"Okay, good. Danki, Mama." Irvin grabbed an apple from the fruit bowl, called for Aaron, and rushed out the back door.

Dorcas cupped an elbow with one hand, while tapping her lips with the index finger on her other hand. *I wonder what is so important that my children believe we should have another family meeting.* Her mouth felt dry, as she considered the possibilities. *I hope my boys haven't decided to give up the lumber mill. The money it's bringing in is providing us with a decent living, and I wouldn't feel good about letting it go.*

Mount Hope

Shortly after Brian left for school, Irma glanced out the living room window and saw the mail truck pull up by the mailbox. Since Myra was still asleep and Clayton hadn't finished his bacon-and-eggs breakfast yet, she decided to go out and get the mail.

They'd had a light rain last night, which had cooled the air, so Irma slipped on a sweater before going out the front door. She was glad she had, for a cool breeze greeted her when she stepped onto the porch.

Irma shivered as she hurried down the driveway to the sound of rustling leaves. It was amazing the way the weather could be hot and sunny one day and turn to damp, chilly weather the next day.

Irma withdrew a stack of mail from the mailbox. The envelope on top caught her attention. In the upper left-hand corner, she noticed her sister Caroline's name and address. Curious to know what Caroline had to say, Irma hurried back to the house. She placed the rest of the mail on LaVern's desk and went to the living room to open the unexpected letter. Pulling the piece of paper from the envelope, Irma read the letter silently:

> *Dear Irma,*
>
> *I hope this letter finds you and your family well. I enjoyed seeing you during the short time you were here for Papa's funeral, but I wish you had been able to stay longer so we could have talked more.*
>
> *There's something about our mother that I think you*

should know. You were not the only one Papa abused. Whenever Mama stuck up for you or when they argued about certain things, Papa often shouted at her and left ugly bruises on Mama's arms—and maybe other places we couldn't see. As you know, our daed had a temper, and Mama feared him. Irvin, Aaron, Hannah, and I did too. Although he never gave us hard whippings, the way he did you, he sometimes talked gruffly to us and threatened us with a trip to the barn. I wonder if you were aware of that. And didn't you suspect, like we did, that Papa's abuse was the cause of our mamm's bruises? I remember one time, after you left St. Ignatius with LaVern, when Mama had a black eye. She made some excuse about how it had happened, but I'd heard Papa yelling at her the night before, so when I saw her eye the next morning, I asked her about it. She said she'd tripped on something and fallen. I figured Papa had hit Mama really hard. I've never talked about this with our brothers and Hannah till recently, but now I know that they all knew what our daed had done to you and Mama too. Sometimes Papa was kind and did nice things for us, but when he got mad about something and started hollering and making threats, I got scared and would hide under my bed.

Mama is really sorry that she couldn't do something to stop Papa from hurting you. I hope you'll find it in your heart to forgive her. Tonight, our family is going to have a meeting and talk about all of this. I am hoping Mama might be willing to speak with one of our church ministers or a counselor. It might help her not to feel guilty and be able to deal with the emotional pain she still feels because of the abuse she went through. Maybe you should think about doing that too. It's not too late for us to deal with this here as a family, and it's not too late for you either.

Take care, Irma, and I hope you write back soon.

Love,

Your sister Caroline

Irma sat staring at Caroline's letter. She was shocked by everything her sister had said. Irma had no idea that her siblings knew about the abuse she'd suffered. None of them had ever said anything to her regarding this until now. She also had not known that Homer had abused her mother. It was a sin and a shame, but the abuse Mama had suffered was no excuse for her allowing Homer to take out his hate and frustrations on Irma.

Anger welled inside of Irma as she thought about the big strap her stepfather had often used on her—sometimes right in front of her mother. Heat flooded Irma's face, and her body tensed. *How could my mother stand there and say nothing while Homer treated her firstborn child so cruelly? Didn't Mama care about me at all? She should never have married Homer, and once she realized that he was an abuser, she should have taken me and the rest of her children and fled.* Irma shook her head vigorously. How many times had she gone over this in her head, and why couldn't she forget about it? *I can't forgive my mother. She's just as guilty for staying with Homer as if she had abused me herself.*

Grabill

"Did you by any chance get the mail?" Doretta asked when her husband arrived home from working at his store that evening.

"As a matter of fact, I did." Warren stepped up to the sink where Doretta stood peeling potatoes and gave her cheek little butterfly kisses. "I placed it on the narrow table near the front door. Would you like me to bring it in here?"

"No, that's okay. I'll look at it after I get these potatoes ready to go on the stove. I doubt there was anything interesting. It's usually just junk mail and bills."

"I noticed a letter from your friend Irma in the pile."

Doretta smiled. "Oh, good. I'm eager to know what she wrote."

"Why don't you let me finish the potatoes so you can read Irma's letter now?"

"I wouldn't feel right about that. You just got home, and you're probably tired and want to spend some time with our son."

Warren shook his head. "Things were slow at the nutrition center today, so I let my helper go home early. And I've already seen sweet William. He's sleeping soundly in his cradle in the living room." Warren took the paring knife from Irma. "Go ahead and enjoy reading your friend's letter."

"All right, if you insist." She reached up and pulled her fingers through his short but nicely filled-in beard.

"I do insist, my dear fraa. You look mied this evening, and I'm guessing you did too much today."

"Not that much," she replied. "I just tire easily since the baby came."

"Which is why you're supposed to be taking things easy." He waved the peeler in her direction. "Now please go relax in the living room with your letter."

Irma did as her husband suggested, and a few minutes later, she had curled up on the couch with Irma's letter. Warren was right: the baby was still asleep. And since the room was so quiet, Doretta could read without distractions. She tore open the envelope, pulled out the piece of notepaper, and began to read:

> *Dear Doretta:*
>
> *I hope you are doing well and regaining your strength. After having a baby, it takes a while to get your energy back. I should know—I have three active children, and now I'm expecting a fourth. I'm dealing with bouts of nausea and don't have much energy, but my real concern is my lack of patience with the children. Sometimes, it seems that they do certain things that tend to irritate me to no end, and I can't say I'm looking forward to the birth of another child in the*

spring of next year: March 22 is my due date.

My nerves are on edge all the time, but it's not just from the naughty things the children do. I've been having dreams and flashbacks about my stepfather and all the pain he caused me from the time he married my mamm until I left St. Ignatius with LaVern. I had thought that going to Homer's funeral would bring closure, but it hasn't. Maybe it's because my mother asked me to forgive her for not doing something when Homer abused me physically and emotionally. I can't find it in my heart to forgive her, Doretta. She knew what he was doing, and that it was wrong, yet she did absolutely nothing to protect me from that man's wrath. I'm angry at him and angry at my mamm, and I hope I never have to see her again. It helps to unload my pent-up emotions in this letter. I'm sorry if I sound so bitter about the past, but I can't seem to let go of the emotional pain. It's plain to see that I have a lot of negative baggage to sort through, and I'm afraid it's affecting how I'm raising my children, along with how I'm dealing with my relationship with my mamm.

You've been a good friend to me all these years, even with the miles between us. Also, you have a lot closer relationship to God than I do these days, so I'm asking you to continue to pray for me, because I can't do it myself.

Your friend,
Irma

Doretta reached up to wipe away tears that had fallen to her cheeks. Her Ohio friend was expecting a baby, and this should be a happy time for her. It saddened Doretta to think that Irma was not looking forward to the birth of her fourth child. In addition, Irma was trying to deal with anger and bitterness toward her stepfather as well as her own mother. Doretta knew from things that had occurred in her own life that without forgiveness, there could be no healing. She was also fully aware of the importance of prayer and putting her trust in God. At a time like this, Irma needed God's guidance more than ever.

She bowed her head and prayed. *Heavenly Father, please give me the right words to say when I respond to my friend's letter. Open Irma's heart to any scriptures I might share, and heal the pain of her past so that she can be the kind of mother her children need.*

When Doretta ended her prayer, she thought about Irma's mother. She remembered spending time at Irma's house when her biological father was alive. Irma was a happy, content child, and Dorcas, although a bit timid, usually wore a smile. After Dorcas' husband died, she was sad, of course, but Doretta couldn't remember ever seeing a smile on the woman's face, even after she remarried.

She didn't remember much about Homer, except that he seemed kind of harsh and talked loudly. As a child, Doretta had never understood why he'd been so determined to leave Grabill and move to Montana, or why Dorcas had agreed to go. But now, as a grown woman, she suspected that he hadn't cared about his new wife's and stepdaughter's happiness. Homer probably never considered how hard it would be for Dorcas and Irma to leave their friends and start over in a strange new place. *Maybe he even wanted to take Dorcas and her daughter away because he had an unhealthy need to be in control,* Doretta thought. From what Doretta had learned on the topic of child abuse, the abuser wanted power and control.

I need to pray for Dorcas too. If Irma refused to accept her apology, then her mother is no doubt hurting as well.

———— ≈ ————

St. Ignatius

When they'd finish supper that evening, Hannah suggested they put the dishes in a sink full of soapy water to soak. "We can wash and dry them after we've had our family meeting," she said.

"What's the hurry?" Dorcas questioned. "I'm sure nothing we have to talk about is so important that we can't do the dishes before we retire to the living room."

Hannah's shoulders slumped as she looked at each of her siblings. When they all nodded, she said, "Okay, Mama, we'll get the dishes done first."

Dorcas had to admit that she too was eager to begin their meeting because she wanted to know what it was all about. But if they had the meeting first, they might be too tired to clean up the kitchen afterward, and that would leave them with a sink full of dirty dishes in the morning. She'd always been one to clean up her kitchen as soon as a meal was finished, and this evening should be no exception.

"While you ladies take care of the dishes, I think I'll head out to the barn and make sure that the horses are doing okay and the cats and dog have been fed." Irvin pushed his chair away from the table.

"I'll go with you," Aaron said, rising from his chair.

Both of Dorcas' sons carried their plates to the counter next to the sink before going out the back door.

"I think my *brieder* ought to do the dishes once in a while and give us a break," Caroline commented as she filled the left side of the separated sink with soapy water. "Why should we women always get stuck with kitchen cleanup when the brothers are perfectly capable?"

"Because they are the ones earning a steady paycheck, which is allowing all of us to have a roof over our heads and to enjoy tasty food in our bellies." Hannah nudged her sister's arm. "Quit complaining, and let's get this job done. Irvin and Aaron will be back in the house before we know it."

Caroline didn't respond as she began washing and rinsing the dishes, which Hannah took care of drying while Dorcas put everything away. They finished up quickly, and Dorcas was about to suggest that they go out to the living room to wait for Aaron and Irvin when the back door opened and her sons entered the kitchen with a nearly gray-haired man she hadn't seen in a good many years. He came right on over and shook her hand. "Good to see you, Dorcas. How are you and the family doing?"

Guess that puts an end to our family meeting, Dorcas thought without responding to his question. *Surely the children will not want to talk about personal things in front of Homer's brother, and I would prefer that Mose doesn't know any of our business either. If he really wanted to be a part of this family, then he wouldn't have missed his brother's funeral.*

Chapter 26

"Sorry for showin' up unannounced, but I have no cell phone, so there was no way of letting you know I was coming." Mose shrugged his shoulders. "Guess I could have borrowed someone's phone." He looked over at each of Dorcas' grown children as though seeing them for the first time, and then he looked back at Dorcas.

"Don't you have a telephone in your house?" she questioned.

"Nope." He shook his head. "I'm done with all that. Sold my place in Colorado six months ago, bought an RV, and hit the road. I've been traveling around the country, seeing the sights ever since."

Her head jerked back slightly. "Seriously?"

"That's right, and I'm enjoying my freedom from all the responsibilities of owning a business."

"You sold your car dealership, Uncle Mose?" The question came from Irvin.

"Sure did." A wide grin stretched across the man's face. "Got a good price for it too. Probably won't have to work again for the rest of my life."

Dorcas' brows pulled downward. "So you never got my message about Homer?"

He shook his head. "What about my brother? I came here to see him because I have something important to say, and—"

"Homer is dead. His funeral was nearly two months ago," she responded.

Mose pressed a fist to his mouth and sank into a chair at the table with a groan. "Wh—what happened?"

"He was working at the lumber mill and suffered a heart attack." Dorcas gestured to her sons, both leaning against the counter near the sink, while the girls stood nearby with curious expressions. "Irvin and Aaron were with him when it happened." She took a glass down from the cupboard, filled it with water, and handed it to Mose. His posture had crumpled, and he took in several shaky breaths. Dorcas figured the poor man might be in a state of shock.

Mose sat staring at the glass before picking it up and taking a drink. "I—I can't believe my brother is gone. I shoulda been here to help you all through it. I wish I'd had a chance to say goodbye."

"It happened so quickly. Our daed died before any of us could say goodbye," Aaron put in.

Dorcas took a seat at the table and asked her children to do the same. The family meeting they'd planned to have would need to be postponed. Right now, they should focus on Mose and helping him deal with his loss. Although Dorcas had never gotten to know Homer's brother very well, she couldn't miss the pained expression on his face.

"I sure would like to hang around here for a few days," Mose said, after a lengthy pause. "I'd like to get to know you all better and talk about my brother."

"That's fine." Dorcas looked across the table at her daughters. "Would you two please go to the guest room and put clean sheets on the bed?"

Before Hannah or Caroline could respond, Mose spoke up. "There's no need to bother with that. My RV has a comfortable bed, and I'm used to sleeping in it. As long as you don't mind, I'll pull my rig on the other side of the yard, not far from the barn. That way, it'll be out of the way. I won't be any trouble to you, I promise."

"That's not a problem. Are you hungry?" Dorcas asked. "I can fix you something to eat if you haven't had supper."

"No, that's okay. I don't have much of an appetite right now."

"Maybe you'll feel like eating in the morning," Dorcas said. "We usually eat breakfast around five thirty, so if you're up by then, feel free to come to the house and join us."

"All right, I will." He pushed away from the table. "I'm feeling more tired than I have all day, so I'm gonna head out to my rig now and move it near the barn. Once I'm settled, I'll try to get some sleep." With slumped shoulders, Mose ambled toward the back door, but then he stopped and turned to face them. "It's good to see you all again. Just wish it was under better circumstances."

All Dorcas could manage was a brief nod. She wasn't sure how she felt about Homer's brother showing up and hoped he wouldn't stick around too long. Although he didn't have a beard and dressed in English clothes, Mose resembled Homer. Now that she'd admitted to herself how she truly felt about her deceased husband, she didn't relish having to look at anyone who resembled him. Of course, Irvin and Aaron both had the same color hair as their father's, and neither of them reminded her of Homer. Maybe it was because the boys were tall and slender, while Homer and his brother were short and stocky.

Mount Hope

"How was your day? I didn't get a chance to ask you during supper because the kids were talking most of the time," LaVern said after the children had been put to bed and he and Irma had gotten settled in the living room with a piece of pie and a glass of milk.

"It was busy and even more stressful than usual," she responded.

"What happened? Didn't the kinner behave?"

"About as much as they normally do." She picked up her glass of milk and took a drink. "The thing that stressed me the most was the letter I got from my sister Caroline."

"Oh?" He took a bite of the apple pie she'd made and set the plate on the coffee table. "What'd she have to say?"

"She informed me that my mother had also been abused."

LaVern tipped his head. "By her father when she was a girl?"

"No, it was Homer."

"Was this during the time you lived with them or after you moved to Ohio with me?"

She shrugged and took another sip from her glass. "Maybe both."

"If Homer abused Dorcas physically while you lived there, surely you would have known about it."

Irma shook her head. "I was hurting so much from all the times he mistreated me, I didn't pay much attention to how he treated Mama." Irma sat quietly for a few seconds, thinking things over. "I remember seeing bruises on her arms on occasion, but she always had some explanation—like she'd fallen or had bumped into something—and Mama always said that she bruised easily." Irma paused to set her glass down next to the plate holding her untouched piece of pie. "I also remember hearing Homer yell at her sometimes, but that was nothing new for him—he was always hollering about something."

"Did he abuse your siblings too?"

Irma shook her head. "He got angry and shouted at them sometimes, but I never saw or heard him punish them harshly—not like he did me."

LaVern moved his hands up to the back of his neck and clasped them. "That man needed help. He must've been full of anger to have behaved so badly. It's too bad your mudder didn't insist that he get help and take responsibility for his hostile actions."

"Humph!" Irma grunted. "Homer would never have admitted that he'd done anything wrong. He never said he was sorry for anything either."

"But if he'd gotten the right kind of help. . ."

"Caroline thinks I should accept the apology our mother gave me."

"She's right. You need to forgive her, Irma."

The muscles in Irma's face tightened. "Why are you taking my mother's side? You should be supporting me, not her."

"I do support you, Irma, but I don't agree with your decision not to forgive Dorcas. Have you thought this through and prayed about the matter?"

"Just forget it," she said sharply. "I should never have said anything." Irma stood. "Enjoy your pie, and feel free to eat my piece too. I've had a rough day, and I'm going to bed." Before her husband could respond, Irma rushed from the room.

———— ≈ ————

LaVern scrubbed a hand over his face and let his fingers pull downward through the coarse hairs of his beard. He wished there was something he could have said to get through to his wife—help her realize the importance of forgiveness and grasp what God's Word said on the topic. He reflected on the verse found in Matthew 6:14: "If you forgive men their trespasses, your heavenly Father will also forgive you." Then the words of 1 John 1:9 came to mind: "If we confess our sins, He is faithful and just to forgive us our sins and to cleanse us from all unrighteousness."

Like all of the rest of us, Irma isn't perfect, and neither is her mother, LaVern thought. *We all need to seek God's forgiveness and be willing to forgive others. Although it may be difficult, Irma also needs to forgive her stepfather for the things he said and did to her.*

LaVern drank the remainder of his milk and finished his piece of pie, all the while listening to the steady *tick-tock* of the clock on the fireplace mantle. *What can I do to help my wife?* he asked himself. *Maybe I should speak to my mamm about this or perhaps the bishop's wife. Whomever I choose to discuss it with, I'm hoping they can get through to Irma. Otherwise, the anger and bitterness she feels, along with an unwillingness to forgive, will fester like a splinter that has been left untreated and continues to cause undue pain.*

———— ≈ ————

St. Ignatius

Morning dawned with gray skies and drizzle, but it didn't stop any of the birds in Dorcas' yard from singing—nor did it keep the rooster from crowing.

The boys had gone outside to do their chores, and the girls were still getting dressed. Dorcas started the coffeepot as soon as she entered the kitchen and had lit the gas light above the table. It wasn't long before the robust coffee aroma filled the room. She sniffed deeply and fought the desire to pour herself a cup before starting breakfast. It could wait. She needed to get busy preparing the morning meal so her sons could eat and be on time to open the mill.

Dorcas peered out the kitchen window, wondering if Mose was awake and still planned to eat breakfast with them. She saw his RV in the distance, but there was no sign of her brother-in-law. She'd often wondered why Mose had not joined the Amish church like his brother had done. Since it was a personal thing, and he might not have appreciated being questioned about it, she would not ask. Homer had never said much about his brother, other than commenting that he lived too far away and didn't come to Montana often enough. Dorcas figured if Mose and Homer's parents had been alive and still living here, Mose might have come to visit more often. In the twenty-some years Dorcas and Homer had been married, she'd only seen his brother on four occasions. Two of those times were when their parents had died. The other times were when Mose brought his wife, Esther, for a visit, and then they'd seen him again when they went to Colorado for Esther's funeral, four years ago. The poor woman had died from a brain aneurysm no one had known about until it was too late. Dorcas had figured Mose might remarry, but he was still single. If he had gotten married again, surely he would have let them know about it while he still had a phone.

Dorcas' thoughts came to a halt when a knock sounded on the back door. She opened it and found Mose on the porch, holding a black umbrella, which he closed before stepping inside. Dorcas led the way to the kitchen, and when they entered the room, Mose tipped his head back and sniffed the air. "Ah. . .just what I've been waiting for—a good cup of *kaffi*."

She thought it seemed odd to hear Mose speak Pennsylvania Dutch, since he drove a vehicle and lived in the English world. But then, he had grown up in an Amish home and had no doubt spoken the language for a good many years before leaving the faith.

Dorcas gestured toward the cupboard where she kept the dishes, glassware, and cups. "Help yourself to one of the bigger mugs, then pour a cup of coffee and take a seat at the table. I'll have some eggs and bacon to offer you soon."

"Thank you." He smiled at her from across the room. "It'll be nice to have a good home-cooked breakfast for a change."

She returned the smile and got the frying pan heated up. While the bacon sizzled in the pan, she broke eggs into a large bowl and beat the mixture. "I hope scrambled eggs are okay with you. They're quicker to make than over-easy, and my sons will be hungry and ready to eat as soon as they come inside from doing their chores."

Mose leaned forward with both arms on the table. "How are you and the family getting along financially with Homer gone?"

"We're doing fine. Irvin and Aaron have been running the lumber mill, and they're doing a good job of it."

"I'm glad to hear that."

Dorcas moistened her lips and decided to ask him a question that had been on her mind since last night. "When you were here last evening, you mentioned that you had wanted to tell Homer something important."

He gave a nod.

"Mind if I ask what it was?"

"I don't have a problem telling you, but it won't do much good now that my brother's not able to hear it."

Dorcas kept cracking eggs as Mose began to tell her about how he and Homer had been physically abused by their father when they were boys, and the mistreatment kept on clear into their teen years. Mose had left home at the age of seventeen and struck out on his own, but for some reason, which he'd never understood, Homer had stuck it out. Mose had given up on the Amish way of life and never looked back after their dad had treated him so badly. He'd figured his brother might do the same, but he had been wrong about that.

"When I met my wife, Esther, I felt good about my life and had a hope for the future." Mose paused and drank some coffee. "Then after Esther died, I missed her so much I started hanging out with some fellows from work, and pretty soon I began drinking too much and often came home all liquored up. Guess I thought I could drown my sorrows in the bottle, but it didn't do anything to keep me from being lonely."

Dorcas had no idea why Mose was telling her all this, but she continued to listen as he kept talking.

"Anyway," he continued, "about a year after Esther's passing, I met Alice, and it wasn't long before we got married. I quit drinking for a while, but I started up again." Mose took another swig of coffee and frowned. "Alice and I had some heated arguments about my drinking, and I didn't handle things well. I found myself getting very angry with my wife, and then one time, after I'd had too much to drink, I roughed her up pretty good. Of course, I blamed it on the alcohol, but deep down, I knew the real problem was not just because I drank and still missed Esther. My deep-seated anger toward my dad and mom had come to the surface for the first time. You see, my mother never tried to do anything to stop Dad from treating me and Homer so bad." Mose drank the rest of his beverage and set the mug down. "I had a real wake-up call when Alice left me and filed for divorce."

"What did you do?" she questioned.

"Nothing at first. I told myself that I was better off without her, and the drinking continued." He stopped talking and looked directly at

Dorcas. "See, Esther was a quiet, submissive wife, and I wasn't drinking when I was married to her. But Alice was more outspoken and didn't hesitate to point out my faults. I'm not blaming her, you understand. I'm just trying to make it clear why I was able to keep my temper under control while Esther and I were married."

Dorcas didn't know what to say, so she just kept listening as she prepared the morning meal.

"Did Homer have a drinking problem?"

She shook her head. "At least, not that I know of. I'm sure I would have smelled it on him if he had been drinking."

"Was he a good husband?"

Dorcas swallowed hard. "Well, um. . ."

"He was an abuser, wasn't he?"

She looked away, unable to face him, and gave a slow nod. "Homer abused my daughter, Irma, and me as well, but he never had any major issues with his flesh-and-blood children."

"I figured something wasn't right the last time I saw you and noticed some bruises on your arms." He cleared his throat real loud. "See, that's what I came here to talk to Homer about. I wanted him to know that I lost my second wife because of my temper and the need to control. It wasn't till Alice walked out on me that I finally admitted to myself that I had a problem and sought help." He pulled in a deep breath and blew it out quickly. "If I had managed to get Homer to admit that he was an abuser, I'd planned to point him in the right direction for help."

Dorcas grabbed the handle on the stove to steady herself, because she suddenly felt kind of shaky. All these years she had wondered if Homer had been an abused child, but knowing the slightest thing could set him off, she'd been afraid to ask.

A horrible thought popped into Dorcas' mind, and she shivered with apprehension. Since Homer had abused Irma, was it possible that Irma, being full of anger and resentment, might be doing the same to her children as had been done to her? Dorcas wished she could speak to her daughter about this, because she wanted to be sure her grandkids were protected. However, after their last phone call, it was doubtful that Irma would listen to anything Dorcas had to say. At this point, all Dorcas felt that she could do was to pray that Irma would never abuse her children and that, by some miracle, her daughter would accept the apology Dorcas had offered and agree to listen to the rest of what she'd wanted to say that day they had talked on the phone.

Chapter 27

Dorcas stood on the front porch, waving goodbye to Homer's brother as he drove his RV out of the yard. The days spent with Mose had gone by quicker than she'd expected. It had been awkward in the beginning to tell him that Homer had passed away—especially when he'd come with the purpose of talking with his brother. The good thing was she had learned several things about Homer's upbringing, and all of her questions about her late husband had been pretty much answered. Mose had been with them a week, but last night during supper, he'd announced that he would be hitting the road. She smiled, thinking about the grin on his face when he'd said, "I have places to go and things to see, and I may as well do it while I still can. One never knows what tomorrow will bring."

So true, Dorcas thought as she turned and went inside. *A year ago, I never would have guessed that my husband would die and I'd become a widow for the second time.*

She made her way to the living room and took a seat in the rocking chair. The boys had left for the mill an hour ago, and since it was Hannah's day off, she and Caroline had gone shopping in town. They'd invited Dorcas to go along, but not knowing what time Mose would head out, she'd declined her daughters' invitation. Besides, it was rather nice, sitting here in the house by herself, where all was quiet and she could think. So many thoughts swirled around in her head—mostly about the things Mose had shared with her during his visit. With the way Homer had liked to control every situation, plus the anger he'd shown when someone didn't do as he said, she'd often wondered if he had been an abused child while growing up. But of course, Dorcas had been afraid to ask him that question. She was glad Mose had come by and relieved that he'd confirmed her suspicions. Unfortunately, knowing that did not change the past—nor did it remove the memories of Homer's abuse toward Dorcas and Irma.

Last night, she and the children had finally had their family meeting, and each of them had shared their knowledge of the abuse that had gone on in their home when their father was alive. They'd all admitted that they'd never talked about Irma's or their mother's abuse until after Homer's death because they were afraid he would take his anger out on them too. Dorcas feared that the scars from the past would always be with her as well as the children.

She pressed her feet firmly against the floor and got the rocker moving faster. *I wish Irma and I could sit down and talk about this. I wonder how she would respond if I made a surprise visit to Mount Hope.* She shook her head. *No, that would probably make things worse, and quite likely she would shut the door in my face.*

Dorcas had shared with Mose about the relationship she had with Irma and how she'd apologized to her but had not been forgiven. He'd been sympathetic and offered a few suggestions, such as another phone call or writing a second letter.

She pondered the topic of spousal abuse, which Mose had said he'd had a problem with until he sought help. She remembered seeing the sadness on his face when he'd said he wished that he could have talked with Homer and encouraged him to acknowledge that he was an abuser and seek help.

Dorcas' lips pressed into a tight grimace. *Even if Mose had been able to share his thoughts and suggestions with Homer while he was still alive, I doubt that he would have listened. My husband was a very stubborn man who was quick to point out everyone's faults but his own.*

One of the things Mose had suggested to Dorcas was talking with their bishop or seeing a Christian counselor—someone who could help her deal with the guilt she felt for allowing Homer to hurt Irma, which had ruined the relationship she'd once had with her daughter. Mose had also pointed out that Dorcas needed to forgive Homer as well as herself. Holding a grudge and allowing anger at her husband to fester would only tear her down, and it would not be helpful to anyone. Mose had talked about some verses in the Bible and quoted several scriptures on the topic of forgiveness. He'd also said that he would be praying for her, as well as Irma and the rest of the family, because they all needed it. She knew her four youngest children had been emotionally scarred by Homer's threats. Even though Homer hadn't been abusive to any of them, they'd all witnessed his out-of-control temper, which had caused them to live in fear that if they said or did the wrong thing, they might also become the victims of his wrath.

Dorcas had to admit—forgiveness did not come easy. Perhaps she should hitch her horse to the buggy and drive over to the bishop's place. *It might be time to bring our family's terrible secret out in the open. I'll ask for guidance and especially prayer.*

———— ≈ ————

As Dorcas sat with Bishop Titus and his wife, Barbara, an hour later, a fluttery stomach and sweaty palms caused her to second-guess her decision to see them. What if she told them about Homer's abuse and they didn't believe her? How would things go if they did believe her but thought she'd been a terrible mother because she'd allowed the abuse to go on? Although Dorcas knew Homer's abuse had been wrong, she'd often put the blame on herself, believing that she'd said or done something wrong to set him off. Dorcas remembered him saying on more than one occasion that she was the problem and needed to keep her mouth shut and let him do his job as head of the family. Maybe if she had handled things differently. . .been more submissive and soft-spoken. . .*I honestly did try to do what he wanted, but it didn't change anything,* she thought with regret.

The bishop cleared his throat and looked at Dorcas. "You said there was something you wanted to talk to us about. Are you and your family struggling financially? Is there anything we can do to help with that?"

She shook her head vigorously. "No, no, we're getting along fine in that regard. I am here because of something of a personal nature—something I've never talked about with anyone outside of our family until now." She clutched her purse, which was lying in her lap, as her breathing accelerated.

"What has you so troubled?" Barbara asked. "Your cheeks are flushed and your breathing appears to be quite heavy. Would you like a glass of water?"

"Danki for asking, but I don't need anything to drink right now. What I do need is some counseling and your prayers."

Barbara left her straight-backed chair and took a seat on the couch beside Dorcas. "We'll help in any way we can." She looked at her husband who sat nearby in his recliner. "Right, Titus?"

He nodded. "Are you still in deep grief over your husband's death, Dorcas? If so, that's understandable, and you probably need more time."

"No, it's not that," she was quick to say. "I'm here to talk about some things that went on in our home while Homer was alive."

The bishop gazed at her steadily while pushing up his glasses that had slipped almost to the middle of his nose. "What kind of things?"

"Physical and emotional abuse." Dorcas could barely get the words out. They'd felt stuck in her throat and she had to swallow a few times before giving her response. *Why does this topic have to be so difficult? I feel ashamed just talking about it.*

"Was Homer the abuser?"

"Jah." Her already warm cheeks heated further. Maybe she did need some water to cool down, but she chose not to ask. Dorcas simply wanted to say what she'd come here for, before she lost her nerve and ran out the door.

"Were you his victim?"

"Sometimes, but most of his abuse was directed at my daughter—both physical and emotional."

"Irma?" This question came from Barbara.

Dorcas nodded.

"I'd suspected it but had no proof, so I never said anything to you or anyone else about it." Barbara's forehead wrinkled, and she looked over at her husband. "Now I wish I had told you my concerns."

"You should have, but then I should have been more aware myself."

"What made you suspicious?" Dorcas asked, looking at Barbara.

"My niece, Melissa, was Irma's teacher for the first few years she attended school in our district." Barbara paused, but kept her gaze on Dorcas. "She mentioned that for the first few years, Irma was shy and withdrawn around the two teachers at the schoolhouse, and she seemed to have trouble making friends with the other children."

"Did your niece make an effort to do anything about it?" Dorcas wanted to know.

"She said that she tried, but Irma didn't respond very well. Melissa figured Irma was simply shy and would get over it once she knew the other children better and felt comfortable attending her new school. She realized that relocating from her home in another state may have been difficult for Irma, and she attempted to make the girl feel welcome."

Dorcas thought back to the way her daughter had been while attending school in Grabill. She certainly wasn't shy back then. In fact, Irma had made friends easily. She'd also kept in contact with a few of her friends from Grabill by sending them postcards.

"Barbara, was Irma's shyness in school the only thing that made you believe she might be a victim of abuse?"

She shook her head. "No, not right away. Children who are new to the area are usually withdrawn at first, but with Irma it was different."

"How so?" her husband questioned.

"When she was about twelve years old, the teacher who taught the older grades realized that Irma had become more aggressive—often getting into disagreements with others her age."

"Did you see this for yourself, or was it based only on your niece's word?" Titus questioned.

"Both. I noticed it at some of our social functions. Irma held back when she was younger and didn't play with the other children much. When she got older, though, I remember hearing her arguing with some of the girls about something, and she wouldn't back down." Barbara fanned her face with her hand, as though she, too, felt overheated discussing this topic. "I used to be a schoolteacher before Titus and I got married, and I learned from the way some of my students acted when there was a problem at home. Guess I was more intuitive than some teachers."

Dorcas sat quietly as the bishop and his wife discussed her daughter's personality changes. When there was a lull in the conversation, she spoke again. "I wish you had said something to me about your suspicions. But then, because I feared my husband's wrath, I probably would have denied there was anything unusual going on in our home." She paused to collect her thoughts. "The reason I'm here now is because my family never talked about Irma's or my abuse when it took place, not even among ourselves. But since Homer's death, it has all come out, and now I'm struggling with guilt for letting the abuse go on all those years and doing nothing about it." She swallowed against the sob rising in her throat. "I've recently discussed it with my children who were not abused by their daed, but when I brought the topic up to Irma and said I was sorry, she refused to listen to me. Irma is bitter, and I know when she and her husband showed up for Homer's funeral that it was difficult for her."

"Is she aware that you were also abused?" Bishop Titus asked.

"I don't think so. If she knew, she never said anything. When I made the phone call to apologize, I was going to tell her that Homer had hit me many times, especially when I stood up for her and tried to calm him down so he wouldn't punish her so severely." Dorcas swiped at the tears dribbling down her cheeks. "But I never got the chance to say any of that, because Irma hung up the phone."

Barbara handed Dorcas a tissue, which she used to wipe her eyes. "I wish we had known about all this sooner so we could have helped," the kindly woman said.

"I'm not sure anyone could have done much unless Homer had acknowledged his sin and sought counseling to change his ways." Dorcas sniffed deeply. "I am so distraught about this and don't know what to do."

"We could have provided a safe haven for you and the children until he agreed to get help." The bishop reached for his Bible, lying on the table beside his chair. He opened it, turned several pages, and read: "For thus says the Lord: . . .'As one whom his mother comforts, so I will comfort you.'" He looked at Dorcas with compassion in his eyes. "Would you like me to reach out to Irma, through a letter or maybe a phone call?"

"I—I'm not sure. That might make things worse, because if you contact her, she would probably figure out that I'd told you about the situation."

"True, but if she listens to what I have to say, it would be worth the risk. Right?"

"But Titus," Barbara interjected, "if Irma suspected that her mother came to us about the problem between them, it could do more damage than good."

He gave his beard a little tug. "Maybe so. Guess for now, the best we can do is pray about this situation and not reach out to Irma until God tells us to do so. In the meantime, however, would it be all right with you, Dorcas, if I came over to your place and talked with your family? I'm certain that your sons and daughters must be dealing with some guilt regarding the fact that they each knew about the abuse but never said anything until after their father's death. And you too, Dorcas. You and your children could all use some biblical counseling."

Dorcas bobbed her head. "I think that's a fine idea, Titus. Jah, I would appreciate it very much." She smiled at Barbara through a fresh set of tears. "I'd like you to be there also, to offer your support."

"Of course." Barbara patted Dorcas' arm. "Just let us know when you want us to come, and we'll be there." She looked at her husband. "Right, Titus?"

"Absolutely."

Before Dorcas could say anything more, the bishop snapped his fingers. "Say, I have an idea. Why don't you and the family come over here for supper one evening next week?" He smiled at his wife. "How's that sound? I'll even help you fix the meal."

"Sounds good to me," she responded.

Dorcas couldn't help feeling a twinge of jealousy, observing how well these two people got along. She closed her eyes to keep more tears from falling. *If only Homer and I could have had that kind of a relationship, things might have been different—for Irma too.*

Chapter 28

Mount Hope

By the time Irma began fixing supper, her nerves were on edge, and she felt like she could scream. Clayton and Myra had been rowdy all day, both vying for her attention. On top of that, when Brian came home from school, he'd tracked mud into the house. It was bad enough that her careless son had left a trail of muddy footprints in the utility room where he should have taken off his boots, but then he'd tromped right into the kitchen—boots and all! Irma had cleaned the kitchen floor earlier in the day, so she hadn't reacted well when she'd seen the muddy boot prints all over her clean floor. Brian hadn't cried when Irma had given him a mop and said he had to scrub the floor, but when she'd hollered at him and said he was a stupid boy who never listened to her and couldn't do anything right, Brian gave in to tears. Irma had no sympathy for him and said he should stop sniffling and quit acting like a baby. Looking back on it now, Irma knew she'd spoken in the heat of anger, and she had apologized to Brian afterward. Even so, it hadn't quieted the agitation she felt from all the unpleasant events she'd dealt with today. Irma determined that what she really needed was some time away from her children.

If LaVern wasn't so busy with multiple auctions lined up for the rest of this month, I would ask him to plan a short getaway for just the two of us, Irma thought as she took out a kettle and filled it with water. *I'm sure Mildred and Paul wouldn't mind keeping the kids while we're gone. They always seem to enjoy having the grandkids at their house. And the great-grandparents who live in the daadihaus there would probably enjoy spending some time with the children too.*

Irma put the potatoes she'd already peeled into a pot of water and set it on the stove. She would wait to turn it on until after LaVern arrived home. In the meantime, she wanted to husk the ears of corn she'd purchased from a neighbor the other day and have them ready to cook when her husband returned.

The place I'd really like to go is to Grabill, Irma mused as she began to peel back the husk on the first ear of corn. *It would be so nice to see Doretta again. If our husbands were outside doing something, or maybe went fishing, it would give me a chance to speak to my friend privately and share my frustrations with her in person.*

Irma reflected on the letter she'd received from Doretta today, and how her friend had seemed excited to hear the news of Irma's pregnancy. "I wish I shared her enthusiasm," Irma mumbled under her breath. *Maybe I would be looking forward to the event if my other three children were older and could help out more. It would also help if they were better behaved. Having to deal with their naughtiness all the time wears on my nerves and zaps what little strength I have these days.*

She moved back to the sink and released a lingering sigh. *What's the point? I just need to accept my situation and learn to live with it. I can handle things,* she determined. *I just can't let my emotions take over.*

When LaVern entered the house that evening, he was greeted in the entryway by two tearful children.

"*Was fehlt du?*" he questioned, asking the children what was wrong with them.

Clayton pointed at his sister and frowned. "She pulled my *haar.*"

"What did you do about that?"

"I pulled her hair right back." Clayton sniffed, while rubbing his backside. "Mama got real mad and gave us some licks with a wooden spoon."

LaVern opened his mouth to speak, but then he paused to sort out his thoughts. If what Clayton had said was true, then Irma had punished the children when she was angry, which was not good parenting. LaVern and Irma had discussed this topic when Brian was a toddler and had agreed that any punishment they felt the child needed would be done in love and never in the heat of anger. Irma must have forgotten the decision they'd made.

LaVern took both children to the living room and got down on his knees in front of them. Pulling his son and daughter into his arms, he said, "It's not nice to pull someone's hair or do anything else that might hurt them. Is that understood?"

Myra and Clayton nodded solemnly as more tears fell.

LaVern took out his hanky and wiped their faces. "Where's your brother?" He directed his question to Clayton.

The boy pointed toward the stairs. "After he got done cleaning the kitchen floor, Mama yelled some more and sent Brian to his room."

"Where's your mamm now?"

"In the *kich*."

"Okay. I am going to let her know that I'm home, and I would like you and Myra to get washed up for supper, because it will likely be on the table soon."

"Okay, Daadi." Clayton hurried from the room and Myra followed.

LaVern pulled in a quick breath and released it slowly. Now he needed to speak with Irma about what had gone on here today.

<hr />

Irma had almost finished setting the table when LaVern came into the kitchen. Instead of his usual cheerful smile and, "How was your day?"

he looked at Irma with eyebrows drawn together and asked a pointed question. "Did you spank Myra and Clayton?"

She looked at him but quickly looked away. "Jah, and they deserved it. Those two have been bickering all day, and when they started pulling hair, I'd had enough."

"They're quite upset and greeted me with tears."

"They got what they deserved."

LaVern stepped in front of her so she had no choice but to look at him. "Were you angry when you punished them?"

Her cheek muscles tightened. "Of course, I was. They'd been pestering each other all day, and hair pulling is not acceptable."

"So, it was acceptable to punish in anger?"

Irma stepped back to put some distance between them. "Why are you questioning me like this? I am their mudder. Don't I have a right to punish our children when they need it? Or should I just let them do whatever they want, no matter how destructive it might be?"

LaVern held up his hand. "Whoa, now. . . . Don't get so defensive. Of course you have a right to discipline the kinner when they've done something unacceptable, but not while you are still angry."

A warm flush swept across Irma's cheeks, and she lowered her gaze. "You're right, LaVern. I should not have doled out any kind of punishment while I was mad." Tears sprang to her eyes. "It's been a difficult day, and I didn't get as much done as I'd hoped because I spent too much time dealing with unruly children." She gestured to the kitchen floor and told LaVern how Brian had worn his muddy boots inside. "I made him clean up the mess and sent him to his room."

"Did you lash out at Brian in anger?"

Irma kept her arms pressed tightly at her sides as she forced herself to look up at him. "Jah, I said some unkind things to Brian, but the words came out before I could stop them."

LaVern pulled her into his arms and patted her back. "I'm sorry I can't be here more to help with the kinner. You have a big responsibility on your shoulders, and I'm sure it's difficult—especially since you haven't felt well with this pregnancy. I'm thinking it might be good if I hired someone to come in during the days I'm at work to help out."

Irma shook her head vigorously. "I do not need a *maad*. What I really need is a vacation—just you and me."

He continued to pat her back while speaking in a gentle tone. "That's not possible right now, Irma. I can't take any time off from my auctioneering duties until things slow down. Maybe after the baby comes and the child is old enough, we could all make a trip to—"

"Don't worry about it. I understand." Irma placed her arms behind her back and gripped one wrist with the other hand. "I'll be fine without a maid, and I won't punish any of the children when I'm angry again. Does that make you feel better?"

He stroked her cheek with his thumb. "All right. But if you start to feel that things are too much for you, please let me know."

"I will." Irma cringed at the lie she'd told. She had no intention of asking LaVern to hire someone to come here to help out. This was her household to run, and she was the children's mother, so she would manage just fine on her own. Irma would simply draw from her inner strength so she wouldn't lose her temper with the children again.

St. Ignatius

"I don't see why we need to have supper at the bishop's house," Aaron complained as Dorcas and her children headed down the road in their family-sized buggy. "I was planning to get together with some of my friends this evening. Since tomorrow's Saturday and the mill will be closed, I was looking forward to staying out late and sleeping in tomorrow morning."

"Aw, quit complaining," Irvin called over his shoulder from the driver's seat. "I'm sure the bishop's *fraa* will serve us a tasty meal. Besides, it's been a week since Mama told us we'd been invited to have supper with

Titus and Barbara. If you'd made other plans, you should have spoken up and said so."

"Jah, okay." Aaron fell quiet, and Dorcas was glad. She was apprehensive enough about what Titus might say to her and the children and didn't need anyone making a fuss before they arrived at the bishop's place.

What if Titus tries to get the children to talk about their daed's abuse, and they don't want to? She stirred restlessly on the seat beside Irvin. *Maybe tonight will be helpful for all of us.* Dorcas thought about Mose, and how she'd gotten a better understanding of things during his visit. It had been especially helpful to learn that Homer and Mose had been abused by their father when they were living at home. It explained a lot about Homer's angry outbursts, and she now understood how and why he'd been an abusive husband and stepfather. *Not that knowing excuses his behavior*, she thought. *Like Mose, Homer could have sought help for his problem. What's been done has been done, and there's nothing anyone can do about it.* She clasped her hands together in a prayer-like gesture. *It's my job now to make sure that the cycle of abuse in this family ends and that none of my children will follow in their daed's footsteps. Hopefully, the bishop will share some things with us tonight that will sink deeply into my children's hearts so that they do not repeat their father's mistakes.*

"This chicken pot pie is sure good," Hannah said after she'd taken a second helping. "Would you mind sharing your recipe with us, Barbara?"

"Not at all. I'll write it out before you go home." Barbara smiled and looked over at her husband. "Titus helped me make it."

"It's very good, and so is the tossed green salad," Dorcas put in. "We appreciate your invitation to join you for supper this evening."

"We're glad you could come," Titus said, helping himself to some of the salad.

The conversation around the table started with a discussion about the weather they'd had recently. Then the bishop asked the boys how everything was going at the lumber mill. Irvin shared a few things, as did Aaron. While that discussion went on at one end of the table, Barbara engaged Dorcas and her daughters in a conversation that involved canning, sewing, and cooking. Hannah contributed a few things of her own and asked Barbara some questions, but Caroline sat quietly— although she did appear to be listening. Dorcas interjected comments a couple of times, but knowing that they would soon be talking about the topic of abuse, she couldn't help wondering how her children would respond to any questions the bishop might ask them. Abuse was a sensitive topic, and it might be difficult for her sons and daughters to talk about—even though they hadn't been the victim of their father's abuse. Knowing about it and being afraid to say anything had to have taken its toll on all of Dorcas' children.

Her thoughts went to Irma. The poor child had suffered so much at the hand of her stepfather, and Dorcas still struggled with the guilt she felt for allowing it to happen. It was hard to forgive herself for something that had occurred in the past and could not be undone.

—❧—

After supper was over and the dishes had been cleared, Titus suggested they all move to the living room. Once everyone was seated, he picked up his Bible and opened it to a page that had been marked with a red ribbon. He'd obviously been preparing for the talk they would have this evening.

The bishop began by reading James 1:19–20: " 'So then, my beloved brethren, let every man be swift to hear, slow to speak, slow to wrath; for the wrath of man does not produce the righteousness of God.' Of course, you realize," he added, "that these verses apply to both men and women. The Bible instructs us to be slow to wrath, or anger, because our anger does not reflect the righteousness of God." He turned to another passage he'd marked with a blue ribbon. "Proverbs 15:1 says, 'A soft answer turns away wrath, but a harsh word stirs up anger.' " He closed the Bible and looked at each of them in turn. "You see, it's never good for someone to lash out or punish another person in anger. Your father became abusive to your mother and your sister Irma because he got angry and took his frustrations out on them. We are all human, and there are times when we become angry, but we must learn to deal with our anger and not take it out on someone by saying unkind things or causing them pain in any way. Do you understand what I'm saying?"

All heads nodded.

"In Ephesians 4:26 we are told: 'Be angry, and do not sin: do not let the sun go down on your wrath.' You see, anger becomes a sin when we direct it at someone in a hurtful way."

The children, as well as Dorcas, gave the bishop their full attention.

"Now, I understand that you were all fearful when Homer abused Irma or your mother. No doubt, you were afraid that if you said anything, he might turn his anger on you." Titus directed his statement to Dorcas' sons and daughters.

They all nodded with solemn expressions.

Titus looked at Dorcas. "You too were frightened. Having been the victim of your husband's harsh words and brutality, you feared more of the same if you didn't keep quiet when he punished Irma. Is that correct?"

Dorcas' throat clogged with unshed tears as she slowly nodded her head.

"You all had good reason to be fearful, and I am truly sorry your family went through such an ordeal without any help or support. But your mother has come forth with the truth, and you have our support now." He glanced over at his wife, and she also nodded.

"There is something else I would like to say on this topic," he continued. "If I'm not mistaken, some or maybe all of you are dealing with guilt because you kept quiet about Homer's abuse."

Caroline emitted a pathetic sob and lifted her hand. Hannah, Irvin, and Aaron raised their hands too.

"If I could undo the past, I surely would," Dorcas said, slowly shaking her head. "But I can't, and I don't know how to make things right with any of my children." She looked at each of them and said, "I'm ever so sorry, and I hope you'll forgive me."

"You did nothing wrong, Mama," Hannah spoke up. "You were not the abuser."

"No, but I allowed the mistreatment to go on because I was scared of your father and too embarrassed to tell others what was happening in our home. I feared they might not believe me or could even take his side."

Barbara reached over and clasped Dorcas' hand. "There may have been some in our community who would've looked the other way or thought you were exaggerating, but if you'd come to Titus or one of our other church leaders, I'm sure they would have investigated the situation until the truth was revealed."

"That's correct," her husband agreed, "but it's in the past, and we must live in the now and do better in the future. We have all made mistakes that we cannot erase. So, in order to live a happy, fulfilled life, we must confess our sins, turns our fears over to God, forgive our own shortcomings, and make every effort to behave in such a way that others will see Christ living in us. Only then will our hearts be filled with peace. Now let us pray." He reached both hands out and clasped Irvin and Aaron's hands. Barbara did the same with Hannah and Caroline, and Dorcas took hold of Caroline's other hand. As she prayed, she thanked the Lord for their bishop and his wife and for God's Holy Word, which had spoken to her tonight. From this point on, with God's help, she would make every effort to be a good mother to the children who lived with her and set a Christian example. Since her other daughter no longer lived with them, all Dorcas could do was pray for Irma—and that, she would continue to do for as long as she lived. If Irma wouldn't talk to her, there wasn't much Dorcas could do except pray.

Chapter 29

Grabill

Pushing her precious baby in the stroller, Doretta headed down the drive-way to get the mail. It was hard to believe little William was already two months old. The days since his birth seemed to be flying by so quickly.

At the mailbox, Doretta bent down to make sure the baby's blanket was still secure and that he hadn't kicked it loose. Those little legs of his could sure move when he became active. What a joy it was to watch each stage of her son's development.

Satisfied that everything looked fine with the covers, Doretta opened the flap of the mailbox and withdrew the mail. Flipping through it quickly, she was pleased to discover a letter from Eleanor. As soon as Doretta got back to the house and put William in his cradle, she planned to sit down with a cup of tea and read her friend's letter. It had been awhile since she'd heard from Eleanor, and Doretta was eager to hear what was new in Paradise, Pennsylvania, and get an update on Eleanor's two children.

Doretta did a quick assessment of the rest of the mail and was disap-pointed to see that there was nothing from Irma. The last letter she'd gotten from her Ohio friend was when she'd received the news that Irma was expecting another child and was having trouble coping with her children.

Maybe Irma hasn't been feeling well, Doretta thought as she put the mail in the shoulder bag she'd brought along. *I should probably write her another letter to see how things are going and give her an update on my life too.*

The November wind picked up as Doretta began the walk back up the driveway. She shivered and hurried along, not wishing to keep the baby outdoors much longer.

When Doretta carried her son into the house a few minutes later, she felt thankful for the warmth that greeted her. Winter was on its way, and it probably wouldn't be long before they got some snow. Since she didn't have to go into town to help at the nutrition center anymore, Doretta was more than happy to stay home where it was warm. When it did snow, she could sit inside and enjoy the pristine white flakes falling outside her windows.

Doretta set her thoughts of winter weather aside and fed the baby. After he'd eaten, she changed his diaper and placed him in the cradle near the couch, where she took a seat with Eleanor's letter. The stamped image of a bluebird made her smile as she began to read:

Dear Doretta,

I hope this letter finds you well and enjoying your baby. Since he's two months old now, I imagine he's grown quite a bit and is getting more active.

Speaking of active, Stephen, my busy toddler, likes to explore, and he's always looking for new things to get into. Rosetta acts like a little mother, often telling him what he can and cannot do. Raising children can be tiring, and sometimes it tries a person's patience, but I wouldn't trade my two for anything. As Vic often says, "Children are a blessing from God, and we've been doubly blessed."

Have you heard anything from Irma lately? I sent her a sympathy card after you told me that her stepfather had died, but I never heard anything in response. I didn't expect a thank-you note for sending the card, but I had hoped Irma

*might write and tell me how she is doing. If you've heard
from her recently, could you please let me know?*

Doretta glanced at the clock across the room. Warren would be home
from work soon, so she needed to get busy making supper. Doretta put
Eleanor's letter back in the envelope and started for the kitchen. She
would have to finish reading it later on.

*I guess any letter reading or writing on my part will have to wait un-
til after we eat. I'll respond to Eleanor's letter and write to Irma again. Or
maybe while Warren spends time with the baby, I'll walk out to the phone
shed to make a call and leave Irma a message.* Doretta paused and looked
over her shoulder where William lay, sleeping peacefully. "Sleep while
you can, little one," she whispered. "Your daadi will be home soon, and
he will be eager to hold you."

Mount Hope

Irma got up from the couch, where she'd been resting, and yawned
while stretching her arms over her head. Today had been rough, and she
was exhausted. Of course, that was nothing new. This pregnancy was taking
a toll on her, and she probably should consent to hiring a maid, but the
thought of someone taking over her job of managing the house and caring
for the children still did not sit well with Irma. That was her responsibility,
no one else's. Besides, paying a helper would take extra money, and as the
children grew they would need new shoes, not to mention replacing the
clothes they'd outgrow. Then they had the expense of having the baby,
especially if Irma ended up giving birth at the hospital instead of having
a home delivery with a midwife like she had planned.

*If we lived closer to LaVern's parents, at least Mildred could have them
at her house sometimes, which would give me a little break and wouldn't cost
us any money.* How many times had she wished for that? It simply wasn't
realistic to expect her husband to move. But remembering back, Irma

had already decided she didn't need her mother-in-law taking over as she'd done when Myra was born.

Irma regretted the fact that she always seemed to be wishing for something other than what she had, but she couldn't seem to help her feelings of discontent. On top of that, she still had trouble holding her temper when the children did something they were not supposed to do or got on her nerves when they became too loud.

Irma hadn't been sleeping well either. Memories of Homer often hounded her dreams, and when she'd wake up in the middle of the night, it was hard to get back to sleep. Sometimes, when Irma tried to control her emotions, it felt like her blood was boiling through her whole body. She didn't know if it was her hormones acting up or if it was caused from the pain of her past that wouldn't let go. Irma wanted desperately to stop thinking about the abuse she had suffered throughout a good deal of her childhood, but the slightest unexpected words from someone or even a thought would cause some unpleasant memory she'd hoped to forget to pop into her head. When that happened, Irma would become irritable and say and do things she later regretted. It seemed like a vicious cycle over which she had no control.

Holding both hands against her growing belly, Irma made her way to the kitchen to begin supper. The nausea she had dealt with during the early months of her pregnancy had abated, but there were times, like now, when she had no appetite for food. This evening, like so many other nights, Irma would have to force herself to eat. If she picked at her food or didn't eat enough, LaVern would remind her that even if she wasn't hungry, for the sake of the baby, she needed to eat. He was right, of course, but Irma was put off by the way her husband kept reminding her of what she should and shouldn't do. She often felt that LaVern treated her like a child instead of a grown woman with a mind of her own.

Irma opened the refrigerator and peered inside. She'd forgotten to thaw any frozen meat for supper, so that left only a few choices. She could mix up some batter and serve pancakes for the meal, or scramble the ten eggs left in the carton. Either choice would probably be fine with the children, who were currently playing in their rooms, but LaVern might not be as easy to please. He was a meat-and-potatoes person and would probably turn his nose up at a supper that didn't include meat.

"I should have thawed some chicken or ground beef," Irma said out loud as she closed the refrigerator door. *I should figure out each day what I'm making for supper the following evening and write myself a note to remember to thaw...* She tapped her forehead and muttered, "My memory isn't as good as it should be these days. Maybe that's because of the pregnancy too."

"Who were you talking to?" LaVern asked when he strolled into the kitchen, causing her to jump.

"Oh, you scared me. I—I was talking to myself and didn't hear your driver's rig pull into the yard, so I had no idea you were home." Her face heated with the embarrassment she felt because he'd caught her jabbering away to herself.

He came over and gave her a hug. "I got out at the end of the driveway so I could check for any messages in the phone shed."

"Were there any?"

"Just two. One was from my mamm, asking if we're still planning to join her and Dad for Thanksgiving next week."

Irma nodded and released a yawn she couldn't hold back. "Did she say what she needs me to bring?"

"No, she did not. Maybe Mom doesn't expect you to contribute anything."

"Oh, we can't go empty-handed."

"I'll check in with her soon and see what she would like us to bring."

"Okay."

LaVern stroked Irma's cheek. "You look mied. Did you have a tiring day? Were the kinner well behaved?"

"It was kind of tiring, and the kids had a few issues, but it was nothing I couldn't deal with. And I did get a short nap."

"You did? How did you manage that?" he asked.

"After having their favorite noodles-and-egg soup and a couple cups each of homemade chocolate goat's milk, it wasn't long before Clayton and Myra were napping on the couch."

LaVern smiled. "Maybe chocolate milk should be served at lunchtime more often."

"Jah, maybe so," she replied. "So, after they were lying down, I sat in your recliner and laid back for what I thought would be a few moments of rest. But when my eyes popped open again, it was thirty minutes later and Myra and Clayton were still asleep." There was no way Irma would admit that the children had gotten on her nerves again today and that she'd struggled not to lose her temper with them. Although she hadn't hit any of the children, Irma had hollered at Myra and Clayton and called Brian a brat when he'd come home from school and hadn't done his chores when she'd asked. She had found him outside playing with his dog instead. She certainly couldn't let him get away with that without saying or doing something. When Irma had shouted and called Brian a brat, he'd looked at her with tears in his eyes and whimpered, "Sorry, Mama. I'll do my chores right now."

"I'm glad your day went okay and you were able to take a nap. It's important for you to get enough rest." LaVern's comment pushed Irma's thoughts aside, and she watched him go over to the sink and wash his hands. "I don't smell anything cooking," he said. "So I assume you haven't started supper yet?"

She shook her head and avoided meeting his gaze. "I forgot to thaw any meat, so I'm afraid our choices for supper are limited to pancakes or scrambled eggs."

LaVern's nose wrinkled. "How about some sandwiches? Do we have any lunch meat and cheese?"

"Jah, I think there's enough of both, and I do have a loaf of bread." Irma didn't know why she hadn't thought of making sandwiches. It was more proof that her brain wasn't working like it should.

"Okay, no problem. If you'll set the table, I'll get out the fixings. Then once the sandwiches are made, we can call the kinner to come join us for supper."

Irma patted his back. "Danki, LaVern. I appreciate your help." That was the truth. She didn't know what she had done to deserve such a good husband.

"Oh, by the way, when I checked for phone messages, there was also one from Doretta," LaVern said as he took mayonnaise and mustard from the refrigerator.

"Oh? What did she say?"

"Just that she hadn't heard from you for quite a while and wondered if everything was okay." He opened the refrigerator again and took out the lunch meat and cheese. "If you don't have time to write a letter, maybe you ought to give her a call."

"Okay. I'll do one or the other when I get the chance."

———— ≈ ————

St. Ignatius

"Could I talk to you for a minute?" Hannah asked when Caroline passed her in the hall after coming out of the bathroom.

"Sure, what's up?"

"I've been meaning to ask you and keep forgetting. Did you ever get a letter from Irma in response to the one you sent her awhile back?"

Caroline shook her head. "I'm thinking she probably didn't appreciate what I said."

"Which part?"

"The one about how our daed abused Mama."

"Why wouldn't Irma appreciate hearing that? It should have made her feel a little better, knowing she wasn't the only person Papa took his anger out on."

"Maybe so, but she might be so angry at our mamm for allowing it to happen that she doesn't even care that Mama was treated badly."

Hannah sighed. "Want me to write Irma a letter? Or I could call if you think that might work better."

"That's probably not a good idea."

"How come?"

"Because she might think I put you up to contacting her, or she might believe the two of us should mind our own business and stay out of the problems between her and Mama."

"Jah, I guess you're right. I will pray about the matter, though, and if God lays it on my heart to contact our sister, I will."

Hurrying to get the last of the supper preparations done, Dorcas scurried around the kitchen. There had been a message from Mose this morning, saying that he would be driving through Montana again and planned to arrive in St. Ignatius early this evening to see the family before he headed south for the winter. Dorcas looked forward to seeing him again and was glad she would have the opportunity to tell Mose that she and the children had talked to their bishop about the abuse that had gone on in their home when Homer was alive. In fact, their whole family had been back to see Titus four more times after their initial visit. Every time they'd met with him and Barbara, he had shared more insightful thoughts and read some important scriptures. Dorcas felt that the counseling sessions had been helpful to all of them. The children seemed calmer and happier, and the guilt she had dealt with diminished considerably. She still felt concerned about Irma, though, and prayed for her daughter regularly. If and when the time felt right, Dorcas planned to either call Irma again or write a letter. There were still some things that needed to be said, but she wanted to give Irma more time and allow the Lord to work in her daughter's life.

Dorcas set her thoughts aside and was about to call the girls to come set the table when a knock sounded on the back door. *I'll bet that's Mose.* She wiped her damp hands on a dish towel and went to see if it was him.

Chapter 30

"Thank you for allowing me to park my RV outside in that same spot again and for inviting me to join you for this delicious Thanksgiving meal." Mose smiled at Dorcas as he helped himself to another piece of the tender turkey breast. "My brother didn't know how lucky he was to have been married to such a good cook."

Dorcas returned his smile, but inwardly she cringed. She wished Mose hadn't mentioned Homer, but she wouldn't let it ruin the day. Just when she thought she'd been successful at forgiving her husband, the mere mention of him had brought the resentment she'd felt during most of their marriage to the surface again. This alerted Dorcas to the fact that she needed to keep praying about forgiving her second husband. She paused to ask God to forgive her unforgiving spirit and help her to think less about Homer's bad behavior. It did no good to dwell on the past. Nothing beneficial could come of it.

Dorcas handed the platter of meat to Hannah. "Would you like to have another piece?"

"No, thanks, Mama. I'll be lucky if I can finish what's left on my plate." Hannah passed the platter on to her sister, and then Caroline offered it to Aaron. He took two hunks of white meat and grinned. "Uncle Mose is right, Mama. You are definitely a good cook."

"Thank you, Son."

"Uncle Mose, how much longer are you planning to stay here?" Irvin asked as he helped himself to a hefty spoonful of mashed potatoes.

"Thought, at first, I might stay a few more days and head out on Monday." He glanced out the window at the graying sky. "Now I'm thinking that I probably should leave sooner, because it looks like we could get some snow."

"So you're gonna spend the winter down south somewhere, huh?" The question came from Aaron.

Mose nodded and took a spoonful of cranberry sauce that he spread on his turkey. "I think my body will appreciate the warm sun more than it would if I stuck around here where it's gonna be cold all winter."

Aaron licked his fingers and wiped them on the napkin beside his plate. "Sure wish I could go with you. I've never been partial to cold weather, and it can get downright frigid here during the harsh winter months."

"I'd take you with me if I could," Mose responded. "But you're needed here to help your brother run the lumber mill."

Aaron slouched in his chair and grimaced. "Don't remind me. Working outside in the cold can be downright miserable."

"Not all of our work is done outdoors," Irvin spoke up. "Some of it is paperwork in the office, and some takes place inside the wooden building where the lumber is cut."

"That building's not very warm either." Aaron stared at his plate. "And in the summer, it can be too hot in there."

"Aw, quit your bellyaching and be thankful that we both have a job." Irvin swatted at the air as if to remove some unknown obstacle.

Spots of color erupted on Aaron's cheeks, and he wrinkled his nose. "Now you sound like Papa. That's the kind of thing he used to say."

Dorcas knew if she didn't reroute this conversation now, her sons' discussion might escalate. She cleared her throat a couple of times and said, "Since we are celebrating Thanksgiving today, why don't we all go around the table and say something we are thankful for?"

"That's a good idea. Mind if I go first?" Mose asked with an uplifted hand.

She gave a nod. "Go right ahead."

"Well, I'm thankful for many things, but I am especially grateful for this opportunity to be with your family today. Since I'm a widower and have no children of my own, I appreciate being able to spend time with my sister-in-law, nieces, and nephews and having this chance of getting to know them all better."

"Danki, Mose. We are pleased that you could join us, and it's been good getting to know you too." Dorcas turned toward Caroline. "What do you have to be thankful for, Daughter?"

Caroline gave her response quickly. "I'm thankful that we used paper plates for this meal, which means there will be fewer dishes to wash when we're done eating."

Everyone except Aaron laughed. He seemed to be deep in thought about something as he pressed his lips and sat with both elbows on the table and a far-off look in his eyes.

"Okay, Hannah," Dorcas said, "it's your turn."

Hannah tilted her head from side to side as if she might be weighing her choices. Several seconds passed before she smiled and said, "I'm thankful for my mamm, who I know loves and cares for each one of her children."

The corners of Dorcas' lips twitched slightly as a feeling of warmth spread throughout her chest. "Danki, Hannah. I'm far from being a perfect mother, and I have made many mistakes in the past, but I am trying to do my best now." Dorcas gestured to Aaron. "What are you thankful for, Son?"

He tapped his fingers on the tabletop a few times and looked over at his brother. "I can't think of anything right now, so why don't you go ahead?"

Irvin shrugged. "Okay, sure. . .why not? I am thankful that our daed taught us so many things about the lumber mill. Because we listened and learned, we were able to take over his job when he passed."

"Do you enjoy your new position?" Mose asked.

"Jah."

"How about you?" Mose looked at Aaron.

Aaron scratched at a spot on his neck that had reddened, then tugged his right ear. "Not particularly. I only work there 'cause I have to. I can think of lots of other things I'd rather do." He barely glanced at his family. "If I could find someone else to take my place at the mill, I'd be out of there for sure."

Dorcas' mouth nearly fell open. She'd never suspected that Aaron didn't like working at the lumber mill. Since Homer had died, both of her sons had been going to work there five days a week without complaint. She wondered why he'd never spoken up and said he didn't enjoy working there before. Dorcas couldn't let this topic go until she had an answer, so she asked him that very question.

In a flat, almost emotionless voice, he said, "No one ever asked me till now."

At this point, Dorcas wasn't sure how to respond. She would have liked to have suggested that her son look for another job, but Irvin couldn't run the mill alone. Aaron's help was needed. Perhaps in time, he would learn to accept—and maybe even appreciate—the work required of him at the lumber mill. If not, then perhaps someday, if Irvin could find a replacement for his brother, Aaron could quit and do something else that he would enjoy more.

"Is anyone ready for dessert yet?" Dorcas asked, hoping the looks of concern she saw on everyone's faces would disappear.

"Think I'm gonna pass on dessert, because I'm too full of turkey, stuffing and everything else you served us Dorcas." Mose patted his stomach and rose from the table. "In fact, I'm going to head out to my RV now and get some sleep before I hit the road."

Dorcas said she understood and tried not to show her disappointment. For all she knew, it could be a good many months before they saw Homer's brother again.

"Could I send some turkey or a slice of pie with you?" Dorcas rose from her spot.

Mose hesitated. "Well, that might be all right. Yes, I'd appreciate it in fact."

"Fine then, I'll get that ready for you to take out to your RV."

He smiled. "Thank you for that, and for the delicious Thanksgiving dinner."

"You're very welcome."

Dorcas got out two plastic containers. She filled one with turkey and the other with a slice of pumpkin pie and placed them both in a paper sack. After handing it to Mose, everyone got up from the table and gathered around him to offer hugs, handshakes, and to say their goodbyes. Dorcas was the last to bid her brother-in-law farewell as she walked him to the door. "God be with you, Mose," she said, trying to keep her emotions in check. "Please find a phone somewhere and give us a call so we know that you got to your destination safely. We'll be praying for you," she added before offering him her hand. Dorcas was taken aback when he pulled her in for a hug and said, "I shall pray for you and your family too."

Baltic

Irma watched her mother-in-law from across the dining room table. On either side of Mildred sat Clayton and Brian, both with happy faces and talking to their grandparents almost nonstop. LaVern's grandparents sat a few chairs down, and they seemed to be enjoying themselves as well.

Irma glanced at Myra, sitting in a booster seat on top of a chair. Her cheeks had a rosy glow, and she giggled frequently when her grandpa said something funny or tickled her bare feet.

The skin beneath Irma's eyes tightened. *Why can't my children be that happy and content when they're with me? And why don't they behave themselves at home the way they have here this afternoon? Maybe they like their grandparents better than me.*

Irma picked up her glass of water and took a drink. She hoped the cool liquid would help calm her down, but it had no effect other than to quench her thirst.

"This meal is *appeditlich*, Mom," LaVern said, reaching for the bowl of savory stuffing to take his second helping. "Danki for all your hard work."

"I'm glad you think it's delicious, but I can't take the credit for fixing all of the food." Mildred gestured to Irma. "Your fraa furnished the green-bean casserole, and we'll get to eat some of her apple pie later on."

"I can't wait for dessert," Brian said. "Do you have any other pies besides the apple one Mama made?"

Mildred nodded. "I made a pumpkin pie, and there's some vanilla ice cream in the freezer to go with whatever pie you decide to eat."

"Can I have a piece of both kinds of pie?" he asked.

"If you eat all your dinner, then I think it'll be fine for you to have two pieces of pie," Mildred replied.

"If he gets two pieces, then I want two." Clayton spoke rapidly and in a bubbly tone. "And I promise to eat everything on my plate." He picked up a piece of turkey meat with his fingers and popped it into his mouth. "Yum. . .this is good."

"Don't talk with your mouth full, and you need to eat with your fork, not your fingers," Irma scolded. "Where are your manners, anyhow?" She was irritated with her son right now and had a hard time keeping her voice down.

Clayton's shoulders slumped and his chin lowered a bit. "Sorry, Mama."

Silence filled the room, and all eyes seemed to be on Irma as though they were waiting to see how she would respond. To hide her irritation, Irma forced a smile and said, "It's okay, Son, but please try to reminder the table manners I have taught you."

He bobbed his head and reached for his napkin to wipe his mouth. The conversation picked up at the table again with Paul talking about his favorite dessert.

Irma glanced at LaVern and noticed his furrowed brows as he looked in her direction. She swallowed hard. *Does he think I'm a terrible mother who finds fault with everything her children do?*

Irma's fingers clenched her glass as she took another drink of water. *Well, maybe I am—especially compared to his mother, who always speaks to the children so kindly. Doesn't my husband realize that it can't be all fun and games at home like it is when our kids come here? Mildred and Paul spoil our three children, and so do the great-grandparents. They give them whatever they want. At home, where I am their primary caregiver and disciplinarian, things aren't nearly so much fun. Is it any wonder they like coming here?*

She noticed that Paul had begun tickling Myra's toes again, making her giggle. *I'll bet if the children behaved here the way they do at home, it would no longer be all fun and games.*

Irma remained silent during the rest of the meal. She felt that she'd been judged and misunderstood by LaVern's parents and grandparents who had all looked at her so strangely. Well, they did not understand how things were for her. Apparently, LaVern didn't either.

———— ≈ ————

After the Thanksgiving meal was finished and they'd had dessert, LaVern's father suggested that they all gather in the living room for a time of devotions, which he'd said he would lead.

"I have no problem with that," LaVern said, "since this is your house, Dad. Besides, with you being a deacon in your church district, I'm sure you know your Bible quite well."

"We should all study the scriptures," Paul said. "That's how we draw closer to the Lord and find answers to our problems and direction for our lives."

Irma was glad that LaVern hadn't been chosen, at this point, to be a minister in their community, and she hoped he never would be called upon for that duty. It would only add more unnecessary pressure to her already hectic life. Trying to keep a clean house, not to mention having to be ready to answer the door to anyone needing to speak to LaVern for counseling, would be quite stressful. Also, she'd have to keep her children in line so they were never sassy in front of guests. Irma's thoughts paused for a moment, but then another thought came to mind. *If my husband was ever chosen by lots, then he'd have to spend what little time he's at home now reading the Bible and studying in order to preach and minister to his congregation.*

Irma's eyes flitted upward as she grabbed her water and headed into the other room with the family. There was no point worrying about this unless it actually happened.

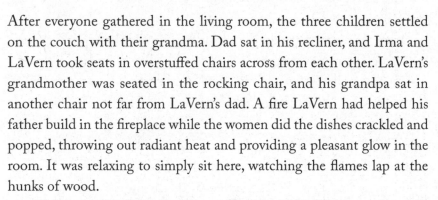

After everyone gathered in the living room, the three children settled on the couch with their grandma. Dad sat in his recliner, and Irma and LaVern took seats in overstuffed chairs across from each other. LaVern's grandmother was seated in the rocking chair, and his grandpa sat in another chair not far from LaVern's dad. A fire LaVern had helped his father build in the fireplace while the women did the dishes crackled and popped, throwing out radiant heat and providing a pleasant glow in the room. It was relaxing to simply sit here, watching the flames lap at the hunks of wood.

Dad opened his New King James Version of the Bible to a place he'd marked with a slip of paper and said, "Since today is Thanksgiving, I have chosen a few passages of scripture to read on the topic of thankfulness. The first passage is found in Psalm 95:2: 'Let us come before His presence with thanksgiving; let us shout joyfully to Him with psalms.'"

He sat quietly for a few seconds, and then turned in the Bible to another marked page. "Psalm 107:1 says: 'Oh, give thanks to the LORD, for He is good! For His mercy endures forever.'"

LaVern's mother nodded in agreement and then leaned over to kiss Myra's flushed cheek. The boys sat as though spellbound while Paul shared another verse.

" 'In everything give thanks; for this is the will of God in Christ Jesus for you.'" Dad paused, and his gaze seemed to focus on each one in the room as he slowly moved his head from left to right. "That verse was

1 Thessalonians 5:18." He leaned slightly forward in his chair. "There are times when giving thanks while we're in the midst of a trial can be difficult, but it is God's will for us to thank Him regardless of our circumstances, so we must strive to remember that." He stopped talking again, as though allowing time for his words to sink in. LaVern knew his children did not understand everything their grandfather had read. Even so, he realized that it was important for Brian, Clayton, and even Myra, to hear the reading of God's Word. As they got older, they would understand it better and hopefully put the scriptures they had heard into practice in their daily lives.

"I have one final passage to share with you," Dad said. "Psalm 100:4–5 says, 'Enter into His gates with thanksgiving, and into His courts with praise. Be thankful to Him, and bless His name. For the LORD is good; His mercy is everlasting, and His truth endures to all generations.'"

As his father gave a short explanation of what the last verse meant, LaVern glanced over at his wife. Her eyes were closed, and he wondered if she'd absorbed all that had been said. Or could Irma be so tired she'd fallen asleep? She certainly hadn't seemed like herself all evening. She hadn't eaten much or said more than a few words today, especially toward the latter part of their meal. Things had been going along fairly well until Irma scolded Clayton for eating with his fingers and talking with his mouth full. From that point on, she'd seemed reluctant to join the conversation at the table.

LaVern had noticed over the last few months that his wife had become quite edgy and had very little patience with the children. *But at least, as far as I know,* he thought, *she hasn't punished any of them out of anger again. If she had, I'm sure one of the kids would have told me about it.*

Chapter 31

St. Ignatius

When Dorcas awoke the following morning, she climbed out of the warm bed, grabbed her robe, and peered out the window. Since this side of the house faced the direction of the barn, she should be able to see Mose's RV if he hadn't left yet. Seeing no sign of it, she felt a bit disappointed. Although they'd said their goodbyes last night, she'd hoped Mose might come back to the house this morning and eat breakfast with them before he pulled out.

"Oh, well," she said aloud. "I guess we'll hear from him when he gets to wherever he's planning to go."

Dorcas hurried to get dressed, and when she arrived in the kitchen, she found Irvin standing near the sink with furrowed brows.

"Is something wrong?" she asked. "You look *verwart*."

"I am perplexed," he responded. "Aaron is missing."

She blinked rapidly. "Wh–what do you mean?"

"He's not here. When I knocked on his door to make sure he was awake, he didn't respond. So I went into his room, and he wasn't there."

"Maybe he got up before you did and went out to the barn to do his chores."

Irvin shook his head vigorously. "I checked there too, but there was no sign of him. I even looked in the buggy shed, the tool shed, the phone shed, and down in the cellar. My brother was not in any of those places."

"You don't suppose he headed for the mill without you?"

"He never goes in this early, and there would be no reason for him to go there ahead of me this morning."

"That makes no sense." Dorcas pinched the skin at her throat as it constricted. "Where did he go? Help me think of some other place your brother may have gone."

"I know exactly where Aaron went." Hannah entered the kitchen, wide-eyed and waving a piece of paper around. "Caroline and I found this note that Aaron wrote for Mama. It was lying on the table, and we noticed it when we came through the dining room." Hannah's voice deepened. "Caroline said I should be the one to give it to you because she couldn't. Then she started crying and ran into the bathroom." Hannah handed the piece of paper to Dorcas.

With trembling fingers Dorcas took the note and read it out loud. "Mama, I am sure you won't like this, but I'm heading out with Uncle Mose. As I said last night, I'm tired of working at the mill, and I need a little adventure. If Uncle Mose comes this way again, I may be with him, unless I decide to strike out on my own. I've never really had the chance to figure out what I want out of life, so this is my opportunity. Sorry for leaving you in the lurch at the mill. Hopefully, Irvin will find someone to take my place soon. With love, your son Aaron."

Dorcas felt a heaviness in her limbs. It was as if every muscle in her body had frozen. She opened her mouth to speak, but the only sound that came out was a little squeak.

"Mama, here. . . You need to sit down."

Dorcas was barely conscious of the chair Irvin had pulled out for her, and it was only with his help that she sat down. Even though Aaron had recently expressed his dislike for working at the lumber mill, she'd never expected that he would run off the very next day without discussing it with her and the rest of the family first. "Irvin, did you know about this?" Dorcas asked once she had found her voice.

"No. No, I didn't. If I had known, I would have tried to stop him from going." Irvin took a sharp breath as he lowered himself into a chair on the other side of the table. "It's going to be difficult to go into work this morning the way I'm feeling right now—especially when I was counting on my brother to help me in the mill. And you know that we've got plenty of orders to fill. Plus, Aaron helped by contributing his share of money to keep our family out of any trouble financially."

Hannah sat down beside Dorcas and patted her arm gently while slowly shaking her head. "Why would Uncle Mose have agreed to let Aaron go with him without talking to you about it first and making sure that you would be okay with Aaron leaving?"

"I don't know the answer to that question, Daughter. I'm just as confused and shocked by all of this as you are right now." Dorcas couldn't help feeling disappointed in Mose. What he'd done was just as wrong as Aaron taking off early this morning and leaving only a note. *They both should have talked to me about this*, she thought. *It was irresponsible and inconsiderate of Aaron to selfishly run off to do his own thing and leave Irvin here to try to run the lumber mill by himself. I must not have taught that boy anything about commitment to the family or his job.*

"I have to say—your uncle Mose is a free-spirited soul, particularly in the way he acts and thinks. Mose just hops into his RV and takes off any old time he gets the urge, going places he's interested in seeing whenever he chooses. Maybe Aaron was looking for an escape, and Uncle Mose granted him his wish." Dorcas sat for a moment after she'd spoken. "Maybe if Aaron spends some time away from home to explore, he might find out that he had it better here all along and will return to work in the mill with an appreciation for it that he didn't have before."

"Mama could be right," Hannah interjected. "Let's just hope and pray that Aaron does return home after seeing whatever it is he thinks he needs to see."

Although this conversation didn't solve the issue at hand, Dorcas figured it was food for thought. It didn't hurt for her to try to be hopeful for the future. Truth was, they all needed a good dose of hope at a time like this.

They sat quietly for several minutes, the only sound coming from the *tick-tock* of the battery-operated clock on the far wall.

Suddenly, Irvin stood up and started filling his lunch box with fruit and cookies.

"What are you doing, Son?" Dorcas asked. "There's no need for you to make your own lunch today. I can do that for you like I always do."

"No, Mama, that's okay. I don't have time to wait for a proper lunch to be made. I need to do my outside chores and head straight to the mill where I will sit down at Papa's old oak desk and try to figure out what to do about this situation."

"There's really nothing you can do," Hannah said. "Uncle Mose doesn't have a cell phone, and neither does Aaron, so we can't get ahold of them and tell our brother to come back home."

Irvin gave a quick shake of his head. "I'm not going to try to get in touch with Aaron—and I wouldn't, even if I could."

"How come?" Hannah questioned. "You need his help at the mill, so—"

"He's obviously made up his mind that he doesn't want to work there anymore, so even if he came back, his heart would not be in it, and it would show. The best thing I can do is figure out who I can count on the most, and then choose that man to take Aaron's second-in-command position." Irvin planted his feet in a wide stance, and leaned forward a bit. "I'll get the word out right away that I'm in need of someone to take my brother's place." Irvin thrust out his chin as he looked at Dorcas. "Don't you worry, Mama; this will all work out."

"I certainly hope so." Dorcas pinched her lips together. "None of us in this family needs one more thing to worry about."

Mount Hope

I'd really like to walk to the phone shed and check to see if there are any messages on the answering machine—preferably before eating our lunch. Irma opened the back door to call Clayton in, but she didn't see him playing in the backyard where he was supposed to be. What she did see, however, was a pile of rocks on the porch—and she would have tripped on them if she hadn't looked down. Irma poked her tongue against the inside of her cheek and inhaled a long breath. "Always trouble somewhere," she murmured. "When is that boy going to learn to do as he's told? And how many times must I tell him that rocks belong in the yard, not on the porch or in the house?"

Irma went back into the house and stopped in the living room to check on Myra, who sat on the floor with two of her dolls. The little girl looked up at Irma and grinned. Irma smiled in return and opened the front door. She blinked several times, trying to process what she saw. Clayton sat in the middle of the yard with a pile of rocks beside him. What shocked her the most, though, was watching him toss one stone after the other in random places on the grass.

Irma stepped off the porch and into the yard, being careful not to step on or trip over any of the rocks. "Young man, what do you think you're doing?"

Clayton leaped to his feet and whirled around to face her. "I was just tossing some rocks to see how far they'd go and where they would land."

"You are nothing but trouble, Clayton!" Irma tensed as her anger increased and heat flushed throughout her body, despite the chilly fall day. "That's a stupid thing to do, Clayton. And don't you know how dangerous it is to leave rocks on the porch? I almost tripped on them. Also, someone could get hurt if they walked across the grass and stepped on one of those stones you threw. Can you just imagine how hard it would be to mow the lawn with a bunch of rocks scattered all over in the grass? It could damage the lawnmower."

He lowered his chin. "Sorry, Mama, I didn't think—"

Irma clamped both hands firmly against her hips. "That's the trouble, Clayton—you don't think! You've got your head in the clouds most of the time, and whenever I tell you not to do something, you go ahead and do it anyway. I've told you so many times to quit fooling around with rocks, but here you are again, playing with the stupid things and putting them where they don't belong."

"Rocks ain't stupid, Mama. They're—"

"Do not interrupt me when I'm talking, young man!" Anger welled up even stronger in Irma, causing her muscles to quiver. She released one hand from her hip and shook her finger at Clayton. "You're a bad boy and deserve to be spanked. I should cut a switch right now!"

He flinched and took a few steps back. "S–sorry, Mama. I won't do it again, I promise."

"You'd better not or you will feel the sting of a switch on your bottom." Irma made a sweeping gesture of the yard and then grabbed hold of his arm. "Now get those rocks picked up and be quick about it. Put every one of them back in the dirt where you found them, and that includes the ones you left on the back porch. Do you understand?" She punctuated her last three words, hoping to get the message across.

Clayton was quick to nod.

"Lunch is ready, and it's on the table, but if you don't get the job done in the next half hour, there will be no lunch for you."

"But, Mama—"

"Don't argue with me, Son." With a shaky hand, Irma pointed. "You'd better get busy now; the clock is ticking." She whirled around and was almost to the house when she remembered that she hadn't gone to the phone shed yet. Irma would do that first, and afterward, she'd check on Clayton to make sure he had done what she asked.

A few minutes later, Irma stepped into the wooden shed and took a seat on the chair. The button on the answering machine blinked, so she pressed it to see what messages had come in.

"Hello, Irma, this is Doretta. I haven't heard from you in some time, so thought I'd give you a call and see how you are doing. I hope by now your morning sickness has passed and you're feeling better about your pregnancy. I've been praying for you and would like to hear from you again. I was sorry to learn that your stepfather had treated you so harshly when you were a girl. It would have been good if he'd gotten some counseling, but it's in the past now and I hope you're able to forgive him and move on with your life."

"Forgive him?" Irma pressed her palms against her hot cheeks. "No way can I ever forgive Homer Schmucker for the horrible way he treated me!"

Back in the house, Irma tried to calm herself as she put Myra in her high chair and cut up the child's peanut butter and jelly sandwich. It was bad enough that she'd had Clayton and his rocks to deal with, but then she'd had to listen to her friend's advice in the phone message. *Doretta doesn't have any idea of the pain Homer inflicted on me. If she'd had to live through something like that, I'm sure she would not be able to forgive the man either. She should have thought that one through before she lectured me. Just let her walk in my shoes for a while, and she might have some understanding of the way I feel.*

Irma placed Myra's sandwich on her tray and tried to concentrate on something other than Doretta's message, but her friend's words kept rolling through her head. *I should call or write her another letter and explain why it's impossible for me to forgive my stepfather and move on with my life.* Irma tapped her foot. *Homer's not the only one I'm angry with either. I'm just as angry with my mamm. Even if he was abusive to Mama, like Caroline said in her letter, she is still at fault for staying with him and subjecting both of us to Homer's wrath.* Irma gripped the back of a chair until her knuckles whitened.

Irma pulled in several deep breaths and was about to go back outside to check on Clayton's progress when he tromped into the kitchen with two rocks in his hands. "I did what you asked me to do, and now I need to find a place to put these pretty rocks while I eat my lunch."

Irma spoke through her teeth with forced restraint. "How many times have I told you, Clayton—rocks do not belong in the house?" She marched across the room, grabbed hold of his ear, and guided him firmly to the back door. "Outside with those rocks, right now, and there will be no lunch for you!"

Clayton let loose with an ear-piercing holler, and then Myra began to cry.

This isn't turning out well, Irma thought. *I'm handling the discipline in anger again. I told LaVern I wouldn't do that anymore, but I can't seem to help myself.* Irma's jaw ached from clenching her teeth. She'd had enough stress for one day, and it was all she could do not to scream. *If LaVern hears about this, he'll want to follow through with hiring someone to help me, and I still don't want anyone coming into my house. I have enough stress to deal with already.*

For some reason, one of the scripture verses her father-in-law had shared with them about being thankful popped into her head. *I am sure not feeling thankful today,* Irma thought. *If I can keep LaVern from finding out that I lost my temper again, then I'll be thankful.*

Chapter 32

A week later, when Brian came home from school, Irma waited for him on the front porch with hands on her hips and a determination not to lose control of her emotions. She watched as he trudged up the driveway through the snow that had come down this morning. "Why are you late?" she asked after he stepped onto the porch. "This is the second time this week that you haven't been home on time."

He gave a brief shrug and looked away.

Irma grabbed him by the shoulders and swiveled him around so that he faced her. "I need to know why you've come home late."

"Can't say," he mumbled without looking at her.

"Were you fooling around in the snow with some of your friends?"

He shook his head.

"So you won't tell me?" Irma's patience had already worn thin, and she needed some answers from Brian right now.

He folded his arms across his chest. "It ain't for you to know, Mama, and—"

"Not for me to know?" *Slap!* The palm of Irma's hand connected with her son's face so quickly, she barely knew it happened. But the telltale red mark was proof enough, in addition to the tears she saw in Brian's eyes. "I will not allow you to speak to me like that. Do you understand?"

"Jah." He sniffed and touched the place she had slapped. "How come you're always so mean? Daadi's never called me names or slapped my face."

"That's because your daddy's hardly ever here. If he was, he'd see what a brat you've become." Irma tried to calm herself by taking a few deep breaths, but it was no use. Her pounding heartbeat and the heat flushing through her body were proof of how angry she was. Brian had mouthed off to her and refused to say why he'd been late, so he deserved whatever punishment he got.

As she remained in place, Irma had a brief flashback of a time she had stood up to Homer. He'd been yelling at her for something she'd said or done, and she had looked right at him defiantly and said, "You're not my father, and I don't have to do what you say." Homer's face and neck had turned bright red, and he'd slapped Irma's face so hard that her head snapped back. She'd felt the sting of that slap for several days.

Irma had just crossed the line and entered into a bad place. . .back into Homer's abusive days. His abuse had stayed hidden from outsiders. No one knew that he had control over Irma, and she'd been too afraid to tell anyone.

I'm just as bad as my stepfather, and I've punished my son in anger. Why am I too proud to admit to LaVern that I need help? I can see that I've become abusive, and it's taking its toll on the children. Irma looked at Brian and swallowed hard. "I—I'm sorry, Son. I shouldn't have hit you like that, but I won't tolerate you talking back to me or refusing to answer my questions. Is that understood?"

"Jah, Mama."

"So why were you late getting home?"

"The teacher kept me and some other kid after school."

"Because you did something bad?"

He lowered his gaze. "I—I guess so."

"What did you and the other kid do that caused your teacher to make you stay late?" She lifted his chin so he was forced to look at her again.

"He was teasin' me and wouldn't let me play ball, so I grabbed the ball, gave it a fling, and it smacked him right in the stomach."

"You can't go around hitting people, with or without a ball," Irma scolded. "If they tease you, you need to ignore them or tell the teacher."

"Then the other kids will call me a *hambariyer schnellposcht.*"

"Better to be called a tattletale than to get in trouble with the teacher." Irma paused to get her thoughts in order. "I'm not going to tell your daed about any of this when he gets home this evening. If he knew how disrespectful you've been to me this afternoon, or heard about the reason you were held after school, he might punish you too." Irma put her hands on Brian's shoulders. "I need you to promise that you won't say anything to him about what happened here. Is that understood?"

He nodded. "Can I go in the house now?"

"Yes, you may, but there will be no snack for you today. I want you to go up to your room and change into your everyday clothes. After that, there's some wood for the fireplace that needs to be brought inside. I expect you to do it without complaint."

Irma saw clearly how sad her son was and how he seemed to avoid eye contact with her. She felt bad. Her insides trembled from the awful way she'd treated Brian. Reflecting on the apology she'd given her son, it was definitely a flimsy one. *"I'm sorry, Son I shouldn't have hit you like that but. . ."* That wasn't a good enough apology, she told herself. *I should've apologized and hugged him.* Tears formed in her eyes and she wiped them with the corner of her apron. Irma looked out toward the front yard and the road beyond. *Wow! I slapped my son right out here in front of the house. What if someone witnessed my actions?*

Her thoughts flitted to the task she'd given her son to do, and she expected it done without complaint. She looked down at Brian and was going to say something, but he turned and raced into the house. Irma followed. *I sure hope Brian doesn't say anything to his father about the hard slap I gave him. What if there's still a mark on his face later on today? If LaVern knew what happened, he might accuse me of child abuse, which I guess would be true,* she mentally added.

St. Ignatius

"How did things go at the lumber mill today?" Dorcas asked when Irvin entered the kitchen with his lips pressed tightly together.

"Not good. Everyone's complaining about the cold, snowy weather we're having, and none of the fellows I've got working for me wants to take Aaron's position." Irvin went to the sink and washed his hands, then ambled across the room and sank into a chair at the table with a groan. "I'm beginning to wish it was me who had taken off with Uncle Mose to find warmer weather in the south."

"Would it help if we could get our hands on a woodstove for the mill?" Dorcas questioned.

"Jah, that could help take some of the edge off with the frigid cold we are dealing with right now. I'm sure the men would use it to warm themselves as they try to work. But purchasing a stove would be an extra expense we can't afford right now."

"That's true, but if the source of heat we're talking about could ease the complaining of the employees, then it would be easier to keep them around."

Irvin shook his head. "Even so, it doesn't lessen the workload. Honestly, Mama, I had no idea how difficult things could get at the mill without Aaron."

Dorcas winced. It appeared that Irvin no longer enjoyed working at the mill, which caused her to wonder if she should have sold the business after all. If she'd chosen to do that, both of her sons might have found different jobs and could be a lot happier. Now, Aaron was gone and Irvin was stuck running things at the mill by himself.

"Have you heard anything from Uncle Mose or Aaron?" Irvin asked after Dorcas handed him a glass of cold apple cider.

She shook her head. "It's been a week since they left, and it's hard not to worry when we don't know where they are or if they've had any problems along the way."

Irvin drank the liquid in his glass and set it on the table. "I hate to say this, but I have a feeling in my gut that Aaron may never come home."

"What makes you think that?"

"He might end up going English, like Uncle Mose did, and only show up here for short visits whenever he feels like it."

Dorcas' heart felt like it had dropped all the way to her toes. "I hope that doesn't turn out to be the case. It saddens me to even think about such a thing."

"I don't like the idea, either, Mama, but we need to face facts. Irma left home, and she probably never would have come back at all if it hadn't been for the obligation she felt to attend Papa's funeral." Irvin flexed his fingers a few times and reached up to rub the back of his neck. "Since Irma disliked Papa so much, I was surprised when she and her husband showed up."

"I was too, but I was happy to see her and know that she was all right." Dorcas didn't want to enter into a self-made pity party, but thinking about her daughter, who didn't want to hear what she had to say, was a bitter pill to swallow. Whenever Dorcas thought about it, she ended up feeling sorry for herself. Well, she wouldn't carry it any further today. She grabbed a fork from the silverware drawer and took her frustrations out on the potatoes that would soon go into the oven to bake. She gave each one of them several pokes. *If Aaron would just contact us, I would feel a whole lot better.*

Myrtle Beach, South Carolina

Aaron stepped out of his uncle's RV and lifted his face toward the sun. "Oh, boy. . .this sure feels good. Beats dealing with the cold weather in Montana, don't you think?" He turned to look at his uncle, who stood beside him.

"Yep. The sun does feel mighty nice. Speaking of Montana, what'd you say in your message when you called home to let your mom and the family know that you're okay?"

Aaron averted his gaze, focusing instead on the beautiful body of water stretching out in front of them. The truth was, he had not called home even once. He was afraid one of his siblings, or even his mother, might be in or near the phone shed when the telephone rang and would answer it. The last thing Aaron wanted was a stern lecture from anyone in the family about him leaving home. He had told his uncle that his mother had given her permission for him to leave with him the morning after Thanksgiving. If Uncle Mose knew otherwise, he'd probably be upset and might even take Aaron right back to St. Ignatius.

I'm done with that place, Aaron told himself. *I shouldn't have to work all the time at a job I don't like, and I deserve to venture out and have some fun for a change.*

Uncle Mose nudged Aaron's arm. "Did you hear my question?"

"Uh. . .yeah. . .sorry. Guess I was too caught up in this wonderful place to form a response."

"So, did you call home or not? And if so, what did you say?"

"Yep, sure did. Left a message saying I was fine and that we were heading to South Carolina."

"Good boy. I'm sure your mamm and the others were relieved to hear that. Sure wouldn't want them to worry about you, right?"

Aaron nodded, then turned his head as a sense of guilt crept in. He pushed it aside, focusing on the rays of sun beating down on his head. *This is the life,* he thought. *My uncle has it made being able to travel from state to state with no cares in the world and no one to answer to.*

Uncle Mose took off his shoes and instructed Aaron to do the same. "Come on, boy, let's go out there on the sand and frolic on the beach for a while!"

Aaron didn't hesitate to do as his uncle said, and he didn't even care that he'd been called a boy. It was so good to be here right now, feeling contented and free.

Grabill

"Did you get today's mail?" Warren asked when he entered the living room where Doretta sat nursing the baby.

She shook her head. "William's been fussy most of the day, and I've spent a good deal of time trying to quiet him."

"Is he *grank*?"

"No, I don't think he's sick, but the poor little guy could be teething."

"Already? I thought most babies didn't cut their first tooth until they were several months old."

"That might be the case for some babies, but every child is different. My mamm was here for a while today, and she said I cut my first tooth before I was two months old."

"Oh, I see." Warren leaned over and kissed Doretta's cheek. Then he stroked the baby's forehead with his index finger. "He seems to have a good appetite."

"He does, but when he's not nursing, he cries a lot."

"No naps then—for you or him?"

"He has slept some today, but not as long as usual."

"And you? Did you manage to get any rest?" Warren's thick eyebrows drew together. "I can't help but worry about you and our son. You are both so precious to me."

"We're fine. I'm sure this is just a passing phase. I do appreciate your concern, however." She smiled up at him. "And I love you very much."

"I love you too, Doretta—with all my heart." Warren went over to his favorite chair, and she assumed he was about to take a seat, but then he stood to his full height and said, "Think I'll go out right now and check the mail. Maybe by the time I get back, William will be done eating and I can hold him for a while."

"That would be nice. I appreciate your thoughtfulness."

"Okay, then. . . I'll return soon."

Doretta had finished nursing her son and burping the baby when Warren returned to the house with a handful of mail. "Anything interesting?" she asked.

"Well, let's see. . ." He took a seat and thumbed through the mail. "Here's one for you, from Irma. Why don't you go ahead and read it and let me hold William?"

"Sounds like a plan." Doretta got up and handed the baby to her husband, and when he gave her Irma's letter, she moved back to her chair and opened it, eager to see what her friend had to say.

> *Dear Doretta,*
>
> *I listened to your phone message last week and decided it was time to write you another letter. I'm still having trouble dealing with my kinner, and I often lose my temper with them. It's gotten so bad here of late that I'm frightened and unsure of what to do.*
>
> *I don't understand what is wrong with me and why I can't control my temper or hold my tongue when I'm disciplining the children. Sometimes I feel like there's another person inside of me, prompting me to lash out in anger and say mean things to Clayton, Brian, and even little Myra. I hated my stepfather for all the terrible things he did to me, and now I feel that if I can't control my anger, I might end up just like him.*
>
> *Would you please continue to pray for me, Doretta? And if you have any words of wisdom concerning how I can keep a clear head and remain calm when the kids misbehave, I'd*

like to hear them. I don't seem to have the strength to make a change for the better on my own.

As Always,
Irma

Doretta's eyes teared up, blurring her vision, and she placed Irma's letter in her lap. She bowed her head and prayed silently, *Heavenly Father, my friend Irma is dealing with anger issues and uncontrolled emotions when she disciplines her children. Please, Lord, give me the right words to share with Irma when I write to her again that will point my dear friend in the right direction to where she can find the kind of help she needs.*

Chapter 33

A week later, Irma found a letter from Doretta in her mailbox. She hoped her friend hadn't been shocked when she'd received her last letter, admitting that she had mistreated her children. Irma was eager to read Doretta's response, hoping that she may have offered some sound advice.

A chilly wind whipped through the trees as Irma made her way back to the house, holding tightly to the mail while avoiding puddles of melted snow. Irma had waited to get the mail until after she'd put Myra down for an afternoon nap and made sure that Clayton was playing quietly in his room. It was the sensible thing to do since Clayton had pestered his sister all morning and would no doubt continue his teasing if the two of them were left in the same room without supervision.

Irma thought about last week's incident with Brian—how she had slapped his face. As far as she knew, LaVern had no clue about the matter. She felt confident that her son hadn't said anything about the harsh treatment he'd received from her. Whenever Irma's anger spilled out, it left her feeling emotionally and physically drained, which wasn't good for her or the child she carried in her womb. In addition to that, her conscience bothered her, and she felt like a failure as a mother.

Irma rubbed her belly. *This isn't the best environment to bring another child into, but how can I control my anger? And why is this happening to me now? I never used to be like this. Although I've always been somewhat impatient with the children, I never felt so out of control as I do now. Could my hormones be causing this? Or does it have something to do with the feelings that got stirred up in me by attending Homer's funeral?*

Irma heaved a sigh. Yesterday, she'd disciplined Brian again—this time for letting Buster in the house without her permission, which resulted in dog hair on the couch and a ruined sofa pillow that the mutt had nearly torn to shreds. Irma had been so upset, she thought she might explode. Needless to say, the dog had been put outside, and Brian had been instructed to clean up the mess. Instead of giving him a good hard spanking, which had been Irma's first option, she'd changed her mind and sent him to his room—but not before calling her son brainless, irresponsible, and a bother. She'd ended her tirade by asking, "Why can't you be like other kids who don't cause so much trouble and are well behaved?" Then when she had been unable to control her tongue, Irma had shouted, "At a time like this, I wish I'd never had any children!"

With each passing day, Irma struggled to hold her temper; and when she dealt harshly with the children, her cruel words and lack of patience seemed to bounce off the walls of their home. The children's personalities seemed to be changing too. They were quieter and held back their affection from her. She couldn't really blame them, but it hurt nonetheless. The dislike Irma had felt toward her stepfather seemed to be growing like mold in a basement, and the hope she'd once had of putting it all behind her seemed to be an impossible task. Irma's goal was to not hit any of her children, even when angry, but how long could she keep it up?

Feeling weighed down with defeat, Irma stepped onto the porch and went inside. She stood in the hall for several seconds, listening for any sounds that might be coming from the children's rooms. All was quiet, and since Brian wouldn't be home from school for another hour, Irma figured this was a good time to read Doretta's letter.

Irma took the mail to the kitchen and placed it on the table. After removing her outer garments, she fixed a cup of herbal tea and took a seat.

Irma glanced through the rest of the mail. Seeing nothing of interest, she set it aside and opened her friend's letter.

Dear Irma,

I received your last letter and am sorry to hear about the things you're going through right now. I will definitely be praying for you. Since you asked if I had any advice, I feel free to make a few comments which I hope might be helpful to you.

A few weeks ago, our bishop preached a sermon on the topic of anger, and he mentioned several verses in the Bible that talk about that subject. One of them is Proverbs 15:1. "A soft answer turns away wrath, but a harsh word stirs up anger." Speaking to your children or punishing them when you are angry could stir up anger in them as well.

Irma, if you haven't been able to bring your anger under control, have you considered seeking help from one of the ministers in your church or going to see a Christian counselor? Sometimes it helps to talk about our problems with someone who will understand and not judge. You may need to deal with the anger you feel toward your stepfather and your mother before you can put out the fire of anger you feel toward your children when they disobey or do something that displeases you. There is hope in the Bible, Irma, and if you are willing to talk about your situation with someone who is trained to counsel, I feel sure that you can get better.

Please remember that I'm here for you anytime you want to call or write. I hope you will keep in touch, dear friend, and remember—I am here for you and want to help in any way I can.

Love & Prayers,
Doretta

Irma closed her eyes while rubbing the middle of her forehead as she tried to pinpoint the source of her discomfort and annoyance with the things her friend had said. Irma knew Doretta felt compassion for her and wanted to help. Trouble was, Irma did not feel comfortable talking about her problems with any of the church ministers or even a counselor outside of their church district. There ought to be some way she could get on top of the anger she felt without opening up her life like a book to read and probably end up being judged for her misdeeds. For now, at least, Irma would continue to reach deep inside herself in an effort to control her anger and swirling emotions. If she could conjure up enough determination, maybe she could manage without any outside help. It made her feel good, however, to know that Doretta had been praying for her and would continue to do so, because these days, Irma couldn't find the words to pray for herself.

Irma's thoughts were whisked away when Clayton came into the kitchen asking for a snack and, like a little shadow, Myra toddled in behind him.

"I'll give you both a couple of cookies and some goat's milk," Irma said. "But nothing else until supper. Understood?"

Clayton bobbed his head and his copycat sister followed suit.

Irma lifted Myra into her high chair, and Clayton took a seat at the table. After Irma had given them both their milk and peanut butter cookies, she tucked Doretta's letter away in a cubby at the back of the desk where LaVern would not be apt to find it. She certainly did not need him reading Doretta's letter and learning about the things she'd shared with her friend. Irma figured if LaVern knew she was still having a problem with anger management, he'd put his foot down and get her some help.

Once Irma was satisfied that the letter was in a safe place, she put the rest of the mail on the counter so LaVern could go through it when he got home. *Whatever time that will be,* she thought. *With his crazy schedule, I never know when to expect him.* LaVern's up-in-the-air schedule, dealing with the children, and her pregnancy kept Irma in a state of stress. If only she and LaVern could get away by themselves for a few days, she might feel better. Even Buster's barking got on Irma's nerves, and she was glad that he wasn't normally in the house or under foot. Irma's longing to get away seemed to be the only remedy she thought would help, and it would be easier for her than doing what Doretta had suggested.

Irma glanced at the kitchen clock. She figured she may as well start working on supper, so she took a roast from the refrigerator. It had helped that, the day before, she'd written herself a note to remind her to thaw the meat. With the brain fog she dealt with so often, it seemed best to write down the meal plan a day or so ahead.

Irma placed the beef in a roasting pan with some broth, and put it in the oven at 375 degrees. In another hour or so, she would add some potatoes, carrots, and onions and then put the lid on to cook until everything was nice and tender. It would be a filling but simple meal, and the only other thing she would need to do was put a few condiments on the table.

She glanced down at her protruding stomach. Just another thirteen weeks until her due date. . .if the baby came on time. It would be nice to get her figure back and lose that top-heavy feeling. However, the thought of having one more child to care for seemed overwhelming to Irma. One thing was for sure: with four children's needs to tend to, she would need some help after the baby was born. But she didn't know who she could trust to come into the house and not take over.

Maybe I could send Clayton and Myra over to their grandparent's house, which would leave me with only the baby to look after during most of the weekdays. Brian wouldn't be out of school for the summer until the latter part of May, but at least he wouldn't be at home for a good chunk of the day, which would help. And maybe, without his younger siblings around, he would behave better and not be so mouthy. When Irma's due date drew closer, she would ask LaVern's parents about keeping Myra and Clayton for a few weeks after the baby came. *I'm sure I can manage by myself until LaVern gets home each day,* Irma determined. *It really shouldn't be too hard if I set my mind to it.*

———— ≋ ————

St. Ignatius

When Dorcas went to the mailbox, she was pleased to discover a postcard from Aaron. Although she would have preferred that he'd called to let his family know where he was and how he and Mose were doing, at least she had finally heard from her son.

Dorcas remained near the mailbox and read Aaron's message:

> Uncle Mose and I are both fine. We're currently in Myrtle Beach, South Carolina. It's warm and sunny here, and we're enjoying the weather. Hope everyone there is okay. I'll write again when we move on to the next place.
>
> —Aaron

Tears welled behind Dorcas' eyes, threatening to spill over. On the one hand, she felt relief, knowing her son was all right. On the other hand, she couldn't help but be concerned. She still couldn't believe Mose had taken her son without discussing it with her, and she feared she might never see Aaron again. Dorcas had been foolish enough to think she could trust Mose, but he had certainly pulled the wool over her eyes.

Dorcas clutched her arms tightly to her chest and trudged wearily up the driveway and back to the house. *If only I'd gotten up sooner that morning, I could have tried to stop Aaron from leaving.*

The warm air that greeted Dorcas when she entered the house did nothing to dispel the chill she felt throughout her body. She'd been praying ever so hard for her son's return, but from the sound of Aaron's note, it didn't look like he'd be coming back home anytime soon—if at all.

She stood like a statue inside the front door, rubbing her forehead.

"You're shivering, Mama. What's wrong?" Caroline asked when she came out of the kitchen. "Are you *kalt* from being outside?"

Dorcas shook her head. "It's not the cold weather that has me shaking. There was a postcard from Aaron in the mailbox, and I'm feeling a bit shook up." Dorcas handed the card to her daughter.

Caroline stood silently reading Aaron's message, then her mouth slackened. "I'm glad we heard from him, Mama, but I think it's possible that we'll never see Aaron again."

Dorcas swept a shaky hand across her forehead. "Those are my thoughts exactly. The thing that upsets me the most, though, is that there's absolutely nothing we can do about it."

Caroline clasped Dorcas' arms. "We can pray."

"Jah, and that I shall continue to do."

———— ≈ ————

Mount Hope

Soon after LaVern entered the house, he spotted Irma lying on the couch with her eyes closed and hands lying on her belly. Assuming she was asleep, and not wanting to wake her, he slipped quietly out of the room.

LaVern's first stop was the kitchen, where he put his lunch pail away, grabbed a few cookies from the jar on the counter, and poured himself a glass of apple cider. The house seemed strangely quiet, and he wondered where the kids could be. Normally, when LaVern came home from work, at least one of them greeted him at the door, but that was not the case today. He hadn't seen any of the children outside either, which made sense since the weather was so cold and nasty with a yard full of melted snow.

I wonder if they're upstairs in their rooms, playing quietly. Now that would be an unexpected surprise. LaVern couldn't help but smile. Except for nighttime, when the kids were all asleep, their house was rarely this quiet.

Enjoying the moment of peace, which he figured could end at any time, LaVern ate the cookies and finished his cider. He spotted the mail on the counter and went over to check it out. Nothing exciting—just one bill and a few catalogs advertising things they didn't need. LaVern took the bill into the room he used for his home office. Then, thinking he ought to check on the kids and see what they were up to, he left the room and climbed the stairs. LaVern paused at the top and listened but didn't hear a single sound from any of their rooms. Surely they couldn't all be taking a nap. Brian was way beyond napping, and Clayton only took naps on rare occasions, after playing too hard or when he didn't feel well. Myra would be the only who might be sleeping, so he headed for her room first. When Myra was just a baby, her bedroom had been downstairs, next to his and Irma's room. But with a new baby coming in a few months, they had moved Myra upstairs last week, and she'd seemed quite happy about it.

LaVern opened the door and was surprised to see her little feet sticking out from under the bed. As he knelt down, he heard his daughter's pathetic whimpers. "Myra, what's wrong? Come out here and tell Daadi why you're under the bed." He spoke Pennsylvania Dutch to his daughter.

When Myra didn't budge, he reached under the bed and gently pulled her out. The whimpers turned to sobs, and after LaVern lifted the child into his arms and stood, she clung tightly to his neck. He asked again what was wrong, but that seemed to make her cry even more. He checked his daughter over, and saw no signs of any cuts, scrapes or bruises on her face, arms, or legs. LaVern could only assume that one of her brothers may have been teasing Myra or taken her favorite toy. *I will need to get to the bottom of this*, LaVern told himself. *But first, I have to get my daughter calmed down.*

Chapter 34

LaVern managed to settle Myra down and took her with him to Clayton's room. He found the boy sniffling and lying face down on the bed.

"What's wrong, Son?" LaVern asked after he'd put Myra at the end of the bed.

A few seconds passed, and then Clayton rolled over onto his side. "Mama came in Myra's room and got really mad at me and Brian 'cause we were teasing Myra about her doll. And then our mamm started hollering real loud, saying she didn't know what she'd done to deserve two bratty boys. Myra got scared, and she started crying real loud and crawled under her bed. After that, Mama told me and Brian to go to our rooms and expect to get punished."

"Did you do as she asked?"

"Sure did. I ran to my room and hid in my closet, hoping Mama wouldn't find me there." Clayton sniffed and swiped a hand across his tear-stained face. "But she did, and I knew when she grabbed hold of my hair and yanked me out of there that she was really mad. Then I saw a big ole' wooden spoon in her hand, and I knew for sure that I was gonna get it. I told her I was sorry for teasing Myra, and that I'd never do it again, but Mama's face was red as a radish, and she didn't listen to me."

"What did your mamm do?"

She shouted at me and said I should lie across the bed."

"Did you do it?"

Clayton sniffed again, and a few tears leaked out of his eyes and dribbled down his cheeks. "Jah. I was scared not to and hoped she wouldn't spank me too hard." He paused again and his chin quivered. "Then she started hitting my backside real hard, and I kept begging her to stop and saying I was sorry and that I'd be a good boy from now on."

LaVern's gut tightened as he gasped. Obviously, Irma had not been able to keep her promise about not punishing when she was angry. His wife's abuse of the children had caused them to fear her. It had also put a strain on his and Irma's marriage—especially where truth and trust were concerned. *My wife has clearly overstepped her authority with the children, and I've got to try to help them through this.*

LaVern still couldn't believe Irma had said she didn't need any help around the house or with the children. She had even added reassurance that she wouldn't punish them anymore when she was angry. *Yet, she did it again.* He shook his head. *I wanted to believe she was being honest with me, but it's clear that my wife is unable to control the manner in which she is disciplining our children. Irma has to see that she's being harsh with them, but it doesn't seem to change her behavior. Apparently, she is not able to keep her emotions in check.*

LaVern sat on the bed beside Clayton and pulled the boy into his arms. "What happened after the spanking was over? Did your mamm say she was sorry and let you know that she loved you?"

"No, Daadi. She said she wished she'd never had any kinner, and then she ran out of my room, screaming, 'Brian Miller. . .you're next!'" Clayton sniffed a few more times and wiped his eyes. "I'm scared of Mama. I don't think she loves us no more neither."

This feels like a nightmare, and I wish I could wake up from it. My children are going through a lot right now. If only Brian, Clayton, and Myra could have a childhood like I had, full of security, love, and a well-grounded upbringing from both Christian parents.

LaVern felt the burn of bile at the back of his throat, but he swallowed it down so he could form a proper response. "Yes, she does love you, Clayton. Your mamm just needs some help for her problems right now." He gestured to Myra, still sitting on the end of Clayton's bed with shimmering tears in her eyes. "Will you please hold your sister's hand and sit here quietly with her while I go to Brian's room and talk to him?"

"Jah, Daadi." Clayton crawled to the end of the bed on his knees and clasped his sister's hand. "I didn't mean to upset Mama. Me and Brian were just having a little fun when we teased Myra about that doll she has with no hair."

"We'll talk about that later, Son." LaVern patted the boy's shoulder and reached out to stroke Myra's cheek, then he rose from the bed and headed for his other son's room. He could only imagine what Brian would have to say.

When LaVern entered Brian's bedroom, he found the boy pacing back and forth at the foot of his bed. Brian's nostrils flared and his breathing had become quite noisy. When he looked at LaVern, there was no sign of tears—just a tightness around his squinted eyes. His lips were pressed together. LaVern knew right away that the boy was angry.

"I just left your brother's room, and I was in Myra's bedroom before that. Clayton is quite upset and said your mother yelled at him and then spanked him real hard." LaVern moved closer to Brian. "Did she do the same thing to you?"

"Jah. She was real mad and hit me many times with that big wooden spoon."

"Did you apologize for teasing your sister?"

"Never had a chance. Mama started whacking on me before I could open my mouth." Brian folded his arms, staring straight ahead. "I can't do nothin' right no more. Mama calls me names all the time, and she makes me wish I'd never been born." He reached around and flinched when he touched his backside. "What's wrong with me, Daadi? How come Mama doesn't love me anymore?"

"I am sure she loves you, Son." LaVern put his hand on Brian's shoulder and gave it a little squeeze. "Your mamm is going through some problems right now, and—"

"She's been yelling a lot and hurting me and Clayton's feelings ever since the two of you got back from Montana."

"I'm real sorry about that." LaVern felt like he'd been stabbed with a knife. It hurt to see the somber expression on his son's face and hear him talking in such a way. He'd seen it on Clayton's face too, but that look was more sadness than the anger Brian exuded. LaVern knew that if he didn't do something about this problem right away, it would only get worse. It was time to go downstairs and confront his wife.

When Irma woke up, her head pounded something awful, and her eyes burned from the tears she'd shed before dozing off after she'd come downstairs to calm down after punishing the boys while she was angry. She didn't know why she'd been unable to control her anger, but she had lost her temper again, and now she needed to go upstairs and tell the children she was sorry. Hopefully, they would keep the incident that had occurred to themselves and not tell their dad. Irma wondered if she should've made them promise not to say anything. After all, she'd gotten away with it the last time when she'd told Brain not to tell his dad about the hard slap she had given him. The fact was this awful secrecy was only scaring her children deeper. And it wasn't helping Irma to end this vicious cycle. Irma lived in fear of being caught, and conjuring up scenarios became second nature to her. If LaVern had any idea what had happened here this afternoon, he might do something drastic like try to take the children from her. *Would he insist that I leave this house?* Irma wondered. *Or would my husband take the children to his parents' home and refuse to let me see them again?*

Irma dried her eyes and gulped in a few quick breaths, then sat up from the couch. She had to make sure all three kids were calmed down before LaVern got home. She couldn't let him know what she had said and done to the boys. Her husband would be very upset and lecture her again about punishing the children when she was angry. Irma had broken her promise to LaVern, and he would no doubt remind her of it.

Irma was almost to the stairway, when she heard footsteps. She looked up and saw LaVern coming down. Her mouth went dry. *If only my nap had ended sooner. Then I could have rushed upstairs and tried to make things right with the kinner before LaVern arrived home.*

Irma turned aside and rushed back to the living room. LaVern had obviously come home while she was asleep, and he'd clearly been upstairs. From the grim expression she'd seen on her husband's face, Irma felt sure that the children had told him everything that had taken place.

LaVern entered the living room and pointed to the couch. "Please sit down, Irma. We need to talk."

She sank to the couch and sat with her head lowered and hands clasped around her knees. "I know what you're thinking, but *kann ich dir des auslege?*"

LaVern took a seat beside Irma and asked her to look at him. "Explain it to me if you must, but I already know that you lashed out at the children and harshly punished the boys in anger." He paused, and a muscle on the side of his neck quivered. "I found our daughter hiding under her bed, whimpering and too scared to come out when I asked her to."

Irma felt her defenses go up as a flush of heat rushed to her cheeks. "Clayton and Brian were teasing their sister again, even after all the times I've asked them not to. Those boys are getting harder to handle, and I had to do something to let them know who's in charge."

"I understand that, and teasing their sister was wrong, but that does not excuse you from losing your temper and spanking the boys while you were angry. Not only that, but it's my understanding that you have done this kind of thing before, in addition to saying mean and hurtful things to the children."

"Did they tell you that?"

He nodded. "They're scared of you, Irma, and they feel like you don't love them anymore."

"That's not true." She shook her head vigorously. "I love my kinner and always have. I just. . ." Unable to finish her sentence, she heaved a heavy sigh and lowered her gaze. "I'm no better than my stepfather, and I hate myself for it. I don't want to lose my temper with the children, but I can't seem to help myself." She put both hands against her chest and swallowed against the pain she felt at the back of her throat. "I—I feel like a horrible mother. I can't do anything right anymore, and I don't know why."

"I can see you are emotionally distraught," he said. "One minute, you defend and even justify your abusive handling of the children's punishment, and the next minute you say you feel like a horrible mother." He looked at Irma with a grave expression. "This matter is way bigger than I'd thought. I had hoped you would be able to work things out for yourself, but I was wrong. I can't trust you not to lose your temper with the children, Irma."

Tears welled in Irma's eyes. The kids were afraid of her, and she'd lost her husband's trust. Irma would need to get her life in order to earn back LaVern's trust—and her children's too. The problem was, she didn't know how.

LaVern lifted her chin, which forced Irma to look at him. "Brian thinks you've been different since we came home from Montana. Could this anger you feel have something to do with the bitter feelings and resentment you have for Homer and, perhaps, your mother?"

"I—I don't know. . . . Well, maybe." She swiped at the hot tears that had dripped onto her cheeks. "I had truly thought that after going to Homer's funeral and seeing his body laid to rest, I would be able to put all thoughts of him aside and feel a sense of peace about myself and my life as your wife and the children's mother."

Irma was surprised when LaVern took hold of her hand. "But that hasn't happened, has it? You still feel anger toward your stepfather, don't you?"

"Jah."

"Do you know why?"

"Because he treated me so terribly." Irma's fingers clenched until her knuckles whitened. "I'm angry at my mamm too, because she never did a single thing to stop it."

"She apologized for that, didn't she?"

Irma slowly nodded.

"Have you accepted her apology?"

"No, and even when Caroline wrote me a letter saying that Mama had also been abused by Homer, I didn't forgive her because I was still angry."

"You know what I think, Irma?" LaVern spoke in a soothing tone.

"What?"

"If you can come to the point where you are able to forgive your mother and stepfather, you'll be able to forgive yourself."

She shook her head. "I don't think I can do that. I still have nightmares about all the terrible things Homer did to me. Sometimes during the day I think about them too. When I have flashbacks, it feels as though it's happening to me all over again."

"Dealing with pain from the past takes time, and sometimes a person needs help in learning how to do that and being able to come to the point where they can forgive freely."

She tipped her head. "What are you saying?"

"You need help, Irma. You need to speak with one of our church ministers or a Christian counselor—someone who is trained and has experience in dealing with the kind of emotional pain you have dealt with for so many years. You may have been able to push the pain you've felt to the back of your mind and squelch your deep-seated feelings during the early part of our marriage, but it's caught up with you now, and you are not able to do that anymore."

"And if I refuse to see someone about my problem?"

"Then I will have no choice but to find someone who'd be willing to come into this house during the hours I'm not here to look after the children." He clasped her fingers tightly in his strong hands and spoke in a firm, but caring voice. "I love you, Irma, and so do our children. They're confused and frightened right now, but things can get better if you agree to go for help." LaVern looked directly at her. "Are you willing to do that?"

Although not happy about it, Irma felt that she had no choice. She loved LaVern and her children and did not want to lose them. "Okay, I'll agree to seek help with a counselor. Maybe one of our ministers knows of a good one who is a Christian."

LaVern smiled. "I'm glad to hear it. This is an important decision, and I'm sure you will not regret it."

"So now that it's all decided, can you please forget about getting someone to come into the house to watch the children when you can't be here?"

He shook his head. "It's either that, or I will ask my parents to take them until things are better with you."

Irma's heart clenched. She couldn't imagine not having the children living here in this house with her and LaVern. She heaved a lingering sigh. "Okay. See who you can find to come in during the daytime to help out and take care of the kinner. If I'm going for counseling, I won't be able to take the children to my appointments, so I would need to have someone here to watch them anyhow."

LaVern leaned forward and kissed her forehead. "You're making the right decision, and I'm sure you won't regret it."

"I hope so," Irma murmured. *But what if I can't be helped? Maybe I'll never get my anger under control or be able to forgive Mama and Homer. Then what? Will I lose my husband and children? And what if whoever LaVern gets to come here to help me and watch the children thinks I'm a terrible person and spreads gossip about me?*

Chapter 35

Millersburg, Ohio

A wave of nausea hit Irma with the force of a strong wind as she entered the counselor's office for the first time and took a seat. She knew without question that the sick feeling in her belly had nothing to do with her pregnancy. It had been brought on by her apprehension about baring her soul to a complete stranger who had been trained to counsel people like her, but Irma knew it was necessary.

The counselor's office held plaques on the wall, stating her credentials, and family photos as well. The furniture looked impressive, and the chair Irma sat in was quite comfortable.

Irma thought about her mother for a moment and wondered what her thoughts would be about all of this. *Would Mama think this was a good idea? And if she did, maybe it would be wise for her to seek some counseling too.*

Irma looked over at the digital clock nearby. She'd arrived early and had been waiting for a while. The curtains were partially open, letting in natural light but keeping distractions from the outside world away. *I hope the counselor can help me. I need to be a good mother and be able to raise my children with love and stability. I don't want any of them to fear me.*

"What brings you to my office today, Irma?" the middle-aged woman who introduced herself as Mrs. Mayes questioned.

"I'm a child abuser, just like my stepfather." Irma could hardly believe she'd blurted those words out so easily. "My children are scared of me, and my husband won't allow me to be in the house with them unless another adult is there." Irma drew in several deeps breaths, hoping it would calm her nerves and settle her stomach.

"Do you know why you have been abusive to your children?" Mrs. Mayes asked after she'd seated herself behind her desk.

Irma shrugged. "My husband thinks it's because I'm angry at my stepfather and won't forgive him even though he's dead and can't hurt me anymore."

Mrs. Mayes leaned forward with both hands on her desk. "Do you agree with your husband?"

Irma's lips pressed together in a tight grimace as she gave a brief nod.

"Here's something you might not be aware of, Irma. It's not unusual for a person who has been abused to follow in their parents' footsteps and abuse their own children. It can easily become a cycle, passed from one generation to the next."

Irma stiffened. "Homer was not my real dad. My biological father died when I was seven."

"That doesn't matter," the counselor said. "You spent most of your childhood under the influence of your stepfather, and though you feared and perhaps even hated him, the bad example he set probably stemmed from the way he was raised."

"Are you saying that Homer's mother or father abused him?"

"Quite possibly."

Irma drew in another quick breath and released it slowly as she tried to process what the counselor had said. "So you think that Homer couldn't help himself?"

"Some people can make positive changes on their own, while others, who are not aware of how their past has affected them and aren't willing to get the help they need, follow the same path their parents took."

Irma's cheeks burned from the embarrassment and shame she felt. Her stomach had settled down a bit, but now she felt the need to cover her mouth in an effort to hold back the sob working its way up her throat. When Irma thought she could talk, she said in a shaky voice, "I—I'm an unfit mother, and I've treated my children in a way I never thought I was capable of. Is there any hope for someone like me?"

"Of course there is. It doesn't matter who you are now. What matters is who you become." Mrs. Mayes explained that she had dealt with numerous cases of abuse—some spousal and some involving children. "Anger and control have always been at the center of the problem," she said. "These issues are important, and we will be talking about them today as well as during your upcoming sessions. Before we begin, however, I would like to take a few moments to pray. Do you have any objections to that?"

Irma shook her head. "In our Amish church we pray silently, and at home it's the same, though some people do pray out loud at times."

"I would like to pray out loud, if that's okay with you."

Although Irma wasn't sure what kind of a prayer this counselor would pray, she gave a nod, bowed her head, and closed her eyes.

"Heavenly Father," Mrs. Mayes prayed, "please bless this time Irma and I have together today. Help her to feel free to say whatever is on her mind and ask any questions she has, as needed. Please give me the words You want me to say as I help Irma deal with the pain of her past and, in so doing, become the person You want her to be. I ask this in Your name, amen."

When Irma opened her eyes, a sense of peace came over her that she hadn't felt in a long while. Was it the prayer her counselor had spoken, or could it be the hope she felt for the first time that, with help, she might get better and become the kind of wife and mother that her family needed?

Myrtle Beach

Since Mose had been trying to get to know his nephew better, it would take many questions to learn what he wanted to know about him. This long road trip together would no doubt be helpful in achieving that goal.

So far, Mose had noticed from talking with Aaron that he had a few of Homer's traits. His nephew liked the outdoors; he enjoyed talking about fishing; and he seemed to be a determined young man. Since Mose's nephew had been raised in an Amish home, whenever there was talk about the English way of life, Aaron would be all ears. It made Mose wonder if his nephew could end up leaving the Amish faith like he had done years ago. Mose could still remember how he felt in his youth about not wanting to stay Amish. Could it be possible that the same thing would happen to Aaron by hanging around with him and, perhaps, seeing Mose as his role model? Aaron would need to consider his future choices carefully before making a life-changing decision. *Even though he's a grown young man, I wouldn't want to be the reason my nephew would leave the Amish faith. It would be hard to face Dorcas and the family if Aaron were to tell them that his uncle Mose had swayed him to become English.*

Mose needed to lighten his thoughts. He and Aaron had been hanging out for a while in this location and had been able to see some impressive things, but Mose needed a change of scenery. He looked at Aaron from across the small, fold-up table where they sat eating breakfast in his RV. "Well, what do you say? Do you think it's about time for us to leave South Carolina?"

⁓

Aaron set his near-empty glass of orange juice down. "You wanna go back to Montana?"

"No, but if you do, I'll take you there. You're probably missing your family by now, and you may want to be home for Christmas next week."

Aaron shook his head. "I'm not homesick, and I really don't need to be there for Christmas. I'm sure they'll enjoy the holiday without me."

"I wouldn't bank on that. Your mamm's probably counting the days until your return. I'll bet that your brother and sisters also miss you."

Aaron shrugged. "No doubt Irvin misses my help at the mill, but he has his own life to lead, and I have mine." Aaron pointed at the map, lying nearby. "If I had my way, I'd visit every single state in America."

"Seriously?" Uncle Mose scratched his head.

"Yep. I've never been happy living in one place, and now that I have this chance to travel with you, I'm planning to enjoy every minute of it."

His uncle smiled. "I'm glad you're having a good time. Having you along has been fun for me too. Sure am glad your mother said it was okay for you to take this trip with me."

"So where did you want to go from here?" Aaron figured a quick topic change was what they needed right now so the guilt wouldn't seep in for leaving without anyone's permission and not telling Uncle Mose the truth.

His uncle picked up the map and studied it a few minutes. Then he pointed to a spot and said, "Let's go and see what this state looks like."

Aaron nodded when he saw where Uncle Mose had pointed. Florida seemed like a good state to visit, and from what he'd heard, they would have plenty of warm weather to enjoy there too.

St. Ignatius

Dorcas looked at the calendar on the kitchen wall and frowned. Christmas was next week, and she hadn't heard anything from Aaron about whether he would be home by then. Surely he'd want to be here with his family that day. She couldn't imagine him, or Mose, spending the holiday on the road or in some strange place where they knew no one except each other.

"The truth is," she murmured, moving over to the kitchen sink, "Aaron doesn't really know his uncle that well either."

"Are you talking to yourself again, Mama?" Caroline touched Dorcas' shoulder.

"Guess I was," Dorcas responded. "I'm feeling a bit sorry for myself because Aaron won't be here to celebrate Christmas with us."

"How do you know he won't? Maybe he will surprise us and show up on Christmas Eve or Christmas Day."

Dorcas shook her head. "It's a nice thought, Daughter, but I'm not holding out any hope for that happening." She picked up a carrot from the pile on the counter, turned on the water, and scrubbed it clean. Someone, namely Caroline, hadn't washed all the carrots when they'd dug out the final batch from the garden last month.

"I miss my bruder too," Caroline said. "But at least we know he's safe and with Uncle Mose."

Dorcas turned to look at her daughter and frowned. "I'm not sure being with your uncle is such a good thing."

"How come?"

"Well, for starters, Mose took Aaron with him without bothering to check with me and see if I was okay with the idea." Dorcas' pulse quickened. "I'm still quite perturbed about that."

"Guess I can't blame you, but Aaron's just as much at fault as Uncle Mose. He's old enough to know that he was selfish and inconsiderate, especially where Irvin was concerned."

"Jah, I'm just glad someone finally came along who Irvin felt was qualified to help him run the mill. That took a lot of pressure off my son. Have you noticed that Irvin seems a lot happier and more relaxed these days?"

"Yes, I have, but I wonder how much of that smile we see on his face is because he finally asked his girlfriend, Mary Alice, to marry him—and she said yes."

"That's true, and I think she'll make him a good wife."

"Have they set a date for their wedding yet?" Caroline asked after she'd washed one of the smaller carrots.

"Not a definite date, but he did tell me it probably wouldn't take place until sometime next year."

"Think Irma and her family might come if they get an invitation?" Caroline popped the hunk of carrot into her mouth and chewed.

"I doubt it. Maybe if I wasn't here, because I'm sure she's still upset with me and might never accept my apology or give me a chance to tell her the truth about the abuse your daed inflicted on me."

Caroline's head lowered, and she turned away from Dorcas.

"What's wrong? Did I say something to make you feel umgerennt?" Dorcas stepped in front of her daughter and fixed her gaze on her.

"I'm not upset, Mama; I feel *schuldich*."

"Guilty for what, Caroline?"

"For not telling you about the letter I wrote to Irma several months ago." Dorcas' mouth opened slightly. "You did?"

"Jah."

"For goodness' sake. Why didn't you tell me you'd sent Irma a letter?"

" 'Cause I thought you'd be upset."

"Why would I be? You have every right to stay in touch with your sister."

Caroline rubbed her hands along the front of her apron. "I--I told Irma that Papa had abused you and that you were frightened of him."

Dorcas processed this information. "So she knows the truth now, yet she has never contacted me. That speaks pretty clearly, doesn't it?"

"I guess so, but she has never sent a response to my letter, so I really don't know what she thought about the information I gave her."

Dorcas moved slowly across the room and sank into a chair at the table. "Irma wouldn't accept my apology or allow me to finish what I was trying to tell her, and she's not responded to your letter. To my way of thinking, that means she's still angry and has not forgiven me." Tears welled in Dorcas' eyes, blurring her vision. "If Aaron never returns and Irma refuses to forgive me, that will mean I've lost two of my children and there's no way I can get them back." She leaned forward with her folded arms on the table and sobbed.

───────≋───────

Mount Hope

When Irma's driver dropped her off in front of her home that afternoon, she was tired and felt the need for a nap. Talking about her past and the anger and resentment she had harbored for so long had been exhausting.

Irma wondered if every session would affect her like this. She had a feeling that she and the counselor had barely scratched the surface of her emotional pain, but at least she had agreed to go and planned to stick it out.

Irma climbed wearily up the porch steps, and Shirley greeted her at the door with a cheerful smile. "The children are in the kitchen," she said. "They're helping me bake kichlin. Would you like to join us?"

Irma shook her head. "Baking cookies sounds nice, but I'm awfully tired. Would you mind if I went to my room and rested for a while?"

"Not at all. It's been a good many years since I was in a family way, but I can still remember how tired I became—especially by late afternoon, before it was time to fix supper." She took Irma's jacket from her and hung it on the clothes tree near the door. "Would you like some water or a cup of tea to take with you to your room?"

"No thank you. I'm fine. I just need to lie down for a bit."

"I understand." Shirley gave Irma's arm a gentle pat. "I'll fix the evening meal, and by the time your husband gets home, it should be ready to put on the table." Shirley's eyes were a soft brown, filled with an inner glow.

"What about your own supper?" Irma questioned. "Shouldn't you be at home right now fixing that?"

"Oh, no. . .not to worry. My dear husband has volunteered to help our daughter, Dianna, do the cooking on the days I'm here helping you."

"That's very kind of them." Irma teared up, beside her best effort not to cry. "I appreciate your willingness to help out here while I'm. . ." Irma's voice trailed off. She wasn't sure how much the bishop had told his wife about her situation.

Shirley gave Irma a few more tender pats. "It's all right. You go ahead and rest now."

Feeling overwhelmed, but in a good way, Irma turned down the hall to her room. She had been on the verge of stopping in the kitchen to say hello to her children, but the thought of seeing them right now made her struggle even more not to cry. Maybe after a short nap she would feel more rested and ready to say hello to the children. Irma hoped their fear of her had subsided some now that sweet, soft-spoken Shirley was in the house seeing to their needs. At least, they didn't have to worry about the bishop's wife shouting at them or getting out the wooden spoon and punishing in anger.

Maybe someday, if I get better, Irma thought after she'd taken off her shoes and reclined on the bed, *my children will have no fear of me either.*

Chapter 36

Over the next few months, Irma went faithfully to her counseling sessions. Each time she came away with a better understanding of herself and her relationships with her mother and stepfather as well as her husband and children. Irma had also learned about various reasons people became angry, such as wanting to be in control, needing to get one's way, unresolved guilt, and in response to having been hurt or mistreated. While she'd been receiving counseling, Irma had decided to get back to reading her Bible. She would take the time to look through the scriptures and pray each day.

Brian, Clayton, and Myra seemed to be getting along nicely with the bishop's wife. In the beginning when Shirley came to stay with them all day, Irma had to adjust her thinking to accept the helping hands of someone else. Shirley was understanding and usually asked Irma before she'd go ahead to do a task. Irma appreciated Shirley's help with the children and was glad for the loving support she'd given so far. Each time Irma would leave her children to go to her sessions, she felt good about having Shirley with them.

Today, as Mrs. Mayes sat across from Irma, she opened her Bible and said that she wanted to read an important scripture to Irma. "This verse is Matthew 6:14," she stated. "Jesus was speaking and said: 'If you forgive men their trespasses, your heavenly Father will also forgive you.'"

Irma squirmed on her chair. Forgiving her flesh-and-blood mother might be easier than forgiving Homer. Mama had asked for Irma's forgiveness. Homer had not, and he never would because he was dead. Even if he were still alive, Irma felt sure that Homer would not have admitted his sin of abuse and apologized for it.

She folded her hands across her bulging stomach and looked down. "I have known for some time what God's Word says about forgiveness, but I don't think I can ever forget or forgive Homer for all the terrible things he said and did to me and for how he mistreated my mother."

"Has she forgiven him?"

Irma shrugged. "I have no idea. I haven't spoken to her since she called some time ago to say she was sorry for allowing me to go through all that I did."

"Let me ask you another question, Irma. Have you apologized to your children for the things you said and did to hurt them?"

Irma looked up and tears sprang to her eyes. "Many times—even before I began seeing you for counseling. The problem is that I did not keep my word when I promised that I would never hurt them again."

"Have you continued to abuse your children?"

"No, I have not. But our bishop's wife is still coming over whenever LaVern's not at home so that my children won't be in any danger of me hurting them."

"Do you think you would abuse them again if she wasn't there?"

A pang of regret shot through Irma and she grimaced. "I—I hope not. With everything I've learned during these sessions, I believe I have my anger under control."

"Are your children still afraid of you?"

"I don't think so. They don't act like it anyway. The kids seem to enjoy spending time with me when I'm there."

"That's good. Now getting back to the apologies you've offered to your children. Have they forgiven you?"

"Yes. . .at least they said they did."

"Do you believe them?"

She nodded and swiped a hand across her damp cheeks where a few tears had fallen.

"How does it make you feel, knowing you have been forgiven?"

"Good. It gives me a sense of peace and makes me love my children all the more."

Mrs. Mayes fixed her gaze on Irma. "You have stated many times that you feel guilty for the way you treated Brian, Clayton, and Myra, and now you have said that you asked for their forgiveness."

"Yes."

"So, my next question is, have you asked God's forgiveness for the things you've said and done that you know were wrong?"

Irma sat a few minutes before finally shaking her head.

"Why not?"

"I've been afraid that He won't forgive me—that I'm not deserving of His love or forgiveness."

"Well, let's see what God's Word has to say about that." The soft-spoken counselor opened her Bible again and flipped through several pages. "Here's 1 John 1:9. Listen to what it says: 'If we confess our sins, He is faithful and just to forgive us our sins, and to cleanse us from all unrighteousness.'" She paused and turned to another passage. "This is from the Old Testament. Nehemiah 9:17 says: 'You are God, ready to pardon, gracious and merciful, slow to anger, abundant in kindness.'"

Irma breathed in and out as she allowed this new revelation to sink in. No doubt she'd heard those same scriptures quoted by one or more of the ministers during the years she'd been attending Amish church. But never, until today, had she let them sink in. She'd listened to ministers preach about Christ's crucifixion and how God sent His Son to earth to die on a cross for the redemption of man's sins, but until today, she hadn't fully realized the necessity of asking God's forgiveness in order to be cleansed of her sins.

Irma's nose began to run, and more tears spilled out of her eyes. Deep, wrenching sobs came forth as Irma closed her eyes and prayed the sinner's prayer, asking God to forgive her sins and fill her heart with His love and peace.

When the tears abated, Irma felt that God's Word had reached into her heart and released the pain. She looked up and saw Mrs. Mayes standing beside her with a box of tissues in one hand. Her other hand rested on Irma's shoulder.

Irma took a tissue gratefully and wiped her eyes and nose. "I've asked the Lord's forgiveness now, and I feel certain that He has pardoned me." She looked up at the counselor and blinked. "Now what should I do?"

"Just as God has forgiven you, you must forgive yourself—as well as those who have hurt you, whether they deserve it or not."

She nodded and sniffed a couple of times. "I need to tell my mother that I forgive her and apologize for shutting her out of my life." She rubbed the bridge of her nose. "What should I do about Homer, though? He's not here, so I can't say that I forgive him to his face. And even if he was, how can I forgive all the things he did to me and my mother when there's no way I can forget about those horrible things?"

"Let me ask you something, Irma." Mrs. Mayes moved back to her desk, but she didn't sit down. "Has the resentment and bitterness you've harbored toward your stepfather since you were a girl made anything better or brought a sense of peace into your life?"

Irma shook her head. "Quite the opposite. It's eaten me alive and caused me to take my frustrations out on my children."

The counselor nodded. "Bitterness blocks healing and prevents the goodness of God from shining through in our life. Bitterness eats away at our peace. Blaming the person who hurt you will increase your pain, and it will affect those around you. The more we are consumed by our pain, the more it will control us. You must move forward, Irma. Pull yourself out of the past and focus on the present. You must let go of your bitterness and allow God to heal your heart and the pain from the past."

Irma agreed, though she knew it would be difficult not to dredge up the past. She also knew there would be days when something would happen or some uninvited thought would pop into her head, and then she would need to run to God and ask for His help.

Irma and Mrs. Mayes continued to talk for another twenty minutes until it was time for their session to end.

When Irma got up from her chair, a sharp pain shot through her lower back and she winced.

Apparently Mrs. Mayes noticed, for she crossed the room quickly. "Are you all right?"

"I'm fine. At least, I think I am. Just feeling some pain in my back. Guess I must have sat too long in one position. I'm sure I'll be okay once I get into my driver's car and am heading for home where I can lie down and take a nap."

"All right then. I'll see you next week." Mrs. Mayes gave Irma a hug. "Unless, of course, your baby is born sometime before then."

Irma shook her head while patting her belly. "That's not likely. I'm not due for two more weeks."

St. Ignatius

"Happy birthday, Mama," Irvin said when he entered the living room where Dorcas sat embroidering some yellow roses on one of the pillow cases she had made. They would be part of the gift she planned to give Irvin and Mary Alice when they got married.

She smiled and said, "Well, thank you, Son, but I believe you gave me a birthday greeting this morning during breakfast."

He grinned and took a seat in the recliner. "So I did, but aren't two birthday wishes better than one?"

"Jah." She glanced at the clock across the room. "It's only three o'clock, Irvin. How come you came home from work so early today?"

"For the same reason I did," Hannah said when she entered the room. "The whole family is taking you out for supper this evening, and we figured we'll need a little extra time to get cleaned up. Caroline's probably in her room right now, getting ready too."

The whole family's not here. Aaron won't be joining us, because he's roaming around the country with Mose. Dorcas didn't voice her thoughts. There was no point in complaining about something that couldn't be changed. Besides, Irvin and Hannah seemed pleased with the idea of taking her out to supper, and she wasn't about to throw cold water on their plans. So Dorcas smiled and said an evening out would be nice. It had been hard to get through Christmas with one member of their family gone, and here they were, getting ready to celebrate her birthday and still no Aaron. The last postcard they'd received from him had arrived in the first part of February. Aaron had sent a Christmas card, however, saying he and Mose were in Orlando, Florida, visiting Disney World. On the February postcard, Aaron had stated that Mose wanted to see a few sights in Missouri, so they'd be heading there next. Dorcas figured she'd better get used to the idea that her youngest son might never return to St. Ignatius, but the thought hurt, nonetheless. When she'd given birth to each of her children, she had never expected that one, much less two of them, would leave home and make little or no contact with her.

Dorcas set her handiwork aside and rose from her seat. "Guess I may as well change into another dress. I've been wearing this black one all day, and after the baking I did this morning, it's not fit to wear out to supper at a restaurant."

Dorcas was about to follow Irvin and Hannah out of the room when the front door swung open and Aaron stepped in. "Happy birthday, Mama!"

"Oh, my, this is such a surprise!" Dorcas rushed across the room and into her son's arms. "Why didn't you let us know you were coming?" She glanced over Aaron's shoulder. "Where's Mose? I assume he's with you?"

"Jah. He's parking his rig. Said he wanted to give me a chance to talk to you by myself for a few minutes before he comes in."

"Talk to me about what?"

Before Aaron could open his mouth to reply, Irvin and Hannah came over and each gave him a hug.

"Welcome home, Brother," Irvin said. "Are you here to stay or just stopping by for a visit?"

"I'm here to stay, if Mama says it's okay. And don't worry, I won't ask for my job back at the mill, 'cause I'm sure by now you've already found someone to replace me."

Irvin bobbed his head. "I have, but there's always room for another man. If you're interested, that is."

Aaron shook his head. "Think I'd rather look for some other job that's more to my liking."

Irvin clasped his brother's shoulders. "Okay, we can talk about that later. Maybe after we all get back from supper."

"Were you invited out to someone's house?"

"Nope," Hannah interjected. "We made plans to take our mamm to a restaurant to celebrate her birthday. Now, you and Uncle Mose can join us." She offered Aaron a wide smile.

"Sounds good, but there's something I need to say to Mama first, and I'd like to say it in private, if that's okay with you."

"No problem." Hannah put her arm in the crook of Irvin's arm. "Let's head upstairs to our rooms to get ready and give these two some privacy."

Once Irvin and Hannah were out of sight, Dorcas invited Aaron to sit on the couch next to her. "What is it you wanted to tell me, Son?"

He swallowed hard, and she watched his Adam's apple move up and down.

"I owe you a big apology, Mama." Aaron gazed downward with hands clasped loosely behind his back. "I should've never left here without telling you first. And to make matters worse, I lied to Uncle Mose and told him you said I could go."

Dorcas spread her fingers out in a fan against her chest. "Oh, Aaron, I can't believe you would do that. All this time, I blamed your uncle, thinking he must have talked you into going and didn't have the courtesy to discuss the matter with me."

Aaron shook his head and looked at her again. "Nope, I'm the one to blame. While we were in Missouri, I finally came clean and told Uncle Mose the truth."

"What did he say?"

"He wasn't happy about it, and he said I ought to go home and set things straight."

"So that's the reason you came back?"

"Partly, but it was mostly because I missed my family and wanted to be home again with all of you. Will you forgive me, Mama, and take me back into your house?"

Dorcas leaned closer and put her hands against her son's clean-shaven face. "Of course I forgive you, Son. And my answer to your question is: 'Welcome home.'"

Upon hearing heavy footsteps out on the front porch, Dorcas looked in the direction of the door and said to Aaron, "That must be Mose. You'd better let him in."

Aaron pulled his arms out from behind his back and gave Dorcas a hug. "I love you, Mama, and I'm really happy to be home."

"And I am ever so glad you're here."

Mount Hope

On the way home, Irma had been thinking over what Mrs. Mayes had said during the session about her children having forgiven her. *"How does it make you feel, knowing you have been forgiven?"*

Irma remembered her response. *"Good. It gives me a sense of peace and makes me love my children all the more."*

She thought about her mother and how much better she would feel if Irma would extend that same loving-kindness to her. *I want to tell Mama that I forgive her and let her know that I love her.* Irma's back twinged again, but she tried to ignore it. *Mama deserves that same sense of peace I feel today.*

When Irma's driver dropped her off, she made her way as quickly as possible into the house. The pain in her back had increased, and Irma was eager to lie down for a while.

After she stepped inside and hung up her outer garments, Irma said hello to Shirley and all three of her children, who sat at the dining room table, drawing pictures on big sheets of paper.

"How was your appointment?" Shirley questioned.

"It went well, but I left there with a *buckelweh.*"

"I'm sorry you have a backache. Maybe it would help if you went to your room to lie down."

Irma nodded. "Jah, that's where I'd planned to go." She commented on the children's drawings, telling them they'd all done well, and then ambled down the hallway and opened her bedroom door. This pregnancy was a little different than her others, feeling back pains this soon before her due date. When she had been pregnant with Myra, Irma had been past her due date and, as she recalled, had felt the same kind of back pain as she had today.

Irma had no more than stepped into the room when she felt warm water dribbling down her legs. Trying not to panic, she stepped out into the hallway and hollered, "Shirley, please go out to the phone shed and call the midwife. The timing isn't good, but ready or not, this baby is coming!" *And with it being my fourth baby, I hope Darlene hurries to get here,* Irma mentally added.

Chapter 37

When LaVern entered the house later that evening, and heard a baby cry, his thoughts swirled so quickly it was hard to follow them. *Is someone with a baby visiting? Could Doretta have made the trip from Indiana to see my wife? Irma has received several letters from her lately filled with encouraging comments concerning her counseling sessions. Maybe Doretta decided to come see her friend in person.*

LaVern set his lunch box on the entry table and walked toward the living room. If any visitors were there, he wanted to say hello. If it was Doretta, it would be nice to thank her in person for all the encouraging letters she'd sent to Irma.

When LaVern entered the living room, he was surprised to see that it was completely quiet and void of visitors. *I'll bet they're in the kitchen visiting.* He turned on his heel and went to the kitchen, but no one was there either. *This is strange. Where is everyone?*

The cries grew louder, and this time LaVern thought they seemed to be coming from his and Irma's bedroom. *I suppose if Doretta and the baby are here, my wife could have taken her into our room to show her something.*

LaVern made it only halfway down the hall when Shirley came from the opposite direction with an upturned face. "Oh, good. I'm glad you're here, LaVern. The children are upstairs in bed, and your wife gave birth to a baby girl a short time ago."

"Wh–what?" LaVern stopped in mid-stride as his heartbeat picked up speed. "But she's not due for another two weeks."

Shirley chuckled. "Some babies come early and some late. I guess your new daughter had her own ideas about when she would make her appearance into this world."

"This is amazing and a little unexpected. Did you help with the delivery?"

"Not really. Darlene, the midwife, is here, and I just assisted as needed. Darlene's in the main bathroom washing up at the moment." She gave LaVern's arm a gentle nudge. "Well, don't stand here with your mouth open. Go in and say hello to the newest member of your family."

With the swiftness of a rabbit being chased, LaVern made a dash for the bedroom he and Irma shared. When he opened the door and saw his wife lying there with a precious baby in her arms, he gave a slow, almost disbelieving shake of his head, "Wow, I can't believe it! Would you look at that?" LaVern stood there soaking up the precious sight of his wife and new baby girl. It was now just the three of them together in the room.

"Come and meet our daughter," Irma said. "Isn't our baby girl schee?"

"Jah." LaVern closed the door and moved closer to the bed. "Even with all her redness and baby wrinkles, she's almost as pretty as her mudder." He leaned in closely, giving his wife a kiss and stroking her face. LaVern did the same to the baby's soft cheek. "I can't believe you gave birth today, Irma, and I wasn't even here to witness the special event."

She smiled. "I certainly didn't plan it that way. Everything happened so fast, there was no way to notify you. I'm just glad my midwife lives close by and got here as soon as she did. Otherwise, Shirley and I would have been on our own."

"When I came into the house, all I heard was the wail of a baby, and I thought at first your friend Doretta might be here visiting with her baby."

"You really believed that?"

"Jah. The thought never occurred to me that you might have given birth."

Irma gave a soft laugh while shaking her head. "No visitors today, and I don't think our baby qualifies as one, either, since she'll be staying and is now part of our family."

LaVern took a seat on the edge of the bed. His gaze traveled from Irma to the baby and back again. "How are you feeling? Was it a hard labor?"

"Not really. It went fast, and my labor was easier than with our other three children." Irma gazed at her husband. "I think it's your turn to hold the newest addition to our family."

LaVern gave a wide grin as he gently picked up the baby. "I'd be honored to hold our sweet little girl."

With the baby in his arms, he couldn't help smiling from ear to ear while thanking God that they had been blessed with a healthy baby girl. The infant was content, all swaddled in a soft blanket. His focus was on her little features. *She's ever so sweet*, he thought. As LaVern continued to hold the baby, it felt so natural and perfect to him.

LaVern thought back to Myra and the boys when they were that small. "It's hard to believe that our older children started out so *bissel* like this."

Irma smiled. "I'm glad they do start out little. Otherwise, it would be a lot harder giving birth."

"When did the pains begin? I know you had an appointment today with your counselor. Were you having signs of labor during your session?"

"No. At least, I didn't think I was. My back hurt, though, and I didn't realize what was happening until I got home. But the way the pain felt reminded me of when I gave birth to Myra. I reasoned that it was too early to have this baby since Myra was born after her due date. However, this little girl had other plans, and soon after my water broke, things began happening fast. That's when I asked Shirley to call Darlene."

"Although I really wish I could have been here, I'm glad everything went well and that you and the baby are both doing okay." LaVern looked down at the precious bundle in his arms.

Irma reached over and stroked the infant's dark hair, which matched the color of her own. "I've been thinking about a name for our little girl."

"Do you have anything particular in mind?"

Irma sat up more in the bed. "As a matter of fact, I do. I was wondering what you might think of calling her Sara. That was my paternal grandmother's name, but you never met her because she died before I knew you. I was twelve at the time of her death."

LaVern smiled. "Sara's a nice name. Jah, I like it. Do you have a middle name in mind too?"

"Actually, I do."

"What is it?"

"How about Dorcas?"

He gave a tentative smile that increased as the surprise he felt set in. "After your mamm?"

"Jah."

"I'm sure if she knew about the baby, she'd be real pleased."

Her forehead wrinkled slightly. "I hope so. I've been so awful, not accepting her apology or making contact with her, and I need to right that wrong."

"How do you plan to do that, Irma? We can't make a trip to Montana right now. It's too soon for you to travel."

"I know, but maybe she'd be willing to come here."

He tipped his head. "Seriously?"

"Yes. I would like to talk to her in person rather than on the phone or by trying to convey what I want to say in a letter." Irma closed her eyes for a moment and then opened them again. "I began thinking about it during my session with Mrs. Mayes today when we talked about forgiveness, and I truly want to make amends with Mama." She reached over and clasped LaVern's arm. "You'll probably want to go out to the phone shed soon to let your parents know about the baby's arrival."

He nodded.

"I would also like you to let Doretta know, and please give my thanks to her for all the letters full of wisdom she's written to me this past year."

"I will do that right now, but I'll need to pass our daughter back to you." LaVern returned little Sara Dorcas to her mom, got off the bed, and was almost to the door when Irma said she had one more favor to ask of him.

"What is it?" He turned around to face her.

"Would you call and leave a message for my mamm, letting her know that I gave birth to a baby girl this afternoon? I would also like you to say that I want her to come here as soon as possible to meet her new granddaughter and talk with me about some important things."

LaVern went back to the bed, bent down, and kissed Irma's cheek. "I'd be more than happy to do that. In fact, I'll call your mamm first thing when I get to the phone shed."

When LaVern left the bedroom, he walked with wide steps and a steady gait. Irma's change of heart toward her mother was an answer to prayer, and he had every confidence that Dorcas would agree to come and things would turn out well between mother and daughter. This was definitely an unexpected occurrence—even more so than their baby making her appearance two weeks before Irma's due date.

St. Ignatius

Dorcas shivered beneath her woolen shawl as she entered the phone shed the following morning to make a call and check for messages. The small wooden building seemed colder today than it did outside. Although the first day of spring was only a few weeks away, the weather hadn't warmed much yet, and a few patches of snow still lay on the ground. It wouldn't be fun if they got another snow to lengthen the winter. Most everyone in her community seemed ready to experience the warmer weather ahead. It would be nice to see the trees bud out and the leaves begin to grow again. All that spring thinking wasn't helping her to feel any better in the chilly cold.

Dorcas was about to pick up the telephone receiver to make a dental appointment for Caroline when she noticed the light on the answering machine blinking, indicating there must be at least one message. *Maybe I'll listen to the messages before I make my phone call,* she decided.

The first message was from the bishop's wife, asking how things were going with Dorcas and her family and inviting Dorcas to a get-together that would be held at her house next week for the widows in their church district.

Dorcas put a pause on the answering machine and smiled. *That kindly woman is always thinking of others and seems to enjoy entertaining and helping those who need it the most.* Dorcas thought about the times she and her children had met with their bishop and his wife to talk about the abuse that had taken place in their home when Homer was alive. The things the caring couple had shared were so helpful, and it was good for Dorcas and her children to openly talk about the feelings, as well as opening up about the fear they'd felt regarding their father. Dorcas was convinced that the time she, along with her sons and daughters, had spent at the bishop's house had been quite beneficial for all of them.

Guess now I'd better see what other messages came in. Dorcas activated the answering machine again and was surprised when the voice she heard said: "This is Irma's husband, LaVern, and my message is primarily for Dorcas. However, the whole family will probably be interested to learn that my wife gave birth to a baby girl this afternoon. Both mother and daughter are doing well." There was a brief pause, and LaVern cleared his throat. "Also, Irma wanted me to give her mother a message. She said that she would like Dorcas to come to our home in Ohio as soon as possible to see the baby and talk with Irma about some important things. Please let us know if you're willing to come, Dorcas, and if so, when we might expect you to arrive. Thank you, and have a blessed evening."

She sat perfectly still on the wooden stool, stunned, and trying to process what she'd just heard in this message that must have been left sometime last evening. *Irma wants me to see my new granddaughter, and there is something important she wishes to talk to me about.* Dorcas' mind raced, searching for answers to all the questions she had. *Is it possible that my daughter might be willing to forgive me for not protecting her from Homer's wrath? Does she want to talk things through so that we can have a better understanding of each other? Oh, I hope that is the case.* She clasped her hands in prayer, bowed her head, and closed her eyes. *Dear Lord, please let it be true. It would bring me such joy and peace to finally have a positive relationship with my daughter and be a part of her family. If it's meant for me to go to Ohio, then please pave the way.*

Mount Hope

A warm feeling spread throughout Irma's body as she lay gazing at her sleeping baby. She'd undone the swaddled blanket some to look at her infant this morning. Sara's little hands were perfectly made, and so were the baby's tiny toes. *The gift of life is a miracle,* Irma thought. *And I am so thankful that God has given me a second chance to make every effort to be a better mother than I was before I got help for my problems and turned my life over to Him.*

"Ready for some company?" Shirley asked quietly when she entered the room. "We have three eager youngsters out there in the hall wanting to meet their new baby sister."

Irma smiled and gestured with her hand. "Well, bring them in. I'm eager to introduce the children to Sara."

Shirley opened the door wider and, speaking in Pennsylvania Dutch, told the children to come into the room.

Brian was the first to come up to the bed. "She sure is red and wrinkly, Mama."

Irma nodded. "That's how all new babies look, but soon her skin will lighten and be smooth as silk." She gestured to Clayton, who had stayed behind his brother. "Come tell me what you think of your tiny little sister."

Clayton hesitated at first, but then he climbed up on the bed and knelt close to the baby. "She looks like one of Myra's dolls, only with lots more hair."

Irma smiled. "That's right. She does resemble a doll, but her name is Sara, and she's your little sister. Someday, when Sara is old enough, she'll be able to join you, Myra, and Brian when you're playing."

Clayton shrugged and got off the bed. Irma figured her son probably thought if his little sister was too young to play with now, there was nothing to get excited about.

Shirley picked Myra up then and placed her next to Irma. For the past two-plus years, Myra had been the baby of the family, so Irma figured having a younger sibling might take some getting used to on Myra's part. She watched carefully to see what her daughter would do, and was pleased when Myra reached out slowly and put her hand on the baby's tummy. *"Mei schweschder,"* she said.

"Yes, Myra." Irma patted the little girl's back. "This baby girl is your sister."

"Well now," Shirley said, "who wants to come with me to the kitchen? I'll be starting breakfast soon, and you can tell me which of the two choices you would like to eat." She winked. "And I'll tell you what those choices are when we go to the kitchen."

"Okay," Brian and Clayton said in unison as they darted out of the room with Shirley following. Myra, however, didn't budge. She reclined on the bed with her head on Irma's chest and one hand on her baby sister.

Joyful tears seeped out of Irma's eyes. She felt certain that Myra had accepted the new baby and probably looked forward to the day when she and her little sister could play together.

Irma thought about Proverbs 2:6–7, a couple of verses of scripture Mrs. Mayes had shared with her during one of their sessions. "The Lord gives wisdom; from His mouth came knowledge and understanding; He stores up sound wisdom for the upright."

Irma felt ever so grateful that through her counselor's guidance and her friend Doretta's letters of wisdom, she had found help and healing for the deep wounds from her past that had plagued her for so long. She also thanked God for giving her such a caring husband who had insisted that she get the help she needed. Irma hoped that someday she would be able to minister to someone who had also struggled with the pain of their past. That would surely be a blessing, and it would make everything she had been through worthwhile.

Epilogue

Two weeks later

Dorcas picked at a hangnail on her thumb, needing something to do to keep her mind off the nervousness she felt. Her trip had been long and sometimes boring. While riding in the car of her driver, Linda, Dorcas had tried to read a book she had started back home, but that didn't work well because she felt a little motion sickness from looking down for too long. And with Dorcas' anxiety, she couldn't seem to relax enough to fall asleep in the passenger seat of Linda's vehicle. Dorcas hadn't slept well at the hotels where she and Linda had stayed along the way either, which contributed to her fatigue. Excitement about seeing her newest grandchild mixed with trepidation concerning the conversation she and Irma would have were the biggest reasons Dorcas had lost sleep. Would it go well or cause more distance between Dorcas and her daughter?

I need to calm myself and stop thinking negative thoughts. It would be wise of me to trust the Lord all the way. Dorcas took a few deep breaths and tried to relax as Linda turned onto the road where Irma's house was located. It seemed nice to be back in a farming community among a slower-paced group of people. An Amish buggy up ahead caused Linda to slow the vehicle, and Dorcas rolled her window down. The fresh country air smelled good as it rushed in on her. After traveling through several states and only seeing motorized vehicles on the highway, being in a rural area and seeing a familiar horse and carriage was a welcome relief. In fact, the *clip-clop* of the horse's hooves connecting with the pavement helped her anxious feelings lessen a bit. *Irma asked me to come here to see the new baby and talk to her about an important matter, so it can't be all bad.* She closed her eyes and prayed. *Lord, please give me the right words to say to my daughter, and let this reunion be a joyous one that will give me and Irma an unbreakable bond that we've never really had.*

———————— ≋ ————————

When Irma heard a vehicle pull into the yard, her pulse quickened. She'd received a message from her mother a few days ago, saying that she had hired a driver to take her to Ohio and that they should arrive sometime today. Buster began barking and carrying on from his kennel. If Brian were home right now, Irma could've sent him out to settle the dog down. But he and his siblings were visiting their Miller grandparents.

I bet that's Mama and her driver. Irma went to the living room window and looked out. A beige-colored car was parked in the driveway, and she watched as the door on the passenger's side opened and her mother stepped out. Mama said a few words to her driver and closed the car door. She carried her purse and headed for the house as the vehicle pulled out. Irma watched as her mother gave the driver a quick wave. Mama looked like she was in good health as she made her way with agility up the sidewalk.

Feeling the throb of her heartbeat, Irma went to the front door. She didn't wait for her mother to knock. Irma opened the door as Mama stepped onto the porch. "Hello, Mama. I'm glad you made it safely." She opened the door fully and moved to one side. "Please, come in."

Irma's mother did as she'd been asked, and once she was inside, Mama, appearing to be a bit hesitant, gave Irma a hug. "It's good to see you, Daughter. Thank you for inviting me to come here. I am eager to see the baby and to spend some time talking with you." She set her purse on the floor.

"Me too, Mama. This conversation with you is long overdue." Irma took her mother's outer garments, hung them up, and invited Mama into the living room. "I'd like you to meet your granddaughter, Sara Dorcas." Irma gestured to the wooden cradle where her daughter lay.

Mama blinked multiple times, and her mouth opened slightly. "You—you used my *naame* for the baby's middle name?"

Irma nodded. "Would you like to hold her?"

"Jah, very much." Mama bent down and picked up the baby. Cradling the infant in her arms, she took a seat in the rocking chair. "Sara's a beautiful little girl. She reminds me so much of you at this age—same dark hair and flawless skin—just like a porcelain doll."

Irma smiled and seated herself on the couch. "Whenever Myra sees her little sister, she calls her a baby doll."

"Where is Myra right now—and her brothers? I was hoping to meet her and the boys too." Mama got the rocking chair moving gently.

"My in-laws, Mildred and Paul, kept them at their place last night. They will bring the children back here in time for supper this evening. While you're here in Mount Hope, we want you to stay with us, Mama. That will give you some quality time to spend with all four of your grandchildren, and they will have the chance to get to know you."

"Oh, that would be wunderbaar. I'll have to let my driver know so she can come back here with my suitcase and find lodging for herself for the night."

"If she is willing to stay longer than one night, that would be good," Irma was quick to say. "I was hoping you could stay for a few days—maybe even a week."

"All right, I'll go out to the phone shed soon and give Linda a call." Mama looked down at the baby. "I love holding this precious child. It's been so long since I've held anyone's baby—especially my own. I still can't believe that my youngest child is sixteen years old or that my oldest son will be getting married next year."

"Irvin's engaged? I didn't even know he had an *aldi*. Of course," Irma added, "since I haven't stayed in contact with any of you, I don't know anything that's gone on since LaVern and I went to St. Ignatius for Homer's funeral."

"Irvin's girlfriend is Mary Alice, and she's a very sweet young woman. It would be nice if you and your family could come to the wedding. It would make Irvin happy, and I'm sure his new wife would love to meet you."

"That would be nice. We'll have to see how it goes." Irma repositioned herself on the couch. "Are you hungerich, Mama? Would you like something to eat or drink?"

"Linda and I stopped for lunch when we got to Mount Hope, so I don't need anything right now. How about you, though? Have you had your lunch yet?"

"Jah, I ate a sandwich a while ago."

"You look tired, Irma. Are you getting enough rest?"

"As much as I can with a new baby in the house. Besides, I've had plenty of help. LaVern's mother spent the first week with us after Sara was born, and our bishop's wife, Shirley, has come by often to fix meals and keep an eye on the kinner. Also, LaVern was able to take some time away from his auctioneering duties—although he was called to do one today." Irma looked down. "The truth is, Mama, Shirley stayed here with the children for a good many weeks before the baby came while I was in Millersburg being counseled."

"You went to see a counselor?"

"Jah. I needed it desperately, because I had begun to abuse my children."

Mama's eyes widened. "Oh, my!" She covered her mouth with one hand. When she released it, she looked at Irma and said, "I blame myself for that, Irma."

"Why? It wasn't your fault I couldn't control my emotions and lashed out at my kinner when I was angry."

"I may not have been directly responsible, but if I had insisted that Homer get help for his temper or taken my children and left him, you would not have had to suffer at his hand, and neither would I." Mama slowly shook her head, and her voice cracked when she spoke again. "Homer abused me too, and I feared that if I stood up to him in your defense, he would treat both of us even worse. I was a coward, and I'm not proud of myself for it."

"Mama, I've forgiven you for that. A couple of the things I learned during my counseling sessions were the importance of forgiveness and not blaming others for my own actions."

"I learned the same thing from talking with our bishop and his wife. In fact, your brothers and sisters went with me, and we all received help for the guilt and shame we felt concerning your stepfather's acts of injustice."

"But I never witnessed Homer inflicting pain on any of my siblings. He always targeted me."

"That's true, but he did yell at them sometimes, and they were all afraid of him—scared that he would do to them what he'd done to you and to me."

"Oh, I see." Irma gulped in some needed breaths as she digested this new information. She couldn't help wondering why none of them had ever said anything to her about the way they felt. *Of course,* she reasoned, *they were all pretty young when I left St. Ignatius. They probably didn't know how to express the feelings of fear they each dealt with at that time.*

"Mama, the reason I asked you to come, in addition to wanting you to meet your new granddaughter, was so that I could say to you in person that I love you very much and hope you'll forgive me for cutting you out of my life and refusing to accept the apology you offered when we talked on the phone not long after Homer's funeral. I was full of anger and bitterness and needed someone to blame. It wasn't right, and I should have accepted your apology and listened to what else you had to say." Irma paused to collect her thoughts, and then she continued. "You may not know this, Mama, but Caroline wrote me a letter, explaining that you had also been mistreated by Homer. But even knowing that, I held onto my bitterness and wouldn't forgive." She swiped at the tears dripping onto her cheeks. "Now I am asking for your forgiveness, Mama. Will you accept my heartfelt apology?"

Irma's mother got up from her chair, placed Sara back in her cradle, and hurried over to the couch. She dropped down beside Irma and pulled her into a hug. "Of course I forgive you, Daughter, and I am grateful that you have forgiven me too."

Irma couldn't miss the tremor in Mama's voice or the tears in her mother's eyes, and as they continued to embrace each other, Irma thanked God for the wisdom He had imparted to both of them. She prayed that from this day forward, even with the miles between their homes, she and her mother would continue to communicate and never let go of God's hand.

Irma's Walnut Coffee Cake

INGREDIENTS FOR CAKE:

3 cups wheat flour

¾ cup honey

5 teaspoons baking powder

12 tablespoons butter

2 teaspoons cinnamon

1½ cups milk

2 eggs

1½ teaspoons salt

2 teaspoons vanilla

INGREDIENTS FOR TOPPING:

½ cup honey

5 tablespoons butter

4 teaspoons cinnamon

1 cup chopped walnuts

Preheat oven to 375 degrees. Combine all ingredients for cake in large bowl and mix well. Pour into greased 9"x13" pan. Mix topping ingredients in small bowl. Cover cake batter with topping and swirl in. Bake 20 minutes.

Author's Note

Dear Reader:

Child abuse comes in many forms. It can be physical, emotional, sexual, or verbal, but the abuse a child suffers always leaves a scar. Physical abuse is when a child is harmed or neglected by someone. This often happens when a child is hurt by someone older, bigger, or stronger than them—especially if it causes an injury. A child who has been physically abused is usually fearful of the one causing the abuse. Emotional abuse occurs when a child is hurt emotionally by words and actions. This may cause a child to withdraw socially. Some children never heal unless the deep-seated wound is properly dealt with. The same holds true for spousal abuse.

Depending on the type of abuse, a child may not even understand that they are being abused. They may believe that they are somehow to blame for their parents' actions. This was the case for me. It wasn't until much later in life that I realized I had been abused by both of my parents. As an adult, looking back on it, I became aware that the abuse I suffered was sometimes physical, and more often, emotional. I lacked confidence and self-worth throughout most of my childhood and didn't understand the reason for all my fears. My husband had also been physically abused as a child, even more so than I was. When our first baby was born, we made the decision to raise him, and any subsequent children, in a Christian home with love, understanding, and the proper needed discipline that was scriptural and not abusive. While we were not perfect parents, with God at the center of lives, we raised two children with love and understanding. My husband and I are thankful that the Lord opened our eyes to the knowledge that, with His help, we could and did break the chains of abuse so they did not follow into the next generation.

If you, or someone you know, is caught in an abusive situation, whether it be child or a spouse, there are places you can go for help. For me, dealing with the pain of my childhood involved numerous sessions with a Christian counselor. If you don't know of a Christian counselor in your area, you can find resources at aacc.net (American Association of Christian Counselors). If you are not comfortable speaking with a counselor, you might consider your church minister or a church-appointed crisis team. Residential counseling centers and clinics for the Plain people are in several states where Amish communities are located. Seeking help doesn't mean a person is helpless or weak. It means that they care enough about themselves and others to make an effort to find an organization or person to speak with about the abuse they have been subjected to or the abuse they are doing to someone else.

Love & Blessings,
Wanda Brunstetter

Discussion Questions

1. In this story, Irma had been abused as a child, but she had never talked about it with anyone until the day she admitted it to her husband. What are some reasons that a person who was abused might not be willing to tell anyone about it?

2. In addition to the dislike Irma felt for her stepfather who had physically and emotionally abused her, Irma felt anger toward her mother because she had allowed it to happen. Why do you think one parent who knew the other parent was abusing their child would not speak up and say anything?

3. When Irma's stepfather died, she thought she could put the past behind her and forget about the pain he had caused. But the nightmares and memories continued, which was disturbing to her. She tried not to think about it, but without success. What should a person do when their past hurts stay with them into their adult life? Is there a way a person such as Irma can move on with their life without painful memories that affect their everyday life?

4. Irma's mother, Dorcas, felt bad because she did nothing to protect Irma from the wrath of her stepfather. After Homer's death, Dorcas apologized to Irma, but the apology was not accepted. When we tell someone we are sorry but they are unwilling to accept the apology, what should we do?

5. Dorcas was also physically and emotionally abused by her husband, but she hid the truth from her family and those in her Amish community. Why do you think the victim of abuse might not be willing to tell anyone about it? If we know of someone who is being abused, what are some things we can do to help?

6. Dorcas' other four children were not abused by their father, but knowing that he had treated their sister so harshly, they were fearful

and never talked about it until after he died. How do you think a child would feel if one of their siblings was being abused but they were not?

7. Dorcas always wondered why her husband was so harsh and full of anger. When Mose, her husband's brother, came to visit, he shed some light on the subject by telling Dorcas and her four grown children that his and Homer's dad had abused them when they were children. Child or spousal abuse can be carried from one generation to the next. Is there a way that abuse can be halted and turned around so an abused child does not grow up to become an abuser?

8. Because Irma couldn't let go of the anger and resentment she felt for her stepfather, she allowed anger to get the best of her when she disciplined her own children. Irma realized that she needed help for the harsh things she said and did to her children. She couldn't find the strength to do it on her own, however, so she reached out to a friend to ask for prayer and advice. Why do you think Irma couldn't make the necessary changes on her own? Should she have told someone about her situation sooner?

9. When Irma's husband, LaVern, learned about the abuse she had suffered at the hand of her stepfather, he was concerned. His worry escalated when he realized for the first time that his wife had been mistreating their children. LaVern wanted to bring a friend or relative into the house to help out, believing that his pregnant wife had too much to deal with and would be less apt to become angry with someone else in the house who was taking charge of the children. Do you think LaVern's idea was a good enough solution? What are some other things that LaVern could have considered?

10. Irma's friend Doretta wrote Irma letters full of advice and wisdom. Doretta also prayed regularly for her friend. What are some ways we can reach out to a friend who might be dealing with issues, either similar to Irma's or something else that is equally destructive to a person and their family?

11. Were there any verses of scripture mentioned in this story that spoke to your heart? What verses helped Irma learn to forgive her mother and stepfather for the mistakes they'd made in the past that had affected Irma so much?

12. Did you learn anything new on the topic of child or spousal abuse by reading this book? Do you think it's a subject that should be brought to light more and be freely discussed? What are the disadvantages of keeping abuse a secret?

The New York Times bestselling and award-winning author Wanda E. Brunstetter is one of the founders of the Amish fiction genre. She has written more than one hundred books translated into four languages. With over twelve million copies sold, Wanda's stories consistently earn spots on the nation's most prestigious bestseller lists and have received numerous awards.

Wanda's ancestors were part of the Anabaptist faith, and her novels are based on personal research intended to accurately portray the Amish way of life. Her books are read and trusted by many Amish people, who credit her for giving readers a deeper understanding of the people and their customs.

When Wanda visits her Amish friends, she finds herself drawn to their peaceful lifestyle, sincerity, and close family ties. Wanda enjoys photography, ventriloquism, gardening, bird-watching, beachcombing, and spending time with her family. She and her husband, Richard, have been blessed with two grown children, six grandchildren, and two great-grandchildren.

To learn more about Wanda, visit her website
at www.wandabrunstetter.com.

The Friendship Letters Series

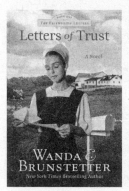

Letters of Trust
Book 1

Life is good on a Pennsylvania Amish farm for newlyweds Vic and Eleanor Lapp—until the day Vic's youngest brother drowns in their pond and Vic turns to alcohol to numb the pain. Things get so bad that Vic loses his job and their marriage is coming apart. Eleanor is desperate to help her husband and writes letters to her friend living in Indiana for advice. The trust Eleanor places in her friend and the gentle words she receives in return are a balm for even darker days to come.
Paperback / 978-1-63609-334-5

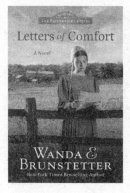

Letters of Comfort
Book 2

Doretta Schwartz used to be so happy and passed her positive attitude along to friends in several letters she wrote each month. But that all changed the day she learned of her fiancé's death and a heavy weight of depression fell upon her. Feeling empty, she puts away her letter writing and won't even respond to calls from friends. William's twin brother, Warren, is also grieving his loss, while at the same time trying to be supportive to his parents and Doretta. Doretta responds to Warren's friendship, but is he just becoming a replacement for the once-in-a-lifetime love she lost?
Paperback / 978-1-63609-487-8